PENGUIN BOOKS

The One Plus One

'A real delight to read . . . a funny, sweet, honest and tender
portrait of modern life in Britain' *The Little Reader Library*

'You will laugh and you will cry. This is possibly the best book
for 2014, with a score of 10/10 for *The One Plus One*'
Two Little Humans and Me

'As with the popular *Me Before You*, *The One Plus One* is
endearing, hilarious and heartbreakingly fantastic. If everyone
isn't reading it this spring, I'll be absolutely shocked'
Judging Covers

'Jojo Moyes writes of our imperfections, the ultimate kindness
of strangers, unlikely heroes and, most of all, hope'
Dolce Bellezza

'Every now and then, a book comes along that is so
absolutely perfect that it stops you in your tracks and you
think you'll never read anything so perfect ever again.
This is one of those books'
Being Anne

'Make sure you put *The One Plus One* by JoJo Moyes on your
"must read" list. You will not be disappointed'
Sophie Annabelle

'My vocabulary can't even begin to do justice to just quite how
brilliant I think this book is' *Beady Jan's Bookshelf*

'As brilliant as we've come to expect from Jojo Moyes'
The Writes of Women

The One Plus One

JOJO MOYES

PENGUIN BOOKS

PENGUIN BOOKS

UK | USA | Canada | Ireland | Australia
India | New Zealand | South Africa

Penguin Books is part of the Penguin Random House group of companies
whose addresses can be found at global.penguinrandomhouse.com.

First published by Michael Joseph 2014
Published in Penguin Books 2014

032

Copyright © Jojo's Mojo Ltd, 2014

The moral right of the author has been asserted

Set in Garamond MT Std
Typeset by Palimpsest Book Production Limited, Falkirk, Stirlingshire

Printed and bound in Great Britain by Clays Ltd, Elcograf S.p.A.

A CIP catalogue record for this book is available from the British Library

ISBN: 978-1-405-90905-1

www.greenpenguin.co.uk

To Charles, as ever.

I.

JESS

The irony did not escape Jessica Thomas that she lost the best job she'd ever had because of a diamond. Not because she stole it but because she didn't.

Jess and Nathalie had cleaned Mr and Mrs Ritter's holiday home for almost three years, since the Beachfront holiday park was part paradise, part building site. Back when the developers promised local families access to the swimming pool, and assured everyone that a large upmarket development would bring benefits to their little seaside town, instead of sucking out what remained of its life. The Ritters were standard occupants. They came down from London most weekends with their children. Mrs Ritter generally stayed on throughout the holidays while her husband stayed in the city. They spent most of their time on the manicured stretch of the beach, and visited the town only to fill up their people-carrier with diesel or to top up their groceries at the retail park. Jess and Nathalie cleaned their spacious, Farrow-&-Ball-painted four-bedroom home twice a week when they were there, and once when they weren't.

It was April and, judging by the empty juice cartons

and wet towels, the Ritters were in residence. Nathalie was cleaning the en-suite bathroom and Jess was changing the beds, humming along to the radio that they carried between jobs. As she whipped off the duvet cover she heard a sound like the crack of a high-velocity air rifle. Living where she did, she knew this sound well. She could have bet money that there were no air rifles at Beachfront.

Her gaze was caught by something glittering on the floor. She stooped by the window and picked up a diamond earring between her thumb and forefinger. She held it up to the light, then walked next door to where Nathalie was on her knees, scrubbing the bath, lines of dark sweat outlining her bra strap. It had been a long morning.

'Look.'

Nathalie climbed to her feet, squinting. 'What is it?'

'Diamond. It fell out of the bed linen.'

'That can't be real. Look at the size of it.'

They gazed at the earring, as Jess rotated it between finger and thumb. 'Lisa Ritter isn't going to have fake diamonds. Not with their money. Can't diamonds cut glass?' She ran it speculatively down the edge of the window.

'Great idea, Jess. You just keep going until her window falls out.' Nathalie stood up, rinsed her cloth under the tap. 'More importantly, where's the other one?'

They shook out the bed linen, peered under the bed, sifted through the deep pile of the beige carpet on their hands and knees, like police at a murder scene. Finally

Jess checked her watch. They looked at each other and sighed.

One earring. Your basic nightmare.

Things they had found while cleaning people's houses:

- False teeth
- An escaped guinea pig
- A long-lost wedding ring (they were given a box of chocolates for this)
- A signed photograph of Cliff Richard (no chocolates; owner denied all knowledge)
- Money. Not just small change, but a whole turquoise wallet stuffed full of fifties. It had fallen behind a chest of drawers. When Jess handed it over to the client – a Mrs Linder, who had rented number four Beachfront for three months over the summer – she had looked at it in mild surprise. 'I was wondering where that had gone,' she said, and pocketed it without a backward look, as you would a mislaid hair slide or a remote control.

Guinea pigs aside, it was not as great as you might think, turning up valuables. One earring or a pile of loose notes, and clients would give you that vague, sideways look, the flicker in their eyes that meant they were wondering if you had pocketed the rest. Mr Ritter would definitely assume they had taken the other earring. He was the kind of man who made them feel guilty just for being in his house. That was on the days he deigned to acknowledge they were there.

'So what do we do?'

Nathalie was bundling up the duvet cover, ready for the laundry. 'Leave it on the side. We'll just write a note saying we couldn't find the other.' They usually left a note or two out during their rounds, saying what they'd done. Or a polite reminder that they were owed money. 'It's the truth.'

'Should we say we shook out all the bedding?'

'Whatever. I just don't want her thinking we took it.'

Jess finished writing, and placed the earring carefully on the piece of paper. 'Mrs Ritter might already have the other one. She might be glad we found it.'

Nathalie made the face that said Jess would look on the bright side of a nuclear apocalypse. 'Personally, I think I would have known if there was a diamond the size of an eyeball in my bed.' She dumped the dirty laundry outside the bedroom door. 'Right. You vacuum the hall, and I'll change the kids' beds. If we get a wiggle on, we can be at the Gordons' by half eleven.'

Nathalie Benson and Jessica Thomas had cleaned together every weekday for four years, the somewhat uninspired moniker Benson & Thomas Cleaning Services on the side of their little white van. Nathalie had stencilled 'A Bit Dirty? Can we Help?' underneath for two whole months until Jess pointed out that half the calls they were getting were nothing to do with cleaning.

Nearly all their jobs were in Beachfront now. Hardly anybody in the town had the money – or the inclination – to hire a cleaner, except for the GPs, the solicitor and the odd client like Mrs Humphrey, whose arthritis stopped her doing it herself. She was one of those old women who believed cleanliness was next to godliness, her life's worth previously measured in starched curtains and a freshly scrubbed front step. Sometimes they suspected she'd saved up a whole forty-eight hours of conversation just for the hour that they were there. Wednesdays they did Mrs Humphrey after their Beachfront jobs, the Ritters and the Gordons, and, if they were lucky, whichever of the holiday cottages the other cleaning firms had failed to turn up for.

Jess was lugging the vacuum cleaner along the hall when the front door opened. Mrs Ritter called up the stairs, 'Is that you, girls?'

She was the kind of woman to whom all women, even those collecting their pensions, were 'girls'. 'I had the best girls' night out on Saturday,' she would say, her eyes rolling with mischief. Or, 'So off I went, to the little girls' room . . .' but they liked her. She was always cheerful, and wore her money lightly. And she never treated them like cleaners.

Nathalie and Jess exchanged looks. It had been a long morning, they'd done two ovens already (what kind of people roasted pork on holiday?), and Mrs Humphrey's tea tended to be the colour and consistency of stair varnish.

Ten minutes later they were sitting round the kitchen table, while Lisa Ritter pushed a plate of biscuits towards them. 'Go on, have one. If you eat them, I can't be tempted.' She squeezed a non-existent roll of fat over her waistband. Nathalie and Jess could never agree if she'd had work. She was the kind of woman who floated somewhere in the carefully maintained hinterlands between forty and sixty-something. Her tinted chestnut hair was set in soft waves, she played tennis three times a week, did Pilates with a private instructor, and Nathalie knew someone at the local salon, who said that she was waxed to within an inch of her life every four weeks.

'How's your Martin?'

'Still alive. To the best of my knowledge,' Natalie said.

'Oh, yes.' She nodded, remembering. 'You did tell me. Finding himself, was it?'

'That's the one.'

'You'd have thought he might have found himself by now. There was enough of him.' Mrs Ritter paused, and gave Jess a conspiratorial smile. 'Your little girl still got her head stuck in a maths book?'

'Always.'

'Oh, they're good children, yours. Some of these mothers round here, I swear they don't know what their lot are doing from dawn till dusk. That Jason Fisher and his friends were throwing eggs at Dennis Grover's windows the other day. Eggs!' It was hard to tell from her voice whether she was more shocked at the act of aggression or the waste of good food.

She was in the middle of a story about her manicurist and a small, incontinent dog, breaking off repeatedly as she was overcome with laughter, when Nathalie held up her phone. 'Mrs Humphrey's tried to call,' she said,

6

pushing back her chair. 'We'd better get off.' She slid off the stool and made her way out to the hallway to fetch the cleaning crate.

'Well, the place looks lovely. Thank you both so much.' Mrs Ritter reached up a hand and patted her hair into place, briefly lost in thought. 'Oh, before you go, Jess, you wouldn't give me a hand with something, would you?'

Most of the clients knew Jess was good at practical things. There was barely a day where somebody didn't want help with some grouting, or picture-hanging, jobs they swore would only take five minutes. Jess didn't mind. 'If it's a big job though I may need to come back,' she said. *And charge*, she added silently.

'Oh, no,' Lisa Ritter said, walking towards the back door. 'I just need someone to help me with my suitcase. I cricked my back on the plane, and I need someone to get it up the steps for me.'

'Plane?'

'I went to see my sister in Mallorca. Well, now the children are at uni, I've got all this time to myself, haven't I? I thought it would be nice to have a few days' mini-break. I left Simon to it, bless him.'

'So when did you get back?'

She looked at Jess blankly. 'You saw me! Just now!'

It took a couple of seconds to hit. And it was a good job that she was already headed outside into the sun because Jess felt the colour actually drain from her face.

*

That was the problem with cleaning. It was a good job on the one hand – if you didn't mind other people's stains and pulling lumps of hair out of other people's plugholes (she didn't, funnily enough). Jess didn't even mind that most of those who rented holiday homes seemed to feel obliged to live like pigs for a week, leaving mess they wouldn't sit in at home because they knew there was a cleaner coming. You could work for yourself, organise your own hours, pick and choose your clients when times were good.

The downside, weirdly, was not the crappy clients (and there always was at least one crappy client), or the dirt, or that scrubbing someone else's toilet somehow left you feeling like you were one step lower on a ladder than you had planned to be. It wasn't even the constant threat from other companies, the leaflets through your clients' doors and the promises of cheaper by the hour. It was that you ended up finding out much more about other people's lives than you really wanted to.

Jess could have told you about Mrs Eldridge's secret shopping habit: the designer-shoe receipts she stuffed into the bathroom bin, and the bags of unworn clothes in her wardrobe, the tags still firmly attached. She could tell you that Lena Thompson had been trying for a baby for four years, and used two pregnancy tests a month (rumour had it she left her tights on). She could tell you that Mr Mitchell in the big house behind the church earned a six-figure salary (he left his payslips on the hall table; Nathalie swore he did it deliberately) and that his daughter smoked secretly in the bathroom and lined up all her cigarette butts in neat rows on the window ledge.

If she was that way inclined, she could have pointed out the women who went out looking immaculate, hair faultless, nails polished, lightly spritzed with expensive scent, who thought nothing of leaving soiled knickers in full view on the floor, or the teenage boys whose stiff towels she didn't want to pick up without a pair of tongs. There were the couples who spent every night in separate beds, the wives insisting brightly when they asked her to change the spare-room sheets that they'd had an 'awful lot of guests lately', the lavatories that required a gas mask and a HAZCHEM warning.

And then every now and then you got a nice client like Lisa Ritter and popped over to vacuum her floors and came home with a whole load of knowledge you could really have done without.

Jess watched Nathalie walking outside, the cleaning crate under her arm, and saw with a terrible clarity what was going to happen next. She saw the bed upstairs, immaculately made with clean linen, the polished surfaces of Mrs Ritter's dressing-table, the cushions neatly plumped on the little sofa in the bay window. She saw that diamond, sitting where she had left it with her scrawled note on the dresser, a tiny glittering hand grenade.

'Actually,' Jess said, hauling the suitcase past Nathalie,

'can I have a quick word, Nat?' She tried to catch her eye, but Nathalie was busy gazing at Mrs Ritter's shoes.

'I love your pumps,' she said breathlessly.

'Do you, Nathalie? I got them while I was away. They were an absolute bargain.'

'Mrs Ritter's been to Spain, Nat,' Jess said pointedly, stopping beside her. 'A *mini-break*.'

Nathalie glanced up and smiled. Nothing.

'She got back *this morning*.'

'Lovely,' said Nathalie, beaming.

Jess felt panic rising inside her, like an unstoppable tide. 'I tell you what, I'll carry this upstairs for you,' she said, pushing past Mrs Ritter.

'You don't have to do that!'

'It's no bother.' She wondered if Lisa Ritter had registered the strange set to her face. She could make it upstairs, she thought. She could run into the bedroom, fetch the earring, stuff it into her pocket and shove Nathalie into the car before she could say anything, and Mrs Ritter would never know. They would decide what to do about it later.

But even as she hurled herself through the back door some part of her already knew what would happen.

'So did Jess tell you?'

She was halfway up the stairs. Nathalie's voice carried, as clear as a bell, through the open window.

'We found one of your earrings. We thought you might have the other one put by.'

'Earrings?' said Mrs Ritter.

'Diamond. I think it's a platinum setting. Fell out of the bed linen. You're lucky we didn't vacuum it up.'

There was a short silence.

Jess closed her eyes, stood very still on the stairs and waited as the inevitable words floated up to her.

'How was I supposed to know Mrs Ritter doesn't have pierced ears?'

They sat in the cleaning van, slumped in their seats. Nathalie was smoking. She had given up six weeks ago. For the fourth time.

'I don't look at people's ears. Do you look at people's ears?'

'I think you must have been mistaken,' Lisa Ritter had said, her voice quivering slightly with the effort, as she held it in her hand. 'It's probably my daughter's, from when she came home last time. She's got a pair just like it.'

'Of course,' Jess said. 'It probably got kicked in here. Or carried in on someone's shoe. We knew it would be something like that.' And she knew right then, when Mrs Ritter turned away from her, that that would be it. Nobody thanked you for bringing bad news to their door.

Nobody wanted a cleaner knowing their bad business.

'Eighty pounds a week, guaranteed. And holiday pay.' Nathalie let out a sudden scream. 'Bloody hell. I actually want to find the tart who owns that bloody earring and thump her for losing us our best job.'

'Maybe she didn't know he was married.'

'Oh, she knew.' Before she'd met Dean, Nathalie had spent two years with a man who turned out to have not one but two families on the other side of Southampton. 'No single man keeps colour-coordinated scatter cushions on his bed.'

'Neil Brewster does,' Jess said.

'Neil Brewster's music collection is sixty-seven per cent Judy Garland, thirty-three per cent Pet Shop Boys.'

At the end of the road a padded toddler toppled gently onto the ground like a felled tree and, after a brief silence, let out a thin wail. Its mother, her two armloads of shopping bags perfectly balanced, stood and stared in mute dismay.

'Look, you heard what she said the other week – she'd get rid of her hairdresser before she'd get rid of us.'

'Before she got rid of "the cleaners". That's different. She won't care whether it's us or Speedicleanz or Maids With Mops.' Nathalie shook her head. 'Nope. To her, from now on, we'll always be the cleaners who know the truth about her husband. It matters to women like her. They're all about appearances, aren't they?'

The mother put down her bags and stooped to pick up the toddler. A few houses away, Terry Blackstone emerged from under the bonnet of his Ford Focus, a car that had not run in eighteen months, and peered out to see what was making all the noise.

Jess put her bare feet up on the dashboard and let her face fall into her hands. 'Bugger it. How are we going to make up the money, Nat? That was our best job.'

'The house was immaculate. It was basically a twice a week polishing job.' Nathalie stared out of the window.

'And she always paid on time.'

'And she used to give us stuff.'

Jess kept seeing that diamond earring. Why hadn't they just ignored it? It would have been better if one of them had stolen it. 'Okay, so she's going to cancel us. Let's change the subject, Nat. I can't afford to cry before my pub shift.'

'So, did Marty ring this week?'

'I didn't mean change the subject to *that.*'

'Well, did he?'

Jess sighed. 'Yup.'

'Did he say why he didn't ring the week before?' Nathalie shoved Jess's feet off the dashboard.

'Nope.' Jess could feel her staring. 'And no, he didn't send any money.'

'Oh, come *on*. You've got to get the Child Support Agency onto him. You can't carry on like this. He should send money for his own kids.'

It was an old argument. 'He's . . . he's still not right,' Jess said. 'I can't put more pressure on him. He hasn't got a job yet.'

'Well, you're going to need that money now. Until we get another job like Lisa Ritter's. How's Nicky?'

'Oh, I went round to Jason Fisher's house to talk to his mum.'

'You're joking. She scares the pants off me. Did she say she'd get him to leave Nicky alone?'

'Something like that.'

Nathalie kept her eyes on Jess and dropped her chin two inches.

'She told me if I set foot on her doorstep once more she'd batter me halfway to next Wednesday. Me and my . . . what was it? . . . me and my "freakazoid kids".' Jess pulled down the passenger mirror and checked her hair, pulling it back into a ponytail. 'Oh, and then she told me her Jason wouldn't hurt a fly.'

'Typical.'

'It's fine. I had Norman with me. And, bless him, he took an enormous dump next to their Toyota and somehow I forgot I had a plastic bag in my pocket.'

Jess put her feet back up.

Nathalie pushed them down again and mopped the dashboard with a wet wipe. 'Seriously, though, Jess. How long has Marty been gone? Two years? You've got to get back on the horse. You're young. You can't wait around for him to sort himself out,' she said, with a grimace.

'Get back on the horse. Nice.'

'Liam Stubbs fancies you. You could totally ride that.'

'Any certified pair of X chromosomes could ride Liam Stubbs.' Jess closed the window. 'I'm better off reading a book. Besides, I think the kids have had enough upheaval in their lives without playing Meet Your New Uncle. Right.' She looked up, wrinkled her nose at the sky. 'I've got to get the tea on and then I've got to get ready for the pub. I'll do a quick ring-round before I go, see if any of the clients want any extras doing. And, you never know, she might not cancel us.'

Nathalie lowered her window, and blew out a long trail of smoke. 'Sure, Dorothy. And our next job is going to be cleaning the Emerald City at the end of the Yellow Brick Road.'

Number fourteen Seacove Avenue was filled with the sound of distant explosions. Tanzie had calculated recently that, since he'd turned sixteen, Nicky had spent 88 per cent of his spare time in his bedroom. Jess could hardly blame him.

She dropped her cleaning crate in the hall, hung up her jacket, made her way upstairs, feeling the familiar faint dismay at the threadbare state of the carpet, and pushed at his door. He was wearing a set of headphones and shooting somebody; the smell of weed was strong enough to make her reel.

'Nicky,' she said, and someone exploded in a hail of bullets. 'Nicky.' She walked over to him and pulled his headphones off, so that he turned, his expression briefly bemused, like someone hauled from sleep. 'Hard at work, then?'

'Revision break.'

She picked up an ashtray and held it towards him. 'I thought I told you.'

'It's from last night. Couldn't sleep.'

'Not in the house, Nicky.' There was no point telling him not at all. They all did it around here. She told herself she was lucky he had only started at fifteen.

'Is Tanzie back yet?' She stooped to pick up stray socks and mugs from the floor.

'No. Oh. The school rang after lunch.'

'What?'

He typed something into the computer then turned to face her. 'I don't know. Something about school.'

It was then that she saw it. She lifted a lock of that dyed black hair, and there it was: a fresh mark on his cheekbone. He ducked away. 'Are you okay?'

He shrugged, looked away from her.

'Did they come after you again?'

'I'm fine.'

'Why didn't you call me?'

'No credit.' He leant back and fired a virtual grenade. The screen exploded into a ball of flame. 'The number's on the table. If it's about me, I was there on Friday. They must have just not seen me.' He replaced his earphones and went back to the screen.

Nicky had come to live with Jess full time eight years previously. He was Marty's son by Della, a woman he'd gone out with briefly in his teens. He had arrived silent and wary, his limbs thin and elongated, his appetite raging. His mother had fallen in with a new crowd, finally disappearing to somewhere in the Midlands with a man called Big Al, who wouldn't look anyone in the eye and clutched an ever-present can of Tennents Extra like a hand grenade in his oversized fist. Nicky had been found sleeping in the locker rooms at school, and when the social workers called again, Jess had said he could come to them. 'Just what you need,' Nathalie had said. 'Another mouth to feed.'

'He's my stepson.'

'You've met him twice in four years. And you're not even twenty.'

'Well, that's how families are, these days. It's not all two point four.'

Afterwards, she sometimes wondered whether that had been the final straw; the thing that had caused Marty to abdicate responsibility for his family altogether. But Nicky was a good kid, under all the raven hair and eyeliner. He was sweet to Tanzie, and on his good days he talked and laughed and allowed Jess the occasional awkward hug, and she was glad of him, even if it sometimes felt as if she had basically acquired one more person to feel anxious about.

She stepped out into the garden with the phone and took a deep breath, her stomach a knot of anxiety. 'Um . . . hello? It's Jessica Thomas here. I had a message to call.'

A pause.

'If it's about Nicky, I did check his study-periods rota. He said he was allowed to do revision at home and I thought that this was how they –'

'Mrs Thomas, I was calling you about Tanzie.'

A clench of panic. She glanced down at the number, registering. 'Tanzie? Is . . . is everything all right?'

'Sorry. I should have said. It's Mr Tsvangarai here, Tanzie's maths teacher.'

'Oh.' She pictured him: a tall man in a grey suit. Face like a funeral director's.

'I wanted to talk to you because a few weeks ago I had

a very interesting discussion with a former colleague of mine who works for St Anne's.'

'St Anne's?' Jess frowned. 'The private school?'

'Yes. They have a scholarship programme for children who are exceptionally gifted in maths. And, as you know, we had already earmarked Tanzie as Gifted and Talented.'

'Because she's good at maths.'

'Better than good. Well, we gave her the paper to sit last week. I don't know if she mentioned it? I sent a letter home but I wasn't sure you saw it.'

Jess squinted at the sky. Seagulls wheeled and swooped against the grey. A few gardens down Terry Blackstone had started singing along to a radio. He had been known to do the full Rod Stewart if he thought nobody was looking.

'We got the results back this morning. And she has done well. Extremely well. Mrs Thomas, if you're agreeable they would like to interview her for a subsidized place.'

She found herself parroting him. 'A subsidized place?'

'For certain children of exceptional ability St Anne's will forgo a significant proportion of the school fees. It means that Tanzie would get a top-class education. She has an extraordinary numerical ability, Mrs Thomas. I do think this could be a great opportunity for her.'

'St Anne's? But . . . she'd need to get a bus across town. She'd need all the uniform and kit. She – she wouldn't know anyone.'

'She'd make friends. But these are just details, Mrs Thomas. Let's wait and see what the school comes up with. Tanzie is an extraordinarily talented girl.' He paused. When she didn't say anything, he lowered his voice: 'I have been teaching maths for almost twenty-two years, Mrs Thomas. And I have never met a child who grasped mathematical concepts like she does. I believe she is actually exceeding the point where I have anything to teach her. Algorithms, probability, prime numbers –'

'Okay. This is where you lose me, Mr Tsvangarai. I'll just go with gifted and talented.'

He chuckled. 'I'll be in touch.'

She put down the phone and sat heavily on the white plastic garden chair that had been there when they'd moved in and had now grown a fine sheen of emerald moss. She stared at nothing, in through the window at the curtains that Marty always thought were too bright, at the red plastic tricycle that she had never got round to getting rid of, at next door's cigarette butts sprinkled like confetti on her path, at the rotten boards in the fence that the dog insisted on sticking his head through. Despite what Nathalie referred to as her frankly mis-guided optimism, Jess found her eyes had filled unexpectedly with tears.

There were lots of awful things about the father of your children leaving: the money issues, the suppressed anger on behalf of your children, the way most of your coupled-up friends now treated you as if you were some kind of potential husband-stealer. But worse than that, worse than the endless, relentless, bloody exhausting financial and energy-sapping struggle, was that being a parent on your own when you were totally out of your depth was actually the loneliest place on earth.

2.

TANZIE

Twenty-six cars sat in the car park at St Anne's. Two rows of thirteen big shiny four-wheel-drives faced each other on each side of a gravel path, sliding in and out of the spaces at an average angle of 41 degrees, before the next in line moved in.

Tanzie watched them as she and Mum crossed the road from the bus stop, the drivers talking illegally into phones or mouthing at bug-eyed blond babies in the rear seats. Mum lifted her chin and fiddled with her keys in her free hand, as if they were actually her car keys and she and Tanzie just happened to have parked somewhere nearby. She kept glancing behind her. Tanzie guessed she was worried she was going to bump into one of her cleaning clients and they were going to ask what she was doing there.

She had never been inside St Anne's, although she'd been past it on the bus at least ten times because the NHS dentist was on this road. From the outside, there was just an endless hedge, trimmed to exactly 90 degrees (she wondered if the gardener used a protractor) and those big trees where the branches hung low and friendly, sweeping out across the playing fields as if they were there to shelter the children below.

The children at St Anne's did not swing bags at each other's heads, or bundle up in huddles by the corner of the playground, backing someone against the wall to tax their lunch money. There were no weary-sounding teachers trying to herd the teenagers into classrooms. The girls had not rolled their skirts six times over at the waistband or backcombed their hair. Not a single person was smoking. A lot of them wore glasses. Her mother gave her hand a little squeeze. Tanzie wanted her to stop looking so nervous. 'It's nice, isn't it, Mum?'

She nodded. 'Yes.' It came out as a squeak.

'Mr Tsvangarai told me that every single one of their sixth-formers who did maths got A or A starred. That's good, isn't it?'

'Amazing.'

Tanzie pulled a bit at Mum's hand so that they could get to the head's office faster. 'Do you think Norman will miss me when I'm doing the long days?'

'The long days.'

'St Anne's doesn't finish till six. And there's maths club on Tuesdays and Thursdays so I'd definitely want to do that.'

'Tanze,' she said, and stopped.

'Mum. *Look*.' There was a girl walking along reading a book. Actually reading a book. Nicky said if you walked across the playground reading a book at McArthur's you got battered. You had to hide them, like cigarettes.

Her mother glanced at her. She looked really tired.

She was always tired, these days. She put on one of those smiles that wasn't really a smile at all, and they went in.

'Hello, Mrs Thomas. Hello, Costanza. It's very good to meet you. Do sit down.'

The headmaster's study had a high ceiling, as white and perfectly decorated as a wedding cake. Little white plaster rosettes sat every twenty centimetres, and tiny rosebuds exactly halfway between them. The room was stuffed with old furniture and through a large bay window a man on a roller could be seen travelling up and down a cricket pitch. On a small table somebody had laid out a tray of coffee and hand-made biscuits. It took Tanzie a few minutes to realize they were for them. 'Can I have one?' she said, and the headmaster pushed them towards her.

'Of course.'

'Mouth closed,' Mum murmured.

They were so good. You could tell they were home-made. Mum used to make biscuits before Dad left and they were just like these. She sat down on the edge of the sofa and gazed at the two men opposite. The one with the moustache smiled like the nurse did before she gave you an injection. Mum had pulled her bag onto her lap and Tanzie could see her holding her hand over the corner where Norman had chewed it. Her leg was jiggling.

'This is Mr Cruikshank. He's the head of maths. And I'm Mr Daly. I've been head here for the past two years.'

She shook their hands and smiled back. Tanzie should have shaken their hands, but all she could hear were the words 'head of maths'. She looked up from her biscuit.

'Do you do chords?'

'We do.'

'And probability?'

'That too.'

Mr Cruikshank leant forward. 'We've been looking at your test results. And we think, Costanza, that you should sit your GCSE in maths next year and get it out of the way. Because I think you'd rather enjoy the A-level problems.'

She looked at him. 'Have you got actual papers?'

'I've got some next door. Would you like to see them?'

She couldn't believe he was asking. She thought briefly of saying, 'Well, DUH', like Nicky did. But she just nodded.

Mr Daly handed Mum a coffee. 'I won't beat around the bush, Mrs Thomas. You are well aware that your daughter has an exceptional ability. We have only seen scores like hers once before and that was from a pupil who went on to be a fellow at Trinity.'

Tanzie nodded, although she was pretty sure she didn't want to be a fellow. Everyone knew girls were better at maths.

He went on and on then. She tuned out a bit because she was trying to see how many biscuits she could eat so what she heard was '. . . for a very select group of pupils who have a demonstrably unusual ability we have created a new equal-access scholarship.' Blah, blah, blah. 'It would offer a child who might not otherwise get the advantages of a school like this the chance to fulfil their potential in . . .' Blah, blah. 'While we are very keen to see how far Costanza could go in the field of maths, we would also want to make sure that she was well rounded in other parts of her student life. We have a full sporting and musical curriculum.' Blah, blah, blah . . . 'Numerate children are often also able in languages . . .' blah, blah '. . . and drama — that's often very popular with girls of her age.'

'I only really like maths,' she told him. 'And dogs.'

'Well, we don't have much in the way of dogs, but we'd certainly offer you lots of opportunities to stretch yourself mathematically. But I think you might be surprised by what else you enjoy. Do you play any instruments?'

She shook her head.

'Any languages?'

The room went a bit quiet.

'Other interests?'

'We go swimming on Fridays,' Mum said.

'We haven't been swimming since Dad left.'

Mum smiled, but it went a bit wonky. 'We have, Tanzie.'

'Once. May the thirteenth. But now you work on Fridays.'

Her smile went really strange then, like she couldn't hold the corners of her mouth up properly.

Mr Cruikshank left the room, and reappeared a

moment later with his papers. She stuffed the last of the biscuit into her mouth, then got up and went to sit next to him. He had a whole pile of them. Stuff she hadn't even started yet!

She began going through them with him, showing him what she had done and what she hadn't, and in the background she could hear Mum and the headmaster's voices rumbling away. 'We're very conscious of the pit-falls, psychological and otherwise, that can occur if children are only encouraged to go in one direction . . . blah, blah, blah . . . If Costanza comes to us, while we would consider her mathematical ability an asset, her pastoral care would be . . .'

It sounded like it was going all right. Tanzie let her attention travel to what was on the page. It might have been renewal theory. 'Yes,' Mr Cruikshank was saying quietly, his finger on the page. 'But the curious feature of renewal processes is that, if we wait some predeter-mined time and then observe how large the renewal interval containing it is, we should expect it to be typi-cally larger than a renewal interval of average size.'

She knew about this! 'So the monkeys would take longer to type *Macbeth*?' she said.

'That's it.' He smiled. 'I wasn't sure you'd have covered any renewal theory.'

'I haven't, really. But Mr Tsvangarai told me about it once and I looked it up on the Internet. I liked the whole monkey thing.' She flicked through the papers. There was tons of it. The numbers sang to her. She could feel her brain sort of humming she wanted to read them so much. She knew she had to go to this school. 'Mum,' she said. She didn't usually interrupt, but she was too excited and forgot her manners. 'Do you think we could get some of these papers?'

Mr Daly looked over. He didn't seem to mind about the missing manners. 'Mr Cruikshank, have we any spares?'

'You can take these.'

He handed them over! Just like that! Tanzie began flicking through them. Outside a bell rang and she could hear children walking past the office window, their feet crunching on the gravel. She poked her head up to look at them. She wanted to see if any others were reading books.

'So . . . what happens next?'

'Well, we'd like to offer Costanza . . . Tanzie . . . a scholarship.' He lifted a glossy folder from the table. 'Here's our prospectus, and the relevant documentation. The scholarship covers ninety per cent of the fees. It's the most generous scholarship this school has ever offered. Usually fifty per cent is our maximum, given the extensive waiting list of pupils hoping to come here. The new scholarship is designed to recognize children with unusual levels of ability.'

'Like me,' Tanzie said.

'Like you.' He held out the plate towards her. Somehow they had replaced the biscuits on the plate with new ones. This really was the greatest school ever.

'Ninety per cent,' Mum said. She put her biscuit back on her saucer.

'I do appreciate that there is still a considerable financial commitment involved. And there would also be uniform and travel costs, and any extras she might want, like music or school trips. But I would like to stress that this is an incredible opportunity.' He leant forward. 'We would love to have you here, Tanzie. Your maths teacher says you're a joy to work with.'

'I like school,' she said, reaching for another biscuit. 'I know lots of my friends think it's boring. But I prefer school to home.'

They all laughed awkwardly.

'Not because of you, Mum,' she said, and helped herself to another. 'But my mum does have to work a lot.'

Everyone went quiet.

'We all do, these days,' said Mr Cruikshank.

'Well. It's a lot for you to think about. And I'm sure you have other questions for us. But why don't you finish your coffee, while we talk, and then I'll get one of our pupils to show you around the rest of the school? Then you can discuss this between yourselves.'

That evening Mum went up to Nicky's room and got him to hook the computer up to Skype. Every Sunday she would text Dad half an hour before, and he would set up the computer at Grandma's so that Tanzie could speak to him. She would sit at Nicky's desk and try not to be distracted by the little image of herself in the corner. It always made her look like she had a really weird-shaped head.

Except it wasn't Sunday.

Tanzie was downstairs in the garden throwing a ball for Norman. She was determined that one day he would fetch it and bring it back. Tanzie had read somewhere that repetition increases the probability of an animal learning how to do something by a factor of four. She wasn't sure Norman could count, though.

They had got Norman from the animal shelter when Dad first left and Mum stayed awake for eleven nights in a row worrying that they would be murdered in their beds once everyone realized he'd gone. Brilliant with kids, a fantastic guard dog, the rescue centre said. Mum kept saying, 'But he's so big.'

'Even more of a deterrent,' they said, with cheery smiles. 'And did we mention he's brilliant with kids?'

Two years on, Mum said Norman was basically an enormous eating and crapping machine. He plodded around the house shedding hair and leaving evil smells behind him. He drooled on cushions and howled in his sleep, his great paws paddling the air as if he was swimming. Mum said the rescue centre had been right: nobody would break into their house for fear Norman would gas them to death.

She had given up trying to ban him from Tanzie's bedroom. When Tanzie woke up in the morning he was always stretched across three-quarters of the bed, hairy legs across her mattress, leaving her shivering under a tiny corner of duvet. Mum used to mutter about hairs and hygiene but Tanzie didn't mind. She and Norman had a special bond. She knew that one day he would show it.

They'd got Nicky when she was two. Tanzie went to bed one night and when she woke he was in the spare room and Mum just said he would be staying and he was her brother. She didn't know if they had a special bond, even though they were actually 50 per cent related. Tanzie had once asked him what he thought their shared genetic material was, and he'd said, 'The weird loser gene.' She thought he might have been joking, but she didn't know enough about genetics to check.

She was rinsing her hands under the outside tap when she heard them talking. Nicky's window was open and their voices floated out into the garden.

'Did you pay that water bill?' Nicky said.

'No. I haven't had a chance to get to the post office.'

'It says it's a final reminder.'

'I know it's a final reminder.' Mum was snappy, like she always was when she talked about money. There was a pause. Norman picked up the ball and dropped it near her feet. It lay there, slimy and disgusting.

'Sorry, Nicky. I . . . just need to get this conversation out of the way. I'll sort it out tomorrow morning. I promise. You want to speak to your dad?'

Tanzie knew what the answer would be. Nicky never wanted to talk to Dad any more.

'Hey.'

She moved right under the window and stood really still. She could hear Dad's voice.

'Everything all right?' Dad sounded tense. She wondered if he thought that something bad had happened.

Perhaps if he thought Tanzie had leukaemia he might come back. She had watched a TV film once where the girl's parents divorced and then got back together because she got leukaemia. She didn't actually want leukaemia though because needles made her pass out and she had quite nice hair.

'Everything's fine,' Mum said. She didn't tell him about Nicky getting battered.

'What's going on?'

A pause.

'Has your mum decorated?' Mum asked.

'What?'

'New wallpaper.'

'Oh. That.'

Grandma's house had new wallpaper? Tanzie felt weird. Dad and Grandma were living in a house that she might not recognize any more. It had been 348 days since she last saw Dad. It was 433 days since she'd seen Grandma.

'I need to talk to you about Tanzie's schooling.'

'Why – is she playing up?'

'Nothing like that, Marty. She's been offered a scholarship to St Anne's.'

'St Anne's?'

'They think her maths is off the scale.'

'St *Anne's*.' He said it like he couldn't believe it. 'I mean I knew she was bright, but . . .'

He sounded really pleased. She pressed her back against the wall and went up on tippy-toes to hear better. Perhaps he'd come back if she was going to St Anne's.

'Our little girl at the posh school, eh?' His voice had puffed up with pride. Tanzie could imagine him already working out what to tell his mates at the pub. Except he couldn't go to the pub. Because he always told Mum he had no money to enjoy himself. 'So what's the problem?'

'Well . . . it's a big scholarship. But it doesn't cover everything.'

'Meaning what?'

'Meaning we'd still have to find five hundred pounds a term. And the uniform. And the registration fee of five hundred pounds.'

The silence went on for so long Tanzie wondered if the computer had crashed.

'They said once we've been there a year we can apply for a hardship fee. Some bursary or something where, if you're a deserving case, they can give you extra. But basically we need to find the best part of two grand to get her through the first year.'

And then Dad laughed. He actually laughed. 'You're having me on, right?'

'No, I am not having you on.'

'How am I meant to find two grand, Jess?'

'I just thought I'd –'

'I've not even got a proper job yet. There's nothing going on round here. I'm . . . I'm only just getting back on my feet. I'm sorry, babe, but there's no way.'

'Can't your mum help? She might have some savings. Can I talk to her?'

'No. She's . . . out. And I don't want you tapping her

32

for money. She's got worries enough as it is.'

'I'm not tapping her for money, Marty. I thought she might want to help her only grandchildren.'

'They're not her only grandchildren any more. Elena had a little boy.'

Tanzie stood very still.

'I didn't even know she was pregnant.'

'Yeah, I meant to tell you.'

Tanzie had a baby cousin. And she hadn't even known. Norman flopped down at her feet. He looked at her with his big brown eyes, then rolled over slowly with a groan, as if it was really, really hard work just lying on the floor. He kept looking at her, waiting for her to rub his tummy, but she was trying too hard to listen.

'Well . . . what if we sell the Rolls?'

'I can't sell the Rolls. I'm going to start the weddings business up again.'

'It's been rusting in our garage for the best part of two years.'

'I know. And I'll come and get it. I just haven't got anywhere to store it safely up here.'

The voices had that edge now. Their conversations often ended up like that. They would start off with Mum being all nice and then something would happen so that they both got really clipped and tense with each other. She heard Mum take a deep breath. 'Can you at least think about it, Marty? She really wants to go to this place. Really, really wants to go. When the maths teacher spoke to her, her whole face lit up like I haven't seen since —'

'Since I left.'

'I didn't mean it like that.'

'So it's all my fault.'

'No, it's not all your fault, Marty. But I'm not going to sit here and pretend that you going has been a barrel of laughs for them. Tanzie doesn't understand why you don't visit her. She doesn't understand why she hardly gets to see you any more.'

'I can't afford the fares, Jess. You know that. There's no point you going on and on at me. I've been ill.'

'I know you've been ill.'

'She can come and see me anytime. I told you. Send them both at half-term.'

'I can't. They're too young to travel all that way alone. And I can't afford the fares for all of us.'

'And I suppose that's my fault too.'

'Oh, for Christ's sake.'

Tanzie dug her nails into the soft parts of her hands. Norman kept looking at her, waiting.

'I don't want to argue with you, Marty,' Mum said, and her voice was low and careful, like when a teacher is trying to explain something to you that you should already know. 'I just want you to think about whether there is any way at all you could contribute to this. It would change Tanzie's life. It would mean she never has to struggle in the way that . . . we struggle.'

'You can't say that.'

'What do you mean?'

'Don't you watch the news, Jess? All the graduates are out of work. It doesn't matter what education you get.

She's still going to have to fight. She's still going to struggle.' He paused. 'No. There's no point us going further into hock just for this. Of course these schools are going to tell you it's all special, and she's special, and her life chances are going to be amazing if she goes, et cetera, et cetera. That's what they do.'

Mum didn't say anything.

'No, if she's bright like they say she is, she'll make her own way. She'll have to go to McArthur's like everyone else.'

'Like the little bastards who spend all their time working out how to bash Nicky's face in. And the girls who wear four inches of makeup and won't do PE in case they break a nail. She won't fit in there, Marty. She just won't.'

'Now you sound like a snob.'

'No, I sound like someone who accepts that her daughter is a little bit different. And might need a school that embraces it.'

'Can't do it, Jess. I'm sorry.' He sounded distracted now, as if he'd heard something in the distance. 'Look. I've got to go. Get her to Skype me Sunday.'

There was a long silence.

Tanzie counted to fourteen.

She heard the door open and Nicky's voice: 'That went well, then.'

She leant over and finally rubbed Norman's tummy. She closed her eyes so she didn't see the tear that plopped onto it.

'Have we done any lottery tickets lately?'

'No.'

That silence lasted nine seconds. Then Mum's voice echoed into the still air:

'Well, I think maybe we'd better start.'

3.

ED

Ed was in the creatives' room drinking coffee with Ronan when Sidney walked in. A man he vaguely recognized stood behind him; another of the Suits. In their sombre grey, with their end-of-the-world expressions, they resembled a pair of Jehovah's Witnesses.

'We've been looking for you.'

'Well, you found us.'

'Not Ronan, you.'

He studied them for a minute, waiting, then threw a red foam ball at the ceiling and caught it. He glanced sideways at Ronan. Investacorp had bought half-shares in the company a full eighteen months ago but they still thought of them as the Suits. It was one of the kinder things they called them in private.

'Do you know a woman called Deanna Lewis?'

'Why?'

'Did you give her any information about the launch of the new software?'

'What?'

'It's a simple question.'

Ed looked from one to the other. The atmosphere was strangely charged. His stomach, a packed elevator, began a slow descent towards his feet. 'We may have chatted about work. No specifics that I remember.'

'Deanna Lewis?' said Ronan.

'You need to be clear about this, Ed. Did you give her any information about the launch of SFAX?'

'No. Maybe. What is this?'

'The police are downstairs searching your office, with two goons from the Financial Services Authority. Her brother has been arrested for insider trading. On the basis of information that you gave them about the launch of the software.'

'Ha-ha-ha! Funny.'

'Deanna Lewis? Our Deanna Lewis?' Ronan began to wipe his spectacles, a thing he did when he was feeling anxious.

'Your Deanna Lewis?'

'We knew her back in college.'

'Did you now? Well, her brother's hedge fund made two point six million dollars on the first day of trading. She alone cleared a hundred and ninety thousand on her personal account.' They weren't laughing.

'Her brother's hedge fund?'

'Yes, his hedge fund.'

'I don't understand,' Ronan said. 'What is this?'

'I'll spell it out. Deanna Lewis is on record talking to her brother about Ed telling her about the launch of SFAX. She says Ed said it was going to be enormous. And guess what? Two days later her brother's fund is among the biggest purchasers of shares. What exactly did you tell her?'

Ronan stared at him. Ed struggled to gather his thoughts. When he swallowed it was shamefully audible. Across the office the development team were peering over the tops of their cubicles. 'I didn't tell her anything.' He blinked. 'I don't know. I might have said something. It's not like it was a state secret.'

'It was a fucking state secret, Ed. It's called insider trading. She told him you gave her dates, times. She told him the company was going to make a fortune.'

'Then she's lying! Shooting her mouth off. We were . . . having a thing.'

'You wanted to bone the girl, so you shot *your* mouth off to impress her?'

'It wasn't like that.'

'You had *sex* with Deanna Lewis?' Ed could feel Ronan's myopic gaze burning into him.

Sidney lifted his hands, turned to the man behind him. 'You need to call your lawyer.'

'But how can I be in trouble? It's not like I got any benefit from it.'

'Michael Lewis's hedge fund was the biggest single investor in Mayfly in the week before SFAX went live.'

'I didn't even know her brother had a hedge fund.'

Sidney glanced behind him. The faces suddenly found something interesting to look at on their desks. And he lowered his voice. 'You have to go now. They want to interview you at the police station.'

'What? This is nuts. I've got a meeting in twenty minutes. I'm not going to any police station.'

'And obviously we're suspending you until we've got to the bottom of this.'

Ed laughed at him. 'Are you kidding me? You can't suspend me. It's my company.' He threw the foam ball up in the air and caught it, turning away from them. Nobody moved. 'I'm not going. This is our company. Tell them, Ronan.'

He looked at Ronan, but Ronan turned away. Ed looked at Sidney, who simply shook his head. Then he looked up at the two uniformed men who had appeared behind him, at his secretary, whose hand was at her mouth, at the carpet path already opening up between him and the office door, and the foam ball dropped silently onto the floor between his feet.

Deanna Lewis. Maybe not the prettiest girl, but definitely the one who scored highest on Ed and Ronan's campus-wide Girls You'd Give One Without Having To Drink A Fourth Pint First points system. As if she'd look at either of them. He guessed that when she walked through the computer-science centre they had worn the same expressions as a basset hound watching a passing hamburger.

He'd bet she'd never once registered him in the whole three years, apart from that time when it was raining heavily and she was at the station and asked him for a lift back to halls in his Mini. He had been so tongue-tied the whole time she was in the passenger seat he had said barely a word, except a vaguely strangled, 'No worries,' when he let her out at the other end. Those two words somehow managed to cover three octaves. She gave him a look that told him he was watching too many Australian soaps, then stooped to peel the empty crisps packet from the sole of her boot, dropping it delicately back into the footwell.

If Ed had it bad, Ronan had it worse. His love weighed him down like a cartoon dumbbell, his hopes for it based on evidence less substantial than dust motes. He wrote her poetry, sent anonymous flowers on Valentine's Day, smiled hopefully at her in the dinner queue and tried not to look crushed when she failed to notice. He grew philosophical in the end. It only took three years. Ed and he had both understood that someone so pretty, so far up the campus pecking order, wouldn't make time for either of them. And after they had graduated, set up their company, and swapped thinking about women for thinking about software until software became the thing they actually preferred thinking about, Deanna Lewis fell into that weird pocket of reminiscence you bring out when you've had too much to drink and want to show your co-workers you had some kind of social life at university and didn't spend the entire three years stuck behind a screen. 'Oh . . . Deanna Lewis,' they would say to each other, their eyes distant, like they could see her floating in slo-mo above the other drinkers' heads. Or occasionally, of some other girl standing at the bar: 'She's nice. But she's no Lewis.'

And then, three months ago, some six months after Lara had left, taking with her the apartment in Rome, half the contents of his stock portfolio, and what remained of Ed's appetite for relationships, Deanna Lewis had contacted him via Facebook. She had been based in New York for a couple of years, but was coming back and wanted to catch up with some of her old friends from uni. Did he remember Reena? And Sam? Was he around for a drink at all?

Afterwards, he was ashamed that he hadn't told Ronan. Ronan was busy with the new software upgrade, he told himself. It had taken him ages to get Deanna out of his system. He was in the early stages of dating that girl from the not-for-profit soup place. Why stir it all up again? The truth was, Ed was still stuck in his post-divorce slough. He hadn't had a date in for ever. And a bit of him wanted Deanna Lewis to see what he had become since the company was sold a year previously.

Because money, it turned out, bought you someone to sort out your clothes, skin and hair. It bought you a personal trainer. Ed Nicholls no longer looked like the tongue-tied geek in the Mini. He wore no obvious signs of wealth, but he knew that, at thirty-three, he carried it like an invisible scent around him.

They met at a bar in Soho. She apologized: Reena – did he remember Reena? – had blown them out at the last minute. She had a *baby*. She lifted a faintly mocking eyebrow as she said this. Sam, he realized long afterwards, never showed. She never once asked about Ronan.

He couldn't stop staring at her. She looked just the same, but better. She had well-cut dark hair that bounced on her shoulders like a shampoo advert, and had lost the traces of puppy fat around her cheeks. She was nicer than he remembered, more human. Perhaps even golden girls were brought down to earth a little, once out of the confines of university. She laughed at all his jokes. Every now and then he glanced sideways to see her blinking at him and registered her brief flash of surprise that he was not the person she remembered. It made him feel good.

They parted after a couple of hours, and a little piece of him was surprised when she called two days later to suggest they hook up again. This time they went to a club and he danced with her, and when she lifted her hands above her head, he had to focus really hard not to picture her pinned to a bed. She was just out of a relationship, she explained, over the third or fourth drink. The break-up had been awful. She was not sure she wanted to be involved in anything serious. He made all the right noises. He told her about Lara, his ex-wife, and how she had said her work was always going to be her first love, and that she had to leave him to save her sanity.

'Bit melodramatic,' Deanna said.

'She's Italian. And an actress. Everything with her is melodramatic.'

'Was,' she corrected him. She kept her eyes on his as she said it. She asked him about work – was blunt in her admiration of what he had done with the company. 'I mean I'm a total tech klutz,' she said. 'But it sounds amazing.' She had picked up the beginnings of an American accent. Her leg rested against his.

He tried to explain it. She watched his mouth as he spoke, which was oddly distracting. He told her everything: the first trial versions he and Ronan had created in his bedroom, the software glitches, the meetings with a media tycoon who had flown them to Texas in his private jet and sworn at them when they refused his buyout offer.

He told her of the day they'd gone public, when he had sat on the edge of his bath watching the share price go up and up on his phone, and begun to shake as he grasped quite how much his whole life was about to change.

'You're that wealthy?'

'I do okay.'

'Define okay.'

He was aware that he was *this* close to sounding like a dick. 'Well . . . I was doing better until I got divorced, obviously . . . I do okay. You know, I'm not really interested in the money.' He shrugged. 'I just like doing what I do. I like the company. I like having ideas and translating them into things that actually work for people.'

'But you sold it?'

'It was getting too big, and I was told that if we did, the guys in suits could handle all the financial stuff. I was never interested in that side of things. I just own a lot of shares.' He stared at her. 'You have really nice hair.' He had no idea why on earth he said this.

She'd kissed him in the taxi. Deanna Lewis had slowly turned his face to hers with a slim, perfectly manicured hand and kissed him. Even though it was more than twelve years since they were at university – twelve years in which Ed Nicholls had been briefly married to a model/actress/whatever – some little voice in his head kept saying: *Deanna Lewis is kissing me.* And she wasn't just kissing him: she hitched up her skirt and slid a long, slim leg over him, apparently oblivious to the taxi driver, pressed into him, and kissed his face, his neck, and slid her hands up his shirt until he couldn't speak or think, and when he came to pay outside his flat, his words came out thick and stupid, and he not only didn't wait for the change but didn't even check what was in the wad of notes he handed the driver.

And the sex was great. Oh, God, it was good. She had porn moves, for Christ's sake. With Lara, in the last months, sex had felt like she was granting him some kind of favour – dependent on some set of rules that only she seemed to understand: whether he had paid her enough attention, or spent enough time with her or taken her out to dinner, or understood how he'd hurt her feelings. Sometimes she would turn silently away from him afterwards like he'd done something awful.

When Deanna Lewis looked at him naked, her eyes seemed to light up from inside with a kind of hunger. Oh, God. Jesus Christ. *Deanna Lewis.*

Afterwards, she had lain in bed, lit a cigarette, and said, 'I hardly smoke any more, but after that . . .' and chuckled throatily.

'I might take it up myself.'

And then, after she had finished her cigarette, she had given him head so good that he had suspected the down-stairs neighbours would be lighting cigarettes too.

She stayed with Ed the night after, and went home reluctantly. She was living with her brother in Fulham in the week, and at weekends in Bristol with her parents. That first week she emailed daily and rang him three times. He didn't tell Ronan. He instant-messaged her from his bed, his laptop a glowing ocean in the middle of his vast duvet, and tried not to think about her. They were just mucking around, he told himself. It was nothing serious. It wasn't as if Ronan was ever likely to bump into her.

Besides, he and Deanna were both just out of bad break-ups. They had discussed how cynical they were about relationships, how it was good to find your feet alone. And then one night he'd had a few drinks. He'd been feeling a bit melancholy. He'd paused for about thirty seconds, then typed: 'Come out with me this week-end.'

'I can't,' came the reply.

'Why?'

'Broke.'

Ed thought of the way her long dark hair felt entwined in his fingers. He thought about how nice it had been just to have someone in his head who wasn't Lara. And he wrote: 'I'll pay. Come.'

She arrived on Friday night. They walked round the local bars, took a trip down the river, had a pub lunch. She linked her arm in his and he found himself staring at her fingers and exclaiming silently, *Deanna Lewis! I'm sleeping with Deanna Lewis!* She was funny and sparky. She had this way of smiling that made you smile right back. And it was just so good to have guilt-free sex with someone whom you weren't afraid might steal your wallet while you were asleep.

On Sunday night they had a good meal, drank a lot of champagne, and then headed back to his place, and she had worn these crazy black silk knickers with ribbons at the sides that you could just pull undone so that they slid slowly down her thighs like a ripple of water. She rolled a joint afterwards, and he didn't normally smoke but he had felt his head spin pleasurably, had rested his fingers in her dark silky hair and felt like life was actually pretty good.

And then she said, 'I told my parents about us.'

He was having trouble focusing. 'Your parents?'

'You don't mind, do you? It's just been so good . . . feeling like . . . I belong in something again, you know?'

Ed found himself staring at a point on the ceiling. It's okay, he told himself. Lots of people tell their parents stuff. Even after two weeks.

'I've been so depressed. And now I just feel . . .' she beamed at him '. . . happy. Like madly happy. Like I wake up and I'm thinking about you. Like everything's going to be okay.'

His mouth felt oddly dry. He wasn't sure if it was the joint. 'Depressed?' he said.

'I'm okay now. I mean, my folks were really good. After the last episode they took me to the doctor and got me pills. And they definitely helped. They do apparently lower your inhibitions, but I can't say that anyone's complained! HA-HA-HA-HA!'

He handed her the joint.

'I just feel things very intensely, you know? My psychiatrist says I'm exceptionally sensitive. Some people bounce through life. I'm not one of those people. Sometimes I can read about an animal dying or a child being murdered somewhere in another country, and I will literally cry all day. Literally. I was like it at college too. Don't you remember?'

'No.'

She rested her hand on his cock. Suddenly Ed felt fairly certain it was not going to spring to life.

She looked up at him. Her hair was half over her face and she blew at it. 'It's such a bummer losing your job and your home. You have no idea what it's like to be really broke.' She gazed at him as if weighing up how much to tell him. 'I mean properly broke.'

'What – what do you mean?'

'Well . . . like I owe my ex a load of money but I've told him I can't pay him. I have too much on my credit card right now. And he still keeps ringing me, going on and on about it. It's very stressful. He doesn't understand how stressed I get.'

'How much are you talking about?'

'Oh. A fair bit.'

'How much?' He wasn't sure he wanted to know.

She told him. As his jaw dropped, she said, 'And don't offer to lend it to me. I wouldn't take money from my boyfriend. Makes things too complicated. But it's a nightmare.'

Ed tried not to think about the significance of her use of the word 'boyfriend'.

He glanced down at her and saw her lower lip tremble. He swallowed. 'Um . . . are you okay?'

Her smile was too swift, too wide. 'I'm good! Thanks to you, I'm really fine now.' She ran a finger along his chest. 'Anyway. It's been lovely not having to think about it. It's been heaven going out for nice dinners without wondering how I can afford it.' She kissed one of his nipples.

That night she slept with one leg slung over him. Ed lay wide awake, wishing he could ring Ronan.

She came back the following Friday, and the Friday after that. She didn't pick up on his hints about things he had said he had to do at the weekend. Her father had given her the money for them to have a meal. 'He says it's such a relief to see me happy again.'

He had a cold, he told her, as she came skipping across the road from the Tube station. Probably best not to kiss him.

'I don't mind. What's yours is mine,' she said, and attached herself to his face for a full thirty seconds.

They ate at the local pizza place. He had started to feel a vague, reflexive panic at the sight of her. She had 'feelings' about things all the time. The sight of a red bus made her happy, the sight of a wilted pot plant in a café window made her vaguely weepy. She was too much of everything. She smiled at too many people. She was sometimes so busy talking that she forgot to eat with her mouth closed. At his apartment she peed with the bathroom door open. It sounded like a visiting horse was relieving itself.

He wasn't ready for this. She was just too needy. Too erratic. Too everything. Ed wanted to be on his own in the apartment. He wanted the silence, the order of his normal routine. He couldn't believe he had ever been lonely.

That night he had told her he didn't want to have sex. 'I'm really tired.'

'I'm sure I could wake you up . . .' She had begun to burrow her way down the duvet and he actually had to haul her upwards. There followed a tussle that might have been funny in other circumstances: her mouth poised to plug onto his genitals, him desperately hauling her up by the armpits.

'Really. Deanna. Not . . . not now.'

'We can snuggle then. Now I know you don't just want me for my body!' She pulled his arm around her and emitted a little whimper of pleasure, like a small animal.

Ed Nicholls lay there, wide-eyed, in the dark. He had forgotten, in the four years that he had been dating and married Lara, how swiftly someone could pivot 180 degrees in your imagination from the most desirable person you had ever seen to someone you would gnaw your own limb off if it meant escaping. He took a breath.

'So . . . Deanna . . . um . . . next weekend I have to go away for business.'

'Anywhere nice?' She ran her finger speculatively along his thigh.

'Um . . . Geneva.'

'Ooh, nice! Shall I stow away in your case?'

'What?'

'I could be there waiting for you in your hotel room. When you come back from your meetings, I could soothe your troubled brow.' She reached out a finger and stroked his forehead. It was all he could do not to flinch.

'Really? That's nice. But it's not that kind of trip.'

'You're so lucky. I love travelling. If I wasn't so broke I'd be back on a plane in an instant.'

'You would?'

'It's my passion. I loved being a free spirit, going where the whim takes me.' She leant over, extracted a cigarette from the packet on the bedside table and lit it.

'So you'd like to travel again?'

'I'd be off like a shot.'

He had lain there for a bit, thinking. 'Do you own any stocks and shares?'

She rolled off him and lay back against her pillow. 'A few. I think my grandma left them to me. A hundred shares in some building society and another two hundred in Woolworths. Hah.' She half laughed. 'And don't suggest I bet on the stock market, Ed. I haven't got enough left to gamble with.'

It was out before he really knew what he was saying. 'It's not a gamble.'

'What isn't?'

'We've got a thing coming out. In a couple of weeks. It's going to be a game changer.'

'A thing?'

'I can't really tell you too much. But we've been working on it for a while. It's going to push our stock way up. Our business guys are all over it.'

She was silent beside him.

'I mean, I know we haven't talked a lot about work but this is going to make a serious amount of money.'

She didn't sound convinced. 'You're asking me to bet my last few pounds on something I don't even know the name of?'

'You don't need to know the name of it. You just need to buy some shares in my company.' He shifted onto his side. 'Look, you raise a few thousand pounds, and I guarantee you'll have enough to pay off your ex-boyfriend within two weeks. And then you'll be free! And you can do whatever you want! Go wherever you like!'

There was a long silence.

'Is this how you make money, Ed Nicholls? You take women to bed and then get them to buy thousands of pounds' worth of your shares?'

'No, it's –'

She turned over and he saw she was joking. She traced the side of his face. 'You're so sweet to me. And it's a lovely thought. But I don't have thousands of pounds lying around right now.'

The words came out of his mouth even before he knew what he was saying. 'I'll lend it to you. If it makes you money, you pay me back. If it doesn't, then it's my own fault for giving you dud advice.'

She started laughing and stopped when she realized he wasn't joking.

'You'd do that for me?'

Ed shrugged. 'Honestly? Five grand doesn't really make a big difference to me right now.' *And I'd pay ten times that if it meant you would leave.*

Her eyes widened. 'Whoa. That is the sweetest thing anyone's ever done for me.'

'Oh . . . I doubt that.'

Before she left the next morning he wrote her a cheque. She had been tying her hair up in a clip, making faces at herself in his hall mirror. She smelt vaguely of apples. 'Leave it blank,' she said, when she realized what he was doing. 'I'll get my brother to do it for me. He's good at all this stocks and shares stuff. What am I buying again?'

'Seriously?'

'I can't help it. I can't think straight when I'm near you.' She slid her hand down his boxers. 'I'll pay you back as soon as possible. I promise.'

'Here.' Ed reached over for a business card, and took a step backwards. 'That's the name of the company. And do this. I promise it'll help. Can't have you feeling hemmed in!'

He smothered the warning voice in his head. His *faux* cheer bounced off the apartment walls.

Ed answered almost all of her emails afterwards. He was cheerful, non-committal. He said how good it was to have spent time with someone who understood how weird it was just to have got out of a serious relationship, how important it was to spend time by yourself. She didn't answer that one. Oddly, she said nothing specific about the product launch or that the stock had gone through the roof. She would have made more than £100,000. Perhaps she was busy sticking pins into a picture of him. Perhaps she had lost the cheque. Perhaps she was in Guadeloupe. Every time he thought about what he had done his stomach lurched. He tried not to think about it.

He changed his mobile-phone number, telling himself it was an accident that he forgot to let her know. Eventually her emails tailed off. Two months passed. He took Ronan on a couple of nights out and they moaned about the Suits; Ed listened to Ronan as he weighed up the pros and cons of the not-for-profit soup girl and felt he'd learned a valuable lesson. Or dodged a bullet. He wasn't sure which.

And then, two weeks after the SFAX launch, he had been lying down in the creatives' room, idly throwing a foam ball at the ceiling and listening to Ronan discuss how best to solve a glitch in the payment software when Sidney, the finance director, had walked in and he had suddenly understood that there were far worse problems you could create for yourself than overly clingy girlfriends.

'Ed?'
   'What?'

A short pause.

'That's how you answer a phone call? Seriously? At what age exactly are you going to acquire some social skills?'

'Hi, Gemma.' Ed sighed, and swung his leg over the bed so that he was seated.

'You said you were going to call. A week ago. So I thought, you know, that you must be trapped under a large piece of furniture.'

He looked around the bedroom. At the suit jacket that hung over the chair. At the clock, which told him it was a quarter past seven. He rubbed the back of his neck. 'Yeah. Well. Things came up.'

'I called your work. They said you were at home. Are you ill?'

'No, I'm not ill, just . . . working on something.'

'So does that mean you'll have some time to come and see Dad?'

He closed his eyes. 'I'm kind of busy right now.'

Her silence was weighty. He pictured his sister at the other end of the line, her jaw set, her eyes raised to Heaven.

'He's asking for you. He's been asking for you for ages.'

'I will come, Gem. Just . . . I'm . . . I'm out of town. I have some stuff to sort out.'

'We all have stuff to sort out. Just call him, okay? Even if you can't actually get into one of your eighteen luxury cars to visit. Call him. He's been moved to Victoria Ward. They'll pass the phone to him if you call.'

'Okay.'

He thought she was about to ring off, but she didn't. He heard a small sigh.

'I'm pretty tired, Ed. My supervisors are not being very helpful about me taking time off. So I'm having to go up there every weekend. Mum's just about holding it together. I could really, really do with a bit of back-up here.'

He felt a pang of guilt. His sister was not a complainer. 'I've told you I'll try and get there.'

'You said that last week. Look, you could drive there in four hours.'

'I'm not in London.'

'Where are you?'

He looked out of the window at the darkening sky. 'The south coast.'

'You're on holiday?'

'Not holiday. It's complicated.'

'It can't be that complicated. You have zero commitments.'

'Yeah. Thanks for reminding me.'

'Oh, come on. It's your company. You get to make the rules, right? Just grant yourself an extra two weeks' holiday. Be the Kim Jong-un of your company. Dictate!'

Another long silence.

'You're being weird,' she said finally.

Ed took a deep breath before he spoke. 'I'll sort something. I promise.'

'Okay. And ring Mum.'

'I will.'

There was a click as the line went dead.

Ed stared at the phone for a moment, then dialled his lawyer's office. The phone went straight through to the answering machine.

The investigating officers had pulled out every drawer in the apartment. They hadn't tossed it all out, like they did in the movies, but had gone through it methodically, wearing gloves, checking between the folds of T-shirts, going through every file. Both his laptops had been removed, his memory sticks and his two phones. He had had to sign for it all, as if this was being done for his own benefit. 'Get out of town, Ed,' his lawyer had told him. 'Just go and try not to think too much. I'll call you if I need you to come in.'

They had searched this place too, apparently. There was so little stuff here it had taken them less than an hour.

Ed looked around him at the bedroom of the holiday home, at the crisp Belgian linen duvet that the cleaners had put on that morning, at the drawers that held an emergency wardrobe of jeans, pants, socks and T-shirts.

'Get out of town,' Sidney had said. 'If this gets out you're seriously going to fuck with our share price.'

Ronan hadn't spoken to him since the day the police had come to the office.

He stared at the phone. Other than Gemma, there was now not a single person he could call just to talk to without explaining what had happened. Everyone he knew was in tech and, apart from Ronan, he wasn't sure right now how many of those would qualify as actual friends. He stared at the wall. He thought about the fact that during the last week he had driven up and down to London four times just because, without work, he hadn't known what to do with himself. He thought back to the previous evening when he had been so angry, with Deanna Lewis, with Sidney, with *what the fuck* had happened to his life, that he had hurled an entire bottle of white wine at the wall and smashed it. He thought about the likelihood of that happening again if he was left to his own devices.

There was nothing else for it. He shouldered his way into his jacket, picked a fob of keys from the locked cupboard beside the back door and headed out to the car.

4.

JESS

There had always been something a bit different about Tanzie. At a year old she would line up her blocks in rows or organize them into patterns, then pull one or two away, making new shapes. By the time she was two she was obsessed with numbers. Before she even started school she would go through those books you can get full of maths problems and ask questions, like, 'Why is a one written as "1" and not "2"?' or tell Jess that multiplication was 'just another way of doing addition'. At six she could explain the meaning of 'tessellate'.

Marty didn't like it. It made him uncomfortable. But then anything that wasn't 'normal' made Marty uncomfortable. It was the thing that made Tanzie happy, just sitting there, ploughing through problems that neither of them could begin to understand. Marty's mother, on the rare occasions that she visited, used to call her a swot. She would say it like it wasn't a very nice thing to be.

'So what are you going to do?'

'There's nothing I can do right now.'

'Wouldn't it feel weird, her mixing with all the private-school kids?'

'I don't know. Yes. But that would be our problem. Not hers.'

'What if she grows away from you? What if she falls in with a posh lot and gets embarrassed by her background?'

'What?'

'I'm just saying. I think you could mess her up. I think she could lose sight of where she comes from.'

Jess looked over at Nathalie, who was driving. 'She comes from the Shitty Estate of Doom, Nat. As far as that goes, I would be happy if she got early-onset Alzheimer's.'

Something weird had happened since Jess had told Nathalie about the interview. It was as if she had taken it personally. All morning she had gone on and on about how her children were happy at the local school, about how glad she was that they were 'normal', how it didn't do for a child to be 'different'.

The truth of it was, Jess thought, that Tanzie had come home from the interview more excited than she had been in months. Her scores had been 100 per cent in maths and 99 per cent in non-verbal reasoning. (She was actually annoyed by the missing one per cent.) Mr Tsvangarai, ringing to tell her, said there might be other sources of funding. Details, he kept calling them, although Jess couldn't help thinking that people who thought money was a 'detail' were the kind who had never really had to worry about it.

'And you know she'd have to wear that prissy uniform,' Nathalie said, as they pulled up at Beachfront.

'She won't be wearing a prissy uniform,' Jess responded irritably.

'Then she'll get teased for not being like the rest of them.'

'She won't be wearing a prissy uniform because she won't be bloody going. I haven't got a hope of sending her, Nathalie. Okay?'

Jess got out of the car, slamming the door and walking in ahead of her so that she didn't have to listen to anything else.

It was only the locals who called Beachfront 'the holiday park'; the developers called it a 'destination resort'. Because this was not a holiday park like the Sea Bright caravan park on the top of the hill, a chaotic jumble of wind-battered mobile homes and seasonal lean-to tents: this was a spotless array of architect-designed 'living spaces' set among carefully manicured paths and lodges, in tended patches of woodland. There was a sports club, a spa, tennis courts, a huge pool complex, which the locals were not allowed to use after all, a handful of overpriced boutiques and a mini-supermarket so that residents did not have to venture into the scrappier confines of the town.

Tuesdays, Thursdays and Fridays Benson & Thomas cleaned the two three-bedroomed rental properties that overlooked the clubhouse, then moved on to the newer properties: six glass-fronted modernist houses that stood on the chalk cliff and looked straight out across the sea.

Mr Nicholls kept a spotless Audi in his driveway that

they had never once seen move. A woman who said she was his sister came once with two small children and a grey-looking husband (they left the place immaculately clean). Mr Nicholls himself rarely visited, and had never, in the year they'd been doing it, used either the kitchen or the laundry room. Jess made extra cash doing his towels and sheets, laundering and ironing them weekly for guests who never came.

It was a vast house; its slate floors echoed, its living areas were covered with great expanses of sea-grass matting and there was an expensive sound system wired into the walls. The glass frontages gazed out onto the wide blue arc of the horizon. But there were no photographs on the walls, or suggestions of any kind of actual life. Nathalie always said that even when he came it was as if he was camping there. There must have been women – Nathalie once found a lipstick in the bathroom, and last year they had discovered a pair of tiny lacy knickers under the bed (La Perla) and a bikini top – but there was little to suggest anything else about him.

Jess thought of her own house, the narrow, creaking stairs, the peeling wallpaper, and unusually (she rarely thought about clients' houses in relation to her own – that truly was the way to madness) she felt briefly wistful for all this space. This was a man who'd never had to put a clothes rail on the upstairs landing, or run out of space for bookshelves. This was a man who'd never fretted about how to find a registration fee.

'He's here,' muttered Nathalie.

As they closed the front door, a man's voice echoed

down the corridor, his voice loud, his tone argumentative, as if on the telephone. Nathalie pulled a face at Jess and walked slowly through the hallway.

'Cleaners,' she called. He did not respond, but he must have heard.

The argument continued the whole time it took to clean the kitchen (he had used one mug, and the bin held two empty takeaway cartons). There was broken glass in the corner by the fridge, small green splinters, as if someone had picked up the larger pieces but couldn't be bothered with the rest. And there was wine up the walls. Jess washed them down carefully. The place smelt like a brewery. And he was still arguing. She couldn't hear what he was saying, as his door was partially closed and too far away, but even muffled and at a distance his frustration was evident. She and Nathalie worked in silence, speaking in murmurs, trying to pretend they couldn't hear.

When they had finished the kitchen Nathalie moved on to the living room and Jess headed down the hall. She did the downstairs loo, then the dining room, with its untouched bleached oak table and perfectly matched chairs. She dusted the picture frames with a soft cloth, tilting the odd one a centimetre or two to show they'd been done. Outside on the decking sat an empty bottle of Jack Daniel's with one glass; she picked them up and brought them inside.

While she washed up, she thought about Nicky, who had returned from school the previous day with a cut ear, the knees of his trousers scuffed with dirt. He shrugged off any attempt to talk about it. His preferred life now consisted of people on the other side of a screen; boys Jess had never met and never would, boys he called SK8RBOI and TERM-N-ATOR who shot and disembowelled each other for fun. Who could blame him? His real life seemed to be the actual war zone.

She thought about Tanzie, and how she'd looked while talking to that maths teacher. Ever since the interview Jess had lain awake, doing calculations in her head, adding and subtracting in a way that would have made Tanzie laugh. The scholarship would not leave her head. It had lodged in there like toothache, and Jess worried away at it, trying every possible way to build financial mountains out of molehills. She sold her belongings. She ran through mental lists of every single person she might be able to borrow money from and who wouldn't mind if it took time to pay it back. She considered the most likely, and the most unlikely people – her mother, her aunt Nell in Dorset, the retired teacher she used to clean for who always said he could see that Tanzie was a bright girl – but while she might have been able to beg fifty pounds here and there, there was nobody who would lend ten times that much. Nobody she knew even had it.

The only people likely to offer Jess money were the sharks who circled the estate with their hidden four-figure interest rates. She had seen neighbours who had borrowed from friendly reps who turned gimlet-eyed, hanging over them like financial vultures. And again and again she came back to Marty's words. Was McArthur's comp really so bad? Some children did well there. There was no reason why Tanzie shouldn't be one of them, if she kept out of the way of the troublemakers.

The hard truth of it was there like a brick wall. Jess was going to have to tell her daughter that she couldn't make it add up. Jess Thomas, the woman who always found a way through, who spent her life telling the two of them that it would All Work Out, couldn't make it work out.

She finished the dining room in which no dining had ever taken place, and observed with some distant part of her that the loud talking had stopped. Mr Nicholls must finally be off the phone. She hauled the vacuum cleaner down the hallway, wincing as it bumped against her shin, and knocked on the door to see if he wanted his office cleaned. There was silence, and as she knocked again he yelled suddenly, 'Yes, I'm well aware of that, Sidney. You've said so fifteen times, but it doesn't mean –'

It was too late: she had pushed the door half open. Jess began to apologize, but with barely a glance the man held up a palm, like she was some kind of a dog – *stay* – then leaned forwards and slammed the door in her face. The sound reverberated around the house.

Jess stood there, shocked into immobility, her skin prickling with embarrassment.

'I told you,' Nathalie said, as she scrubbed furiously at the guest bathroom a few minutes later. 'Those private schools don't teach them any manners.'

Forty minutes later they were finished. Jess gathered Mr Nicholls's immaculate white towels and sheets into her holdall, stuffing them in with more force than was strictly necessary. She walked downstairs and placed the bag next to the cleaning crate in the hall. Nathalie was polishing the doorknobs. It was one of her things. She couldn't bear fingerprints on taps or doorknobs. Sometimes it took them ten minutes to leave an address.

'Mr Nicholls, we're going now.'

He was standing in the kitchen, just staring out through the window at the sea, one hand on the top of his head like he'd forgotten it was there. He had dark hair and was wearing those glasses that are supposed to be trendy but just make you look like you've dressed up as Woody Allen. He wore a suit like a twelve-year-old forced to go to a christening.

'Mr Nicholls.'

He shook his head slightly, then sighed and walked down the hallway. 'Right,' he said distractedly. He kept glancing down at the screen of his mobile phone. 'Thanks.'

They waited.

'Um, we'd like our money, please.'

Nathalie finished polishing, and folded her cloth, unfolding it and folding it again. She hated money conversations.

'I thought the management company paid you.'

'They haven't paid us in three weeks. And there's never anyone in the office. If you want us to continue we need to be up to date.'

He scrabbled around in his pockets, pulled out a wallet. 'Right. What do I owe you?'

'Thirty times three weeks. And three weeks of laundry.'

He looked up, one eyebrow raised.

'We left a message on your phone, last week.'

He shook his head, as if he couldn't be expected to remember such things. 'How much is that?'

'One hundred and thirty-five all together.'

He flicked through the notes. 'I don't have that much cash. Look, I'll give you sixty and get them to send you a cheque for the rest. Okay?'

On another occasion Jess would have said yes. On another occasion she would have let it go. It wasn't as if he was going to rip them off, after all. But she was suddenly sick of wealthy people who never paid on time, who assumed that because seventy-five pounds was nothing to them it must be nothing to her too. She was sick of clients who thought she meant so little that they could slam a door in her face without so much as an apology.

'No,' she said, and her voice was oddly clear. 'I need the money now, please.'

He met her eye for the first time. Behind her Nathalie rubbed manically at a doorknob. 'I have bills that need paying. And the people who send them won't let me put off paying week after week.'

She couldn't get it out of her head: the flat dismissal of his palm, the way he had just slammed the door in her face.

He frowned at her, as if she was being particularly difficult. It made her dislike him even more. She wondered, for a moment, whether to tell him to stick his stupid job. But there were some principles you couldn't afford.

'I'll have to look upstairs,' he said, disappearing. They stood in uncomfortable silence as they heard drawers being shut emphatically, the clash of hangers in a wardrobe. Finally he came back with a handful of notes.

He peeled some off without looking at Jess and handed them over. She was about to say something – something about how he didn't have to behave like an utter dickhead, about how life went that little bit more smoothly when people treated each other like human beings, something that would no doubt make Nathalie rub half the door handle away with anxiety. She didn't care. Even the way he handed out the money suggested he was giving her something she wasn't quite entitled to. But just as she opened her mouth to speak his phone rang. Without a word Mr Nicholls spun away from her and was striding down the hallway to answer it.

'What's that in Norman's basket?'

'Nothing.'

Jess was unpacking the groceries, hauling items out of the bags with one eye on the clock. She had a three-hour shift at the Feathers and just over an hour to make tea and get changed. She shoved two cans to the back of the shelves, hiding them behind the cereal packets. She was sick of the supermarket's cheery 'value' label. It was as if every time she opened the cupboard someone was yelling at her, 'HEY! YOU'RE POOR!'

Nicky stooped, and tugged at the piece of fabric, so

that the dog reluctantly got to his feet. 'It's a white towel. Jess, it's an expensive one. Norman's got hair all over it. And dribble.' He held it up between two fingers.

'I'm going to wash it later.' She didn't look at him.

'Is it Dad's?'

'No, it is not your dad's.'

'I don't understand –'

'It's just making me feel better, okay? Can you put that stuff over there in the freezer?'

He slouched against the kitchen units, peering out into the front garden. In the breeze the clothes dryer whirled around, the pegged cleaning cloths flying out like pennants above the potted geraniums and the bicycle Jess had painted a glittery pink that peeled off like clumps of nail varnish.

'Shona Bryant was taking the mickey out of Tanzie at the bus stop. Because of her clothes.'

'What about her clothes?' Jess turned to Nicky, a can of tinned tomatoes in her hand.

'Because you make them.'

'How does she know I make them?'

'She asked Tanzie where they came from and Tanzie just told her. You know what she's like.'

'But she likes what I make. I mean – she's happy in them.'

'Shona Bryant's the one who said our house was weird because we had too many books.'

'Shona Bryant's an idiot.'

He leant down to stroke Norman. 'Oh. And we got a reminder from the electric company.'

Jess let out a small sigh. 'How much?'

He walked over to the pile of papers on the sideboard and flicked through. 'Comes to more than two hundred altogether.'

She took out a packet of cereal. 'I'll sort it.'

Nicky opened the fridge door. 'You should sell the car.'

'I can't sell it. It's your dad's only asset.'

'But he could be using it to earn money. And then he could pay you some.'

Sometimes Jess wasn't entirely sure why she kept defending him. 'There isn't anywhere safe to keep it at his mum's. Anyway. He'll sort it out when he's back on his feet. Now, go on upstairs. I've got someone coming.' She could see her walking up the back path.

'We're buying stuff off Aileen Trent?' Nicky watched her open the gate and close it carefully behind her.

Jess couldn't hide the way her cheeks coloured. 'Just this once.'

He stared at her. 'You said we had no money.'

'Look, it's to take Tanzie's mind off the school thing when I have to tell her.' Jess had made her decision on the way home. The whole idea was ridiculous. They could barely keep their heads above water as it was. There was no point even trying to entertain it.

He kept staring at her. 'But Aileen Trent. You said – '

'And you're the one who just told me Tanzie was getting bullied because of her clothes. Sometimes, Nicky . . .' Jess threw her hands into the air. 'Sometimes the ends justify the means.'

Nicky's look lasted longer than she felt entirely comfortable with. And then he went upstairs.

'So I've brought a lovely selection of things for the discerning young lady. You know they all love their designer labels. I took the liberty of bringing a few extra bits, even though you said you weren't interested.'

Aileen's 'shop' voice was formal, with overly precise diction. It was quite odd, emerging as it did, from someone Jess had seen regularly ejected by force from the King's Arms. She sat cross-legged on the floor and reached into her black holdall, pulling out a selection of clothes and laying them carefully on the carpet, co-ordinating separates in layers.

'There's a Hollister top here. They're all into Hollister, the girls. Shocking expensive in the shops. I've got some more designer stuff in my other bag, although you did say you didn't require high-end. Oh, and two sugars, if you're making one.'

Aileen did a weekly round of this end of the estate, her skin waxy, her big black holdall on wheels trundling behind her. She was as much a local fixture as the postman, and as regular. 'You've got to be professional to thrive in business,' she would observe sagely, pale eyes blinking slowly within her spectral face.

Jess had always issued a firm thanks-but-no-thanks. Nobody on the estate ever talked about where Aileen got her bargains, her knock-down prices with the tags still on, but everyone knew. Jess always told Marty she didn't like the example it set the kids.

But that was before.

She picked up the layered tops, one stripy, the other a soft rose. She could already see Tanzie in them. 'How much?'

'Ten for the top, five for the T-shirt, and twenty for the trainers. You can see from the tag they retail for eighty-five. That's a serious discount.'

'I can't do that much.'

'Well, as you're a new client, I can do you an introductory bonus.' Aileen held up her notebook, squinting at the figures. 'You take the three items and I'll let you have the jeans too. For goodwill.' She smiled, her missing tooth gaping cheerfully. 'Thirty-five pounds for a whole outfit, including footwear. And this month only I'm throwing in a little bracelet. You won't get those prices in TK Maxx.'

Jess stared at the perfect clothes laid out on the floor. She wanted to see Tanzie smiling. She wanted her to feel that life held the potential for unexpected happy things, not just a harassed, overworked mother who never had time to spend with her, and an absent father who communicated once a week through a computer screen.

She wanted her to have something to feel good about when she gave her the news.

'Hold on.'

She walked through to the kitchen, pulled the cocoa tin from the cupboard where she kept the electricity money. She counted out the coins and dropped them into Aileen's clammy palm before she could think about what she was doing.

'Pleasure doing business with you,' Aileen said, folding the remaining clothes and placing them carefully in the bin bag. 'I'll be back in two weeks. Anything you want in the meantime, you know where to find me.'

'I think this will be it, thanks.'

She gave Jess a knowing look. *Yeah. They all say that, love.*

Nicky didn't look up from his computer when Jess walked in.

'Nathalie's going to bring Tanzie back after maths club. Are you going to be okay here by yourself?'

'Sure.'

'No smoking.'

'Mm.'

'You going to do some revision?'

'Sure.'

Sometimes Jess fantasized about the kind of mother she could be if she wasn't always working. She would bake cakes with the children and let them lick the bowl. She would smile more. She would sit on the sofa and actually talk to them. She would stand over them at the kitchen table while they did their homework, pointing out mistakes and ensuring they got the best possible marks. She would do the things they wanted her to do, instead of always answering:

- Sorry, love, I just have to get the supper on.
- After I've put this wash on.
- I've got to go, sweetie. Tell me when I get back from my shift.

She gazed at him, his unreadable expression, and she had a weird sense of foreboding. 'Don't forget to walk Norman. But don't go round near the off-licence.'

'As if.'

'And don't spend the whole evening on the computer.'

He had already turned back to the screen.

She hoicked up the back of his jeans. 'And put your pants away before I can't help myself and give you the world's biggest wedgie.'

He turned and she glimpsed his brief smile. As Jess walked out of his room she realized she couldn't remember the last time she'd seen it.

5.

NICKY

My dad is such an arsehole.

6.

JESS

The Feathers public house sat between the library (closed since January) and the Happy Plaice (11 a.m.–11 p.m., all year round), and in the right light, inside, it was possible to believe it was still 1989. Des, the landlord, had never been seen in anything but faded tour T-shirts, jeans and, if it was cold, a blouson leather jacket. On a quiet night, if you were unlucky, he would detail the merits of a Fender Stratocaster against a Rickenbacker 330 or recite with a poet's reverence all the words to 'Money For Nothing'.

The Feathers was not smart, in the way that the Beach-front bars were smart, and it did not serve fresh seafood or fine wines and family-friendly menus to screaming children. It served various kinds of dead animal with chips, and it scoffed at the word 'salad' (what it really liked was crisps: it stocked no fewer than twenty-eight varieties). There was nothing more adventurous than Tom Petty on the jukebox, a battered dartboard on the wall, and a carpet from which, in the mornings, the odour of beer and old cigarettes was so strong that locals had been known to arrive at work partially drunk because they had strolled past too slowly.

But it was a formula that worked. The Feathers was that rare thing in a seaside town: busy all year round.

'Is Roxanne here?' Jess pinned up a new strip of pork scratchings as Des emerged from the cellar, where he had been tying on a fresh barrel of real ale.

'Nah. She's doing something with her mother.' He thought for a minute. 'Healing. No, fortune-telling. Psychiatrist. Psychologist.'

'Spiritualist?'

'The one where they tell you stuff you already know and you're meant to look impressed.'

'Psychic.'

'Thirty pound a ticket, they're paying, to sit there with a glass of cheap white wine and shout, "Yes!" when someone asks did someone in the audience have a relative whose name began with J.' He stooped, slamming the cellar door shut with a grunt. 'I could predict a few things, Jess. And I won't charge you thirty pound for it. I predict that man is sitting at home right now, rubbing his hands and thinking, What a bunch of muppets.'

Jess hauled the tray of clean glasses out of the dishwasher and began stacking them on the shelves above the bar.

'Do you believe all that old bollocks?'

'No.'

'Course you don't. You're a sensible girl. I don't know what to say to her sometimes. Her mother's the worst. She reckons she's got her own guardian angel. An angel.' He mimicked her, looking at his own shoulder and tapping it. 'She reckons it protects her. Didn't protect her from spending all her compensation on the shopping channels, did it? You'd think that angel would have had a word. "Here, Maureen. You really don't want that luxury ironing-board cover with a picture of a dog on it. Really, love. Put a bit into your pension instead.'"

Miserable as Jess felt, she couldn't help but laugh. It was hard not to in the pub. The men at the bar were gentlemanly (as far as men who belched the alphabet could be called gentlemanly), the talk was cheerful, and it meant that for two nights and two lunchtimes a week she did not sit at home with a pile of someone else's laundry worrying about things she could not control.

'You're early.' Des looked pointedly at his watch.

'Shoe emergency.' Chelsea slung her handbag under the bar, and fixed her hair. 'I got chatting online to one of my dates,' she said, to Jess, as if Des wasn't there. 'He's absolutely gorgeous.'

All Chelsea's Internet dates were gorgeous. Until she met them.

'David, his name is. He's looking for someone who likes cooking, cleaning and ironing. And the odd trip out.'

'To the supermarket?' said Des.

Chelsea ignored him. She picked up a dishcloth and began drying glasses. 'You want to get yourself on there, Jess. Get out and about a bit instead of mouldering in here with this lot of droopy old ballsacks.'

'Less of the old, you.'

The football was on, which meant that Des put out free crisps and cheese cubes, and, if he was feeling particularly generous, mini sausage rolls. Jess had taken home the leftover cubes, with Des's blessing, to make macaroni cheese, until Nathalie had told her the statistic for how many men actually washed their hands after going to the loo.

The bar filled, the match started, the evening passed without note; she poured pints in the commentary gaps, silent against the blare of the satellite television on the far wall, and thought, yet again, about money. The end of the month, the school had said. If she didn't register by then, that was it. Jess could save for a year and see if she could try to get her in at twelve, but there was no guarantee that the scholarship would still exist.

She was so deep in thought that she almost didn't hear Des until he dumped a bowl of Quavers on the bar beside her. 'I meant to tell you. Next week we've got a new till coming. It's one of those where everything's written down. All you have to do is touch the screen.'

She turned away from the optics. 'A new till? Why?'

'That one is older than I am. And not all the barmaids can add up as well as you, Jess. The last time Chelsea was on by herself I cashed up and we were eleven quid out. Ask her to add up a double gin, a pint of Webster's and a packet of dry-roasted and her eyes cross. We've got to move with the times.' He ran his hand across an imaginary screen. 'Digital accuracy. You'll love it. You won't have to use your brain at all. Just like Chelsea.'

'Can't I just stick with this? I'm hopeless with computers.'

'You'll be fine. We're going to do staff training.'

'Staff training.'

'Half a day. Unpaid, I'm afraid. I've got a bloke coming.'

'Unpaid?'

'Just tap-tap-swipe on a screen. It'll be like *Minority Report*. But without the bald people. Mind you, we'll still have Pete. PETE!'

Liam Stubbs came in at a quarter past nine. Jess had her back to the bar and he leant over it and murmured, 'Hey, hot stuff,' into her ear.

She didn't turn round. 'Oh. You again.'

'There's a welcome. Pint of Stella, please, Jess.' He glanced around the bar, then said, 'And whatever else you have on offer.'

'We have some very nice dry-roasted peanuts.'

'I was thinking of something a bit . . . wetter.'

'I'll get you that pint, then.'

'Still playing hard to get, eh?'

She had known Liam since school. He was one of those men whom you knew would break your heart into tiny pieces if you let him; the kind of blue-eyed, smart-mouthed boy who ignored you all the way through years ten and eleven, laughed you into bed when you lost your braces and grew your hair, then gave you nothing more than a cheery wave and a wink for ever after. His hair was chestnut brown, his cheekbones high and lightly tanned. He ran a flower stall in the market and whenever she passed he would whisper, 'You. Me. Behind the dahlias, now,' just seriously enough to make her miss her stride. His wife had left him about the same time as Marty had departed ('A little matter of serial infidelity. Some women are so picky'), and six months ago, after one of Des's lock-ins, they had ended up in the ladies' loos with his hands up her shirt and Jess walking round wearing a lopsided smile for days.

She and Marty had lived like an irritable brother and sister by the time he left. Sometimes he said he was tired. Mostly he said she put him off with her nagging.

Jess sometimes thought she missed it, but she didn't miss him.

She was taking the empty cardboard crisps boxes out to the bins when Liam appeared at the back gate. He walked up to her with a sort of silent swagger so that she had to back slowly against the wall of the pub garden. He had a smile on his face like they were both in on some private joke. He stood so that the entire length of his body was just inches from hers and said softly, 'I can't stop thinking about you.' He held his cigarette hand well away from her. He was a gentleman like that.

'I bet you say that to all the girls.'

'I like watching you move around that bar. Half the time I'm watching the football, and half the time I'm imagining bending you over it.'

'Who says romance is dead?'

God, he smelt good. Jess wriggled a bit, trying to get herself out from under him before she did something she'd regret. Being near Liam Stubbs sparked bits of her to life that she had forgotten existed, like those joke birthday candles that insist on reigniting long after you'd blown them out.

'So let me romance you. Let me take you out. You and me. A proper date. Come on, Jess. Let's make a go of it.'

Jess pulled back from him. 'What?'

'You heard.'

She stared. 'You want us to have a *relationship*?'

'You say it like it's a dirty word.'

She slid out from under him, glancing towards the back door. 'I've got to get back to the bar, Liam.'

'Why won't you go out with me?' He took a step closer. 'You know it would be great . . .' His voice had dropped to a whisper.

'And I also know I have two kids and two jobs and you spend your whole life in your car, and it would take about three weeks for you and me to be bickering on a sofa about whose turn it was to take the rubbish out.' She smiled sweetly at him. 'And then we would lose the heart-stopping romance of exchanges like this for ever.'

He picked up a lock of her hair and let it slide through his fingers. His voice was a soft growl. 'So cynical. You're going to break my heart, Jess Thomas.'

'And you're going to get me fired.'

He was the man you never dared take seriously. She thought he probably liked her because she was the only woman round here who didn't.

'I take it this means a quickie's out of the question?'

She extricated herself and made her way towards the back door, trying to make the colour subside from her cheeks. Then she stopped. 'Hey, Liam.'

He looked up from stubbing his cigarette out.

'You don't want to lend me five hundred quid, do you?'

'If I had it, babe, you could have it.' He blew a kiss as she disappeared back indoors.

She was walking around the bar to pick up empties, her cheeks still pink, when she saw him. She actually did a double-take. He was sitting in the corner alone, and there were three empty pint glasses in front of him.

He had changed into Converse trainers, jeans and a T-shirt and he sat staring at his mobile phone, flicking at the screen and occasionally glancing up when everyone cheered a goal. As Jess watched, he picked up a beer and downed it. He probably thought that in his jeans he blended in, but he had 'incomer' written all over him. As he glanced towards the bar, she turned away swiftly, feeling her brief happy mood evaporate.

'Just popping downstairs for some more snacks,' she said to Chelsea, and made for the cellar. 'Ugh,' she muttered, under her breath. 'Ugh. Ugh. Ugh.' When she re-emerged he had a fresh pint and barely looked up from his phone.

The evening stretched. Chelsea discussed her Internet options, Mr Nicholls drank three more pints and Jess disappeared whenever he got up to the bar, juggled debts and imaginary lottery wins and tried not to meet Liam's eye. By ten to eleven, the pub was down to a handful of stragglers – the usual offenders, Des called them. Chelsea put on her coat.

'Where are you going?'

She stooped to apply her lipstick in the mirror behind the optics. 'Des said I could leave a bit early.' She pursed her lips. 'Date.'

'Date? Who goes on a date at this time of night?'

'It's a date at David's house. It's all right,' she said, as Jess stared at her. 'My sister's coming too. He said it would be nice with the three of us.'

'Chels, have you ever heard the expression "booty call"?'

'What?'

Jess looked at her for a minute. 'Nothing. Just . . . have a nice time.'

She was loading the dishwasher when he appeared at the bar. His eyes were half closed and he swayed gently, as if he was about to embark on some free-form dance.

'Pint, please.'

She shoved another two glasses to the back of the wire rack. 'We're not serving any more. It's gone eleven.'

He looked up at the clock. His voice slurred. 'It's one minute to.'

'You've had enough.'

He blinked slowly, stared at her. His short, dark hair was sticking up slightly on one side, as if at some point during the last hour, he had started to slide down the banquette. 'Who are you to tell me I've had enough?'

'The person who serves the drinks. That's usually how it works.' Jess held his gaze. 'You don't even recognize me, do you?'

'Should I?'

She stared at him a moment longer. 'Hold on.' She let herself out from behind the bar, walked over to the swing door, and as he stood there, bemused, she opened it and let it swing back in her face, lifting a hand and opening her mouth as if to say something.

She opened the door again and stood there in front of him. 'Recognize me now?'

He blinked. Jess could almost hear the cogs of his brain working.

'Are you . . . Did I see you yesterday?'

'The cleaner. Yes.'

He ran a hand through his hair. 'Ah. The whole door thing. I was just . . . having a tricky conversation.'

'"Not now, thanks" tends to work just as well, I find.'

'Right. Point taken.' He leant on the bar. Jess tried to keep a straight face when his elbow slipped off.

'So that's an apology, is it?'

He peered at her blearily. 'Sorry. I'm really, really, really sorry. Very sorry, O Bar Lady. Now can I have a drink?'

'No. It's gone eleven.'

'Only because you kept me talking.'

'I haven't got time to sit here while you nurse another pint.'

'Give me a shot, then. Come on. I need another drink. Give me a shot of vodka. Here. You can keep the change.' He slammed a twenty on the bar. The impact reverberated through the rest of him so that his head whiplashed back slightly. 'Just one. Actually, make it a double. It'll take me all of two seconds to down it. One second.'

'No. You've had enough.'

Des's voice broke in from the kitchen. 'Oh, for Christ's sake, Jess, give him a drink.'

Jess stood for a moment, her jaw rigid, then turned and emptied the optic twice into a glass. She rang up the money, then silently placed his change on the bar. He downed the vodka, swallowing audibly as he put the glass down, and turned away, staggering slightly.

'You forgot your change.'

'Keep it.'

'I don't want it.'

'Put it in your charity box, then.'

She gathered it up and shoved it at his hand. 'Des's charity of choice is the Des Harris Holiday In Memphis Fund,' she said. 'Really. Just take your money.'

He blinked at her, and took two unbalanced steps to the side as she opened the door for him. It was then she noticed what he had just pulled from his pocket. And the super-shiny Audi in the car park.

'You're not driving home.'

'I'm fine.' He batted away her protest. 'There aren't any cars around here at night anyway.'

'You can't drive.'

'We're in the middle of nowhere, in case you haven't noticed.' He gestured at the sky. 'I'm miles away from everything, and stuck here, in the middle of fucking nowhere.' He leant forward, and his breath was a blast of alcohol. 'I'll go very, very, slowly.'

He was so drunk that peeling the keys from his hand was embarrassingly easy. 'No,' she said, turning back to the bar. 'I won't be responsible for you having an accident as well as everything else. Go back inside, and I'll call you a taxi.'

'Give me my keys.'

'No.'

'You're stealing my keys.'

'I'm saving you from a driving ban.' She held them aloft, and turned back towards the bar.

'Oh, for Chrissakes,' he said. He made it sound like she was the last in a long line of irritations. It made her want to kick him.

'I'll get you a taxi. Just – just sit there. I'll give you your keys back once you're safely inside it.'

She texted Liam from the phone in the back hall.

Does this mean I get lucky? he replied.

If you like them hairy. And male.

She walked back outside and Mr Nicholls was gone. His car was still there. She called him twice, wondering if he'd headed off to a bush to relieve himself, then glanced down and there he was, fast asleep on the outside bench. The angle of his limbs suggested he had simply keeled over sideways from his seated position and passed out.

She thought, briefly, about leaving him there. But it was chilly, and the sea mists were unpredictable, and he would likely wake up without his wallet.

'I'm not taking that,' Liam said, through the driver's window, as his taxi pulled into the car park.

'He's fine. He's just asleep. I can tell you where he's got to go.'

87

'Nuh-uh. Last sleeper I had woke up and vomited all down my new seat covers. Then somehow perked up enough to do a runner.'

'He lives on Beachfront. He's hardly going to do a runner.' She glanced down at her watch. 'Oh, come on, Liam. It's late. I just want to get home.'

'Then leave him. Sorry, Jess.'

'Okay. How about I stay in the car while you drop him off? If he's ill, I'll clean it up. Then you can drop me home. He can pay.' She picked up Mr Nicholls's change from where he had dropped it on the ground beside the bench, and sifted through it. 'Thirteen pounds should do it, yes?'

He pulled a face. 'Ah, Jess. Don't make it hard for me.'

'Please, Liam.' She smiled. She placed a hand on his arm. 'Pretty please.'

He gazed down the road. 'All right. But if he's sick it's thirty quid for the lost earnings. And you'll have to clean it up.'

She lowered her head to Mr Nicholls's sleeping face, then straightened and nodded. 'He says that's fine.'

Liam shook his head. The flirtatious air of earlier had evaporated.

'Oh, come on, Liam. Help me get him in. I need to go home.'

He lay with his head on her lap, like a sick child. She didn't know where to put her hands. She held them across the back of the rear seat, and spent the whole journey praying that he wouldn't be sick. Every time he groaned, or shifted, she wound down a window, or leaned across to check his face. Don't you dare, she told him silently. Just don't you dare. They were two minutes from the holiday park when her phone buzzed. It was Belinda, her neighbour. She squinted at the illuminated screen: *Boys have been after your Nicky again. Got him outside the chip shop. Nigel's taken him to hospital.*

A large cold weight landed on her chest. *On my way* she typed.

Nigel says he'll stay with him till you're there. I'll stay here with Tanzie.

Thanks Belinda. I'll be as quick as I can.

A drumbeat of anxiety began a tattoo in her chest. Mr Nicholls shifted and let out an elongated snore. She stared at him, at his expensive haircut and his too blue jeans, and was suddenly furious. She might have been home by now if it wasn't for him. It would have been her walking the dog, not Nicky.

'Here we are.'

Jess directed him to Mr Nicholls's house, and they dragged him in between them, his arms slung over their shoulders, Jess's knees buckling a little under his surprising weight. He stirred a little when they reached his front door, and she fumbled through his keys, trying to find the right one, before she decided it would be easier to use her own.

'Where do you want him?' said Liam, puffing.

'Sofa. I'm not lugging him upstairs.'

'He's lucky we lugged him anywhere at all.'

She pushed him briskly into the recovery position. She took his glasses off, threw a nearby jacket over him, and dropped his keys on the side table that she had polished earlier that day.

And then she felt able to speak the words: 'Liam, can you drop me at the hospital? Nicky's had an accident.'

The car sped through the empty lanes in silence. Her mind was racing. She was afraid of what she might find. *What had happened? How badly was he hurt? Had Tanzie seen any of it?* And then, under the fear, the stupid, mundane stuff, like, *Will I be hours at the hospital? A taxi from there would be at least fifteen pounds. Bugger Mr Nicholls and his stupid vodka.*

'You want me to wait?' said Liam, when he pulled up at A&E.

'Could you? I'll only be two minutes. I just need to find out how bad it is.'

She was out of the door before he had even stopped the car.

He was in a side cubicle. When the nurse showed her in through the curtain, Nigel rose from his plastic chair, his kind, doughy face taut with anxiety. Nicky was turned away, his cheekbone covered with a dressing and the beginnings of a black eye leaking colour into the socket above it. A temporary bandage snaked its way around his hairline.

It was all she could do not to let out a sob.

'They're going to stitch it. But they want to keep him in. Check for fractures and whatnot.' Nigel looked awkward. 'He didn't want me to call the police.' He gestured in the general direction of outside. 'If you're all right, I'll be getting back to Belinda. It's late . . .'

Jess whispered her thanks, and moved over to Nicky. She placed her hand on the blanket, where his shoulder was.

'Tanzie's okay,' he whispered, not looking at her.

'I know, sweetheart.' She sat down on the plastic chair beside his bed. 'What happened?'

He gave a faint shrug. Nicky never wanted to talk about it. What was the point, after all? Everyone knew the score. You looked like a freak, you got battered. You still looked like a freak, they still kept coming after you. That was the immovable logic of a small seaside town.

And, just for once, she didn't know what to say to him. She couldn't tell him it would all be all right, because it patently wasn't. She couldn't tell him the police would get the Fishers, because they never did. She couldn't tell him that things would change before he knew it, because when you were a teenager your life really only stretches in your imagination about two weeks ahead, and they both knew that it wasn't going to get better by then. Or, probably, any time soon after that.

She took his grazed hand and held it in both of hers. 'It'll be okay, you know,' she said quietly. 'It does get better than this. You need to keep hold of that. Really. It does get better.'

His gaze slid briefly over and met hers, and then he looked away.

'He all right?' said Liam, as she walked slowly back out to the car. The adrenalin had leached out of her, and

Jess's shoulders slumped with exhaustion. She opened the rear door to fetch her jacket and bag, and his eyes, in the rear-view mirror, took it all in.

'He'll live.'

'Little bastards. I was just talking to your neighbour. Someone ought to do something.' He adjusted his mirror. 'I'd teach them a lesson myself if I didn't have to watch out for my licence. Boredom, that's what it is. They don't know what else to do with themselves but pick on someone. Make sure you got all your stuff, Jess.'

She had to half climb into the car to reach her coat. And as she did, she felt something under her feet. Semi-solid, cylindrical. She moved her foot, reached down into the footwell, and came up with a fat roll of bank notes. She stared at it in the half-dark, then at what had fallen down beside it. A laminated identity card, the kind you would use at an office. Both must have fallen out of Mr Nicholls's pocket when he was slumped on the back seat. Before she could think about it she stuffed them into her bag.

'Here,' she said, reaching into her purse, but Liam raised a hand.

'No. I've got it. You've enough on your plate.' He gave her a wink. 'Give one of us a ring when you want picking up. On the house. Dan's cleared it.'

'But –'

'No buts. Out you get now, Jess. Make sure that boy of yours is okay. I'll see you at the pub.'

She felt almost tearful with gratitude. She stood there, one hand raised, as he circled the car park, so that she heard him as he shouted out of the driver's window: 'You should tell him, though, if he'd just try to look a bit more normal, he might not get his head bashed in so often.'

7.

JESS

She dozed through the small hours on the plastic chair, waking occasionally from discomfort and the sound of distant tragedies in the ward beyond the curtain. She watched the newly stitched Nicky as he finally slept, wondering how she was supposed to protect him. She wondered what was going on in his head. She wondered, with a clench of her stomach that no longer seemed to go away, what was coming next. A nurse popped her head around the curtain at seven and said she'd made her some tea and toast. This small act of kindness caused her to fight back embarrassed tears. The consultant stopped by shortly after eight, and said Nicky would probably spend another night in while they checked that there was no internal bleeding. There was a shadow they hadn't quite got to the bottom of on the X-ray and they wanted to be sure. The best thing Jess could do would be to go home and get some rest. Nathalie rang to say she'd taken Tanzie to school with her kids and that everything was fine.

Everything was fine.

She got off the bus two stops before her house, walked round to Leanne Fisher's, knocked on her door and told

94

her, with as much politeness as she could muster, that if Jason came anywhere near Nicky again she would have the police on him. Whereupon Leanne Fisher spat at her and said if Jess didn't fuck right off she'd put a brick through her effing window. There was a burst of laughter from within the house as Jess walked away.

It was pretty much the response she'd expected.

She let herself into her empty home. She paid the water bill with the council-tax money. She paid the electric with her cleaning money. She showered and changed and did her lunchtime shift at the pub, so lost in thought that Stewart Pringle rested his hand on her arse for a full thirty seconds before she noticed. She poured his half-pint of best bitter slowly over his shoes.

'What did you do that for?' Des yelled, when Stewart Pringle complained.

'If you're so okay with it, you stand there and let him rest his hand on *your* arse,' she said, and went back to cleaning the glasses.

'She has a point,' Des said.

She vacuumed the entire house before Tanzie came home. She was so tired that she should have been comatose, but in fact she was so angry it was possible she did it all at double speed. She couldn't stop herself. She cleaned and folded and sorted because if she didn't she would take Marty's old sledgehammer down from the two hooks in the musty garage, walk round to the Fishers' house and do something that would finish them all off completely. She cleaned because if she didn't she would stand in her overgrown little back garden, lift her face to the sky and scream and scream and scream and she wasn't sure she'd be able to stop.

By the time she heard the footsteps on the path, the house floated in a toxic fug of furniture polish and kitchen cleaner. She took two deep breaths, coughed a bit, then made herself take one more before she opened the door, a reassuring smile already plastered on her face. Nathalie stood on the path, her hands on Tanzie's shoulders. Tanzie walked up to her, put her arms around her waist and held her tightly, her eyes shut.

'He's okay, sweetheart,' Jess told her, stroking her hair. 'It's all right. It's just a silly boys' fight.'

Nathalie touched Jess's arm, gave a tiny shake of her head, and left. 'You take care,' she said.

Jess made Tanzie a sandwich and watched her wander away into the shady part of the little garden with the dog to do algorithms and told herself she would tell her about St Anne's tomorrow. She would definitely tell her tomorrow.

And then she disappeared into the bathroom and unrolled the money she had found in Mr Nicholls's taxi. Four hundred and eighty pounds. She laid it out in neat piles on the floor with the door locked.

Jess knew what she should do. Of course she did. It wasn't her money. It was a lesson she drummed into the kids every day: *You don't steal. You don't take what is not yours. Do the right thing, and you will be rewarded for it in the end.*

Do the right thing.

So why didn't she take it back?

A new, darker voice had begun a low internal hum in

her ear. *Why should you give it back? He won't miss it. He was passed out in the car park, in the taxi, in his house. It could have fallen out anywhere. It was only luck that you found it, after all. And what if someone else from round here had picked it up? You think they would have handed it back to him? Really?*

His security card said the name of his company was Mayfly. His first name was Ed.

She would take the money back to Mr Nicholls. Her brain whirred round and round in time with the clothes-airer.

And still she didn't do it.

Jess never used to think about money. Marty handled the finances, and they generally had enough for him to go down the pub a couple of nights a week, and for her to have the odd night out with Nathalie. They took the occasional holiday. Some years they did better than others, but they got by.

And then Marty got fed up with making do. There was a camping holiday in Wales where it rained for eight days solid and Marty became more and more dissatisfied, as if the weather was something to be taken personally. 'Why can't we go to Spain, or somewhere hot?' he'd mutter, staring out through the flaps of the sodden tent. 'This is crap. This isn't a bloody holiday.' He got fed up with driving; he found more and more to complain about. The other drivers were against him. The controller was cheating him. The passengers were tight. And then he started with the schemes. The pyramid scheme they joined two weeks too late. The knock-off

T-shirts for a band that fell out of the charts as quickly as it had arrived. Import-export was the thing, he told Jess confidently, arriving home from the pub one night. He had met a bloke who could get cheap electrical goods from India, and they could sell them on to someone he knew.

And then – surprise, surprise – the someone who was going to sell them on turned out not to be the sure thing Marty had been promised. And that year's summer turned into the wettest on record. And the few people who did buy them complained that they blew their electricity supply, and the rest of them rusted, even in the garage, so their meagre savings turned into a pile of useless white goods that had to be loaded, fourteen a week, into Marty's car and taken to the dump. She still had the plugs under the stairs.

And then came the Rolls-Royce. Jess could at least see the sense in that one: Marty would spray it metallic grey, then rent himself out as a chauffeur for weddings and funerals. He'd bought it off eBay from a man in the Midlands, and made it halfway down the M6 before it conked out. Something to do with the starter motor, they said, peering under the bonnet. But the more they looked at it, the more seemed wrong with it. The first winter it spent on the drive, mice got into the upholstery so they needed money to replace the back seats before he could rent it out – because who wanted to sit on seats held together with duct tape on their wedding day? And then it turned out that replacement upholstered Rolls-Royce seats were about the only thing you couldn't get on eBay.

So it sat there in the garage, a daily reminder of how they never quite managed to get ahead, and the reason why her freezer had to live in the downstairs hall.

She'd taken over the money when Marty had got ill and started to spend most of each day in bed. Depression was an illness, everyone said so. Although, from what his mates said, he didn't seem to suffer it on the two evenings he still managed to drag himself to the pub. She had peeled all the bank statements from their envelopes, and retrieved the savings book from its place in the hall desk and had finally seen for herself the trouble they were in. She'd tried to talk to him a couple of times, but he'd just pulled the duvet over his head and said he couldn't cope. It was around then that he'd suggested he might go home to his mum's for a bit. If she was honest, Jess was relieved to see him go. It was hard enough coping with Nicky, who was still a silent, skinny wraith, Tanzie and two jobs.

'Go,' she'd said, stroking his hair. She remembered thinking how long it had been since she'd touched him. 'Go for a couple of weeks. You'll feel better for a bit of a break.' He had looked at her silently, his eyes red-rimmed, and squeezed her hand.

That had been two years ago. Neither of them had ever seriously raised the possibility of him coming back.

She tried to keep things normal until Tanzie went to bed, asking what she'd had to eat at Nathalie's, telling her what Norman had done while she was out. She combed Tanzie's hair, then sat on her bed and read her a story, like she was a much younger child, and just for once Tanzie didn't tell her that actually she'd rather do some maths.

When Jess was finally sure she was asleep she rang the hospital, who said that Nicky was comfortable, and that the consultant was coming around again first thing, after which they thought he could probably be discharged. The X-rays had thrown up no evidence that his lung was punctured, and the small facial fracture would have to heal by itself.

She rang Marty, who listened in silence, then asked, 'Does he still wear all that stuff on his face?'

'He wears a bit of mascara, yes.'

There was a long silence.

'Don't say it, Marty. Don't you dare say it.' She put the phone down before he could.

And then the police rang at a quarter to ten and said that Fisher had denied all knowledge.

'There were fourteen witnesses,' she said, her voice tight with the effort of not shouting. 'Including the man who runs the fish-and-chip shop. They jumped my son. There were four of them.'

'Yes, but witnesses are only any use to us if they can identify the perpetrators, madam. And Mr Brent says it wasn't clear who was actually doing the fighting.' He let out a sigh, as if these sorts of calls were an endless chore, as if she should know what teenage boys were like. 'I have to tell you, madam, the Fishers claim your son started it.'

'He's about as likely to start a fight as the Dalai bloody

Lama. We're talking about a boy who can't put a duvet in its cover without worrying it might hurt someone.'

'We can only act on the evidence, madam.' His flat tone said he had heard it all before.

The Fishers, she thought, as she slammed down the phone. With their reputation, she'd be lucky if a single person 'remembered' what they'd seen.

For a moment Jess let her head fall into her hands. They would never let up. And it would be Tanzie next, once she started secondary school. She would be a prime target with her maths and her oddness and her total lack of guile. The thought of it made her go cold. She thought about Marty's sledgehammer in the garage. She thought about how it would feel to walk down to the Fishers' house and –

The phone rang. She snatched it up. 'What now? Are you going to tell me he beat himself up too? Is that it?'

'Mrs Thomas?'

She blinked.

'Mrs Thomas? It's Mr Tsvangarai.'

'Oh. Mr Tsvangarai, I'm sorry. It – it's not a great time –' She held out her hand in front of her. It was shaking.

'I'm sorry to call you so late but it's a matter of some urgency. I have discovered something of interest. It's called a Maths Olympiad.' He spoke the words carefully.

'A what?'

'It's a new thing, in Scotland, for gifted students. A maths competition. And we still have time to enter Tanzie.'

'A maths competition?' Jess closed her eyes. 'You

know, that's really nice, Mr Tsvangarai, but we have quite a lot going on here right now and I don't think I –'

'Mrs Thomas. Hear me out. The prizes are five hundred pounds, a thousand pounds and five thousand pounds. Five thousand pounds. If she won, you'd have at least the first year of your St Anne's school fees sorted out.'

'Say that again?'

He repeated it. Jess sat down on the chair, as he explained in greater depth.

'This is an actual thing?'

'It is an actual thing.'

'And you really think she could do it?'

'There is a category especially for her age group. I cannot see how she could fail.'

Five thousand pounds, a voice sang in her head. *Enough to get her through at least the first year.*

'What's the catch?'

'No catch. Well, you have to do advanced maths, obviously. But I can't see that this would be a problem for Tanzie.'

She stood up and sat down again.

'And of course you would have to travel to Scotland.'

'Details, Mr Tsvangarai. Details.' Her head was spinning. 'This is for real, right? This isn't a joke?'

'I am not a funny man, Mrs Thomas.'

'Fuck. FUCK. Mr Tsvangarai, you are an absolute beauty.'

She could hear his embarrassed laugh. She thought he was less embarrassed by her swearing than that she was probably the first woman ever to have called him a beauty.

'So . . . what do we do now?'

'Well, they waived the qualifying test after I sent over some examples of Tanzie's work. I understand they are very keen to have children from less advantaged schools. And, between you and me, it is, of course, an enormous benefit that she's a girl. But we have to decide quickly. You see, this year's Olympiad is only five days away.'

Five days. The deadline for registration at St Anne's was tomorrow.

She stood in the middle of the room, thinking. Then she ran upstairs, pulled Mr Nicholls's money from its nest among her tights, and before she could think she stuffed it into an envelope, scrawled a note, and wrote the address in careful letters on the front.

She would pay it back. Every penny.

But, right now, she didn't have a choice.

That night, Jess sat at the kitchen table, studied the figures and worked out a rough plan. She paid off the minimum on her credit card, sent a holding letter to the gas company disputing her bill (that should buy her at least a month), and wrote cheques to the creditors whom she knew wouldn't wait, like the housing association. She looked up the cost of three train tickets to Edinburgh, laughed a bit hysterically, then looked up coach tickets (£187, including the £13 it would cost to get to the coach station) and the cost of putting Norman in kennels for a week (£94). She put the palms of her hands into her eye sockets and let them stay there for a bit. And then, when the children were asleep, she dug out the keys to the Rolls-Royce, went outside, brushed the mouse droppings off the driver's seat and tried the ignition.

It turned over on the third attempt.

Jess sat in the garage that always smelt of damp, even in high summer, surrounded by old garden furniture, bits of car, plastic buckets and spades and the empty boxes for air-conditioning units, letting the engine run and thinking. Then she leant forward and peeled back the faded tax disc. It was almost two years out of date. And she was uninsured.

She stared at it, then turned off the ignition and sat in the dark as the engine ticked down and the smell of oil gradually faded from the air, and she thought, for the hundredth time: *Do the right thing*.

8.

ED

Ed.Nicholls@mayfly.com: Don't forget what I told you. Can remind you of deets if you lose the card.

Deanna1@yahoo.com: I won't forget. Whole night engraved on my memory. ;-)

Ed.Nicholls@mayfly.com: Did you do what I told you?

Deanna1@yahoo.com: I did. Thanx.

Ed.Nicholls@mayfly.com: Let me know if you get good results!

Deanna1@yahoo.com: Well, based on your past performance, I'd be amazed if it was anything but! ;-0

Deanna1@yahoo.com: Nobody's ever done for me what you did for me.

Ed.Nicholls@mayfly.com: Really. It was nothing.

Deanna1@yahoo.com: You want to hook up again, next weekend?

Ed.Nicholls@mayfly.com: Bit busy at the mo. I'll let you know.

Deanna1@yahoo.com: I think it worked out well for both of us ;-)

The detective let him finish reading the two sheets of paper, then slid them towards Paul Wilkes.

'Have you got any comment on those, Mr Nicholls?'

There was something excruciating about seeing private emails laid out in an official document. The eagerness of his early replies, the barely veiled *double-entendres*, the smiley faces (what was he? Fourteen?) viewed in the cold light of an interview room, made something inside him shrivel.

'You don't have to say anything,' Paul said.

'That whole exchange could be about anything.' Ed pushed the documents away from him. "Let me know if you get good results." I could have been telling her to do something sexual. It could be, like, email sex.'

'At eleven fourteen a.m.?'

'So?'

'In an open-plan office?'

'So I'm uninhibited.'

The detective removed his glasses and gave him a hard look. 'Email sex? Really? That's what you were doing here?'

'Well, no. Not in that case. But that's not the point.'

'I would suggest it is totally the point, Mr Nicholls. There are reams of this stuff. There's a paper trail of the two of you meeting twice. You talk about keeping in touch . . .' he flicked through the papers '. . . "to see if I can help you out some more".'

'But it's not how it sounds. She was depressed. She was having a bad time getting rid of her ex. I just wanted to . . . make things a little easier for her. I keep telling you.'

'Ed . . .' Paul's voice was a warning bell.

'Just a few more questions.'

They had questions, all right. They wanted to know how often he had met Deanna. Where they had gone. What the exact nature of their relationship was. They didn't believe him when Ed said he didn't know much about her life. They didn't believe him when he said he knew nothing about her brother.

'Oh, come on!' he protested. 'You've never had a relationship based on sex?'

'Miss Lewis doesn't say it was based on sex. She says the two of you were involved in a "close and intense" relationship, that you had known each other since your college days, and that you were determined to make her go ahead with this deal, that you pressed it on her. She says she had no idea that in taking your advice she was doing anything illegal.'

'But she's — she's making it sound like we had much more of a relationship than we did. And I didn't force her to do anything.'

'So you admit that you gave her the information.'

'I'm not saying that! I'm just saying —'

'I think what my client is saying is that he cannot be

held responsible for any misconceptions Ms Lewis might have held about their relationship,' Paul Wilkes interjected. 'Or what information she might have passed on to her brother.'

'And we were not having a relationship. Not that kind of relationship.'

The detective shrugged. 'You know what? I don't really care what the nature of your relationship was. I don't care if you knobbed her halfway to next Wednesday. What is of interest to me, Mr Nicholls, is that you are on record as having given this young woman information, which, on the twenty-eighth of February, she told a friend was "going to bring us some serious profit". And which her and her brother's fund's bank accounts show did in fact bring them some "serious profit".'

An hour later, bailed for a fortnight, Ed sat in Paul Wilkes's office. Paul poured them both a whisky, and they sat in silence while Ed drank his. He was becoming oddly used to the taste of strong alcohol in daylight hours.

'I can't be held responsible for what she told her brother. I can't go around checking whether every potential partner has a brother who works in finance. I mean who does that? Surely they're going to see that.'

Paul leant back in his chair and sighed, like someone well used to explaining the obvious. 'The chain comes back to you. She and her brother made a barrow-load of money, and they did it illegally on information you gave her.'

'I was trying to help her.'

'Well, you certainly did that. But the SFA and the SOCA won't care what your motives were, Ed.'

'Can we stop talking in acronyms? I have no idea who you're talking about.'

'Well, basically, try and imagine every serious crime-fighting body that has anything to do with finance. Or crime. That's basically who is investigating you right now.'

'You make it sound like I'm actually going to be charged.' Ed put the whisky on the table beside him.

'I think it's extremely likely, yes. And I think we may be in court pretty quickly. They're trying to speed up these cases.'

Ed stared at him. Then his head sank into his hands. 'This is a nightmare. I just . . . I just wanted her to go away, Paul. I want this to go away.'

'Well, the best we can hope for at the moment is that we can convince them that you're basically just a geek who was in over his head.'

'Great.'

'You got any better ideas?'

Ed shook his head.

'Then just sit tight.'

'I need to do something, Paul. I need to get back to work. I don't know what to do if I'm not working. I'm going nuts down there in Nowheresville.'

'Like I said, I know the prosecutors want to get this sewn up quickly. But if I were you I'd stay put for now. The SFA may well leak this and then the shit is really going to hit the fan. I've drawn up a statement saying you're completely innocent and that we have every confidence your name will be cleared once this goes to court. But the moment this gets out, the media are going to be all over you like a bad suit. The best thing you can do is hide out down there in Nowheresville for another week or so.' Paul scribbled a note on his legal pad.

Ed gazed at the upside-down writing. 'Do you think this will get into the papers?'

'I don't know. Probably. It might be a good idea to talk to your family, anyway, just so they're prepared for any negative publicity.'

Ed rested his hands on his knees. 'I can't.'

'You can't what?'

'Tell my dad about all this. He's sick. This would . . .' He shook his head. When he finally looked up, Paul was watching him steadily.

'Well, that's got to be your decision. But, as I said, I think it would be wise for you to remain somewhere out of reach when it all blows up. Mayfly obviously doesn't want you anywhere near its offices until it's all sorted. There's too much money riding on the product launch. So you need to steer clear of anyone associated with the company. No calls. No emails. And if anyone does happen to locate you, for God's sake, don't say anything. To anyone.' He tapped his pen, signalling the end of the conversation.

'So basically I hide in the middle of nowhere, keep *schtum*, and twiddle my thumbs until I get sent to prison.'

The lawyer just stood, closed the file on his desk.

'Well, we're putting our best team on it. We'll do our best to make sure it doesn't come to that.'

Ed stood, and made to leave, slowly digesting the fact that his lawyer had not denied any of it. Paul opened the door to show him out. 'And next time, Ed? Just tell her you're not really interested. Saves a whole lot of trouble.'

Ed stood blinking on the steps of Paul's office, surrounded by office workers and lead-stained buildings, couriers tugging helmets from sweaty heads, bare-legged secretaries laughing on their way to eat sandwiches in the park, and felt a sudden pang for his old life. The one with his Nespresso machine in his office and his secretary nipping out for sushi, and his apartment with the views over the city, and the worst thing that afternoon being the prospect of having to lie on the couch in his office and listen to the Suits drone on about profit and loss. He had never really measured his life by that of anyone else but now he felt cripplingly envious of the people around him with their everyday concerns, their ability to get on a Tube back to their own homes, their families. The simple pleasures of going for a meal with friends, to stretch out in front of the television with his arm around someone. What did he have? Weeks of being stuck in an empty house, with nobody to talk to, facing the prospect of imminent prosecution.

He thought back to the previous week, to waking up on his sofa at Beachfront with no idea how he had got there, his mouth as dry as if it had been packed with cotton wool, his glasses neatly folded on the coffee-table. It was the third time in as many weeks that he'd been so drunk he couldn't remember how he'd got home, the first time he had woken with empty pockets.

He wasn't really a drinker. Lara had always insisted alcohol gave you belly fat and complained that he snored if he had more than two. He wanted a drink right now like he had rarely wanted anything.

Because here was the thing: he missed work more than he had ever missed his wife. He missed it like a constant mistress; he missed having a routine. For almost five years now his day had run to the world's most regular timetable:

- 7.00 a.m. get up, drink coffee
- 7.30 a.m. meet personal trainer, shower, walk to work, second coffee with Ronan
- 9.00 a.m. work
- 8.30 p.m. finish work, maybe have a quick drink at the bar downstairs with Ronan, walk home, maybe stay up and do a bit more work

It had been orderly. Reassuring. Satisfying. And now every morning that Ed Nicholls woke up he had to think of a reason just to get dressed. He had to convince himself that his life wasn't over.

Get a grip, Nicholls. He took a breath. Think logically. There is a way round every problem. There is always a way round.

He checked his phone (new, only three imported contacts). There were two voicemail messages from Gemma. Nobody else had called. Ed sighed and pressed delete, then set off along the sun-baked pavement towards the car park.

Ed sat for a while in his empty flat, got a bite to eat at a pizza restaurant, sat again in his flat, and then, because he had no reason to stay in the city, he climbed back into his car and drove towards the coast. Deanna Lewis danced before him the whole way out of London, spinning around against the rain-spattered windscreen like a cut-price dervish. He thought about those big brown eyes, half closed in apparent pleasure, wrinkling in delight at one of his jokes. He saw them gazing directly into his, as if allowing him to see straight into her. His thoughts darted around like silverfish. How could he have been so stupid? Why had he not thought about the possibility that she would tell someone else? Or was he actually missing something more sinister here? Had she and her brother planned this? Was it some sort of psychotic revenge strategy for dumping her?

He drove and his brain hummed with questions. His skin prickled with anger, and with every mile it grew. He might as well have given her the keys to his flat, his bank-account details, like his ex-wife, and let her wipe him out. That would actually have been better. At least he would have kept his job, his friend. Shortly before the Godalming exit, overcome with rage, he pulled over on the motorway and dialled her mobile number. He had to try to remember it, as the authorities had taken his old phone, with all the contacts on, as part of their search for evidence. *What the hell did you think you were doing?* he wanted to yell at her. *Why would you even do that to somebody? What the hell did I ever do to you that justified demolishing my whole life and leaving me in so much rubble?*

But the number was dead.

Ed sat in a layby, his phone in his hand, feeling his rage dissipate. He hesitated, then rang Ronan's number. It was one of only a handful he knew off by heart.

It rang several times before he answered.

'Ronan –'

'I'm not allowed to talk to you, Ed.' He sounded weary.

'Yeah. I know. I just – I just wanted to say –'

'Say what? What do you want to say, Ed?'

The anger in his voice was a silencer.

'You know what? I don't actually care so much about the insider-trading thing. Although obviously it's a bloody disaster for the company. But you were my mate. My oldest friend. I would *never* have done that to you.'

A click, and the phone went dead.

Ed sat there and allowed his head to drop onto the wheel for a few minutes. He waited until the humming in his mind leached away to nothing, and then he indicated, pulled out slowly and drove towards Beachfront.

*

The phone rang just as he was coming off the dual carriageway. He looked at the glowing screen, sighed, and pressed a button on the hands-free set.

'What do you want, Lara.' He didn't say it like a question.

'Hey, baby. How are you?'

'Uh . . . not so good.'

'Oh, no! What is the matter?'

He never knew if it was an Italian thing, but she had a way, his ex-wife, of making you feel better. She would cradle your head, run her fingers through your hair, fuss around you, cluck maternally. By the end it had irritated him, but now, on the empty road at dead of night, he felt nostalgic for it.

'It's . . . a work thing.'

'Oh. A *werk* thing.' That instinctive bristle in her voice. Ed wondered if she had thought he was going to say he missed her.

He had known marrying Lara wasn't a good idea. You know that thing where people say, 'Even as we stood at the altar I knew in my gut that it wasn't right,' and you think, You idiot! Why the hell did you go ahead with it, then? Well, that was him. He had been that man. They had got married because he knew Lara really, really wanted it and he'd thought it would make her happy. It had taken him about two weeks to realize marriage wasn't going to make her happy at all. Or, at least, marriage to him.

'It's fine, Lara. How are you?'

'Mamma is driving me crazy. And there is a problem with the roof at home.'

'Any jobs?'

She made a sound with her teeth against her lips. 'I got a call-back for a West End show and then they say I look too old. Too old!'

'You don't look too old.'

'I know! I can look sixteen! Baby, I need to talk to you about the roof.'

'Lara, it's your place. You got a settlement.'

'But they say it's going to cost lots of money. Lots of money. I have *nothing*.'

He kept his voice steady. 'What happened to the settlement?'

'There is nothing. My brother needed some money for his business, and you know Papi's health is not good. And then I had some credit cards . . .'

'All of it?'

'I don't have enough for the roof. It's going to leak this winter, they said. *Eduardo* . . .'

'Well, you could always sell the print you took from my apartment in December.' His solicitor had implied it was his own fault for not changing the locks on the doors. Everyone else did, apparently.

'I was sad, Eduardo. I miss you. I just wanted a reminder of you.'

'Right. Of the man you said you couldn't stand to even look at any more.'

'I was angry when I said that.' She pronounced it *engry*. By the end she was always *engry*. He rubbed at his eyes, flicked the indicator to signal his exit onto the coast road.

'I just wanted some reminders of when we were *heppy*.'

'You know, maybe the next time you miss me you could take away, like, a framed photo of us, not a four-teen-thousand-pound limited-edition print of Mao Tse-tung.'

Her voice dropped to a whisper. It filled the dark confines of the car, almost unbearably intimate. 'Don't you care that I have no one to turn to?'

Her voice was feline, a soft, sad growl. It made his balls tighten reflexively. And she knew it.

Ed glanced in his rear-view mirror. 'Well, why don't you ask Jim Leonards?'

'What?'

'His wife called me. She's not very happy, funnily enough.'

'It was only once! Once I went out with him. And it is nobody's business who I date!' He heard her roar of outrage. Could picture her, one perfectly manicured hand raised, fingers splayed in frustration at having to deal with 'the most annoying man on earth'. 'You left me! Am I supposed to be a nun my whole life?'

'You left me, Lara. On the twenty-seventh of May, on the way back from Paris. Remember?'

'Details! You always twist my words with details! This is exactly why I had to leave you!'

'I thought it was because I only loved my work and didn't understand human emotions.'

'I left you because you have a tiny dick! Tiny, TINY dick! Like a pawn!'

'You mean prawn.'

'PRAWN. CRAYFISH. Whatever is smallest thing! Tiny!'

'Then I think you actually mean shrimp. You know, given you just walked off with a valuable limited-edition print, I think you could at least have granted me "lobster". But sure. Whatever.'

He heard the Italian curse, the clumsy slamming down of her phone. He drove for several miles that later he would not recall driving. And then he sighed, turned on the radio, and fixed his gaze on the seemingly endless black road ahead.

Gemma rang just as he was turning down the coast road. Her name flashed up on the hands-free and Ed answered before he'd had time to think about why he shouldn't. It felt like every time his phone rang it was just so that somebody could yell at him.

'Don't tell me. You're really busy.'

'I'm driving.'

'And you have a hands-free thing. Mum wanted to know if you're going to be there for their anniversary lunch.'

'What anniversary lunch?'

'Oh, come on, Ed. I told you about it months ago.'

'I'm sorry. I haven't got access to my diary right now.'

He could hear her taking a breath.

'They're going to let Dad out next Tuesday. So Mum's doing a special lunch at home for them. She wanted us to be there. You said you'd be able to come.'

'Oh. Yeah.'

'Yeah what? You remember? Or yeah, you're coming?'

He tapped his fingers on the steering-wheel. 'I don't know.'

'Look, Dad was asking for you yesterday. I told him you're tied up with a work project but he's so frail, Ed. This is really important to him. To both of them.'

'Gemma, I've told you –'

Her voice exploded into the interior of the car. 'Yeah, I know, you're too busy. You've told me you've got a lot on. You've told me you've got stuff going on.'

'I have got stuff going on! You have no idea!'

'Oh, no, I couldn't possibly hope to understand, could I? Just the stupid social worker who doesn't earn a six-figure fucking salary. This is our dad, Ed. This is the man who sacrificed everything to buy you a fucking education. He thinks the sun shines out of your backside. And he's not going to last much longer. You need to get down there and show your face and say the things that sons are meant to say to their dying fathers, okay?'

'He's not dying.'

'How the fuck would you know? You haven't been to see him in two months!'

'Look, I will go. It's just I've got to –'

'Why do you keep making excuses?'

'I'm not making excuses, Gem –'

'Bullshit. You're a businessman. You make stuff happen. Make this happen. Or I swear I –'

'I'm losing you, Gem. Sorry, the reception's really

patchy here. I –' He began to make *ssssh* noises, then reached over, pressed a button. The phone went dead, but not before he detected the muffled cry of '*Arsehole!*'

He turned on the radio. It was a monotone programme about milk yields. He changed the channel, but the music was abrasive and shrieky and reminded him too much of his sister. He tried a classical music station (too melancholy) and commercial local radio (DJ too irritating) before giving up and turning it off again.

The phone rang. He looked at the number and ignored it. It rang again. He ignored it. The third time he sighed, then pressed the button.

'One lunch,' she said, her social-work voice on, all calm and conciliatory. 'One little lunch, Ed. That's all I'm asking.'

He spotted a police car up ahead, and checked the speedometer, half braced for tangled metal. A filthy Rolls-Royce, one headlight dimmed, sat half up on the verge under the orange glow of a sodium light. A small girl stood beside it holding an enormous dog on a lead. Her head swivelled slowly as he passed.

'I do understand that you have a lot of commitments, and your job is really important. We all understand that, Mr Big Swinging Technodick. But just one awkward family lunch with your sick father and your overworked, underpaid do-gooder sister. Would that be too much to ask?'

'Hang on, Gem. There's an accident.'

Beside her a ghostly teenager – boy? girl? – with a

shock of dark hair, stood with his hands in his pockets, his shoulders slumped and, turning briefly away from a policeman who was writing something, another child – no, a small woman, her hair tied back into a scrappy ponytail. She was lifting her hands in exasperation in a gesture that reminded him of Lara. *You are so annoying!*

He had driven a further hundred yards before he understood the jolt that went through him. He knew that woman. He racked his brain: bar? Holiday park? He had a sudden image of her taking his car keys, a memory of her removing his glasses in his house. What was she doing out there with children at this time of night? He pulled over and glanced into the rear-view mirror, watching. He could just make out the group. The little girl had sat down on the dark verge, the dog a mountainous black lump beside her.

'Ed? Are you okay?' Gemma's voice broke into the silence.

Afterwards he wasn't entirely sure what made him do it. Perhaps it was an attempt to delay his arrival back in that empty house to sit staring at a television screen until the small hours. Perhaps it was the strangeness of it – that making himself part of such a scene seemed no longer an odd thing to do in a life that had gone so far off the rails.

Perhaps it was just that he wanted to convince himself, against all available evidence, that he was not entirely an arsehole.

'Gem, I'll have to call you back. It's someone I know.'

He pulled over and did a three-point turn, driving back down the dimly lit road slowly until he reached the police car. He pulled up on the other side of the road.

'Hi,' Ed said, lowering the window. 'Can I help?'

9.

TANZIE

They let Nicky out at a quarter to five. Tanzie handed over the Nintendo she'd brought on the bus from home and watched silently as he played with grazed fingers. Her happy mood had disappeared a bit when she first saw Nicky's swollen face. It didn't really look like him and she'd had to make her eyes stay very firmly on his when they would have liked to go somewhere else, even to the stupid picture of galloping horses on the wall opposite, which didn't even look like horses. She wanted to tell him about how they'd registered at St Anne's, but it was hard to think about it too much in that little room, with the smell of hospitals in her nose and Nicky's eye all the wrong shape.

He made funny little sounds as he walked, and tried to close his mouth over them, like he didn't want to let on how much it hurt. Tanzie found herself thinking, *The Fishers did this, the Fishers did this,* and she felt a bit scared because she couldn't believe anyone they knew would do this for no reason. Mum had to have all the usual arguments with the hospital people about how, no, she wasn't his actual mum, but as good as. And, no, he didn't have a social worker. And it always made Tanzie feel a bit odd, like Nicky wasn't a proper part of their family, even though he was.

When Nicky got up to go down the corridor she put her hand gently into his, and even though normally he would have told her to 'Scoot, small fry' or one of the other stupid things he said, he just squeezed her fingers a bit and his swollen mouth gave her this little smile, like just for once she was allowed (or at least until he said, 'Tanze, mate, I do actually need to go to the loo now').

Mum's face was all pale, and she kept chewing her lip, like she wanted to say a lot more than she did. Nicky didn't look at her once.

And then, when lots of doctors and people arrived in his room, Mum told Tanzie to wait outside and she walked up and down the long antiseptic corridors, reading her papers and working on her algebra. Numbers always made her feel better. If you treated them properly they always did what they were meant to do – like there was a magical order all around that you could unlock if you had the right key.

Nicky was dressed when she went back in. He walked out of the room really slowly, and he remembered to thank the nurse.

'Nice lad, isn't he?' she said. 'Polite.'

Mum was gathering up his things. 'That's the worst bit,' she said. 'He just wants to be left alone.'

'Doesn't really work like that round here, though, does it?' The nurse smiled at Tanzie. 'Take care of your brother, eh?'

As she walked towards the main entrance behind him,

Tanzie wondered what it said about their family when every single conversation they had now seemed to end with a funny look and the words 'Take care.'

Mum made dinner and gave Nicky three different-coloured pills to take, and they sat watching television on the sofa together. It was *Total Wipeout*, which normally made Nicky pretty much wee himself laughing, but he had barely spoken since they returned home, and she didn't think it was because his jaw hurt. He looked weird. Tanzie thought about the way those boys had jumped on him and the woman who had dragged her into the shop so that she wouldn't see and she tried to block out the thought because the sound of them hitting him still made her stomach go a bit funny, even though Mum said she would never, ever let it happen again, and she was not to think about it, okay?

Mum was busy upstairs. Tanzie could hear her dragging drawers out and going backwards and forwards across the landing. She was so busy she didn't even notice it was way past bedtime.

She nudged Nicky very gently with her finger. 'Does it hurt?'

'Does what hurt?'

'Your face.'

'What do you mean?' He looked at her like he didn't know what she was talking about.

'Well . . . it's a funny shape.'

'So's yours. Does that hurt?'

'Ha-ha.'

'I'm fine, Titch. Drop it.' And then, when she stared at him, 'Really. Just . . . forget it. I'm fine.'

Mum came in and put the lead on Norman. He was lying on the sofa and didn't want to get up and it took her about four goes to drag him out of the door. Tanzie was going to ask her if she was taking him for a walk but then the really funny bit was on where the wheel knocks the contestants off their little pedestals into the water and she forgot. Then Mum came back in.

'Okay, kids. Get your jackets.'

'Jackets? Why?'

'Because we're leaving. For Scotland.'

She made it sound perfectly normal.

Nicky didn't even look round from the television. 'We're leaving for Scotland.' He pointed the remote control at the screen, just to check.

'Yup. We're going to drive.'

'But we haven't got a car.'

'We're taking the Rolls.'

Nicky glanced at Tanzie, then back at Mum. 'But you haven't got insurance.'

'I've been driving since I was twelve years old. And I've never had an accident. Look, we'll stick to the B roads, and do most of it overnight. As long as nobody pulls us over we'll be fine.'

They both stared at her.

'But you said —'

'I know what I said. But sometimes the ends justify the means.'

'What does that mean?'

Mum threw her hands up in the air. 'There's a maths competition that could change our lives and it's in Scotland. Right now, we haven't got the money for the fares. That's the truth of it. I know it's not ideal to drive, and I'm not saying it's right, but unless you two have a better idea then let's just get into the car and get on with it.'

'Um, don't we need to pack?'

'It's all in the car.'

Tanzie knew Nicky was thinking what she was thinking – that Mum had finally gone mad. But she had read somewhere that mad people were like sleepwalkers – it was best not to disturb them. So she nodded really slowly, like this was all making perfect sense, and she fetched her jacket and they walked through the back door and into the garage, where Norman was sitting in the back seat and giving them the look that said, 'Yeah. Me too.' She climbed in. It smelt a bit musty, and she didn't really want to put her hands down on the seats because she had read somewhere that mice wee all the time, like non-stop, and mouse wee could give you about eight hundred diseases. 'Can I just run and get my gloves?' she said. Mum looked at her like she was the crazy one, but she nodded, so Tanzie ran and put them on and thought she probably felt a bit better.

Nicky eased his way gingerly into the front seat, and wiped at the dust on the dashboard with his fingers. Tanzie wanted to tell him about the mouse wee but she didn't want to alert Mum to the fact that she knew.

Mum opened the garage door, started the engine, reversed the car carefully out onto the drive. Then she climbed out, closed and locked the garage securely, then sat and thought for a minute. 'Tanze. Have you got a pen and paper?'

She fished around in her bag and handed her one. Mum didn't want her to see what she was writing but Tanzie peeped through the seats.

FISHER YOU LITTLE WASTE OF SKIN I HAVE TOLD THE POLICE THAT IF ANYONE BREAKS IN IT WILL BE YOU AND THEY ARE WATCHING

She got out of the car and pinned it to the bottom part of the door, where it wouldn't be visible from the street. Then she climbed back into the half-eaten driver's seat and, with a low purr, the Rolls set off into the night, leaving the glowing little house behind them.

It took them about ten minutes to work out that Mum had forgotten how to drive. The things that even Tanzie knew – mirror, signal, manoeuvre – she kept doing in the wrong order, and she drove leaning forwards over the steering-wheel and clutching it like the grannies who drove at fifteen m.p.h. around the town centre and scraped their doors on the pillars in the municipal car park.

They passed the Rose and Crown, the industrial estate with the five-man car wash, and the carpet warehouse. Tanzie pressed her nose to the window. They were officially leaving town. The last time she had left town was on the school journey to Durdle Door when Melanie

Abbott was sick all down herself in the coach and started a vomit chain reaction around the whole of Five C.

'Just keep calm,' Mum muttered to herself. 'Nice and calm.'

'You don't look calm,' said Nicky. He was playing Nintendo, his thumbs a blur on each side of the little glowing screen.

'Nicky, I need you to map-read. Don't play Nintendo right now.'

'Well, surely we just go north.'

'But where is north? I haven't driven around here for years. I need you to tell me where I should be going.'

He glanced up at the signpost. 'Do we want the M3?'

'I don't know. I'm asking you!'

'Let me see.' Tanzie reached through from the back and took the map from Nicky's hands. 'What way up do I hold it?'

They drove round the roundabout twice, while she wrestled with the map, and then they were on the ring road. Tanzie vaguely remembered this road: they had once come this way when Mum and Dad were trying to sell the air-conditioners. 'Can you turn the light on at the back, Mum?' she said. 'I can't read anything.'

Mum swivelled in her seat. 'The button should be above your head.'

Tanzie reached up and clicked it with her thumb. She could have taken her gloves off, she thought. Mice couldn't walk upside down. Not like spiders. 'It's not working.'

'Nicky, you'll have to map-read.' She looked over, exasperated. 'Nicky.'

'Yeah. I will. I just need to get these golden stars. They're five thousand points.' Tanzie folded the map as best she could and pushed it back through the front seats. Nicky's head was bent low over his game, lost in concentration. To be fair, golden stars were really hard to get.

'Will you put that thing down!'

He sighed, snapped it shut. They were going past a pub she didn't recognize, and now a new hotel. Mum said they were looking for the M3 but Tanzie hadn't seen any signs for the M3 for ages. Beside her Norman started a low whine: she figured they had around thirty-eight seconds before Mum said it was shredding her nerves.

She made it to twenty-seven.

'Tanzie, please stop the dog. It's making it impossible to concentrate. Nicky. I really need you to read the map.'

'He's drooling everywhere. I think he needs to get out.' She shifted to the side.

Nicky squinted at the signs in front of them. 'If you stay on this road I think we'll end up in Southampton.'

'But that's the wrong way.'

'That's what I said.'

The smell of oil was really strong. Tanzie wondered whether something was leaking. She put her glove over her nose.

'I think we should just head back to where we were and start again.'

With a grunt Mum swung the car off at the next exit and went round the roundabout. Turning corners made the tendons in her neck stand out like little steel cables.

They all tried to ignore the grinding noise as she turned the wheel to the right, and headed back down the other side of the dual carriageway.

'Tanzie. Please do something with the dog. Please.' She looked up and pointed towards the turn-off for the town. 'What am I doing, Nicky? Coming off here?'

'Oh, God. He's farted. Mum, I'm suffocating.'

'Nicky, please can you read the map.'

Tanzie remembered now that Mum hated driving. She wasn't good at processing information quickly enough. She always said she didn't have the right synapses. Plus, to be fair, the smell now seeping through the car was so bad it made it hard to think straight.

She began to gag. 'I'm dying!'

Norman turned his big old head to look at her, his eyes sad, like she was being really mean.

'But there are two turnings. Do I take this one or the next?'

'Definitely the next. Oh, no, sorry – it's this one.'

'What?' Mum wrenched the car off the dual carriageway, narrowly avoiding the grass verge, and onto the exit slip. The car juddered as they hit the kerb and Tanzie had to let go of her nose to grab Norman's collar.

'For Christ's sake, can you just –'

'I meant the next one. This one takes us miles out of the way.'

'We've been on the road almost half an hour and we're further away than when we started. Jesus, Nicky, I –'

It was then that Tanzie saw the flashing blue light.

She stared up at the rear-view mirror, then turned to

look out of the back windscreen, disbelieving. She willed it to go past, to be racing to the scene of some accident. But instead it drew nearer and nearer, until those cold blue lights filled the car.

Nicky swivelled painfully in his seat. 'Um, Jess, I think they want you to pull over.'

'Shit. *Shit shit shit.* Tanzie, you didn't hear that.' Mum took a deep breath, adjusted her hands on the wheel as she started to slow. 'It will be fine. It will all be fine.'

Nicky slumped a little lower in his seat. 'Um, Jess?'

'Not now, Nicky.'

The blue light was pulling over too. Her palms had begun to sweat. *It will all be fine.*

'I guess this isn't the time to tell you I brought my stash with me.'

10.

JESS

So there she was, standing on the grass verge of a dual carriageway at eleven forty at night with two policemen who were both acting not like she was a major criminal, which was sort of what she'd expected, but worse – like she was just really, really stupid. Everything they said had a patronising edge to it: *So are you often in the habit of taking your family out for a late-night drive, madam? With only one headlight working? Were you not actually aware, madam, that your tax disc is two years out of date?* They hadn't actually looked up the whole no-insurance thing yet. So there was that to look forward to.

Nicky was sweating on the verge, waiting for them to locate his stash. Tanzie was a pale, silent ghost a few feet away, hugging Norman's neck for reassurance.

Jess had only herself to blame. It could hardly get any worse.

And then Mr Nicholls turned up.

Jess almost laughed then: the whole thing was so ridiculously awful. She felt the remaining colour drain from her face as his window wound down and she saw who it was. And she realized exactly what was going to happen next, which was that he was going to tell the policemen: 'You know what? As well as driving a car that is uninsured and without a valid tax disc and probably contains a quarter-ounce of skunk somewhere in that mouse-infested upholstery, this woman is a THIEF.'

And a million thoughts flashed through her head – like who was going to mind the children when she went to prison, and if it was Marty, would he remember things like the fact that Tanzie's feet grew occasionally and buy her new shoes instead of waiting until her toenails curled in on her toes? And who would look after Norman? And why the hell hadn't she done what she should have done in the first place and just given Ed Nicholls back his stupid roll of money?

But he didn't say any of that. He just took in the scene and said, 'Need some help?'

Policeman Number One turned slowly to look him over. He was a barrel-chested man with an upright bearing, the kind who took himself seriously, and bristled if everyone else didn't too. 'And you are . . .'

'Edward Nicholls. I know this woman. What is it? Car trouble?' He stared at the Rolls as if he couldn't believe it was actually on the road.

'You could say that,' said Policeman Number Two.

'Out-of-date tax disc,' Jess muttered, trying to ignore the hammering in her chest. 'I was trying to drive the kids somewhere. And now I guess I'm driving it home again.'

'You're not driving anywhere,' said Policeman Number One. 'Your car is now impounded. The tow truck is on its way. It is an offence under Section Thirty-three of the Vehicle Excise and Registration Act to drive on a public road without a valid tax disc. Which also means your insurance will be invalidated.'

'I don't have any.'

They both turned towards her.

'The car isn't insured. I'm not insured.'

She could see Mr Nicholls staring. What the hell? The moment they entered the details they would see it anyway. 'We've had a bit of trouble. I was desperate. It was the only way I could see to get the kids from A to B.'

'You are aware that driving your car without tax and insurance is a crime.'

She stared at her feet.

'And carries a possible jail sentence.'

'And it's not my car.' She kicked at a stone on the grass. 'That's the next thing you're going to see when you do your whole database thing.'

'Did you steal the vehicle, madam?'

'No, I did not steal the vehicle. It's been sitting in my garage for two years.'

'That's not an answer to my question.'

'It's my ex-husband's car.'

'Does he know you've taken it?'

'He wouldn't know if I had a sex change and called myself Sid. He's been in north Yorkshire for the past –'

'You know, you really might want to stop talking now.' Mr Nicholls ran a hand over the top of his head.

'Who are you, her lawyer?'

'Does she need one?'

'Driving without tax and insurance is an offence under Section Thirty-three –'

'Yeah. You said. Well, I think you might want to get some advice before you say any more –'

'Jess.'

'Jess.' He looked at the policemen. 'Officers, does this woman actually need to go to the station? Because she's obviously really, really sorry. And given the hour, I think the kids need to go home.'

'She'll be charged with driving without tax and insurance. Your name and address, madam?'

Jess gave it to Policeman Number One. She couldn't muster a 'sorry' face. She was so cross with herself that she could barely get the words out. She watched him turn away and repeat it into his walkie-talkie. Whatever came over the airwaves seemed to satisfy him because when he turned back he looked at the kids and nodded.

'The car is registered to that address, yes. But it's registered under a SORN, which means –'

'That it shouldn't be driven on a public road. I know.'

'You know. Shame you didn't think about that before you came out, then, isn't it?' He gave her the kind of look that teachers reserve for making eight-year-olds feel small. And something in that look pushed Jess over the edge.

'You know what?' she said. 'You honestly think I would have driven my kids anywhere at eleven o'clock at night if I hadn't been desperate? You really think I just sat there this evening in my little house and thought, I

136

know. I'll take my kids and my bloody dog and just go and get us all into a whole heap of trouble and –'

'It's not my business what you were thinking, madam. My issue is you bringing an uninsured, possibly unsafe vehicle onto a public road.'

'I was desperate, okay? And you won't find me on your damned database because I've never done anything wrong –'

'Or you just never got caught.'

Mr Nicholls's hand landed on her shoulder. 'Uh, Jess? I think maybe you should stop now.'

The two policemen gazed at her steadily. On the verge, Norman flopped down with a great sigh. Tanzie watched it all in silence, her eyes great hollows. *Oh, God,* Jess thought. *All she sees around her now is chaos.* She bit back her words, mumbled an apology.

'You will be charged with driving without the appropriate documents, Mrs Thomas,' Policeman Number One said, handing her a slip of paper. 'I have to warn you that you will receive a court summons, and that you face a possible fine of up to five thousand pounds.'

'Five grand?' Jess started to laugh.

'But you can go now.'

'Five *grand*?'

'And you'll need to pay to get this . . .' the officer couldn't bring himself to say 'car' '. . . out of the police pound. I have to tell you there is a fifteen-pound charge for every day that it remains there.'

'Perfect. And how am I supposed to get it out of the pound if I'm not allowed to drive it?'

She was testing his patience, she could see. But she couldn't stop herself. *Five grand.*

'You tax it and insure it like everybody else and then you can take it away. Or you pay a garage to fetch it. I'd advise you to remove all your belongings before the tow truck arrives. Once it leaves here we cannot be held responsible for the vehicle's contents.'

'Of course. Because obviously it would be way too much to hope for a car to be safe in a police pound,' she muttered.

'Jess –'

'But, Mum, how are we going to get home?'

There was a brief silence. The policemen turned away.

'I'll give you a lift,' Mr Nicholls said.

Jess stepped away from him. 'Oh. No. No, thank you. We're fine. We'll walk. It's not far.'

'It's three miles.'

Tanzie squinted at her, as if trying to assess whether she was serious, then clambered wearily to her feet. Jess remembered that under her coat Tanzie was in her pyjamas. Mr Nicholls glanced at the children. 'I'm headed back that way.' He nodded towards the town. 'You know where I live.'

Tanzie and Nicky didn't speak, but Jess watched Nicky limp towards the car and start to haul out the bags. She couldn't make him carry all that stuff home. She wasn't sure he could even walk that far in his present state.

'Thank you,' she said stiffly. 'That's very kind of you.' She couldn't look him in the eye.

'What happened to your boy?' Policeman Number Two said, as Nicky dropped his holdall at her feet.

'Look it up on your database,' she snapped, and walked over to the pile of bags.

They drove away from the police in silence. Jess sat in the passenger seat of Mr Nicholls's immaculate car, staring straight ahead at the road. She wasn't sure she had ever felt more uncomfortable. She could feel, even if she couldn't see, the children's stunned silence at the evening's turn of events. She had let them down. She watched the hedgerows turn to fencing and brick walls, the black lanes turn to streetlights. She couldn't believe they had only been gone an hour and a half. It felt like a lifetime. A five-thousand-pound fine. An almost-certain driving ban. And a court appearance. Marty would go mental. And she had just blown Tanzie's last chance of going to St Anne's.

For the first time that evening Jess felt a lump rise in her throat.

'You okay?'

'Fine.' She kept her face turned away from Mr Nicholls. He didn't know. Of course he didn't know. For a brief, terrifying moment after she had agreed to get into his car, she had wondered if this was a trick. He would wait until the police had gone, then do something dreadful to pay her back for her theft.

But it was worse. He was just trying to be helpful.

'Um, can you turn left here? We're down there. Go to the end, turn left, then the second turning on the right.'

The picturesque part of town had fallen away half a mile back. Here on Danehall, the trees were skeletal even in summer and burnt-out cars stood on piles of bricks, like civic sculptures on little pedestals. The houses came in three vintages, depending on your street: terraced, pebble-dashed, or tiny and built in maroon brick with uPVC windows. He swung the car round to the left and into Seacole Avenue, slowing as she pointed to her house. She looked round at the back seat and saw that during the short drive Tanzie had nodded off, her mouth hanging slightly open, her head resting against Norman, who leant half his bulk against Nicky's body. Nicky looked out of the window impassively. They were turning them out of the Hare and Terrier, and groups of men stood smoking on the corner, some preparing to go home, others looking for an excuse not to.

'You might not want to hang around too long,' she said, nodding towards them. 'Your car is the same model as the local skunk dealer's.'

'So where were you trying to get to?'

'Scotland.' She rubbed her nose. 'It's a long story.'

He waited.

Her leg had started to jiggle involuntarily. 'I need to get my daughter to a Maths Olympiad. The fares were expensive. Although not as expensive as getting pulled over by the Old Bill, it turns out.'

'A Maths Olympiad.'

'I know. I'd never heard of one either until a week ago. Like I said, it's a long story.'

'So what are you going to do?'

Jess looked into the back seat, at Tanzie, who snored gently. She shrugged. She couldn't say the words.

Mr Nicholls suddenly caught sight of Nicky's face. He stared, as if seeing it for the first time.

'Yeah. That's another story.'

'You have a lot of stories.' He turned back in his seat and looked straight ahead at the men on the corner.

Jess couldn't work out if he was deep in thought or if he was just waiting for her to get out of the car. 'Thanks. For the lift. It was kind of you.'

'Yeah, well, I owe you one. I'm pretty sure it was you who got me home from the pub the other night. I woke up on my sofa with my car safely in the pub car park and the world's most malevolent hangover.' He paused. 'I also have a vague memory of being an arsehole. Possibly for the second time.'

'It's fine,' she said, as blood rushed to her ears. 'Really.'

Nicky had opened the car door. The cool air made Tanzie stir. She rubbed her eyes and blinked at Jess. Then she gazed slowly around her at the car, the last hour re-registering on her face. 'Does this mean we're not going?'

Jess gathered up the bags at her feet. This was not a conversation to have in front of an audience. 'Let's go inside, Tanze. It's late.'

'Does this mean we're not going to Scotland?'

She smiled awkwardly at Mr Nicholls. 'Thanks again.' She hauled her bags out onto the pavement. The air was surprisingly chill. Nicky stood outside the gate, waiting.

Tanzie's voice crackled with sudden knowledge. 'Does this mean I don't get to go to St Anne's?'

She tried to smile. 'Let's not talk about it now, sweetie.'

'But what are we going to do?' said Nicky.

'Not now, Nicky. Let's just get indoors.'

'You now owe the police five grand. How are we going to get to Scotland?'

'Kids? Please? Can we just go indoors?'

With a groan, Norman heaved himself off the back seat and ambled out of the car.

'You didn't say we'll sort something out.' Tanzie's voice was panicked. 'You always say we'll sort something out.'

'We'll sort something out,' Jess said, dragging the duvets out of the boot.

'That's not the voice you use when we're really going to sort something out.' Tanzie began to cry.

It was so unexpected, that at first Jess could do nothing but stand there in shock. 'Take these.' She thrust the duvets at Nicky, and leant her upper half into the car, trying to manoeuvre Tanzie out. 'Tanzie . . . sweetheart. Come out. It's late. We'll talk about this.'

'Talk about me not going to St Anne's?'

Mr Nicholls was staring at his steering-wheel, like this was all too much for him. Jess began apologizing under her breath. 'She's tired,' she said, trying to put her arm around her daughter. Tanzie shifted away. 'I'm so sorry.'

It was at that point Mr Nicholls's phone rang.

'Gemma,' he said wearily, as if he'd been expecting it. She could hear an angry buzzing, as if a wasp had been trapped in the receiver.

'I know,' he said quietly.

'I just want to go to St Anne's,' Tanzie cried. Her glasses had fallen off – Jess hadn't had time to take her to the optician to fix them – and she covered her eyes with her hands. 'Please let me go. Please, Mum. I'll be really good. Just let me go there.'

'Sssh.' A lump rose in Jess's throat. Tanzie never begged for anything. She just wasn't made that way. 'Tanze . . .' On the pavement, Nicky turned away, as if he couldn't watch it.

Mr Nicholls said something into his phone that she couldn't make out. Tanzie had begun to sob. She was a dead weight. It was as if she was refusing to leave the car.

'Come on, sweetheart,' Jess said, tugging at her.

She had braced herself against the door. 'Please, Mum. Please. Please. I'll be really good.'

'Tanzie, you cannot stay in the car.'

'Please . . .'

'Out. C'mon, baby.'

'I'll drive you,' Mr Nicholls said.

Jess's head bumped against the door frame. 'What?'

'I'll drive you to Scotland.' He had put down his phone and was staring at his steering-wheel. 'Turns out I've got to go to Northumberland. Scotland's not that much further. I'll drop you there.'

Everyone fell silent. At the end of the street there was a burst of laughter and a car door slammed. Jess straightened her ponytail, which had gone askew. 'Look, it's really nice of you to offer but we can't accept a lift from you.'

'Yeah,' said Nicky, leaning forward. 'Yeah, we can, Jess.' He glanced at Tanzie. 'Really. We can.'

'But we don't even know you. I can't ask you to –'

Mr Nicholls didn't look at her. 'It's just a lift. It's really not a big deal.'

Tanzie sniffed and rubbed at her nose. 'Please? Mum?'

Jess looked at her, and at Nicky's bruised face, then back at Mr Nicholls. She had never wanted to sprint from a car so badly. 'I can't offer you anything,' she said, and her voice emerged with a weird break in the middle. 'Anything at all.'

He raised one eyebrow, swivelled his head towards the dog. 'Not even vacuum my back seats afterwards?'

The breath that left her chest probably sounded slightly more relieved than was diplomatic. 'Well . . . okay, that I can do.'

'Right,' he said. 'Then I suggest we all get a few hours' sleep and I'll pick you up first thing tomorrow.'

11.

ED

It took Edward Nicholls about fifteen minutes after he had left Danehall estate to question what the bloody hell he had just done. He had agreed to transport his stroppy cleaner, her two weird kids and an enormous reeking dog all the way to Scotland. What the hell had he been thinking? He could hear Gemma's voice, the scepticism with which she had repeated his statement: 'You're taking a little girl you don't know and her family to the other end of the country and it's an "emergency". Right.' He could hear the inverted commas. A pause. 'Pretty, is she?'

'What?'

'The mother. Big tits? Long eyelashes? Damsel in distress?'

'That's not it. Er . . .' He couldn't say anything with them all in the car.

'I'll take both those as a yes, then.' She sighed deeply. 'For Christ's sake, Ed.'

Tomorrow morning he would pop by first thing, apologize and explain that something had come up. She'd understand. She probably felt weird about sharing a car with a near-stranger too. She hadn't exactly jumped at the offer.

He would donate something towards the kid's train fare. It wasn't his fault the woman – Jess? – had decided to drive an untaxed, uninsured car, after all. If you looked at it on paper – the cops, the weird kids, the night-time joyriding – she was trouble. And Ed Nicholls did not need any more trouble in his life.

With these thoughts in his head, he washed, brushed his teeth and fell into the first decent sleep he'd had in weeks.

He pulled up outside the gate shortly after nine. He had meant to be there earlier but couldn't remember where the house was, and given that the estate was a sprawling mass of identikit streets, he had driven up and down blindly for almost thirty minutes until he recognized Seacole Avenue. It was only the pub that got him there in the end.

It was a damp, still morning, the air heavy with moisture. The street was empty, apart from a ginger cat, which stalked its way along the pavement, its tail a question mark. Danehall seemed a little less unfriendly in daylight, but he still found himself double-checking he'd locked the car once he'd stepped out of it.

He gazed up at the windows, hoping he'd got the right place. Pink and white bunting hung in one of the upstairs rooms, and two hanging baskets swung listlessly from the front porch. A car sat under a tarpaulin in the next driveway. But the real giveaway was lumbering slowly around the front garden, pausing only to lift its leg against a child's bicycle. Jesus. That dog. The size of it. Ed pictured it lolling over his back seat the previous evening. A faint echo of its scent had remained when he climbed back in this morning.

He opened the latch of the gate warily, in case it went for him, but it simply turned its enormous head with mild disinterest, walked to the shade of a weedy tree and flopped down on its side, lifting a desultory front leg as if in the vague hope it might get its stomach scratched.

'I'll pass, thanks,' Ed said.

He walked up the path and paused at the door. He had his little speech all prepared.

Hi, I'm really sorry but something very important has come up with work and I'm afraid I'm not going to be able to take the next couple of days off. However, I'd be happy to contribute something to your daughter's Olympiad fund. I think it's great that she's working so hard at her studies. So here's her train fare.

If it sounded a little less convincing in his head this morning than it had done last night, well, it couldn't be helped. He was about to knock when he saw the note, half attached to the door with a pin, flapping in the breeze:

FISHER YOU LITTLE WASTE OF SKIN I HAVE TOLD THE POLICE THAT IF ANYONE BREAKS IN IT WILL BE YOU AND THEY ARE WATCHING

As he straightened up the door opened. The little girl stood there. 'We're all packed,' she said, squinting, her head tilted to one side. 'Mum said you wouldn't come but I knew you would so I said I wouldn't let her unpack the suitcases until ten. And you made it with fifty-three minutes to spare. Which is actually about thirty-three minutes better than I estimated.'

He blinked.

'*Mum!*' She pushed the door open. Jess was standing in the hallway, as if she had stopped dead halfway down it. She was wearing a pair of cut-off jeans and a shirt with the sleeves rolled up. Her hair was clipped up. She did not look like someone preparing to travel the length of the country.

'Hi.' Ed smiled awkwardly.

'Oh. Okay.'

She shook her head. And he realized the child had been telling the truth: she really hadn't expected him to turn up. 'I'd offer you a coffee, but I got rid of the last of the milk before we set off last night.'

Before he could answer, the boy sloped past, rubbing his eyes. His face was still swollen, and now coloured an impressionist palette of purples and yellows. He gazed at the pile of holdalls and bin bags in the hall and said, 'Which of these are we taking?'

'All of them,' said the little girl. 'And I packed Norman's blanket.'

Jess looked at Ed warily. He made to open his mouth, but nothing came out. The entire length of the hallway was lined with battered paperbacks. He wasn't sure why that surprised him.

'Can you pick up this bag, Mr Nicholls?' The little girl tugged it towards him. 'I did try and lift it earlier because Nicky can't pick stuff up right now but it's too heavy for me.'

'Sure.' He found himself stooping, but stopped for a moment before he lifted it. *How was he going to do this?*

'Listen. Mr Nicholls . . .' Jess was in front of him. She looked as uncomfortable as he did. 'About this trip –'

And then the front door flew open. A woman stood in jogging bottoms and a T-shirt, a baseball bat raised in her hand.

'DROP THEM!' she roared.

He froze.

'PUT YOUR HANDS UP!'

'Nat!' Jess shouted. 'Don't hit him!'

He lifted them slowly, turning to face her.

'What the –' The woman looked past Ed at Jess. 'Jess? Oh, my God. I thought someone was in your house.'

'Someone *is* in my house. Me.'

The woman dropped the bat, then looked in horror at him. 'Oh, my God. It's – Oh, God, oh, God, I'm so sorry. I saw the front door and I honestly thought you were a burglar. I thought you were . . . you know who.' She laughed nervously, then pulled an agonized face at Jess, as if he couldn't see her.

Ed let out a breath. The woman put the bat behind her and tried to smile. 'You know how it is around here . . .'

He took a step backwards and gave a small nod. 'Okay, well . . . I just need to get my phone. Left it in the car.'

He edged past her with his palms up and headed down the path. He opened and shut the car door, then locked it again, just to give himself something to do, trying to think clearly over the ringing in his ears. *Just drive off,* a little voice said. *Just go. You never have to see her again. You do not need this right now.*

Ed liked order. He liked to know what was coming. Everything about this woman suggested the kind of . . . *boundarylessness* that made him nervous.

He walked halfway back up the path, trying to formulate the right words. As he approached the house, he could just hear them talking behind the half-closed door, their voices carrying across the little garden.

'I'm going to tell him no.'

'You can't, Jess.' The boy's voice. 'Why?'

'Because it's too complicated. I work for him.'

'You clean his house. That's not the same thing.'

'We don't know him, then. How can I tell Tanzie not to get in cars with men she doesn't know, and then do exactly that?'

'He wears glasses. He's hardly going to be a serial killer.'

'Tell that to Dennis Nielsen's victims. And Harold Shipman's.'

'You know way too many serial killers.'

'We'll set Norman on him if he does anything bad.' The boy's voice again.

'Yes. Because Norman has been so useful, protecting this family in the past.'

'Mr Nicholls doesn't know that, does he?'

'Look. He's just some bloke. He probably got caught up in the drama last night. It's obvious he doesn't want to do it. We'll – we'll just let Tanzie down gently.'

Tanzie. Ed watched her running around the back garden, her hair flying out behind her. He watched the dog shambling back towards the door, half dog, half yak, leaving an intermittent snail trail of drool behind him.

'I'm wearing him out so that he'll sleep most of the journey.' She appeared in front of him, panting.

'Right.'

'I'm really good at maths. We're going to an Olympiad so I can win money to go to a school where I can do A-level maths. Do you know what my name is, converted to binary code?'

He looked at her. 'Is Tanzie your full name?'

'No. But it's the one I use.'

He blew out his cheeks. 'Um. Okay. 01010100 01100001 01101110 01111010 01101001 01100101.'

'Did you say 0101 at the end? Or 1010?'

'0101. Duh.' He used to play this game with Ronan.

'Wow. You actually spelt it right.' She walked past him and pushed the door. 'I've never been to Scotland. Nicky keeps trying to tell me there are herds of wild haggis. But that's a lie, right?'

'To the best of my knowledge they're all farmed these days,' he said.

Tanzie stared at him. Then she beamed, and sort of growled at the same time.

And Ed Nicholls realized he was headed for Scotland.

The two women fell silent as he pushed the door open. Their eyes dropped to the bags that he picked up in each hand.

'I need to get some stuff before we go,' he said, as he let the door swing behind him. 'And you missed out Gary Ridgway. The Green River Killer. But you're fine. They were all short-sighted. And my glasses are long.'

It took three-quarters of an hour to leave town. The lights were out on the top of the hill and that, combined with Easter-holidays traffic, slowed the queue of cars to a bad-tempered crawl. Jess sat in the car beside him, silent and oddly awkward, her hands pressed together between her knees. He guessed she knew that he'd over-heard the whole conversation. She had barely said a single word since they'd left her house.

The boy – Nicky – sat on the other side of the dog to his sister. He had the air-con on, but it couldn't disguise the smell of the dog, so he turned it off and they sat with all four windows open instead. And into this odd silence, Tanzie kept up a constant stream of chatter.

'Have you been to Scotland before?'

'Where do you come from?'

'Do you have a house there?'

'Why are you staying here then?'

He had some work to sort out, he said. It was easier than 'I'm awaiting possible prosecution and a jail term of up to seven years.'

'Do you have a wife?'

'Not any more.'

'Were you unfaithful?'

'Tanzie,' said Jess.

He blinked. Glanced into the rear-view mirror. 'Nope.'

'On *Jeremy Kyle* one person is usually unfaithful. Sometimes they have another baby and they have to do a DNA test and usually when it's right the woman looks like she wants to hit someone. But mostly they just start crying.'

She squinted out of the window.

'They're a bit mad these women, mostly. Because the men have all got another baby with someone else. Or lots of girlfriends. So statistically they're really likely to do it again. But none of the women ever seem to think about statistics.'

'I don't really watch *Jeremy Kyle*,' he said, glancing at the satnav.

'Nor do I. Only when I go to Nathalie's house when Mum's working. She records it while she's cleaning so she can watch it in the evenings. She has forty-seven episodes on her hard drive.'

'Tanzie. I think Mr Nicholls probably wants to concentrate.'

'It's fine.'

Jess was twisting a strand of her hair. She had her feet up on the seat. Ed really hated people putting their feet on seats. Even if they did take their shoes off.

'So why did your wife leave you?'

'Tanzie.'

'I'm being polite. You said it was good to make polite conversation.'

'I'm sorry,' Jess said.

'Really. It's fine.' He addressed Tanzie through the rear-view mirror: 'She thought I worked too much.'

'They never say that on *Jeremy Kyle*.'

The traffic cleared, and they headed out onto the dual carriageway. Ed put his foot down. It was a beautiful day, and he was tempted to take the coast road, but he didn't want to risk getting caught in traffic again. The dog whined, the boy played silently with a Nintendo, his head down in intense concentration, and Tanzie grew quieter. He turned the radio on – a hits channel – and for a moment or two he started to think this could be okay. It was just a day out of his life, if they didn't hit too much traffic. And it was better than being stuck in the house.

'The satnav reckons about eight hours if we don't hit any jams,' he said.

'By motorway?'

'Well, yeah.' He glanced left. 'Even a top-of-the-range Audi doesn't have wings.' He tried to smile, to show her he was joking, but she was still straight-faced.

'Uh . . . there's a bit of a problem.'

'A problem.'

'Tanzie gets sick if we go fast.'

'What do you mean "fast"? Eighty? Ninety?'

'Um . . . actually, fifty. Okay, maybe forty.'

Ed glanced into the rear-view mirror. Was it his imagination or had the child grown a little paler? She was gazing out of the window, her hand resting on the dog's head. 'Forty?' He slowed. 'You're joking, right? You're saying we have to drive to Scotland via B roads?'

'No. Well, maybe. Look, it's possible she's grown out of it. But she doesn't travel by car very much and we used to have big problems with it and . . . I just don't want to mess up your nice car.'

Ed glanced into the rear-view mirror again. 'We can't take the minor roads – that's ridiculous. It would take days to get there. Anyway, she'll be fine. This car is brand new. It has award-winning suspension. Nobody gets sick in it.'

She looked straight ahead. 'You don't have kids, do you?'

'Why do you ask?'

'No reason.'

It took twenty-five minutes to disinfect and shampoo the back seat, and even then every time he put his head inside the interior Ed got a faint whiff of vomit. Jess borrowed a bucket from a petrol station and used shampoo that she had packed in one of the kids' bags. Nicky sat on the verge beside the garage, hiding behind a pair of oversized shades, and Tanzie sat with the dog, holding a balled tissue to her mouth, like a consumptive.

'I'm so sorry,' Jess kept saying, her sleeves rolled up, her face set in a grim line of concentration.

'It's fine. You're the one cleaning it.'

'I'll pay for you to get your car valeted afterwards.'

He raised an eyebrow at her. He was laying a plastic

bin bag over the seat so that the kids wouldn't get damp when they sat down again.

'Well, okay, I'll do it. It will smell better, whatever.'

Some time later they climbed back into the car. Nobody remarked on the smell. He ensured his window was as low as it could go, and began reprogramming the satnav.

'So,' he said. 'Scotland it is. Via B roads.' He pressed the 'destination' button. 'Glasgow or Edinburgh?'

'Aberdeen.'

He looked at Jess.

'Aberdeen. Of course.' He looked behind him, trying not to let the despair seep into his voice. 'Everyone happy? Water? Plastic bag on seat? Sick bags in place? Good. Let's go.'

Ed heard his sister's voice as he pulled back onto the road. *Ha-ha-ha Ed. SERVED.*

It began to rain shortly after Portsmouth. Ed drove through the back roads, keeping at a steady thirty-eight all the way, feeling the fine spit of raindrops from the half-inch of window he had not felt able to close. He found he had to focus on not putting his foot too far down on the accelerator the whole time. It was a constant frustration, going at this sedate speed, like having an itch you couldn't quite scratch. In the end he switched on cruise control.

Nicky fell asleep. Jess muttered something about him only coming out of hospital the previous day. He half wanted to ask her what had happened, but he wasn't sure he wanted to know quite how much trouble this family was likely to be.

Given the snail's pace, he had time to study Jess surreptitiously. She remained silent, her head mostly turned away from him, as if he had done something to annoy her. He remembered her in her hallway now, demanding money, her chin tilted (she was quite short) and her unfriendly eyes unblinking. And then he remembered her behaviour at the bar, that she had had to babysit him all the way home. She still seemed to think he was an arsehole. Come on, he told himself. Two, three days maximum. And then you never have to see them again. Let's play nice.

'So . . . do you clean many houses?'

She frowned a little. 'Yes.'

'You have a lot of regulars?'

'It's a holiday park.'

'Did you . . . Was it something you wanted to do?'

'Did I grow up wanting to clean houses?' She raised an eyebrow, as if checking that he had seriously asked that question. 'Um, no. I wanted to be a professional scuba diver. But I had Tanze and I couldn't work out how to get the pram to float.'

'Okay, it was a dumb question.'

She rubbed her nose. 'It's not my dream job, no. But it's fine. I can work around the kids and I like most of the people I clean for.'

Most of.

'Can you make a living out of it?'

Her head shot round. 'What do you mean?'

'Just what I said. Can you make a living? Is it lucrative?'

Her face closed. 'We get by.'

'No, we don't,' said Tanzie, from the back.

'Tanze.'

'You're always saying we haven't got enough money.'

'It's just a figure of speech.' She blushed.

'So what do you do, Mr Nicholls?' said Tanzie.

'I work for a company that creates software. You know what that is?'

'Of course.'

Nicky looked up. In the rear-view mirror Ed watched him remove his ear-buds. When the boy saw him looking, he glanced away.

'Do you design games?'

'Not games, no.'

'What, then?'

'Well, for the last few years we've been working on a piece of software that will hopefully move us closer to a cashless society.'

'How would that work?'

'Well, when you buy something, or pay a bill, you wave your phone, which has a thing a bit like a bar code, and for every transaction you pay a tiny, tiny amount, like nought point nought one of a pound.'

'We would pay to pay?' said Jess. 'No one will want that.'

'That's where you're wrong. The banks love it. Retailers like it because it gives them one uniform system instead of cards, cash, cheques . . . and you'll pay less per transaction than you do on a credit card. So it works for both sides.'

'Some of us don't use credit cards unless we're desperate.'

'Then it would just be linked to your bank account. You wouldn't, like, have to do anything.'

'So if every bank and retailer picks this up, we won't get a choice.'

'That's a long way off.'

There was a brief silence. Jess pulled her knees up to her chin and wrapped her arms around them. 'So basically the rich get richer – the banks and the retailers – and the poor get poorer.'

'Well, in theory, perhaps. But that's the joy of it. It's such a tiny amount you won't notice it. And it will be very convenient.'

Jess muttered something he didn't catch.

'How much is it again?' said Tanzie.

'Point nought one per transaction. So it works out as a little less than a penny.'

'How many transactions a day?'

'Twenty? Fifty? Depends how much you do.'

'So that's fifty pence a day.'

'Exactly. Nothing.'

'Three pounds fifty a week,' said Jess.

'One hundred and eighty-two pounds a year,' said Tanzie. 'Depending on how close the fee actually is to a penny. And whether it's a leap year.'

Ed lifted one hand from the wheel. 'At the outside. Even you can't say that's very much.'

Jess swivelled in her seat. 'What does one hundred and eighty-two pounds buy us, Tanze?'

'Two supermarket pairs of school trousers, four school blouses, a pair of shoes. A gym kit and a five pack of white socks. If you buy them from the supermarket. That comes to eighty-five pounds ninety-seven. The one hundred is exactly nine point two days of groceries, depending on whether anyone comes round and whether Mum buys a bottle of wine. That would be supermarket own-brand.' She thought for a minute. 'Or one month's council tax for a Band D property. We're Band D, right, Mum?'

'Yes, we are. Unless we get re-banded.'

'Or an out-of-season three-day holiday at the holiday village in Kent. One hundred and seventy-five pounds, inclusive of VAT.' She leant forward. 'That's where we went last year. We got an extra night free because Mum mended the man's curtains. *And* they had a waterslide.'

There was a brief silence.

Ed was about to speak when Tanzie's head appeared between the two front seats. 'Or a whole month's cleaning of a four-bedroom house from Mum, laundering of sheets and towels included, at her current rates. Give or take a pound.' She leant back in her seat, apparently satisfied.

They drove three miles, turned right at a T-junction, left onto a narrow lane. Ed wanted to say something but found his voice had temporarily disappeared. Behind him, Nicky put his ear-buds back in and turned away. The sun hid briefly behind a cloud.

'Still,' said Jess, putting her bare feet up on the dashboard, and leaning forward to turn up the music, 'let's hope you do really well with it, eh?'

12.

JESS

Jess's grandmother had often stated that the key to a happy life was a short memory. Admittedly that was before she got dementia and used to forget where she lived, but Jess took her point. She had to forget about that money. She was never going to survive being stuck in a car with Mr Nicholls if she let herself think too hard about what she had done. Marty used to tell her she had the world's worst poker face: her feelings floated across them like reflections on a still pond. She would give herself away within hours and blurt out a confession like one of those North Koreans. Or she would go crazy with the tension and start plucking at bits of the upholstery with her fingernails.

She sat in the car and listened to Tanzie chatting, and she told herself she would find a way to pay it all back before he discovered what she had done. She would take it out of Tanzie's winnings. She would work it out somehow. She told herself he was just a man who had offered them a lift and with whom she had to make polite conversation for a few hours a day.

And periodically she glanced behind her at the two kids and thought, What else could I have done?

It shouldn't have been hard to sit back and enjoy the ride. The country lanes were banked with wild flowers, and when the rain cleared the clouds revealed skies the azure blue of 1950s postcards. Tanzie wasn't sick again, and with every mile they travelled from home she found her shoulders starting to inch downwards from her ears. She saw now that it had been months since she had felt even remotely at ease. Her life these days held a constant underlying drumbeat of worry: what were the Fishers going to do next? What was going on in Nicky's head? What was she to do about Tanzie? And the grim bass percussion underneath it all: *Money. Money. Money.*

'You okay?' said Mr Nicholls.

Hauled from her thoughts, Jess muttered, 'Fine. Thanks.' They nodded awkwardly at each other. He hadn't relaxed. It was obvious in his intermittently tightened jaw, in the way he was deep in thought behind his sunglasses, at the way his knuckles showed white on the steering-wheel. Jess wasn't sure what on earth had been behind his decision to offer to drive, but she was pretty sure he had regretted it from the moment Tanzie had first wailed that she needed a sick bag.

'Um, is there any chance you could stop with the tapping?'

'Tapping?'

'Your feet. On the dashboard.'

She looked at her feet.

'It's really distracting.'

'You want me to stop tapping my feet.'

He looked straight ahead through the windscreen. 'Yes. Please.'

She let her feet slide down, but she was uncomfortable, so after a moment she lifted them and tucked them under her on the seat. She rested her head on the window.

'Your hand.'

'What?'

'Your hand. You're hitting your knee now.'

She had been tapping it absentmindedly. 'You want me to stay completely still while you drive.'

'I'm not saying that. But the tapping thing is making it hard for me to focus.'

'You can't drive if I'm moving any part of my body?'

'That's not it.'

'What is it, then?'

'It's tapping. I just find . . . tapping . . . irritating.'

Jess took a deep breath. 'Kids, nobody is to move. Okay? We don't want to irritate Mr Nicholls.'

'The kids aren't doing it,' he said mildly. 'It's just you.'

'You do fidget a lot, Mum.'

'Thanks, Tanze.' Jess clasped her hands in front of her. She sat and clenched her teeth and concentrated on staying still, trying to focus on the good, which was that Mr Nicholls hadn't changed his mind. It had been almost sixty miles now and he hadn't changed his mind. And when you were basically responsible for an entire household, it was kind of nice not to be in charge for a while.

She let her head fall back against the headrest, closed her eyes and cleared her mind of money, of Marty's stupid car, of her worries for the children, letting them float away with the miles, and she tried to let the quiet hum of an expensive engine pass through her; she let the breeze from the open window ripple over her face and the music fill her ears and just briefly she felt like a woman in a different sort of life altogether.

They stopped for lunch at a pub somewhere outside Oxford, unfurling themselves and letting out little sighs of relief as they cracked joints and stretched cramped limbs. Mr Nicholls disappeared into the pub and she sat on a picnic table and unpacked the sandwiches she had made hastily that morning when it turned out they were going to get a lift after all.

'Marmite,' said Nicky, arriving back and peeling apart two slices of bread.

'I was in a rush.'

'Have we got anything else?'

'Jam.'

He sighed, and reached into the bag. Tanzie sat on the end of the bench, already lost in maths papers. She couldn't read them in the car, as it made her nauseous, so she wanted to take every opportunity to work. Jess watched her scribbling algebraic equations on her exercise book, lost in concentration, and wondered for the hundredth time where she had come from.

'Here,' said Mr Nicholls, arriving with a tray. 'I thought we could all do with some drinks.' He pushed two bottles of cola towards the kids. 'I didn't know what you wanted so I got a selection.' He had bought a bottle of

Italian beer, what looked like a half of cider, a glass of white wine, another cola, a lemonade and a bottle of orange juice. He had a mineral water. A small mountain of different-flavoured crisps sat in the middle.

'You bought all that?'

'There was a queue. I couldn't be bothered to come back out to ask.'

'I – I haven't got that much cash.'

He looked at her as if she was the weird one. 'It's a drink. I'm not buying you a house.'

And then his phone rang. He grabbed it and strode off across the car park, already talking as he went.

'Shall I see if he wants one of our sandwiches?' Tanzie said.

Jess watched him stride along the lane, one hand thrust deep in a pocket, until he was out of sight. 'Not just now,' she said.

Nicky said nothing. When she asked him which bit hurt the most, he just muttered that he was fine.

'It'll get easier,' Jess said, reaching out a hand. 'Really. We'll have this break, get Tanze sorted and work out what to do. Sometimes you need time away to sort things out in your head. It makes everything clearer.'

'I don't think what's in my head is the problem.'

She gave him his painkillers, and watched him wash them down with cola, then stretch out his gangly limbs tentatively. In the car, she had tried to move the dog so that Nicky wasn't pressed up against the door, but it was tough. Norman was too wide to fit in the footwell. He could sit up in the middle of the back seat – they actually

166

put a belt round him for a while — but then he would gradually slump until he was horizontal; a canine landslip, his head on Tanzie's lap, his great backside shoving Nicky along the leather seat.

Nicky took the dog off for a walk, his shoulders hunched, and his feet dragging. She wondered if he had cigarettes. He was out of sorts because his Nintendo had run out of charge some twenty miles back. Jess wasn't sure he knew what to do with himself when he wasn't surgically attached to a gaming device.

They watched him go in silence.

Jess thought of the way his few smiles had steadily grown fewer, his watchfulness, the way he now seemed like a fish out of water, pale and vulnerable, in the rare hours he was out of his bedroom. She thought of his face, resigned, expressionless, in that hospital. Who was it who had said you were only as happy as your unhappiest child?

Tanzie bent over her papers. 'I'm going to live somewhere else when I'm a teenager, I think.'

Jess looked at her. 'What?'

'I think I might live in a university. I don't really want to grow up near the Fishers.' She scribbled a figure in her workbook, then rubbed out one digit, replacing it with a four. 'They scare me a bit,' she said quietly.

'The Fishers?'

'I had a nightmare about them.'

Jess swallowed. 'You don't need to be scared of them,' she said. 'They're just stupid boys. What they did is what cowards do. They're nothing.'

'They don't feel like nothing.'

'Tanze, I'm going to work out what to do about them, and we're going to fix it. Okay? You don't need to have nightmares. I'm going to fix this.'

They sat in silence. The lane was silent, apart from the sound of a distant tractor. Birds wheeled overhead in the infinite blue. Mr Nicholls was walking back slowly. He had straightened up, as if he had resolved something, and his phone was loose in his hand. Jess rubbed at her eyes.

'I think I've finished the complex equations. Do you want to see?'

Tanzie held up a page of numbers. Jess looked at her daughter's lovely open face. She reached forward and straightened her glasses on her nose. 'Yes,' she said, her smile bright. 'I would totally love to look at some complex equations.'

It took two and a half hours to do the next leg of the journey. Mr Nicholls tapped the steering-wheel as if they were stuck in a jam (they weren't), took two calls during the journey, one from the woman called Gemma, which he cut off (his ex-wife?) and one that was obviously to do with his business. He said he would ring them later. He was silent for a whole forty minutes after he'd taken the second. A woman with an Italian accent called just after they pulled into a petrol station, and at the words 'Eduardo, baby' Mr Nicholls ripped his phone from the hands-free holder and went and stood outside by the pump. 'No, Lara,' he said, turning away from them. 'We've discussed this ... Well, your solicitor is wrong ... No, calling me a lobster really isn't going to make any difference.'

Nicky slept for an hour, his blue-black hair flopping over his swollen cheekbone, his face briefly untroubled in sleep. Tanzie sang under her breath and stroked the dog. Norman slept, farted audibly several times, and slowly infused the car with his odour. Nobody complained. It actually masked the lingering smell of vomit.

'Do the kids need to grab some food?' Mr Nicholls said, as they finally drove into the suburbs of some large town. Jess had already stopped noting which. Huge, shining office blocks punctuated each half-mile, their frontages bearing management- or technology-based names she'd never heard of: ACCSYS, TECHNOLOGICA and MEDIAPLUS. The roads were lined with endless stretches of car parks. Nobody walked.

'We could find a McDonald's. There's bound to be loads of them around here.'

'We don't eat McDonald's,' she said.

'You don't eat McDonald's.'

'No. I can say it again, if you like. We don't eat McDonald's.'

'Vegetarian?'

'No. Actually, could we just find a supermarket? I'll make sandwiches.'

'McDonald's would probably be cheaper, if it's about money.'

'It's not about the money.'

Jess couldn't tell him: if you were a single parent, there

were certain things you could not do. Which were basically the things that everyone expected you to do: claim benefits, smoke, live on an estate, feed your kids McDonald's. Some things she couldn't help, but others she could.

He let out a little sigh, his gaze fixed ahead. 'Okay, well, we could find somewhere to stay and then see whether they have a restaurant attached.'

'I had kind of planned we'd just sleep in the car.'

Mr Nicholls pulled over to the side of the road and turned to face her. 'Sleep in the car?'

Embarrassment made her spiky. 'We have Norman. No hotel's going to take him. We'll be fine in here.'

He pulled out his phone and began tapping into a screen. 'I'll find a dog-friendly place. There's bound to be somewhere, even if we have to drive a bit further.'

Jess could feel the colour bleeding into her cheeks. 'Actually, I'd rather you didn't.'

He kept tapping on the screen.

'Really. We – we don't have the money for hotel rooms.'

Mr Nicholls's finger stilled on the phone. 'That's crazy. You can't sleep in my car.'

'It's only a couple of nights. We'll be fine. We would have slept in the Rolls. It's why I brought the duvets.'

Tanzie watched from the rear seat.

'I have a daily budget. And I'd like to stick to it. If you don't mind.' Twelve pounds a day for food. Maximum.

He looked at her like she was mad.

'I'm not stopping *you* getting a hotel,' she added. She didn't want to tell him she'd actually prefer it if he did.

'This is nuts,' he said finally.

It was only when he turned back to the wheel that it occurred to her he might not want to leave them alone in his car.

They drove the next few miles in silence. Mr Nicholls had the air of a man who was quietly pissed off. In a weird way, Jess preferred it. Two, three days max, she told herself. In fact, she'd just let him drop them at the maths competition and tell him they would make their own way back. She wasn't sure she could take more than another forty-eight hours of being stuck in a car with him. And if Tanzie did as well as everyone seemed to think she would, they could blow a little of her winnings on train tickets.

The thought of ditching Mr Nicholls made her feel so much better that she didn't say anything when he pulled into the Travel Inn.

'I'll be back in a minute,' he said, and walked off across the car park. He took the keys with him, jangling them impatiently in his hand.

'Are we staying here?' Tanzie said, rubbing at her eyes and looking around.

'Mr Nicholls is. We're going to stay in the car. It will be an adventure!' Jess said.

There was a brief silence.

'Yay,' said Nicky.

Jess knew he was uncomfortable. But what else could she do? 'You can stretch out in the back. Tanze and I will sleep in the front. It will be fine.'

Mr Nicholls walked back out, shielding his eyes against the early-evening sun. She realized he was wearing the exact same outfit she had seen him wear in the pub that night.

'They had one room left. A twin. You guys can take it. I'll see if there's somewhere else nearby.'

'Oh, no,' she said. 'I told you. I can't accept any more from you.'

'I'm not doing it for you. I'm doing it for your kids.'

'No,' she said, trying to sound a little more diplomatic. 'It's very kind of you, but we'll be fine out here.'

He ran a hand through his hair. 'You know what? I can't sleep in a hotel room knowing that there's a boy who just got out of hospital sleeping in the back seat of a car twenty feet away. Nicky can have the other bed.'

'No,' she said, reflexively.

'Why?'

She couldn't say.

His expression darkened. 'I'm not a pervert.'

'I didn't say you were.'

'So why won't you let your son share a room with me? He's as tall as I am, for Christ's sake.'

Jess flushed. 'He's had a tough time lately. I just need to keep an eye on him.'

'What's a pervert?' said Tanzie.

'I could charge up my Nintendo,' said Nicky, from the back seat.

'You know what? This is a ridiculous discussion. I'm hungry. I need to get something to eat.' Mr Nicholls

172

poked his head in through the door. 'Nicky. Do you want to sleep in the car or in the hotel room?'

Nicky looked sideways at Jess. 'Hotel room. And I'm not a pervert either.'

'Am I a pervert?' said Tanzie.

'Okay,' said Mr Nicholls. 'Here's the deal. Nicky and Tanzie sleep in the hotel room. You can sleep on the floor with them.'

'But I can't let you pay for a hotel room for us, then make you sleep in the car. Besides, the dog will howl all night. He doesn't know you.'

Mr Nicholls rolled his eyes. He was clearly losing patience. 'Okay, then. The kids sleep in the hotel room. You and I sleep in the car with the dog. Everyone's happy.' He didn't look happy.

'I've never stayed in a hotel. Have I stayed in a hotel, Mum?'

There was a brief silence. Jess could feel the situation sliding away from her.

'I'll mind Tanze,' said Nicky. He looked hopeful. His face, where it wasn't bruised, was the colour of putty. 'A bath would be good.'

'Would you read me a story?'

'Only if it has zombies in it.' Jess watched as he half smiled at her. And that smile was what broke her.

'Okay,' she said. And tried to fight the wave of nausea at what she had just agreed to.

The mini-mart squatted, illuminated, in the shadow of a logistics company across the road, its windows bright with exclamation marks and offers on crispy fish bites and fizzy drinks. She bought rolls and cheese, crisps and overpriced apples, and made the kids a picnic supper, which they ate on the grassy slope around the car park. On the other side the traffic thundered past in a purple haze towards the south. She offered Mr Nicholls some, but he peered at the contents of her bag and said thanks but he'd eat in the restaurant. She suspected he wanted a break from them.

Once he was out of sight, Jess relaxed too. She set the kids up in their room, feeling faintly wistful that she wasn't in with them. It was on the ground floor, facing the car park. She had asked Mr Nicholls to park as close to their window as possible, and Tanzie made her go outside three times, just so she could wave at her through the curtains and squash her nose sideways against the glass.

Nicky disappeared into the bathroom for an hour, the taps running. He came out, switched on the television and lay on the bed, looking simultaneously exhausted and relieved.

Jess laid out his pills, got Tanzie bathed and into her pyjamas, and warned them not to stay up too late. 'And no smoking,' she warned him. 'Seriously.'

'How can I?' he said, grumpily. 'You've got my stash.'

Tanzie lay on her side, working her way through her maths books, locked into a silent world of numbers. Jess fed and walked the dog, sat in the passenger seat with the door open, ate a cheese roll and waited for Mr Nicholls to finish his meal.

It was a quarter past nine, and she was struggling to read a newspaper in the fading light when he appeared. He was holding a phone in a way that suggested he had just come off another call, and he seemed about as pleased to see her as she was him. He opened the door, climbed in and shut it.

'I've asked Reception to ring me if anyone cancels their booking.' He stared ahead at the windscreen. 'Obviously I didn't tell them I'd be waiting in their car park.'

Norman was lying on the tarmac, looking like he'd been dropped from a great height. She wondered whether she should bring him in. Without the children in the back, and with the encroaching darkness, it felt even odder to be in the car beside Mr Nicholls.

'Are the kids okay?'

'They're very happy. Thank you.'

'Your boy looks pretty bashed up.'

'He'll be fine.'

There was a long silence. He looked at her. Then he put both hands on the wheel, and leant backwards in his seat. He rubbed his eyes with the heels of his hands, and turned to face her. 'Okay . . . so have I done something else to upset you?'

'What?'

'You've acted like I'm bugging you all day. I apologized for the thing in the pub the other night. I've done what I can to help you out here. And yet still I get the feeling I've done something wrong.'

'You – you haven't done anything wrong,' she stammered.

He studied her for a minute. 'Is this, like, a woman's "There's nothing wrong" when actually what you mean is that I've done something massive and I'm actually supposed to guess? And then you get really mad if I don't?'

'No.'

'You see, now I don't know. Because that "no" might be part of the woman's "There's nothing wrong."'

'I'm not speaking in code. There's nothing wrong.'

'Then can we just ease up around each other a bit? You're making me really uncomfortable.'

'I'm making *you* uncomfortable?'

His head swivelled slowly.

'You've looked like you regretted offering us this lift since the moment we got into the car. In fact, since before we got in.' *Shut up, Jess,* she warned herself. *Shut up. Shut up. Shut up.* 'I'm not even sure why you did it.'

'What?'

'Nothing,' she said, turning away. 'Forget it.'

He stared ahead of him out of the windscreen. He looked suddenly really, really tired.

'In fact, you could just drop us at a station tomorrow morning. We won't bother you any more.'

'Is that what you want?' he said.

She drew her knees up to her chest. 'It might be the best thing.'

They sat there in the silence. The skies darkened to pitch around them. Twice Jess opened her mouth to speak, but nothing came out. Mr Nicholls stared through the windscreen at the closed curtains of the hotel room, apparently deep in thought.

She thought of Nicky and Tanzie, sleeping peacefully on the other side, and wished she was with them. She felt sick. Why couldn't she have just pretended? Why couldn't she have been nicer? It would only have been for a couple of days. She was an idiot. She had blown it all again.

It had grown chill. Finally, she pulled Nicky's duvet from the back seat and thrust it at him. 'Here,' she said.

'Oh.' He looked at the huge picture of Super Mario. 'Thanks.'

She called the dog in, reclined her seat just far enough for it not to be touching him, and then she pulled Tanzie's duvet over herself. 'Goodnight.' She stared at the plush interior a matter of inches from her nose, breathing in the new-car smell, her mind a jumble. How far away was the station? How much would the fare cost? They would have to pay for an extra day's bed and breakfast somewhere, at least. And what was she going to do with the dog? She could hear Norman's faint snore from behind her and thought grimly that she was damned if she would vacuum that rear seat now.

'It's half past nine.' Mr Nicholls's voice broke into the silence.

Jess lay very still.

'Half. Past. Nine.' He let out a deep sigh. 'I never thought I'd say it, but this is actually worse than being married.'

'What – am I breathing too loud?'

He opened his door abruptly. 'Oh for Christ's sake,' he said, and set off across the car park.

Jess pushed herself upright and watched him jogging across the road to the mini-mart, disappearing into its fluorescent-lit interior. He reappeared a few minutes later with a bottle of wine and a packet of plastic cups.

'It's probably awful,' he said, climbing back into the driver's seat. 'But right now I couldn't give a toss.'

She gazed at the bottle.

'Truce, Jessica Thomas? It's been a long day. And a shitty week. And, spacious as it is, this car isn't big enough for two people who aren't talking to each other.'

He looked at her. His eyes were exhausted and stubble was starting to show through on his chin. It made him seem curiously vulnerable.

She took a cup from him. 'Sorry. I'm not used to people helping us out. It makes me . . .'

'Suspicious? Crabby?'

'I was going to say, it makes me think I should get out more.'

He let out a breath. 'Right.' He glanced down at the bottle. 'Then let's . . . Oh, for crying out loud.'

'What?'

'I thought it was a screw top.' He stared at it as if it was just one more thing designed to annoy him. 'Great. I don't suppose you have a bottle opener?'

'No.'

'You think they'll exchange it?'

'Did you take the receipt?'

He let out a deep sigh, which she interrupted. 'No need,' she said, taking it from him. She opened her door and climbed out. Norman's head shot up.

'You're not going to smash it into my windscreen?'

'Nope.' She peeled off the foil. 'Take off your shoe.'

'What?'

'Take off your shoe. It won't work with flip-flops.'

'Please don't use it as a glass. My ex did that once with a stiletto and it was really, really hard pretending that champagne smelling of feet was an erotic experience.'

She held out her hand. He finally took his shoe off and handed it to her. As he looked on, Jess placed the base of the wine bottle inside it and, holding the two together carefully, she stood alongside the hotel and thumped them hard against the wall.

'I suppose there's no point me asking you what you're doing.'

'Just give me a minute,' she said, through gritted teeth, and thumped again.

Mr Nicholls shook his head slowly.

She straightened up and glared at him. 'You're more than welcome to suck the cork out, if you'd rather.'

He held up his hand. 'No, no. You go ahead. Broken glass in my socks is exactly how I hoped to end tonight.'

Jess checked the cork and thumped again. And there – a centimetre of it protruded from the neck of the bottle. *Thump*. Another centimetre. She held it carefully, gave it one more thump, and there it was: she pulled the rest of the cork gently from the neck and handed it to him.

He stared at it, and then at her. She handed him back his shoe.

'Wow. You're a useful woman to know.'

'I can also put up shelves, replace rotting floorboards and make a fan belt out of a tied stocking.'

'Really?'

'Not the fan belt.' She climbed into the car and accepted the plastic cup of wine. 'I tried it once. It shredded before we'd got thirty yards down the road. Total waste of M&S opaques.' She took a sip. 'And the car stank of burnt tights for weeks.'

Behind them, Norman whimpered in his sleep.

'Truce,' Mr Nicholls said, and held up his cup.

'Truce. You're not going to drive afterwards, are you?' she said, holding up her own.

'I won't if you won't.'

'Oh, very funny.'

And suddenly the evening became a little easier.

13.

ED

So these were the things Ed discovered about Jessica Thomas, once she'd had a drink or two (actually, four or five) and stopped being chippy. The facts of her life, other than the other things he just observed, which were that she tied her hair back for no reason when she felt awkward, as if she needed to be doing something, and that she had a laugh like a seal's bark – big, abrupt and awkward, at odds with her size and shape. Her lean figure betrayed that she did physical work for a living, her roots had grown out some months earlier, and she wore cheap jeans. He slightly hated himself for noticing, but Lara used to point out things like denim colour and stitching and it was one of those weird things, unlike the date of Lara's birthday, that had stuck with him.

1. The boy wasn't actually her kid. He was the son of her ex and her ex's ex and, given that both of them had effectively walked out on him, she was pretty much the only person he had left. 'Kind of you,' he said.

   'Not really,' she said. 'Nicky is as good as mine. He's been with me since he was eight. He looks

181

out for Tanzie. And, besides, families are different shapes now, right? It doesn't have to be two point four any more.' The defensive way she said it made him think she had had this conversation many times before.

2. The little girl was ten. He did some mental arithmetic, and Jess cut in before he said a word. 'Seventeen.'

'That's . . . young.'

'I was a wild kid. I knew everything. I actually knew nothing. Marty came along, I dropped out of school, and then I got pregnant. I wasn't always going to be a cleaner, you know. My mum was a teacher.' Her gaze had slid towards him, as if she knew this fact would shock.

'Okay.'

'Retired now. She lives in Cornwall. We don't really get on. She doesn't agree with what she calls my life choices. I never could explain that once you have a baby at seventeen there are no choices.'

'Not even now?'

'Nope.' She twisted a lock of hair between her fingers. 'Because you never quite catch up. Your friends are at college, you're at home with a tiny baby. Your friends are starting their careers, you're down the housing office trying to find somewhere to live. Your friends are buying their first cars and houses and you're trying to find a job that you can fit round childcare. And all the jobs you can fit round school hours have really crappy wages. And that was before the economy went splat. Oh, don't get me wrong. I don't regret having Tanzie, not for a minute. And I don't regret taking Nicky on. But if I had my time again, sure, I'd have had them after I had done something with my life. It would be nice to be able to give them . . . something better.'

She hadn't bothered to put the seat back up while she told him this. She lay propped on her elbow facing him under the duvet and her bare feet rested on the dashboard. Ed found he didn't mind them so much.

'You could still have a career,' he said. 'You're young. I mean . . . you could get an after-school nanny or something?'

She actually laughed. A great seal-bark 'Ha!' that exploded into the interior of the car. She sat bolt upright, and took a swig of her wine. 'Yeah. Right, Mr Nicholls. Sure I could.'

3. She liked fixing things. She did odd jobs around the estate, from rewiring plugs to tiling people's bathrooms. 'I did everything around the house. I'm good at making stuff. I can even block-print wallpaper.'

'You make your own wallpaper.'

'Don't look at me like that. It's in Tanzie's room. I made her clothes too, until recently.'

'Are you actually from the Second World War? Do you save jam jars and string too?'

'So what did you want to be?'

'What I was,' he said. And then he realized he didn't want to talk about it and changed the subject.

4. She had seriously tiny feet. As in she bought child-sized shoes. (Apparently they were cheaper.) After she'd said this he had to stop himself sneaking looks at her feet like some kind of weirdo.

5. Before she'd had children she could drink four double vodkas in a row and still walk a straight line. 'Yup, I could hold my drink. Obviously not enough to remember birth control.' He believed her: they drank two bottles of wine and he thought she had twice as much as he did, and while she did relax a bit, there wasn't a point at which he thought she was even a bit drunk.

She almost never drank at home. 'When I'm working at the pub and someone offers me one I just take the cash. And when I'm at home I worry that something might happen to the kids and I'll need to be together.' She stared out of the window. 'Now I think about it, this is the closest thing I've had to a night out in ... five months.'

'A man who shut a door in your face, two bottles of rot-gut wine and a car park.'

'I'm not knocking it.'

She didn't explain what made her worry so much about the kids. He thought back to Nicky's face and decided not to ask.

6. She had a scar under her chin from when she'd fallen off a bike and a piece of gravel had lodged in it for two whole weeks. She tried to show him but the light in the car wasn't strong enough. She also had a tattoo on the base of her spine. 'A proper tramp stamp, according to Marty. He wouldn't talk to me for two whole days after I got it.' She paused. 'I think that's probably why I got it.'

7. Her middle name was Rae. She had to spell it out every single time.

8. She didn't mind cleaning but she really, really hated people treating her like she was 'just' a cleaner. (He had the grace to colour a little here.)

9. She hadn't had a date in the two years since her ex had left.

'You haven't had sex for two and a half years?'

'I said he left two years ago.'

'It's a reasonable calculation.'

She pushed herself upright, and gave him a sideways look. 'Three and a half. If we're counting. Apart from one – um – episode last year. And you don't have to look so shocked.'

'I'm not shocked,' he said, and tried to rearrange his face. He shrugged. 'Three and a half years. I mean, it's only, what, a quarter of your adult life? No time at all.'

'Yeah. Thanks for that.' And then he wasn't sure what happened, but something in the atmosphere changed. She mumbled something that he couldn't make out, pulled her hair into another ponytail and said maybe it was really time for them to be getting some sleep.

Ed thought he would lie awake for ages. There was something oddly unsettling about being in a darkened car just arm's length from an attractive woman you had just shared two bottles of wine with. Even if she was huddled under a *SpongeBob SquarePants* duvet. He looked out of the sunroof at the stars, listened to the lorries rumbling past towards London, listened to the dog in the rear seats whimper in his sleep and thought that his real life – the one with his company and his office and the never-ending hangover of Deanna Lewis – was now a million miles away.

'Still awake?'

He turned his head, wondering if she'd been watching him. 'No.'

'Okay,' came the murmur from the passenger seat. 'Truth game.'

He raised his eyes to the roof.

'Go on, then.'

'You first.'

He couldn't come up with anything.

'You must be able to think of something.'

'Okay, why are you wearing flip-flops?'

'That's your question?'

'It's freezing out. It's been the coldest, wettest spring since records began. And you're wearing flip-flops.'

'Does it bug you that much?'

'I just don't understand it. You're obviously cold.'

She pointed a toe. 'It's spring.'

'So?'

'So. It's spring. Therefore the weather will get better.'

'You're wearing flip-flops as an expression of faith.'

'If you like.'

He couldn't think how to reply to this.

'Okay, my turn.'

He waited.

'Did you think about driving off and leaving us this morning?'

'No.'

'Liar.'

'Okay. Maybe a bit. Your neighbour wanted to smash my head in with a baseball bat and your dog smells really bad.'

'Pfft. Any excuse.'

He heard her shift in the seat. Her feet disappeared under the duvet. He could smell her shampoo. It made him think of Bounty bars.

'So why didn't you?'

He thought for a minute before he responded. Perhaps it was because he couldn't see her face. Perhaps it was because some time between the third and fourth glass he had decided she was okay. Perhaps the drink and the late hour had lowered his defences because he wouldn't normally have answered like he did. 'Because I've done some stupid stuff lately. And maybe some part of me just wanted to do something I could feel good about.'

Ed thought she was going to say something. He sort of hoped she would. But she didn't.

He lay there for a few minutes, gazing out at the sodium lights and listening to Jessica Rae Thomas's breathing and thought how much he missed just sleeping near another person. Most days he felt like the loneliest man on the planet. He thought about those tiny feet and their highly polished toenails. Then he saw his sister's raised eyebrow and realized he had probably had too much to drink. Don't be an idiot, Nicholls, he told himself, and turned so that he had his back to her.

Ed Nicholls thought about his ex-wife and Deanna Lewis until the soft, melancholy thoughts evaporated and only the stone-hard anger remained. And then suddenly it was cold and pale grey outside and his left arm had gone to sleep and he was so groggy that it took two whole minutes to figure out that the banging he could hear was the security guard knocking on the driver's window to tell them they couldn't sleep there.

14.

TANZIE

There were four different types of Danish pastry at the breakfast buffet, and three different types of fruit juice and a whole rack of those little individual packets of cereal that Mum said were uneconomical and would never buy. She had knocked on the window at a quarter past eight to tell them they should wear their jackets to breakfast and stuff as many of each of them as they could into their pockets. Her hair had flattened on one side and she had no makeup on. Tanzie guessed the car hadn't been that much of an adventure after all.

'Not the butters or jams. Or anything that needs cutlery. Rolls, muffins, that kind of thing. Don't get caught.' She looked behind her to where Mr Nicholls seemed to be having an argument with a security guard. 'And apples. Apples are healthy. And maybe some slices of ham for Norman.'

'Where am I meant to put the ham?'

'Or a sausage. Wrap them in a napkin.'

'Isn't that stealing?'

'No.'

'But –'

'It's just taking a bit more than you're likely to eat at that exact moment. You're just . . . Imagine you're a guest with a hormone disorder and it makes you really, really hungry.'

'But I haven't got a hormone disorder.'

'But you could have. That's the point. You're that hungry, sick person, Tanze. You've paid for your breakfast, but you need to eat a lot. More than you would normally eat.'

Tanzie folded her arms. 'You said it was wrong to steal.'

'It's not stealing. It's just getting your money's worth.'

'But we didn't pay for it. Mr Nicholls did.'

'Tanzie, just do as I say, please. Look, Mr Nicholls and I are going to have to leave the car park for half an hour. Just do it, then come back to the room and be ready to leave at nine. Okay?' She leant through the window and kissed Tanzie, then trudged back towards the car, her jacket wrapped around her. She stopped, turned back and shouted, 'Don't forget to brush your teeth. And don't leave any of your maths books.'

Nicky came out of the bathroom. He was wearing his really tight black jeans and a T-shirt that said WHEVS across the front.

'You're never going to get a sausage in those,' she said, staring at his jeans.

'I bet I can hide more than you can,' he said.

Her eyes met his. 'You're on,' Tanzie said, and ran to get dressed.

*

Mr Nicholls leant forward and squinted through his windscreen as Nicky and she walked across the car park. To be fair, Tanzie thought, she would probably have squinted at them too. Nicky had stuffed two large oranges and an apple down the front of his jeans and waddled across the asphalt like he'd had an accident in his trousers. She was in her jacket, despite feeling too hot, because she'd packed the front of her hoodie with little packets of cereal and if she didn't wear her jacket she looked like she might be pregnant. With baby robots.

They couldn't stop laughing.

'Just get in, get in,' said Mum, throwing their overnight bags into the boot and almost shoving them into the car as she glanced behind her. 'What did you get?' Mr Nicholls set off down the road. Tanzie could see him glancing in the mirror as they took turns to unload their haul and hand it forward to her.

Nicky pulled a white package from his pocket. 'Three Danish pastries. Watch out – the icing got a bit stuck to the napkins. Four sausages and a few slices of bacon in a paper cup for Norman. Two slices of cheese, a yoghurt, and . . .' He tugged his jacket over his crotch, reached down, grimacing, tensing, and pulled out the fruit. 'I can't believe I managed to fit those in there.'

'There's nothing I can say to that that's in any way appropriate mother-son conversation,' Mum said.

Tanzie had six small packets of cereal, two bananas, and a jam sandwich that she'd made out of toasted white bread. She sat eating while Norman stared at her and two stalactites of drool grew longer and longer from his lips until they were pooling on the seat of Mr Nicholls's car.

'That woman behind the poached eggs definitely saw us.'

'I told her you had a hormone disorder,' Tanzie said. 'I told her you had to eat twice your bodyweight three times a day or you would faint in their dining room and you might actually die.'

'Nice,' said Nicky.

'You win on numbers,' she said, counting out his items. 'But I win extra points for skill.' She leant forward and, as everyone watched, she carefully lifted the two polystyrene cups of coffee from her pockets, packed out with paper napkins so that they would stay upright. She handed one to Mum and the other she placed in the cup holder next to Mr Nicholls.

'You are a genius,' Mum said, peeling off the lid. 'Oh, Tanze, you have no idea how much I needed this.' She took a sip, closing her eyes. Tanzie wasn't sure if it was that they'd done so well with the buffet, or just that Nicky was laughing for the first time in ages, but for a moment she looked happier than she had done since Dad left.

Mr Nicholls just stared like they were a bunch of aliens.

'Okay, so we can make sandwiches for lunch with the ham, cheese and sausages. You guys can eat the pastries now. Fruit for pudding. Want one?' She held an orange towards Mr Nicholls. 'It's a bit warm still. But I can peel it.'

'Uh . . . kind of you,' he said, tearing his gaze away. 'But I think I'll just stop at a Starbucks.'

The next part of the journey was actually quite nice. There were no traffic jams once they'd got out of town and Mum persuaded Mr Nicholls to put on her favourite radio station and sang along to six songs, getting louder with each one. She would do this thing where when she didn't know the lyrics she just substituted random words like 'custard tarts' or 'bald-headed policeman' and sometimes it made Tanzie cringe but today it was really funny. She made Tanzie and Nicky join in too and Mr Nicholls looked fed up at first but Tanzie noticed that after a few miles he was tapping the steering-wheel like he was sort of enjoying himself. The sun got really hot and Mr Nicholls slid the roof back. Norman sat bolt upright so that he could scent the air as they were going along and it meant that he didn't squish them into each door, which was also nice.

It reminded Tanzie a bit of when Dad lived with them and they would sometimes go on outings in his car. Except Dad always drove too fast and got grumpy when Mum asked him to slow down. And they could never agree on where to stop and eat. And Dad would say he didn't understand why they couldn't just blow some money on a pub lunch and Mum would say that she'd made the sandwiches now and it would be silly to waste them. And Dad would tell Nicky to get his head out of whatever game he was playing and enjoy the damn scenery and Nicky would mutter that he hadn't actually asked to come, which would make Dad even madder.

And then Tanzie thought that while she did love Dad she probably preferred this trip without him.

After two hours Mr Nicholls said he needed to stretch, and Norman needed to wee, so they stopped at the edge of a country park. Mum put some of the buffet haul out and they sat in a little clearing in the shade at a proper wooden picnic table and ate. Tanzie did some revision (prime numbers and quadratic equations), then took Norman for a walk around the woods. He was really happy and stopped every two minutes to sniff at something, and the sun kept sending little moving spotlights through the trees and they saw a deer and two pheasants and it was like they were actually on holiday.

'You okay, lovely?' Mum said, walking up with her arms crossed. From where they stood they could just see Nicky talking to Mr Nicholls at the table through the trees. 'Feeling confident?'

'I think so,' she said.

'Did you go through the past papers last night?'

'Yes. I do find the prime-number sequences a bit difficult, but I wrote them all down and when I saw the sequencing laid out I found it easier.'

'No more nightmares about the Fishers?'

'Last night,' Tanzie said, 'I dreamt about a cabbage that could rollerskate. It was called Kevin.'

Mum gave her a long look. 'Right.'

They walked a bit further. It was cooler in the forest, and it smelt of good damp, mossy and green and alive, not like the damp in the back room, which just smelt mouldy. Mum stopped on the path and turned back towards the car. 'I told you good things happen, didn't I?' She waited for Tanzie to catch up. 'Mr Nicholls is going to get us there tomorrow. We'll have a quiet night, get you through this competition, and you'll start at your new school. Then, hopefully, all our lives will change a little for the better. And this is fun, isn't it? This is a nice trip?'

She kept her eyes on the car as she spoke and her voice did that thing where she was saying one thing and thinking about something else. Tanzie noticed she'd put her makeup on while they were in the car. She had half turned away from Mr Nicholls, held up her compact and put on the mascara even though every time it went over a bump she ended up with a black blob on her face. Tanzie wasn't really sure why she bothered. She looked perfectly nice without it. 'Mum,' she said.

'Yes?'

'We did sort of steal the food from that buffet, didn't we? I mean, if you look at it proportionally, we did take more than our share.'

Mum stared at her feet for a minute, thinking. 'If you're really worried, when we get your prize money we'll put five pounds in an envelope and send it to them. How does that sound?'

'I think, given the items we took, it would probably be nearer six pounds. Probably six pounds fifty,' Tanzie said.

'Then that's what we'll send them. And now I think

we should work really, really hard to get this fat old dog of yours to run around a bit, so that (a) he's tired enough to sleep the next leg of the journey, and (b) it might encourage him to go to the loo here and not fart his way through the next eighty miles.'

They hit the road again. It rained. Mr Nicholls had had One of His Phone Calls with a man called Sidney and talked about share prices and market movements and looked a bit serious, so Mum didn't sing for a bit. Everyone was quiet. She tried not to sneak looks at her maths papers (Mum said it would make her sick) and Nicky's Nintendo had run out of power again so he just stared out of the window and sighed a lot. That part of the journey seemed to take for ever. Nicky was having one of his quiet days. Tanzie wanted to talk to him, but you could tell when he didn't want to talk as his mouth just turned into a straight line and he wouldn't meet your eye. Tanzie's legs kept sticking to Mr Nicholls's leather seats and she was sort of regretting wearing her shorts. Plus Norman had rolled in something in the woods and she kept getting this whiff of something really bad, but she didn't want to say anything in case Mr Nicholls decided he'd had enough of them and their stinky dog so she just held her nose with her fingers and tried to breathe through her mouth and only let herself open her nostrils every thirty lampposts.

It rolled on. The weather cleared. They headed past Coventry and up towards Derby, with its ring roads and its big dark red factories, and she gazed at the landscape as it got wilder and woollier, and let the numbers run through her head in little strings, trying to do calculations in her head without actually looking at them so she wouldn't get nauseous.

Mr Nicholls's phone rang and a woman immediately started shouting at him in Italian. He just turned it off without saying anything.

Mum sat in the front and counted the money in her purse. She had £63.91, but she hadn't yet seen that one of the ten-pence pieces was actually foreign money so it was going to be £63.81 unless she could get someone else to take it.

'Nicky.'

He looked up. Mr Nicholls was watching him in the rear-view mirror.

'You want to borrow my phone? It doesn't have many games on it, but you could log onto Twitter or Facebook or whatever it is you lot are into these days.'

'Really?' Nicky pushed himself upright from his slumped position.

'Sure. It's in the pocket of my jacket.'

Mum took it out and handed it to him. 'Be very careful with it, Nicky.'

'I've deactivated the PIN. Just . . . you know, no movies.'

'Cool.' Nicky didn't actually smile – he didn't really do smiling much any more, Tanzie thought – but you could tell he was pleased.

'Not you, Tanzie.' Mum's voice came across the seats. 'Don't you look at it or you'll get sick.'

Tanzie sighed. It was SO boring being her sometimes. Norman's head was really heavy on her lap and she tried to move it gently because her legs were getting pins and needles. She wondered how long it would take them to get to Scotland. She was really, really bored, but she knew that if she said so Mum would get all *We're all bored, Tanzie. There's nothing I can do about it.* She started to doze off, her head bumping against the window frame. Mum and Mr Nicholls started talking. It was possible they'd forgotten anyone else was in the car.

'So, tell me about your wife.'

'Ex-wife. And no thanks.'

'Why not? You weren't unfaithful. I'm guessing she wasn't, or you would have made that face.'

'What face?'

There was a short silence. Maybe ten lampposts.

'I'm not sure I would ever have made that face. But no. She wasn't. And, no, I don't really want to discuss it. It's . . .'

'Private?'

'I just don't like talking about personal stuff. Do you want to talk about your ex?'

'In front of his children? Yup, that's always a great idea.'

They carried on in silence for a few miles. Mum started tapping on the window. Tanzie glanced over at Mr Nicholls. Every time Mum tapped a little muscle tweaked in his jaw.

'So what shall we talk about, then? I'm not very interested in software and I'm guessing you have zero interest in what I do. And there are only so many times I can point at a field and say: "Oh, look, cows."'

Mr Nicholls sighed.

'Come on. It's a long way to Scotland.'

There was a thirty-lamppost silence.

'I could sing if you like. We could all sing. Let me see if I can find something –'

'Lara. Italian. Model.'

'Model.' Mum laughed this great big laugh. 'Of course.'

'What's that supposed to mean?' Mr Nicholls said grumpily.

'All men like you go out with models.'

'What do you mean, men like me?'

Mum pressed her lips together.

'What do you mean, men like me? Come on.'

'Rich men.'

'I'm not rich.'

Mum shook her head. 'Noooo.'

'I'm not.'

'I think it depends how you define rich.'

'I've seen rich. I'm not rich. I'm well-off, yes. But I'm a long way from rich.'

Mum turned to him. He really had no idea whom he was dealing with. 'Do you have more than one house?'

He signalled and swung the wheel. 'I might.'

'Do you have more than one car?'

He glanced sideways. 'Yes.'

'Then you're rich.'

'Nope. Rich is private jets and yachts. Rich is staff.'

'So what am I?'

Mr Nicholls shook his head. 'Not staff. You're . . .'

'What?'

'I'm just trying to imagine your face if I'd referred to you as my staff.'

Mum started to laugh. 'My woman-servant. My cleaning wench.'

'Yeah. Or those. Okay, well, what would you say is rich?'

Mum pulled one of the buffet apples from her bag and bit into it. She chewed for a minute before speaking. 'Rich is paying every single bill on time without thinking about it. Rich is being able to have a holiday or get through Christmas without having to borrow against January and February. Actually, rich would be just not thinking about money all the bloody time.'

'Everyone thinks about money. Even rich people.'

'Yes, but you're just thinking what to do with it to make more money. Whereas I'm thinking how the hell we can get enough of it to get through another week.'

Mr Nicholls made a sort of harrumphing sound. 'I can't believe I'm driving you to Scotland and you're giving me a hard time because you've misguidedly decided I'm some kind of Donald Trump.'

'I'm not giving you a hard time.'

'Noooo.'

'I'm just pointing out that there's a difference between what you consider to be rich and what is actually rich.'

There was a sort of awkward silence. Mum blushed like she'd said too much and started eating her apple with big, noisy bites, even though she would have told Tanzie off if she had eaten like that. She had come awake again by then and she didn't want Mum and Mr Nicholls to stop talking to each other because they were having quite a nice day, so she put her head through the front seats. 'Actually, I read somewhere that to qualify for the top one per cent in this country you would need to earn more than a hundred and forty thousand pounds a year,' she said helpfully. 'So if Mr Nicholls doesn't earn that much then he probably isn't rich.' She smiled and sat back in her seat.

Mum looked at Mr Nicholls. She kept looking at him.

Mr Nicholls rubbed his head. 'I tell you what,' he said, after a while, 'shall we stop off and get some tea?'

Moreton Marston looked like it had been invented for tourists. Everything was made of the same grey stone and really old, and everyone's gardens were perfect, with tiny blue flowers creeping over the tops of walls, and immaculate little baskets of trailing leaves, like something out of a book or maybe *Midsomer Murders*. There was a faint smell of sheep in the air, and you could hear them in the far distance, and there was this chill in the breeze, as if it was warning you what it could be like on a day that wasn't sunny. The shops were all the kind you get on Christmas cards, in the market square a woman dressed as a Victorian was selling buns from a tray and groups of tourists wandered around taking pictures of everything. Tanzie was so busy gazing out of the window at it that she didn't notice Nicky at first. It was only when they pulled into the parking space that she noticed he had gone really quiet. He wasn't looking at the phone – even though, she knew, he had really, really wanted it – and his face was all white. She asked him whether his ribs were hurting, and he said no, and when she asked if he had an apple down his trousers that he couldn't get out, he said, 'No, Tanze, just drop it,' but the way he said it, there was definitely something. Tanzie looked at Mum but she was busy not looking at Mr Nicholls and Mr Nicholls was busy making this big to-do about finding the best parking space. Norman just looked up at Tanzie, like 'Don't even bother asking.'

Everyone got out and stretched and Mr Nicholls said they were all having tea and cake and it was his treat and please could we not make a big financial deal out of it as it was just tea, okay, and Mum raised her eyebrows like she was going to say something and then just muttered, 'Thank you,' but not with good grace.

They sat down in a café whose name was Ye Spotted Sowe Tea Shoppe, even though Tanzie would bet there were no tea shoppes in medieval times. She was pretty sure they didn't even have tea then. Nobody else seemed to mind. Nicky got up to go to the loo. And Mr Nicholls and Mum were at the counter choosing what to eat so she clicked on Mr Nicholls's phone and the first thing that came up was Nicky's Facebook page. She waited for a minute because Nicky got really annoyed if people looked at his stuff, and then when she was sure he really was in the loo she made the screen go bigger so she could read it and then she went cold. The Fishers had posted messages and pictures of men doing rude things to other men all over Nicky's timeline. They had called him GIMP and FAGBOY, and even though Tanzie didn't know what the words meant she knew they were bad and she suddenly felt sick. She looked up and Mum was coming back holding a tray.

'Tanzie! Be careful with Mr Nicholls's phone!'

The phone had clattered onto the edge of the table. She didn't want to touch it. She wondered if Nicky was crying in the loos. She would have done.

When she looked up Mum was staring at her. 'What's wrong?'

'Nothing.'

She sat down and pushed an orange cupcake on a plate across the table. Tanzie wasn't hungry any more, even though it was covered with sprinkles.

'Tanze. What's wrong? Talk to me.'

She pushed the phone slowly across the wooden table with the tip of her finger, like it was going to burn her or something. Mum frowned, and then looked down at it. She clicked on it and stared. 'Jesus Christ,' she said, after a minute.

Mr Nicholls sat down beside her. He had the biggest slice of chocolate cake Tanzie had ever seen. 'Everyone happy?' he said. He looked happy.

'The little bastards,' Mum said. And her eyes filled with tears.

'What?' Mr Nicholls had a mouthful of cake.

'Is that like a prevert?'

Mum didn't seem to hear her. She pushed the chair

back with a massive screech and began striding towards the toilets.

'That's the Gents, madam,' a woman called, as Mum pushed the door open.

'I can read, thank you,' Mum said, and she disappeared inside.

'What? What's going on now?' Mr Nicholls struggled to swallow his mouthful. He glanced over at where Mum had gone. Then, when Tanzie didn't say anything, he looked down at his phone and tapped it twice. He didn't say anything, just kept staring. Then he moved the screen around like he was reading everything. Tanzie felt a bit weird. She wasn't sure he should be looking at that.

'Did . . . Is this something to do with what happened to your brother?'

She wanted to cry. She felt like the Fishers had ruined the nice day. She felt like they had followed them here, like they would never get away from them. She couldn't speak.

'Hey,' he said, as a great big tear plopped down on the table. 'Hey.' He held out a paper napkin towards her and Tanzie wiped her eyes and when she couldn't hide the sob that burst upwards he moved around the table and put an arm around her and pulled her in for a hug. He smelt of lemons and men. She hadn't smelt that man smell since Dad left and it made her even sadder.

'Hey. Don't cry.'

'Sorry.'

'Nothing to be sorry for. I'd cry if someone did that to my sister. That's – that's . . .' He clicked the phone off.

'Sheez.' He shook his head and blew out his cheeks. 'Do they do that to him a lot?'

'I don't know.' She sniffed. 'He doesn't say much any more.'

Mr Nicholls waited until she had stopped crying and then he moved back around the table and ordered a hot chocolate with marshmallows, chocolate shavings and extra cream. 'Cures all known ills,' he said, pushing it towards her. 'Trust me. I know everything.'

And the weird thing was, it was actually true.

Tanzie had finished her chocolate and her cupcake by the time Mum and Nicky came out of the loos. Mum put on this bright smile, like nothing was wrong, and had her arm around Nicky's shoulders, which actually looked a bit odd now he was half a head taller than her. He slid into the seat beside her at the table and stared at his cake like he wasn't hungry. His face had gone back to how it was before they went away: like a shop dummy so you couldn't see what he was thinking. Tanzie watched Mr Nicholls watching him and wondered if he was going to say anything about what was on his phone but he didn't. She thought maybe he didn't want Nicky to get embarrassed. Either way, the happy day, she thought sadly, was over.

And then Mum got up to check on Norman who was tied up outside and Mr Nicholls ordered a second cup of coffee and started stirring it slowly like he was thinking about something. And then he looked up at Nicky from under his eyebrows, and said quietly, 'So. Nicky. You know anything about hacking?'

She got the feeling she wasn't supposed to listen so she just stared really hard at the quadratic equations.

'No,' said Nicky.

Mr Nicholls leant forward over the table and lowered his voice. 'Well, I think now might be a good time to start.'

When Mum came back, Mr Nicholls and Nicky had disappeared. 'Where are they?' she said, looking around the room.

'They've gone to Mr Nicholls's car. Mr Nicholls said they're not to be disturbed.' Tanzie sucked the end of her pencil.

Mum's eyebrows shot somewhere into her hairline.

'Mr Nicholls said you'd look like that. He said to tell you he's sorting it out. The Facebook thing.'

'He's doing what? How?'

'He said you'd say that too.' She rubbed at a 2, which looked a bit too much like a 5 and blew away the rubbings. 'He said to tell you to please give them twenty minutes and he's ordered you another cup of tea and you should have some cake while you're waiting. They'll come back and fetch us when they're finished. And also to tell you the chocolate cake is really good.'

Mum didn't like it. Tanzie sat and finished her unit until she was happy with the answers, while Mum fidgeted and looked out of the window and made as if to speak, then closed her mouth again. She didn't eat any chocolate cake. She just left the five pounds that Mr Nicholls had put on the table sitting there and Tanzie put her rubber on it because she was worried that when someone opened the door it would blow away.

Finally, just as the woman was sweeping up close enough to their table to send a silent message, the door opened, a little bell rang and Mr Nicholls walked in with Nicky. Nicky had his hands in his pocket and his hair over his eyes but there was a little smirk on his face.

Mum stood up and looked from one to the other. You could tell she really, really wanted to say something but she didn't know what.

'Did you try the chocolate cake?' Mr Nicholls said. His face was all bland, like a game-show host's.

'No.'

'Shame. It was really good. Thank you! Your cake is the best!' he called to the woman, who went all smiley and twinkly even though she hadn't looked at Mum like that. Then Mr Nicholls and Nicky went straight back out again, striding across the road like they'd been mates all their lives, leaving Tanzie and Mum to gather up their things and hurry out after them.

15.

NICKY

There was this article in the newspaper once, about a hairless baboon. Her skin wasn't black all over, like you'd expect, but kind of mottled, pink and black. Her eyes were black-rimmed, like she had this really cool eyeliner on, and she had one long pink nipple and one black one, like a sort of simian, booby David Bowie.

But she was all on her own. It turns out baboons don't like difference. And literally not one baboon was prepared to hang out with her. So she was photographed picture after picture, just out looking for food, all bare and vulnerable, without a single baboon mate. Because even though all the other baboons, like, knew she was still a baboon, their dislike of difference was stronger than any genetic urge they had to stick with her.

Nicky thought this one thing quite often: that there was nothing sadder than a lonely hairless baboon.

Obviously Mr Nicholls was about to give him a lecture on the dangers of social networking or say that he had to report it all to his teachers or the police or something. But he didn't. He opened his car door, pulled out his laptop from the boot, plugged the power lead into a connector near his gearstick, and then plugged in a dongle so that they had broadband.

'Right,' he said, as Nicky eased himself into the passenger seat. 'Tell me everything you know about this little charmer. Brothers, sisters, dates of birth, pets, address – whatever you've got.'

'What?'

'We need to work out his password. Come on – you must know something.'

They were sitting in the car park. Around them, people loaded shopping into their cars, strolled around in search of a nice pub or tea room. There was no graffiti here, no discarded shopping trolleys. This was the kind of place where they walked actual miles to return a shopping trolley. Nicky would have bet money they had one of those Best Kept Village signs too. A grey-haired woman loading her car beside them caught his eye and smiled. She actually smiled. Or maybe she smiled at Norman, whose big head was hanging over Nicky's shoulder.

'Nicky?'

'Yeah. I'm thinking.' He tried to clear his head. He reeled off everything he knew about Fisher. He went through his address, his sister's name, his mum's name. He actually knew his birthday as it was only three weeks previously and his dad had bought him one of those quad bikes and he'd smashed it up within a week.

Mr Nicholls kept tapping away. 'Nope. Nope. Come on. There must be something else. What music does he like? What team does he support? Oh, look – he's got a hotmail address. Great – we can put that in.'

Nicky told him everything he knew. Nothing worked. And then he had a sudden thought. 'Tulisa. He's got a thing about Tulisa. The singer.'

Mr Nicholls tapped away at his keyboard, then shook his head.

'Try Tulisa's Arse,' Nicky said.

Mr Nicholls typed. 'Nope.'

'IShaggedTulisa. All one word.'

'Nope.'

'Tulisa Fisher.'

'Mmm. Nope. Nice try, though.'

They sat there, thinking.

'You could just try his name,' said Nicky.

Mr Nicholls shook his head. 'Nobody's stupid enough to use their name as their password.'

Nicky looked at him. Mr Nicholls typed a few letters then stared at the screen. 'Well what do you know?' he said, and leant back in his seat. 'You're a natural.'

'So what are you doing?'

'We're just going to have a little play with Jason Fisher's Facebook page. Actually, I'm not going to do it. I'm . . . uh . . . I can't really risk anything on my IP address right now. But I know someone who can.' He dialled a number.

'But won't he know it's down to me?'

'How? We're basically him right now. There'll be nothing tracing this to you. He probably won't even notice. Hang on. Jez? . . . Hey. It's Ed . . . Yeah. Yeah, I'm just under the radar for a bit. I need you to do me a favour. It'll take five minutes.'

Nicky listened as he told 'Jez' Jason Fisher's password and email address. He said that Fisher had been 'creating a few difficulties' for a friend. He looked at Nicky sideways as he said this. 'Just have a bit of fun with it, yeah? Read through his stuff. You'll get the picture. I'd do it myself but I've got to keep my hands super-clean right now ... Yeah ... Yeah, I'll explain when I see you. Appreciate it.'

He couldn't believe it was so easy. 'Won't he hack me back, though?'

Mr Nicholls put down his phone. 'I'm going to take a punt here. But a boy who can't think further than his own name for a password is not really overflowing with computer skills.'

They sat there in the car and waited, refreshing Jason Fisher's Facebook page again and again. And, like magic, things began to change. Man, Fisher was such a douche. His wall was full of how he was going to 'do' this girl or that girl from school, or how so-and-so was a slag and how he'd battered pretty much everyone outside his crew. His messages were much the same. Nicky glimpsed one message that had his name in it, but Mr Nicholls read it really fast and just said, 'Yeah. You don't need to see that one,' and scrolled up. The only time he didn't sound like a douche was when he messaged Chrissie Taylor and told her that he really liked her and did she want to come round his house? She didn't sound too keen, but he kept messaging her. He said he'd take her out somewhere 'really dope' and that he could borrow his dad's car (he couldn't – he was under-age). He told her she was the prettiest girl in school and that she was doing his head in and that if his mates knew she'd made him like this they'd think he was 'a mentalist'.

'Who says romance is dead?' Mr Nicholls murmured.

And so it began. Jez messaged two of Fisher's friends and told them that he had decided he was anti-violence, and didn't want to hang out with them any more. He messaged Chrissie and told her that he still liked her but he had to get himself sorted out before he went out with her because he'd 'picked up some stupid infection what the doctor says I need to get medicine for. I'll be nice and clean when we get together though, eh?'

'Oh, man.' Nicky was laughing so much that his ribs hurt. 'Oh, man.'

'Jason' told another girl called Stacy that he really liked her and that his mum had picked out some really nice clothes for him if she ever wanted to go out, and the same thing to a girl called Angela in his year whom he had once called a scuzz. And Jez deleted a new message from Danny Kane, who had tickets for some big football match and said Jason could have one but he'd have to let him know by the end of the day. Which was today.

He changed Fisher's profile picture for an image of a braying donkey. And then Mr Nicholls stared at the screen, thinking, and picked up his mobile. 'Actually, I think we should leave it there, mate, just for now,' he told Jez.

'Why?' said Nicky, when he put down the phone. The donkey thing was kind of excellent.

'Because it's better to be subtle. If we just stick to his private messages for now it's entirely likely that he won't even spot them. We send them, then delete them at this end. We'll turn off his email notifications. And so his friends, and this girl, will just think he's become even more of an idiot. And he won't have a clue why. Which is kind of the point.'

He couldn't believe it. He couldn't believe someone could just mess with Fisher's life like that.

Jez rang back to say he'd logged out, and they shut down Facebook. 'And that's it?' Nicky said.

'For now. It's only a bit of fun. But it made you feel better, right? And he's going to clean up your page so that none of the stuff Fisher put up is there any more.'

It was a bit embarrassing then because when Nicky breathed out he did this kind of shudder. He did feel better. It wasn't like it really solved anything, but for once it was nice not to feel like the butt of the joke.

He messed with the hem of his T-shirt until his breathing went back to normal. It was possible Mr Nicholls knew because he looked out of the window like he was really interested even though there was nothing there apart from cars and old people.

'Why would you do all this? The hacking thing and driving us all the way to Scotland. I mean, you don't even know us.'

Mr Nicholls stared out of the window at the car park and just for a moment it was like he wasn't really talking to

Nicky any more. 'I sort of owe your mum one. And I guess I just don't like people crapping all over other people. Bullies didn't start with your generation, you know.'

Mr Nicholls sat there for a minute, and Nicky was suddenly fearful that he was going to try to make him talk about stuff. That he'd do that thing the counsellor did at school, where he tried to act like he was your mate and said about fifty times that anything you said would be 'just between us' until it sounded a little creepy.

'I'll tell you one thing.'

Here it comes, Nicky thought. He wiped at his shoulder, where Norman had left a drool.

'Everyone I've ever met who was worth knowing was a bit different at school. You just need to find your people.'

'Find my people.'

'Your tribe.'

Nicky pulled a face.

'You know, you spend your whole life feeling like you don't quite fit in anywhere. And then you walk into a room one day, whether it's at university or an office or some kind of club, and you just go, "Ah. There they are." And suddenly you feel at home.'

'I don't feel at home anywhere.'

'For now.'

Nicky considered this. 'So where was yours?'

'Computing room at university. I was a bit of a geek. I met my best mate Ronan there. And then . . . my company.' He looked a bit serious after he'd said that.

'But I'm stuck there until I finish school. And there's

215

nothing like that where we live, no tribes.' Nicky pulled his fringe down over his eyes. 'You do things Fisher's way or you stay out of his way.'

'So find your people online.'

'How?'

'I don't know. Look up online groups for things you're . . . interested in? Lifestyle choices?'

Nicky registered his expression. 'Oh. You think I'm gay too, right?'

'No, I'm just saying, the Internet's a big place. There's always someone out there who shares your interests, whose life is like yours.'

'Nobody's life is like mine.'

Mr Nicholls shut his laptop and slid it into a case. He unplugged everything and glanced over towards the café.

'We should head back. Your mum will be wondering what we're up to.' He opened his door and then turned back. 'You know, you could always write a blog.'

'A blog?'

'Doesn't have to be under your real name. But it's a good way of talking about what's going on in your life. You put a few keywords in, and people will find you. People like you, I mean.'

'People who wear mascara. And who like neither football nor musical theatre.'

'And who have enormous stinking dogs and sisters who are maths prodigies. I bet you there's at least one person like that somewhere.' He thought for a minute. 'Maybe. Perhaps in Hoxton. Or Tupelo.'

'I'm not a hairless baboon, you know.'

'What?'

'Nothing.' Nicky pulled at his fringe some more, trying to cover the bruise. It had gone this really grim yellow, which made him look like he had some weird disease. 'Thanks, but blogs are . . . not really my thing. Blogs are like for middle-aged women writing about their divorces and cats and stuff. Or nail varnish obsessives.'

'Just putting it out there.'

'Do you write one?'

'Nope.' He climbed out of the car. 'But I don't particularly want to talk to anyone.' Nicky climbed out after him. Mr Nicholls pointed his fob and the car locked down with an expensive thunk. 'In the meantime,' he said, lowering this voice, 'we didn't have this conversation, okay? It wouldn't go down too well if anyone knew I was teaching innocent kids how to hack into private information.'

'Jess wouldn't mind.'

'I'm not just talking about Jess.'

Nicky held his gaze. 'First rule of Geek Club. There is no Geek Club.'

'Good man. Right. You going to walk this disgusting dog of yours before we head off?'

16.

TANZIE

Nobody really wanted to get back in the car. The novelty of spending hours in a car, even one as nice as Mr Nicholls's, had worn off pretty quickly. This, Mum announced, like someone about to give an injection, would be the longest day. They were all to make themselves comfortable and make sure they'd been to the loo because Mr Nicholls's aim was to drive almost to Newcastle, where he had found a B&B that took dogs. They would arrive at around 10 p.m. After that, he had calculated that with one more day's driving they should arrive in Aberdeen. Mr Nicholls would find them somewhere to stay close to the university, then Tanzie would be bright and fresh for the maths competition the next day. He looked at her hopefully. 'Unless you think you've got used to this car enough for me to go above forty now?'

She shook her head.

'No.' His face fell a bit. 'Oh, well.'

He caught sight of the back seat then and blinked. A couple of chocolate buttons had melted into the cream leather seats, and although Tanzie had picked away at them as best she could there was definitely a brown mark. The footwell was covered with mud and leaves from where they had been walking around the woods. Norman's drool had traced snail trails everywhere. At home she could wipe his jowls with a cloth, but trying to do it in the car made her feel sick. Mr Nicholls saw her looking and gave a half-smile, like it really didn't matter, even though you could tell that it probably did, and turned back to the wheel.

'Okay then,' he said, and started the engine.

Everyone was silent for about an hour, while Mr Nicholls listened to something on Radio 4 about technology. Mum read one of her books. Since the library had closed, she'd bought two paperbacks a week from the charity shop but only ever had time to read one. Sometimes, if Mum was doing extra shifts, Tanzie would find her in the morning lying there with her mouth open and a book propped on her pillow. Because she was not very good at understanding simple equations, their whole house was now full of tattered paperbacks that she swore she was about to read.

The afternoon stretched and sagged, and the rain came down in thick, glassy sheets. They drove past endless rolling green fields, through village after village, moving restlessly in their seats and pulling rucked shirts from the small of their backs. All the villages had started to look pretty much the same after Coventry. Tanzie gazed out of the window and tried to do maths problems in her head but it was hard to focus when she couldn't do workings out on a pad. It was about six o'clock when Nicky began shifting around, like he couldn't get comfortable.

'When are we next stopping?'

Mum had nodded off briefly. She pushed herself upright abruptly, pretending she hadn't, and peered at the clock.

'Ten past six,' Mr Nicholls said.

'Could we stop for some food?' said Tanzie.

'I really need to walk around. My ribs are starting to hurt.' Nicky's legs were too long for even this car. His knees were folded up against Mr Nicholls's seat, and he looked like he was being squashed into the corner by Norman, who lay across him, his big pink tongue lolling out through his teeth.

'Let's find somewhere to eat. We could divert into Leicester for a curry.'

'We'll be fine with sandwiches.'

Nicky groaned quietly.

'Do you guys eat nothing but sandwiches?'

'Of course not. But sandwiches are convenient. And we don't have time to sit down and eat a curry.'

'I love curry,' Nicky said mournfully.

'Well, perhaps we'll have one in Aberdeen.'

'If I win.'

'You'd better, small fry,' said Nicky, quietly. 'If I eat another stale cheese sandwich I'm going to start curling up at the edges.'

Mr Nicholls drove through a small town, then another, and followed the signs to a retail park. It had begun to get dark. The roads were thick with Saturday-evening traffic and beeping cars filled with football supporters, celebrating a match involving teams nobody had ever heard of, their faces joyous, pressed against the windows. The Audi crawled through it all, its windscreen wipers beating a dull, insistent tattoo, then finally stopped outside a supermarket and Mum climbed out with a loud sigh and ran in. They could see her through the rain-lashed window, standing in front of the chiller cabinets, picking things up and putting them down again.

'Why doesn't she just buy the ready-made sandwiches?' muttered Mr Nicholls, looking at his watch. 'She'd be back out in two minutes.'

'Too expensive,' said Nicky.

'And you don't know whose fingers have been in them.'

'Jess did three weeks making sandwiches for a supermarket last year. She said that the woman next to her picked her nose in between shredding the chicken for the chicken Caesar wraps.'

'And none of them wore gloves.'

Mr Nicholls went a bit quiet.

Jess emerged several minutes later with a small shopping bag, holding it over her head as she ran the short distance to the edge of the kerb.

'Five to one it's own-brand ham,' said Nicky, watching. 'Plus apples. She always buys apples.'

'Own-brand ham is two to one,' Tanzie said.

'Five to two it's rubber bread. On special.'

'I'm going to go right out there and say sliced cheese,' said Mr Nicholls. 'What odds will you give me on sliced cheese?'

'Not specific enough,' said Nicky. 'You have to go for

Dairylea or cheaper own-brand orange-coloured slices. Probably with a made-up name.'

'Pleasant Valley Cheese.'

'Udderly Lovely Cheddar.'

'That sounds disgusting.'

'Grumpy Cow Slices.'

'Oh, come on now, she's not that bad.'

Tanzie and Nicky started laughing.

Mum opened the door, and held up her carrier bag. 'Right,' she said brightly. 'They had tuna paste on special. Who wants a sandwich?'

'You never want our sandwiches,' Mum said, as Mr Nicholls drove through the town.

Mr Nicholls indicated, and pulled out onto the open road. 'I don't like sandwiches. They remind me of being at school.'

'So what do you eat?' Mum was tucking in. It had taken only a matter of minutes for the whole car to smell of fish. Tanzie thought Mr Nicholls was too polite to say so.

'In London? Toast for breakfast. Maybe some sushi or noodles for lunch. I have a takeout place I order from in the evening.'

'You have a takeaway? Every night?'

'If I'm not going out.'

'How often do you go out?'

'Right now? Never.'

Mum gave him a hard look.

'Well, okay, unless I'm getting drunk in your pub.'

'You seriously eat the same thing every day?'

Mr Nicholls seemed a bit embarrassed now. 'You can get different curries.'

'That must cost a fortune. So what do you eat when you're at Beachfront?'

'I get a takeaway.'

'From the Raj?'

'Yeah. You know it?'

'Oh, I know it.'

The car fell silent.

'What?' said Mr Nicholls. 'You don't go there? What is it? Too expensive? You're going to tell me it's easy to cook a jacket potato, right? Well, I don't like jacket potato. I don't like sandwiches. And I don't like cooking.' It might have been because he was hungry, but he was suddenly quite grumpy.

Tanzie leant forwards through the seats. 'Nathalie once found a hair in her chicken Jalfrezi.'

Mr Nicholls opened his mouth to say something, just as she added, 'And it wasn't from someone's head.'

Twenty-three lampposts went by.

'You can worry too much about these things,' Mr Nicholls said.

Somewhere after Nuneaton Tanzie started sneaking bits of her sandwich to Norman because the tuna paste didn't really taste like tuna, and the bread kept sticking to the roof of her mouth. Mr Nicholls pulled into a petrol station that squatted by the side of the road, a UFO that had just landed.

'Their sandwiches will be awful,' said Mum, gazing inside the kiosk. 'They'll have been there for weeks.'

'I'm not buying a sandwich.'

'Do they do pasties?' said Nicky, peering inside, and his voice was full of longing. 'I love pasties.'

'They're even worse. They're probably full of dog.'

Tanzie put her hands over Norman's ears.

Mum glanced at Nicky and sighed.

'Are you going in?' she said to Mr Nicholls, rummaging around in her purse. 'Will you get these two some chocolate? Special treat.'

'Crunchie, please,' said Nicky, who had cheered up.

'Aero. Mint, please,' Tanzie said. 'Can I have a big one?'

Mum was holding out her hand. But Mr Nicholls was staring off to his right. 'Can you get them? I'm just going to pop across the road,' he said.

'Where are you going?'

He patted his stomach and he suddenly looked really cheerful. 'There.'

Keith's Kebabs had six plastic seats that were bolted to the floor, fourteen cans of Diet Coke arranged in its window, a neon sign that was missing its first b, and a rum baba that looked as though it had been there for several decades. Tanzie peered through the window of the car, and watched Mr Nicholls's walk become almost jaunty as he entered its strip-lit interior. He stared at the wall behind the counter, then spoke to the man, who gestured towards some trays behind a glass screen, then pointed to a huge hunk of brown meat turning slowly on a spit. Tanzie considered what animal was shaped like that, and could only come up with buffalo. Maybe an amputee buffalo.

'Oh, man,' said Nicky, as the man began to carve, and his voice was a low moan of longing. 'Can't we have one of those?'

'No,' said Mum.

'How much do you think they are?'

'Too much.'

'I bet Mr Nicholls would buy us one if we asked,' he said.

Mum snapped, 'Mr Nicholls is doing quite enough for us. We're not going to scrounge off him any more than we already have. Okay?'

Nicky rolled his eyes at Tanzie. 'Fine,' he said moodily.

And then nobody said anything.

'I'm sorry,' said Mum, after a minute. 'I just . . . I just don't want him thinking we're taking advantage.'

'But is it still taking advantage if someone just offers you something?' Tanzie said. She was really, really bored of eating cold food out of plastic bags. And she had the feeling that, if they asked him, Mr Nicholls would buy them one.

'Eat an apple if you're still hungry. Or one of the breakfast muffins. I'm sure we've got a few left.' Mum began rummaging around in the plastic bag again. Nicky raised his eyes silently. Tanzie let out a sigh.

Mr Nicholls opened the car door, bringing with him the smell of hot, fatty meat. He was grinning as he sat down. His kebab was swaddled in white, grease-stained paper, and shredded green salad bushed from both sides of the meat, like Kitchener's moustache. Two twin bungee ropes of drool dropped immediately from Norman's mouth. 'You sure you don't want some?' he said cheerfully, turning towards Nicky and Tanzie. 'I only put a bit of chilli sauce on.'

'No. That's very kind, but no thank you,' said Mum, firmly, and gave Nicky a warning look.

'No, thanks,' Tanzie said quietly. It smelt delicious.

'No. Thank you,' said Nicky, and turned his face away.

'Right. Who wants another sandwich?' said Mum.

Nuneaton, Market Bosworth, Coalville, Ashby de la Zouch, the signs passed by in a steady blur. They could have said Zanzibar and Tanzania for all Tanzie knew of where they actually were. She found herself repeating Ashby de la Zouch, Ashby de la Zouch, and thinking it would be a good name to have. Hi – what's your name? I'm Ashby de la Zouch. Hey, Ashby! That's so cool! Costanza Thomas was five syllables too, but it didn't have the same rhythm. She considered Costanza de la Zouch, which was six, and then Ashby Thomas, which sounded flat by comparison.

Costanza de la Zouch.

The car slowed for a traffic jam that seemed to be caused by nothing, and they had to double back once when Mr Nicholls took a wrong turning. He seemed a bit distracted.

Costanza de la Zouch.

They had been back on the open road for 389 lamp-posts when Mr Nicholls said he had to stop the car. Usually it was one of them who asked to stop. Tanzie kept getting dehydrated and drinking too much, then needing a wee. Norman whined to go every twenty minutes, but they could never tell if he genuinely needed one or was as bored as they were and just wanted a little sniff around. Mum was reading again, with the passenger light on, and Mr Nicholls kept shifting around in his seat, until finally he said, 'That map . . . is there a restaurant or something up ahead?'

'You're still hungry?' Mum looked up.

'No. I – I need the loo.'

Mum went back to her book. 'Oh, don't mind us. Just go behind a tree.'

'Not that kind of loo,' he muttered.

'Oh.' Mum picked the map out of his glove compartment. 'Well, judging by this, Kegworth is the nearest town. I'm sure there'll be somewhere you could go. Or there might be a services if we can get to the dual carriageway.'

'Which is closest?'

Mum traced the map with her finger. 'Hard to say. Kegworth?'

'How far?'

'Ten minutes?'

'Okay.' He nodded, almost to himself. 'Ten minutes is okay.' He said it again, and his face was weirdly shiny. 'Ten minutes is doable.'

Nicky had his ear-buds in and was listening to music.

Tanzie was stroking Norman's big soft ears and thinking about string theory. And then suddenly Mr Nicholls swerved the car abruptly into a lay-by. Everyone lurched forward. Norman nearly rolled off the seat. Mr Nicholls threw open the driver's door, ran round the back, and as she turned in her seat, he crouched down by a ditch, one hand braced on his knee, and began heaving. It was impossible not to hear him, even with the windows closed.

They all stared.

'Whoa,' said Nicky. 'That's a lot of stuff coming out of him. That's like . . . whoa, that's like the Alien.'

'Oh, my God,' said Mum.

'It's disgusting,' Tanzie said, peering over the back shelf.

'Quick,' said Mum. 'Where's that kitchen roll, Nicky?'

They watched as she got out of the car and went to help him. He was doubled over, like his stomach was really hurting. When she saw Tanzie and Nicky were staring out of the back window, she flicked her hand like they shouldn't look, even though she had been doing the exact same thing.

'Still want a kebab?' Tanzie said to Nicky.

'You're an evil sprite,' he said, and shuddered.

Mr Nicholls walked back to the car like someone who'd only just learnt how to do it. His face had gone this weird pale yellow. His skin was dusted with tiny beads of sweat.

'You look awful,' Tanzie told him.

He eased himself back into his seat. 'I'll be fine,' he whispered. 'Should be fine now.'

Mum reached back through the seats and mouthed, 'Plastic bag.' Tanzie handed over hers. 'Just in case,' she said cheerfully, and opened her window a bit.

Mr Nicholls drove really slowly for the next few miles. So slowly that two cars kept flashing them from behind and one driver sat on his horn really angrily as he passed. Sometimes he veered a bit across the white line, like he wasn't really concentrating, but Tanzie registered Mum's determined silence and decided not to say anything.

'How long now?' Mr Nicholls kept muttering.

'Not long,' said Mum, even though she probably had no idea. She patted his arm, like he was a child. 'You're doing really well.'

When he looked at her, his eyes were anguished.

'Hang on in there,' she said quietly, and it was like an instruction.

And then, about half a mile further along, 'Oh, God,' he said, and slammed the brakes on again. 'I need to –'

'Pub!' Mum yelled, and pointed towards one, its light just visible on the outskirts of the next village. 'Look! You can make it!'

Mr Nicholls's foot went down on the accelerator so that Tanzie's cheeks were pulled back in G-force. He skidded into the car park, threw the door open, staggered out and hurled himself inside.

They sat there, waiting. The car was so quiet that they could hear the engine ticking.

After five minutes, Mum leant across and pulled his door shut to keep the chill out. She looked back and smiled at them. 'How was that Aero?'

'Nice.'

'I like Aeros too.'

Nicky, his eyes closed, nodded to the music.

A man pulled into the car park with a woman wearing a high ponytail and looked hard at the car. Mum smiled. The woman did not smile back.

Ten minutes went by.

'Shall I go and get him?' said Nicky, pulling his ear-buds from his ears and peering at the clock.

'Best not,' said Mum. Her foot had started tapping.

Another ten minutes passed. Finally, when Tanzie had taken Norman for a walk around the car park and Mum had done some stretches on the back of the car because she said she was bent out of shape, Mr Nicholls emerged.

He looked whiter than anyone Tanzie had ever seen, like paper. He looked like someone had rubbed at his features with a cheap eraser.

'I think we might need to stop here for a bit,' he said.

'In the pub?'

'Not the pub,' he said, glancing behind him. 'Definitely not the pub. Maybe . . . maybe somewhere a few miles away.'

'Do you want me to drive?' Mum said.

'No,' everyone said at once, and she smiled and tried to look like she wasn't offended.

*

The Bluebell Haven was the only place within ten miles that wasn't fully booked. It had eighteen static caravans, a playground with two swings and a sandpit, and a sign that said 'No Dogs'.

Mr Nicholls let his face drop against the steering-wheel. 'We'll find somewhere else.' He winced and doubled over. 'Just give me a minute.'

'No need.'

'You said you can't leave the dog in the car.'

'We won't leave him in the car. Tanzie,' said Mum. 'The sunglasses.'

There was a mobile home by the front gate marked 'Reception'. Mum went in first, and Tanzie put the sunglasses on and waited outside on the step, watching through the bubbled-glass door. The fat man who raised himself wearily from a chair said she was lucky as there was only one still available, and they could have it for a special price.

'How much is that?' said Mum.

'Eighty pound.'

'For one night? In a static?'

'It's Saturday.'

'And it's seven o'clock at night and you had nobody in it.'

'Someone might still come.'

'Yeah. I heard Madonna was having a swift half down the road and looking for somewhere to park her entourage.'

'No need to be sarky.'

'No need to rip me off. Thirty pounds,' Mum said, pulling the notes from her pocket.

'Forty.'

'Thirty-five.' Mum held out a hand. 'It's all I've got. Oh, and we've got a dog.'

He lifted a meaty hand. 'Read the sign. No dogs.'

'He's a guide dog. For my little girl. I'd remind you that it's illegal to bar a person on the grounds of disability.'

Nicky opened the door and, holding her elbow, guided Tanzie in. She stood motionless behind her dark glasses while Norman stood patiently in front of her. They had done this twice when they'd had to catch the coach to Portsmouth after Dad had left.

'He's well trained,' Mum said. 'He'll be no trouble.'

'He's my eyes,' Tanzie said. 'My life would be nothing without him.'

The man stared at her hand, and then at her. His jowls reminded Tanzie of Norman's. She had to remember not to glance up at the television.

'You're busting my balls, lady.'

'Oh, I do hope not,' Mum said cheerfully.

He shook his head, withdrew his huge hand, and moved heavily towards a key cabinet. 'Golden Acres. Second lane, fourth on the right. Near the toilet block.'

Mr Nicholls was so ill by the time they reached the static that it was possible he didn't even notice where they were. He kept moaning softly and clutching his stomach and when he saw the word 'Toilets' he let out a little cry and disappeared. They didn't see him for the best part of an hour.

Golden Acres wasn't gold and didn't look anything like even half an acre, but Mum said any port in a storm. There were two tiny bedrooms, and the sofas in the living room turned into another bed. Mum said that Nicky and Tanzie could stay in the one with twin beds, Mr Nicholls could go in the other and she would have the sofa. It was actually okay in their bedroom, even if Nicky's feet did hang over the end of his bed and everywhere smelt of cigarettes. Mum opened some windows for a bit, then made up the beds with the duvets and ran the water until it came hot because she said Mr Nicholls would probably want a shower when he came back in.

Tanzie opened all the cupboards, which were made of chipboard, one after another, shut the floral curtains, and inspected the chemical loo in the bathroom, then pressed her nose to the window and counted all the lights in the other static caravans. (Only two seemed to be occupied. 'That lying git,' said Mum.)

While they waited for Mr Nicholls to come back, she studied the map from his car, running her fingers along the routes. 'We've got plenty of time,' she said. 'Plenty. It'll be fine. And look! More quiet time for you to revise.' She sounded as if she was actually reassuring herself.

She had put her phone on to charge for precisely fifteen seconds when it rang. She started and picked it up, still plugged into the wall.

'Hello?' She sounded like she thought it might be Mr Nicholls, calling from the toilet block for more paper again. 'Des?' Her hand flew to her mouth. 'Oh, God. Des, I'm not going to make it back in time.'

A series of muffled explosions at the other end.

'I'm really sorry. I know what I said. But things have gone a bit crazy. I'm in . . .' She pulled a face at Tanzie. 'Where are we?'

'Near Ashby de la Zouch,' she said.

'Ashby de la Zouch,' Mum repeated. And then, her hand in her hair, 'Ashby de la Zouch. I know. I'm really sorry. The journey didn't quite go as I planned and our driver got sick and my phone ran out and with all the . . . What?' She glanced at Tanzie. 'I don't know. Probably not before Tuesday. Maybe even Wednesday. It's taking longer than we thought.'

Tanzie could definitely hear him shouting then.

'Can't Chelsea cover it? I've done enough of her shifts . . . I know it's the busy period. I know. Des, I'm really sorry. I've said I –' She paused. 'No. I can't get back before then. No. I'm really . . . What do you mean? I've never missed a shift this past year. I – Des? . . . Des?' She broke off and stared at the phone.

'Was that Des from the pub?' Tanzie liked Des from the pub. Once she had sat outside with Norman on a Sunday afternoon, waiting for Mum, and he had given her a packet of scampi fries.

At that minute, the door to the caravan opened, and Mr Nicholls pretty much fell in. 'Lie down,' he muttered, pulled himself briefly upright, then collapsed onto the floral sofa cushions. He looked up at Mum with a grey face and big hollow eyes. 'Lying down. Sorry,' he mumbled.

Mum just sat there, staring at her mobile.

He blinked at her, registering the phone, and muttered, 'Were you trying to reach me?'

'He's sacked me,' Mum said. 'I don't believe it. He's bloody sacked me.'

17.

JESS

She wouldn't have slept much anyway, given that she now had to worry about having lost her job at the Feathers, as well as everything else. But Jess spent most of that night looking after Mr Nicholls. She had never seen a man be so ill without actually coughing up a kidney. By midnight he was a shell. There was literally nothing left in him. 'I feel better, I feel better,' he would insist, trying to sound reassuring. And then half an hour later he would grab at the bucket she had pulled from under the sink and cough up a thin string of green bile.

The night took on a weird, disjointed quality, the hours running into each other, fluid and endless. She gave up trying to sleep. She stared at the caramel-coloured, wipe-clean walls of the caravan, read a bit, dozed. Mr Nicholls groaned beside her, occasionally getting up to shuffle backwards and forwards to the toilet block. She closed the kids' door and sat waiting for him in the little caravan, sometimes dozing on the far end of the L-shaped sofa, handing him water and tissues when he staggered in.

Shortly after three, Mr Nicholls said he wanted a shower. She made him promise to leave the bathroom door unlocked, took his clothes down to the launderette

236

(a washer-dryer in a shed) and spent three pounds twenty on a sixty-degree cycle. She didn't have any change for the dryer.

He was still in the shower when she arrived back at the caravan. She draped his clothes from hangers over the heater, hoping they might dry a bit by morning, then knocked quietly on the door. There was no answer, just the sound of running water, and a belch of steam. She peeped around the door. The glass was clouded but she could make him out, slumped and exhausted on the floor. She waited a moment, staring at his broad back pressed against the glass panel, an oddly beautiful, pale inverted triangle, then watched as he lifted his hand and ran it wearily over his face.

'Mr Nicholls?' she whispered, behind him, then again, when he didn't say anything. 'Mr Nicholls?'

He turned then, and saw her, and perhaps it was the water, but she wasn't sure she had ever seen a man look more defeated. His eyes were red-rimmed and his head sunk deep into his shoulders.

'Fucksake. I can't even get up. And the water's starting to go cold,' he said.

'Want me to help?'

'No. Yes. Jesus.'

'Hold on.'

She held up the towel, whether to shield him or herself, she wasn't sure, reached in and turned off the shower, soaking her arm. Then she crouched down, so that he could cover himself, and leant in. 'Put your arm around my neck.'

'You're tiny. I'll just pull you over.'

'I'm stronger than I look.'

He didn't move.

'You're going to have to help me here. I'm not up to a fireman's lift.'

His wet arm slid around her, he hooked the towel around his waist. Jess braced herself against the wall of the shower, and finally, shakily, they stood. Usefully, the caravan was so small that at every step there was a wall for him to lean on. They made their way unsteadily to what would have been the living room and he collapsed onto the sofa cushions.

'This is what my life has come to.' He groaned, eyeing the bucket as she placed it beside the bed.

'Yup.' Jess viewed the peeling wallpaper, the nicotine-stained paintwork. 'Well, I've had better Saturday nights myself.'

She made herself a cup of tea. It was a little after four. Her eyes were gritty and sore, and she felt light-headed. She sat down and closed them for a minute.

'Thanks,' he said, weakly.

'What for?'

He pushed himself upright. 'For bringing loo roll out to me in the middle of the night. For washing my disgusting clothes. For helping me out of the shower. And for not once acting like it was my own fault for buying a dodgy doner from a place called Keith's Kebabs.'

'Even though it was your own fault.'

'See? Now you're spoiling it.'

He lay back on the pillow, his forearm over his eyes.

She tried not to look at the broad expanse of chest above the strategically placed towel. She couldn't remember when she had last seen a man's naked torso other than at Des's ill-advised Pub Beach Volleyball Match the previous August.

'Go and lie down in the bedroom. You'll be more comfortable.'

He opened one eye. 'Do I get a SpongeBob duvet?'

'You get my pink stripy one. But I promise not to regard it as any reflection whatsoever on your masculinity.'

'Where will you sleep?'

'Out here. It's fine,' she said, as he started to protest. 'I'm not sure I'll sleep much now anyway.'

He let her lead him into the tiny bedroom. He groaned as he collapsed onto the bed, as if even that caused him discomfort, and she pulled the duvet over him gently. The shadows under his eyes were ash-coloured and his voice had become drowsy. 'I'll be ready to go in a couple of hours.'

'Sure you will,' she said, observing the ghostly pallor of his skin. 'Take your time.'

'Where the hell are we, anyway?'

'On the Yellow Brick Road.'

'Is that the one with the God-like Lion who saves everyone?'

'You're thinking of Narnia. This one is cowardly and useless.'

'Figures.'

And finally he slept.

Jess left the room silently, and lay down on the narrow

sofa under a peach-coloured blanket that smelt of damp and furtively smoked cigarettes, and tried not to look at the clock. She and Nicky had studied the map while Mr Nicholls was in the toilet block the previous evening and had reconfigured the journey as best they could.

We still have plenty of time, she told herself. And then, finally, she, too, slept.

All was silent within Mr Nicholls's room well into the morning. Jess thought about waking him, but each time she made a move towards his door, she remembered the sight of him slumped against the shower cabinet and her fingers stilled on the handle. She opened the door only once, when Nicky pointed out that it was just possible he had choked to death on his own vomit. He seemed the faintest bit disappointed when it turned out Mr Nicholls was just in a really deep sleep. The children took Norman up the road, Tanzie in her dark glasses for authenticity, bought supplies from a convenience store and breakfasted in whispers. Jess converted the remaining bread into sandwiches ('Oh, good,' said Nicky), cleaned the caravan, for something to do, went outside and left a message on Des's answerphone, apologizing again. He didn't pick up.

At ten thirty the door of the little room opened with a squeak and Mr Nicholls emerged, blinking, in his T-shirt and boxers. He raised a palm in greeting. He looked disoriented, a castaway waking on an island. A long crease bisected his cheek from the pillow. 'We are in . . .'

'Ashby de la Zouch. Or somewhere nearby. It's not quite Beachfront.'

'Is it late?'

'Quarter to eleven.'

'Quarter to eleven. Okay.' His jaw was thick with stubble, and his hair stuck up on one side. Jess pretended to read her book. He smelt of warm, sleepy male. She had forgotten what a weirdly potent scent that was.

'Quarter to eleven.' He rubbed at the stubble on his chin, then walked unsteadily to the window and peered out. 'I feel like I've been asleep for a million years.' He sat down heavily on the sofa cushion opposite her, running his hand over his jaw.

'Dude,' said Nicky from beside her. 'Jailbreak alert.'

'What?'

Nicky waved a biro. 'You need to put the prisoners back in the pen.'

Mr Nicholls stared at him, then turned to Jess, as if to say, 'Your son has gone mad.'

'Oh, God.'

He frowned. 'Oh God what?'

Following Nicky's gaze, Jess looked down and swiftly away. 'You could at least have taken me out to dinner first,' she said, standing to clear the breakfast things.

'Oh.' Mr Nicholls looked down and adjusted himself. 'Sorry. Right. Okay.' He stood, and made for the bathroom. 'I'll – uh – I . . . Am I okay to have another shower?'

'We saved you some hot water,' said Tanzie, who was head-down over her exam sheet in the corner. 'Well, actually, all of it. You smelt really bad yesterday.'

He emerged twenty minutes later, his hair damp and smelling of shampoo, his jaw clean-shaven. Jess was busy whisking salt and sugar into a glass of water and trying not to think about what she had just seen. She handed it to him.

'What's that?' He pulled a face.

'Rehydrating solution. To replace some of what you lost last night.'

'You want me to drink a glass of salty water? After I've spent all night being sick?'

'Just drink it.' She was too tired to argue with him. While he was grimacing and gagging, she fixed him some plain toast and a black coffee. He sat across the little Formica table, took a sip of coffee and a few tentative bites of toast, and ten minutes later, in a voice that held some surprise, acknowledged that he did actually feel a bit better.

'Better, as in able-to-drive-without-having-an-accident better?'

'By having an accident, you mean . . .'

'Not crashing into a lay-by.'

'Thank you for clarifying that.' He took another, more confident, bite of toast. 'Yeah. Give me another twenty minutes, though. I want to make sure I'm . . .'

'. . . safe in cars.'

'Ha.' He grinned, and it was curiously pleasing to see him smile. 'Yes. Quite. Oh, man, I do feel better.' He ran a hand across the plastic-covered table and took a swig of coffee, sighing with apparent satisfaction. He finished the first round of toast, asked if there was any more going, then looked around the table. 'Although, you know, I might feel even better if you weren't all staring at me while I eat. I'm worried some other part of me is poking out.'

'You'll know,' said Nicky. 'Because we'll all run screaming.'

'Mum said you pretty much brought up an organ,' said Tanzie. 'I was wondering what it felt like.'

He glanced up at Jess and stirred his coffee. He didn't shift his gaze until she had blushed. 'Truthfully? Not so different from most of my Saturday nights, these days.' He drank the rest and put down his cup. 'Okay. I'm good. The rogue kebab is defeated. Let's hit the road.'

The landscape altered by the mile as they drove through the afternoon, the hills growing steeper and less bucolic, the walls that banked them morphing from hedgerows into flinty grey stone. The skies opened, the light around them grew brighter and they passed the distant symbols of an industrial landscape: red-brick factories, huge power stations that belched mustard-coloured clouds. Jess watched surreptitiously as Mr Nicholls drove, at first wary that he would suddenly clutch his stomach, and then later with a vague satisfaction at the sight of normal colour returning to his face.

'I don't think we're going to make Aberdeen today,' he said, and there was a hint of apology in his voice.

'Let's just get as far as we can and do the last stretch early tomorrow morning.'

'That's exactly what I was going to suggest.'

'Still loads of time.'

'Loads.'

She let the miles roll by, dozed intermittently and tried not to worry about all the things she needed to worry about. She positioned her mirror surreptitiously so that she could watch Nicky in the back seat. His bruises had faded, even in the short time they had been away. He seemed to be talking more than he had been. But he was still closed to her. Sometimes Jess worried he would be like that for the rest of his life. It didn't seem to make any difference how often she told him she loved him, or that they were his family. 'You're too late,' her mother had said, when Jess had told her he was coming to live with them. 'With a child that age, the damage has been done. I should know.'

As a schoolteacher, her mother could keep a class of thirty eight-year-olds in a narcoleptic silence, could steer them through tests like a shepherd streaming sheep through a pen. But Jess couldn't remember her ever smiling at her with pleasure, the kind of pleasure you're meant to get just from looking at someone you gave birth to.

She had been right about many things. She had told Jess on the day she started secondary school: 'The choices you make now will determine the rest of your life.' All Jess heard by then was someone telling her she should pin her whole self down, like a butterfly. That was the thing: when you put someone down all the time, eventually they stopped listening to the sensible stuff.

When Jess had had Tanzie, young and daft as she had

been, she'd had enough wisdom to know she was going to tell her how much she loved her every day. She would hug her and wipe her tears and flop with her on the sofa with their legs entwined like spaghetti. She would cocoon her in love. When she was tiny Jess had slept with her in their bed, her arms wrapped around her, so that Marty would haul himself grumpily into the spare room, moaning that there wasn't any room for him. She barely even heard him.

And when Nicky had turned up two years later, and everyone had told her she was mad to take on someone else's child, a child who was already eight years old and from a troubled background – you know how boys like that turn out – she'd ignored them. Because she could see instantly in the wary little shadow who had stood a minimum twelve inches away from anyone, from his father even, a little of what she had felt. Because she knew that something happened to you when your mother didn't hold you close, or tell you all the time that you were the best thing ever, or even notice when you were home: a little part of you sealed over. You didn't need her. You didn't need anyone. And, without even knowing you were doing it, you waited. You waited for anyone who got close to you to see something they didn't like in you, something they hadn't seen initially, and to grow cold and disappear, like so much sea mist, too. Because there had to be something wrong, didn't there, if even your own mother didn't really love you?

It was why she hadn't been devastated when Marty left. Why would she be? He couldn't hurt her. The only thing Jess really cared about was those two children, and letting them know they were okay by her. Because even if the whole world was throwing rocks at you, if you still had your mother or father at your back, you'd be okay. Some deep-rooted part of you would know you were loved. That you deserved to be loved. Jess hadn't done much to be proud of in her life, but the thing she was most proud of was that Tanzie knew it. Strange little bean that she was, Jess knew she knew it.

She was still working on Nicky.

'Are you hungry?' Mr Nicholls's voice woke her from a half-doze.

She pushed herself upright. Her neck had calcified, as bent and stiff as a wire coat hanger. 'Starving,' she said, turning awkwardly towards him. 'You want to stop somewhere for lunch?'

The sun had emerged. It shone in actual rays off to their left, strobing a vast, open field of green. God's fingers, Tanzie used to call them. Jess reached for the map in the glove compartment, ready to look up the location of the next services.

Mr Nicholls glanced at her. He seemed almost embarrassed. 'Actually . . . you know what? I could really murder one of your sandwiches.'

18.

ED

The Stag and Hounds B&B wasn't listed in any accommodation guides. It had no website, no brochures. It wasn't hard to work out why. The pub sat alone on the side of a bleak, windswept moor, and the mossy plastic garden furniture that stood outside its grey frontage suggested an absence of casual visitors or, perhaps, the triumph of hope over experience. The bedrooms were apparently last decorated several decades previously, and bore shiny pink wallpaper, doilied curtains and a smattering of china figurines in place of anything useful like, say, shampoo or tissues. There was a communal bathroom at the end of the upstairs corridor, where the sanitary-ware was a non-ironic avocado and the pink soap was bisected by dark grey fissures. A small box-shaped television in the twin room deigned to pick up three channels, and each of those with a faint static buzz. When Nicky discovered the plastic Barbie doll in a crocheted wool ball dress that squatted over the loo roll, he was awestruck. 'I actually love this,' he said, holding her up to the light to inspect her glittery synthetic hem. 'It's so bad it's actually cool.'

Ed couldn't believe places like this still existed. But he

had been driving for a little over eight hours at forty m.p.h., the Stag and Hounds was twenty-five pounds per night per room – a rate even Jess was happy with – and they were happy to let Norman in.

'Oh, we love dogs.' Mrs Deakins waded through a small flock of excitable Pomeranians. She patted her head, on which a carefully pinned structure sat like a small ginger cottage loaf. 'We love dogs more than humans, don't we, Jack?' There was a grunt from somewhere downstairs. 'They're certainly easier to please. You can bring your lovely big fella into the snug tonight, if you like. My girls love to meet a new man.' She gave Ed a faintly saucy nod as she said this.

She opened the two doors and waved a hand inside.

'So you'll be in this one, Mr and Mrs Nicholls. And your children will be next door. There's only the two rooms this side so you have the whole upstairs to yourself. We have a selection of cereals for breakfast or Jack will do you egg on toast. He does a lovely egg on toast.'

'Thank you.'

She handed him the keys, held his gaze a millisecond longer than was strictly necessary. 'I'm going to guess you like yours . . . gently poached. Am I right?'

Ed glanced behind him, checking that she was addressing him.

'I am, aren't I?'

'Um . . . however they come.' He didn't really want to dwell on the thought of gelatinous white eggs.

'However . . . they . . . come,' she repeated slowly, her eyes not leaving his. She raised one eyebrow, smiled at him again, then headed downstairs, her pack of small dogs a moving hairy sea around her feet. From the corner of his eye he could see Jess smirking.

'Don't.' He dropped their bags onto the bed.

'I bags first bath.' Nicky rubbed at the small of his back.

'I need to revise,' said Tanzie. 'I have exactly seventeen and a half hours until the Olympiad.' She gathered her books under her arm and disappeared into the next room.

'Come and give Norman a walk first, sweetheart,' Jess said. 'Get some fresh air. It'll help you sleep later.'

She unzipped a holdall, and pulled a hoodie over her head. When she lifted her arms, a crescent of bare stomach was briefly visible, pale and startling. Her face emerged through the neck opening. 'I'll be gone for at least half an hour. Or I . . . could make it longer.' As she adjusted her ponytail she glanced towards the stairs and lifted an eyebrow at him. 'Just . . . saying.'

'Funny.'

He could hear her laughing as they disappeared. Ed lay down on the nylon bedspread, feeling his hair lift slightly with static electricity, and pulled his phone from his pocket.

'So here's the good news,' said Paul Wilkes. 'The police have completed their initial investigations. The preliminary results show no obvious motive on your side. There is no evidence that you extracted a profit from Deanna Lewis or her brother's trading activities. More pertinently, there is no sign that you made any money at all from the launch of SFAX, other than the same share gains that would be made by any employee. Obviously there would be a higher proportion of profit, given your overall shareholding, but they can find no links to offshore accounts, or any attempt to conceal on your side.'

'That's because there were none.'

'Also, the investigating team says that they have uncovered a number of accounts in Michael Lewis's family's names, which suggests a clear attempt to conceal his actions. They have obtained trading records which show that he was trading large volume immediately prior to the announcement – another red flag for them.'

'Okay.' He was still talking but the signal was patchy, and Ed struggled to hear him. He stood and walked over to the window. Tanzie was running round and round the pub garden, shrieking happily. The small yappy dogs were following her. Jess was standing, her arms folded, laughing. Norman was in the middle of the space, gazing at them all, a bemused, immovable object in a sea of madness. Ed thought he knew how he felt. He put his hand over his other ear. 'Does that mean I can come back now? Is it sorted?' He had a sudden vision of his office: a mirage in a desert.

'Hold your horses. Here's the less good news. Michael Lewis wasn't just trading stocks, he was trading options on the stock.'

'Trading what?' He blinked. 'Okay. You're now speaking Polish.'

'Seriously?' There was a short silence. Ed pictured him in his wood-panelled office, rolling his eyes. 'Options allow a trader to leverage his or, in this case, her investment, and generate substantially more in profits.'

'But what does that have to do with me?'

'Well, the level of profits he generated from the options is significant, so the whole case moves up a gear. Which brings me to the bad news.'

'That wasn't the bad news?'

He sighed.

'Ed, why didn't you tell me you'd written Deanna Lewis a damn cheque?'

Ed blinked. The cheque.

'She cashed a cheque written by you for five thousand pounds to her bank account.'

'So?'

'So,' and here, from the elaborately slow and careful tenor of his voice, it was possible to picture the eye roll again, 'it links you financially to what Deanna Lewis was doing. You enabled some of that trade.'

'But it was just a few grand to help her out! She had no money!'

'Whether or not you extracted a profit from it, you had a clear financial interest in Lewis, and it came just before SFAX went live. The emails we could argue were inconclusive. But this means it's not just her word against yours, Ed.'

He stared out at the moorland. Tanzie was jumping up and down and waving a stick at the slobbering dog. Her glasses had gone askew on her nose and she was laughing. Jess scooped her up from behind and hugged her.

'Meaning?'

'Meaning, Ed, defending you just got a whole lot tougher.'

Ed had only properly disappointed his father once in his whole life. That's not to say he wasn't a general disappointment – he knew his father would have preferred a son who was more obviously in his own mould: upright, determined, driven. A sort of filial marine. But he managed to override whatever private dismay he felt at this quiet, geeky boy, and decided instead that as he so clearly couldn't sort him out an expensive education would.

The fact that the meagre funds their parents saved over their working years sent Ed to private school and not his sister was the great Unacknowledged Resentment of their family. He often wondered whether, if they had known then what a huge emotional hurdle they were planting in front of her, they would still have done it. Ed never could convince her that it was purely because she was so good at everything that they never felt the need to send her. He was the one who spent every waking hour in his room or glued to a screen. He was the one who was hopeless at sports. The day he told his father that he had started running every day (the personal trainer had been right – he did eventually love it), he wore the same expression he would have worn at the announcement of an imminent grandchild.

But no, against all available evidence he was convinced that an expensive minor public school, with the motto 'Sports Maketh the Man', would maketh his son. 'This is a great opportunity we're giving you, Edward. Better than your mother or I ever had,' he said repeatedly. 'Don't waste it.' So when he opened the report at the end of Ed's first year, which used the words *disengaged*, and *lacklustre performance* and, worst of all, *not really a team player*, he stared at the letter and Ed watched uncomfortably as the colour drained from his face.

He couldn't tell him he didn't really like the school, with its braying packs of bullying over-entitled Henries. He couldn't tell him that no matter how many times they made him run round the rugby pitch he was never going to like rugby. He couldn't explain that it was the possibilities of the pixellated screen, and what you could create from it, that really interested him. And that he felt he could make a life out of it. His father's face actually sagged with disappointment, with the sheer bloody waste of it all, and he realized he had no choice.

'I'll do better next year, Dad,' he said.

Ed Nicholls was due to report to the City of London police in a matter of days.

He tried to imagine the expression his father would wear when he heard that his son, the son he now boasted about to his ex-army colleagues, the pride with which he would say, 'Of course I don't understand what it is he actually does, but apparently all this software stuff is the Future', was quite possibly about to be prosecuted for insider trading. He tried to picture his father's head turning on that frail neck, the shock and disappointment pulling his weary features down even as he tried to disguise it, and his gently pursed lips as he grasped there was nothing he could say or do. The faint nod as he acknowledged that his son was, indeed, no better than he had ever really expected him to be.

And Ed made a decision. He would ask his lawyer to prolong the proceedings as long as possible. He would throw every penny of his own money at the case to delay the announcement of his supposed crime. But he could not go to that family lunch, no matter how ill his father was. He would be doing his father a favour. By staying away he would actually be protecting him.

Ed Nicholls stood in the little pink hotel bedroom that smelt of air freshener and disappointment and stared out at the bleak moors, at the little girl who had flopped onto the damp grass and was pulling the ears of the dog as he sat, tongue lolling, an expression of idiotic ecstasy on his great features, and he wondered why – given that he was so evidently doing the right thing – he felt like a complete shit.

19.

JESS

Tanzie was nervous, even though she would only admit to 'thirty-seven per cent nervous, maybe thirty-eight'. She refused supper, and declined to come downstairs even for a break, preferring to curl up on the pink nylon coverlet and plough through her maths papers while nibbling at what remained of the breakfast picnic. Jess was surprised: her daughter rarely suffered from nerves when it came to anything maths related. She did her best to reassure her, but it was hard when she had no idea what she was talking about.

'We're nearly there! It's all good, Tanze. Nothing to worry about.'

'Do you think I'll sleep tonight?'

'Of course you'll sleep tonight.'

'But if I don't I might do really badly.'

'Even if you don't sleep you'll do fine. And I've never known you not sleep.'

'I'm worried that I'll worry too much to sleep.'

'I'm not worried that you'll worry. Just relax. You'll be fine. It will all be fine.'

When Jess kissed her she saw that she had chewed her nails right down to the quick.

Mr Nicholls was in the garden. He walked up and down where she and Tanzie had been half an hour earlier, talking avidly into his phone. He stopped and stared at it a couple of times, then stepped up onto a white plastic garden chair, presumably to get better reception. He stood there, wobbling, utterly oblivious to the curious glances of those inside as he gesticulated and swore.

Jess gazed through the window, unsure whether to go and interrupt him. There were a few old men in the bar, gathered around the landlady as she chatted from the other side. They looked at her incuriously over their pints.

'Work, is it?' The landlady followed her gaze through the window.

'Oh. Yes. Never stops.' Jess raised a smile. 'I'll take him a drink.'

Mr Nicholls was seated on a low stone wall when she finally walked out. His elbows were on his knees and he was staring at the grass.

Jess held out the pint and he stared at it for a moment, then took it from her. 'Thanks.' He looked exhausted.

'Everything okay?'

'No.' He took a long gulp of his beer. 'Nothing's okay.'

She sat down a few feet away. 'Anything I can help with?'

'No.'

They sat in silence. The pub was shabby but she quite liked it. It was so peaceful there, with nothing around them except the breeze rippling across the moors, the distant cries of birds and the gentle hum of conversation from inside. She was going to say something about the landscape, when a voice broke into the still air.

'Fuck it,' Mr Nicholls said vehemently. 'Just fuck it.'

It was so startling that Jess flinched.

'I just can't believe my fucking life has turned into this ... mess.' His voice cracked. 'I can't believe that I can work and work for years and the whole thing can fall apart like this. For what? For fucking what?'

'It's only food poisoning. You'll –'

'I'm not talking about the fucking kebab.' He dropped his head into his hands. 'But I don't want to talk about it.' He shot her an angry look.

'Okay.'

Jess took a sip of her beer. She didn't really like beer, but it had been on special. Upstairs the bathroom window opened and a little burp of steam emerged.

'That's the thing. Legally, I'm not meant to talk to anyone about any of this.'

She didn't look at him. She had learnt this trick long ago: when Nicky first came to them, the social worker had said he would open up a lot more if Jess didn't make eye contact with him. They were like animals, men. They found too much direct contact threatening.

'I can't tell a soul. I mean legally.'

She stretched out a leg and gazed at the sunset. 'Well, I don't count, do I? I'm a cleaning wench.'

He let out a breath. 'Fuck it,' he said again.

And then he told her, his head down, his hands raking his short dark hair. He told her about a girlfriend whom he couldn't think how to let down nicely, and an ex-wife who never quite left him alone, and how his whole life had come crashing down. He told her about his company and how he should have been there now, celebrating the launch of his last six years' obsessive work. And how instead he had to stay away from everything and everyone he knew all the while facing the prospect of prosecution. He told her about his dad who was sick, and who was going to be even sicker when he heard what had happened. And he told her about the lawyer who had just rung to inform him that shortly after he returned from this trip his presence would be required at a police station in London where he would be charged with insider trading, a charge that could win him up to twenty years in prison. By the time he'd finished she felt winded.

'Everything I've ever worked for. Everything I cared about. I'm not allowed to go into my own office. I can't even go back to my flat in case the press hear of it and I do another stupid thing and let slip what's happened. I can't go and see my own dad because then he'll die knowing what a bloody idiot his son is.'

Jess digested this for a few minutes. He smiled bleakly at the sky. 'And you know the best bit? It's my birthday.'

'What?'

'Today. It's my birthday.'

'Today? Why didn't you say anything?'

'Because I'm thirty-four years old, and a thirty-four-year-old man sounds like a dick talking about birthdays.' He took a swig of his beer. 'And what with the whole food-poisoning thing, I didn't feel I had much to cele-brate.' He looked sideways at her. 'Plus you might have started singing "Happy Birthday" in the car.'

'I'll sing it out here.'

'Please don't. Things are bad enough.'

Jess's head was reeling. She couldn't believe all the stuff Mr Nicholls was carrying around. If it had been anyone else she might have put her arm around them, attempted to say something comforting. But Mr Nicholls was prickly. And who could blame him? It felt like offering an Elasto-plast to someone who had just had an arm amputated.

'Things will get better, you know,' she said, when she couldn't think of anything else to say. 'Karma will get that girl who stitched you up.'

He pulled a face. 'Karma?'

'It's like I tell the kids. Good things happen to good people. You just have to keep faith . . .'

'Well, I must have been a complete shit in a past life.'

'Come on. You still have property. You have cars. You have your brain. You have expensive lawyers. You can work this out.'

'How come you're such an optimist?'

'Because things do come right.'

'And that's from a woman who doesn't have enough money to catch a train.'

Jess kept her gaze on the craggy hillside. 'Because it's your birthday, I'm going to let that one go.'

Mr Nicholls sighed. 'Sorry. I know you're trying to help. But right now I find your relentless positivity exhausting.'

'No, you find driving hundreds of miles in a car with three people you don't know and a large dog exhausting. Go upstairs and have a long bath and you'll feel better. Go on.'

He trudged inside, the condemned man, and she sat and stared out at the slab of green moorland in front of her. She tried to imagine what it would be like to be facing prison, not to be allowed near the things or the people you loved. She tried to imagine someone like Mr Nicholls doing time. And then she decided not to think about it and hoped quite hard that Nicky hadn't used up all the hot water.

After a while, she walked inside with the empty glasses. She leant over the bar, where the landlady was watching an episode of *Homes Under the Hammer*. The men sat in silence behind her, watching it too or gazing rheumily into their pints.

'Mrs Deakins? It's actually my husband's birthday today. Would you mind doing me a favour?'

Mr Nicholls finally came downstairs at eight thirty, wearing the exact clothes he'd worn that afternoon. And the previous afternoon. Jess knew he had bathed, as his hair was damp and he had shaved.

'So what's in your bag, then? A body?'

'What?' He walked over to the bar. He gave off a faint scent of Wilkinson Sword soap.

'You've worn the same clothes since we left.'

He looked down, as if to check. 'Oh. No. These are clean.'

'You have the exact same T-shirt and jeans? For every day?'

'Saves thinking about it.'

She looked at him for a minute, then decided to bite back what she had been about to say. It was his birthday after all.

'Oh. You look nice, though,' he said suddenly, as if he'd only just noticed.

She had changed into a blue sundress and a cardigan. She had been going to save it for the Olympiad, but had figured that this was important. 'Well, thank you. One has to make the effort to fit one's surroundings, doesn't one?'

'What – you left your flat cap and dog-haired jeans behind?'

'You're about to be sorry for your sarcasm. Because I have a surprise in store.'

'A surprise.' He looked instantly wary.

'It's a good one. Here.' Jess handed him one of two glasses she had prepared earlier, to Mrs Deakins's amusement. 'I figure you're well enough.'

'What is this?' He stared at it suspiciously. They hadn't made a cocktail here since 1987, Mrs Deakins had observed, as Jess checked the dusty bottles behind the optics.

'Scotch, triple sec and orange juice.'

He took a sip. And then a larger one. 'This is all right.'

'I knew you'd like it. I made it specially for you. It's called a Mithering Bastard.'

*

The white plastic table sat in the middle of the thread-bare lawn, with two place settings of stainless-steel cutlery and a candle in a wine bottle in the middle. Jess had wiped the chairs with a bar cloth so that there was no green left on them and now pulled one out for him.

'We're eating al fresco. Birthday treat.' She ignored the look he gave her. 'If you would like to take your seat, I'll go and inform the kitchen that you're here.'

'It's not breakfast muffins, is it?'

'Of course it's not breakfast muffins.' She pretended to be offended. As she walked towards the kitchen, she muttered, 'Tanzie and Nicky had the rest of those.'

When she arrived back at the table, Norman had flopped down on Mr Nicholls's foot. Jess suspected Mr Nicholls would quite like to have moved it, but she had been sat on by Norman before and he was a dead weight. You just had to sit there and pray that he shifted before your foot went black and fell off.

'How was your aperitif?'

Mr Nicholls gazed at his empty cocktail glass. 'Delicious.'

'Well, the main course is on its way. I'm afraid it's just the two of us this evening, as the other guests had prior arrangements.'

'*Waterloo Road* and some completely insane algebraic equations.'

'You know us too well.' Jess sat down in her chair and, as she did, Mrs Deakins picked her way across the lawn, the Pomeranians yapping at her feet. With the same care as a head waiter holds up cordon bleu dishes in a five-star restaurant, she held aloft two plates upon each of which sat a huge foil-clad pie and chips.

'There you go,' she said, placing them on the table. 'Steak and kidney. From Ian up the road. He does a lovely meat pie.'

Jess was so hungry by then she thought she could probably have eaten Ian. 'Fantastic. Thank you,' she said, laying a paper napkin on her lap.

Mrs Deakins stood and gazed around, as if seeing the setting for the first time. 'We never eat out here. Lovely idea. I might offer it to my other customers. And those cocktails. I could make a package of it.'

Jess thought about the old men in the bar. 'Shame not to,' she said, passing the vinegar across to Mr Nicholls. He seemed temporarily stunned.

Mrs Deakins rubbed her hands on her apron. 'Well, Mr Nicholls, your wife is certainly determined to show you a good time on your birthday,' she said, with a wink.

He glanced up at her. 'Oh. There's never a quiet moment with Jess,' he said, letting his gaze slide back to hers.

'So how long have you two been married?'

'Ten years.'

'Three years.'

'The children are from my previous marriages,' Jess said, slicing into the pie.

'Oh! That's —'

'I rescued her,' said Mr Nicholls. 'From the side of the road.'

'He did.'

'That's very romantic.' Mrs Deakins's smile wavered a little.

'Not really. She was being arrested at the time.'

'I've explained all that. God, these chips are delicious.'

'You have. And those policemen were very understanding. Considering.'

Mrs Deakins had started to back away. 'Well, that's lovely. It's nice that you're still together.'

'We get by.'

'We have no choice right now.'

'That's true too.'

'Could you bring out some red sauce?'

'Oh, good idea. Darling.'

As she disappeared, Mr Nicholls nodded towards the candle, and the plates. And then he looked up at Jess and he was no longer scowling. 'This is actually the best pie and chips I've ever eaten in a weird bed-and-breakfast somewhere I've never heard of on the north Yorkshire moors.'

'I'm so glad. Happy birthday.'

They ate in companionable silence. It was astonishing how much better a hot meal and a fearsomely strong cocktail could make you feel. Upstairs Jess could hear Nicky watching television, occasional growls of frustration echoing through the open window when the static electricity interrupted his programme. Crows cawed obscenely from a nearby telephone wire. Norman groaned and flopped over onto his side, releasing Mr Nicholls's foot. Mr Nicholls stretched his leg speculatively, perhaps trying to see whether he still could.

He looked up at her, and raised his refreshed cocktail glass. 'Seriously. I do feel better. Thank you.' Without his glasses on, she noticed now that he had ridiculously long eyelashes. It made her feel weirdly conscious of the candle in the middle of the table. It had been a bit of a joke when she'd asked for it.

'Well . . . it was the least I could do. You did rescue us. From the side of the road. I don't know what we would have done.'

He speared another chip and held it aloft. 'Well, I like to look after my staff.'

'I think I preferred it when we were married.'

'Cheers.' He grinned at her. And it was so genuine and unexpected that she found herself grinning back.

'Here's to tomorrow. And Tanzie's future.'

'And a general absence of more crap.'

'I'll drink to that.'

The evening crept into night, eased by strong alcohol, and the happy knowledge that nobody had to sleep in a car, or needed frequent, urgent access to a bathroom. Nicky came down, ate his pie and chips, gazed suspiciously from under his fringe at the men in the snug, who gazed equally suspiciously back at him, and retreated to his bedroom to watch television. Jess drank three glasses of acidic Liebfraumilch, went inside to check on Tanzie and take her some food. She made her promise she would not revise later than ten o'clock. 'Can I keep working in your room? Nicky has the telly on.'

'That's fine,' Jess said.

'You smell of wine,' Tanzie said pointedly.

'That's because we're sort of on holiday. Mums are allowed to smell of wine when they're sort of on holiday.'

'Hmm.' She gave Jess a severe look and turned back to her books.

Nicky was sprawled on one of the single beds watching television. She shut the door behind her and sniffed the air.

'You haven't been smoking, have you?'

'You've still got my stash, if you remember. You said you were going to throw it away.'

'Oh, yes.' She had completely forgotten. 'But you slept without it. Last night and the night before.'

'Mm.'

'Well, that's good, right?'

He shrugged.

'I think the words you were looking for are "Yes, it's great that I no longer need illegal substances simply to fall asleep." Right, up you get for a minute. I need you to help me lift a mattress.' When he didn't move, she said, 'I can't sleep in there with Mr Nicholls. We'll make another bed on the floor of your room, okay?'

He sighed, but he got up and helped. He didn't wince any more when he moved, she noticed. On the carpet beside Tanzie's bed, the mattress left just enough room for them to slide in and out of the door, which now only opened six inches.

'This is going to be fun if I need the loo in the night.'

'Go last thing. You're a big boy.' She told Nicky to

turn off the television at ten so as not to disturb Tanzie, and left them both upstairs.

The candle had long since expired in the stiff evening breeze, and when they could no longer see each other to talk they moved indoors, seating themselves in the corner of the snug as far as possible from Mrs Deakins and the silent men at the bar. They had moved from parents and first jobs onto relationships. Jess told him about Marty and how he had once bought her an extension lead for her birthday, protesting, 'But you said you needed one!' In turn, he told her about Lara the Ex and how on her birthday he had once arranged for a chauffeur-driven car to pick her up for a surprise breakfast at a posh hotel with her friends, then spend the morning in Harvey Nichols with a personal shopper and an unlimited budget, and how when he'd met her for lunch she had complained bitterly because he hadn't taken the whole day off work. Jess thought she'd quite like to slap Lara the Ex quite hard around her overly made-up face (she had invented this face: it was probably more dragqueen than was strictly necessary).

'Did you have to pay her maintenance?'

'Didn't have to but I did. Until she let herself into the apartment and helped herself to my stuff for the third time.'

'Did you get it back?'

'It wasn't worth the hassle. If a screen-print of Mao Tse-tung is that important to her she can have it.'

'What was it worth?'

'What?'

'The painting.'

'A few grand.'

'You and I speak different languages, Mr Nicholls.' She studied him. 'Have you changed the locks now?'

He shuffled a little awkwardly in his seat. 'It's just stuff . . .' Jess must have pulled a face, because he said, 'Okay, then, how much maintenance does your ex pay you?'

'Nothing.'

'Nothing?' His eyebrows had lifted to somewhere round his hairline. 'Nothing at all?'

'He's a mess. You can't punish someone for being a mess.'

'Even if it means you and the kids have to struggle? You're right – you and I do speak different languages.'

How could she explain? It had taken her two years to work it out herself. She knew the kids missed him, but she was secretly relieved Marty had gone. She was relieved that she didn't have to worry about whether he was going to hijack their futures with his next ill-thought-out scheme. She was weary of his black moods and that he was permanently exhausted by the children. Mostly she was tired of never doing anything right. Marty had liked the sixteen-year-old Jess – the wild, impulsive, responsibility-free version. Then he had weighed her down with responsibility and hadn't liked who had emerged from it. 'When he's sorted himself out I'll make sure he contributes his share again, yes. But we're okay.' Jess glanced upstairs to where Nicky and Tanzie were sleeping. 'I think this will be our turning point. And, besides, you probably won't understand this, and I know everyone thinks they're a bit odd, but I'm the lucky one having them. They're kind and funny. They have ideas about stuff.' She poured herself another glass of wine and took a gulp. It was definitely getting easier to drink. She just wasn't sure how much tooth enamel she'd have afterwards.

'They're nice kids.'

'Thank you,' she said. 'Actually, I realized something today. The last few days have been the first time I can remember where I just got to be with them. Not working, not running around doing housework or shopping or trying to catch up on all the stuff. It's been nice just hanging out with them, if that doesn't sound daft.'

'It doesn't.'

'And Nicky's sleeping. He never sleeps. I'm not sure what you did for him, but he seems . . .'

'Oh, we just redressed the balance a little.'

Jess raised her glass. 'Then one nice thing happened on your birthday — you cheered my boy up.'

'That was yesterday.'

She thought for a moment. 'You didn't vomit once.'

'Okay. Stop now.'

She could no longer see him properly as they were side by side on the bench but, whether it was just the food, or perhaps the four pints of beer on top of the cocktail, or perhaps even just not having to look her in the eye, Mr Nicholls's whole body had finally relaxed. He leant back, his long legs stretched out under the table. For some time now one of them had been resting against hers. She had thought fleetingly that she should move it, and hadn't, and now she couldn't without it looking as if she was making a point. She felt it, an electric presence, against her bare leg.

She quite liked it.

Because something had happened somewhere between the pie and chips and the last round, and it wasn't just drink, or being away from everything, or the fact that they were finally so close to their destination. Jess wasn't quite sure what it was. She wanted Mr Nicholls not to feel angry and hopeless. She wanted to see that big sleepy grin of his, the one that seemed to defuse all the suppressed anger so you could see what he might have been like if all the crap hadn't happened to him. And when he did unleash one of those smiles it was so joyful and unexpected that she couldn't help a huge, involuntary grin spreading in answer across her own face. And so they sat, talking quietly, listening to the hum of the television at the bar, the murmured conversation, and periodically grinning like a pair of idiots.

'You know, I've never met anyone like you,' he said.

He was gazing at the table, apparently deep in thought. Jess had been about to make a joke about cleaners and baristas and staff but instead she just felt this great lurch in the pit of her belly and found herself picturing the taut V of his bare torso in the shower and wondering what it would be like to sleep with him.

The shock of this thought was so great that she nearly said it out loud. *I think it would be quite nice to have sex with Mr Nicholls.* She looked away and gulped the remaining half-glass of wine, feeling the burn of complaint as it went down.

Mr Nicholls was looking at her. 'Don't take offence. I meant it in a good way.'

'I'm not taking offence.' Her ears had gone pink.

'You're just the most positive person I've ever met. You're practical. You fix stuff. You never seem to feel sorry for yourself. Every obstacle that comes your way, you just scramble over it.'

'Ripping my trousers and falling over in the process.'

'But you keep going.'

'When someone helps me.'

'Okay. This simile is becoming confusing.' He took a swig of his beer. 'I just . . . wanted to tell you. I know it's nearly over. But I've enjoyed this trip. More than I expected to.'

It was out before she knew what she was saying. 'Yeah. Me too.'

They sat. He was gazing at her leg. She wondered if he was thinking what she was thinking.

'Do you know something, Jess?'

'What?'

'You've stopped fidgeting.'

They looked up at each other and a question passed silently between them. She wanted to look away but she couldn't. Mr Nicholls had just been a means of moving forward out of an impossible mess. Now all Jess could see were his big dark eyes, the way his hair left his forehead in an impossibly thick, lush line. The hypnotic way his top lip sculpted itself into a tiny cradle.

You need to get back on the horse.

He looked away first.

'Whoa! Look at the time. It's late. We should really get some sleep. You said we had to get up early.' His voice was just a bit too loud. 'Yup. Nearly eleven already. I think I calculated that we need to leave here by seven to make it there for midday. Does that sound right to you?'

'Uh . . . sure.'

She swayed a little when she stood up, and reached for his arm, but he'd already moved away.

They arranged an early breakfast, bade Mrs Deakins a slightly-too-hearty goodnight and made their way slowly up the stairs at the back of the pub. Jess was barely aware of what was said. For she was acutely conscious of him behind her. Of the unsteady way her hips moved when she walked. Of her bare shoulders. Is he watching me? Her mind swirled and dipped in unexpected directions. She wondered, briefly, what it would feel like if he were to lean forward and kiss her bare shoulder. She thought she might have made a small, involuntary sound at the thought of it.

They stopped on the landing, and she turned to face him. It felt as if, three days in, she'd only just seen him.

'Goodnight, then, Jessica Rae Thomas. With an a and an e.'

Her hand came to rest on the door handle. She gazed up at him then – at his broad shoulders and his clean identikit T-shirt and his soft, sad eyes – and her breath caught in her throat. It had been so long. Would it really be such a bad idea? She pushed down on the handle and leant in. 'I'll see you in the morning.'

'I'd offer to make you coffee. But you're always up first anyway.'

She didn't know what to say. It was possible she was just gazing at him.

'Um . . . Jess?'

'What?'

'Thanks. For everything. The sickness stuff, the birthday surprise . . . In case I don't get a chance to say this tomorrow . . .' he gave her a lopsided smile '. . . as ex-wives go, you were definitely my favourite.'

Jess tried to smile back, but her answer dried in her throat. She pushed at the door. She was going to say something else, but she was distracted by the fact that the door didn't move.

She turned and pushed down on the handle again. It gave, opened an inch, and no more.

'What?'

'I can't open the door,' she said, putting both her hands on it. Nothing.

Mr Nicholls walked over and pushed. It gave the tiniest amount. 'It's not locked,' he said, working the handle. 'There's something blocking it.'

She squatted down, trying to see, and Mr Nicholls turned on the landing light. Through the two inches of door space, she could just make out Norman's bulk on the other side of the door. He was lying on the mattress, his huge back to her.

'Norman,' she hissed. 'Move.'

Nothing.

'Norman.'

'If I push, he'll have to wake up, right?' Mr Nicholls began leaning on the door. He rested his full weight on it. Then he pushed. 'Jesus Christ,' he said.

Jess shook her head. 'You don't know my dog.'

He let go of the handle and the door shut with a gentle click. They stared at each other.

'Well . . .' he said finally. 'There are two beds in here. It'll be fine.'

She grimaced. 'Um. Norman is sleeping on the other single. I moved the mattress in there earlier.'

He looked at her wearily then. 'Knock on the door?'

'Tanzie is stressed. I can't run the risk of waking her. It's fine. I'll . . . I'll . . . just sleep on the chair.'

Jess headed down to the bathroom before he could contradict her. She washed and brushed her teeth, gazing at her alcohol-flushed skin in the plastic-framed mirror and trying to stop her thoughts chasing themselves in circles.

When she arrived back at the room, Mr Nicholls was holding up one of his dark grey T-shirts. 'Here,' he said, and threw it at her as he walked past to the bathroom. Jess changed into it, trying to ignore the vague eroticism of its clean male smell, pulled the spare blanket and a pillow out of the wardrobe and curled up in the chair, struggling to bring her knees up to a position that made it comfortable. It was going to be a long night.

Some minutes later, Mr Nicholls opened the door and turned off the overhead light. He was wearing a white T-shirt and a pair of dark blue boxers. She saw that his legs bore the long, visible muscles of someone who does no-excuses exercise. She knew immediately how they would feel against her own. The thought made her mouth go dry.

The little bed sagged audibly as he climbed in.

'Are you comfortable like that?' He looked at her over the lavender-coloured bedspread.

'Totally fine!' she said brightly. 'You?'

'If one of these springs impales me while I sleep, you have my permission to take the car the rest of the way.'

He gazed at her across the room for a moment longer, then turned out the bedside light.

The darkness was total. Outside, a faint breeze moaned through unseen gaps in the stone, trees rustled and a car door slammed, its engine roaring a protest. In the next room, Norman whined in his sleep, the sound only partially muffled by the thin plasterboard wall. Jess could hear Mr Nicholls breathing, and although she had spent the previous night only inches from him, she was acutely conscious of his presence in a way she hadn't been twenty-four hours earlier. She thought of the way he had made Nicky smile, of the way his fingers rested on a steering-wheel. She thought of him slumped on the dry stone wall, his head in his hands, as he talked about what he had lost, the hurt and anger etched deep on his face.

She thought about some expression she had heard Nicky use a few weeks ago – YOLO – You only live once – and remembered how she had told him she thought it was just an excuse idiots used for doing pretty much anything they felt like doing, no matter what the consequences.

She thought about Liam, and how she knew in her gut that he was probably having sex with someone right this minute – that ginger barmaid from the Blue Parrot, maybe, or the Dutch girl who drove the flower van. She thought about a conversation she'd had with Chelsea when Chelsea had told her she should lie about her kids because no man would ever fall in love with a single mother of two, and how Jess had got angry with her because deep down she knew she was probably right.

She thought about the fact that even if Mr Nicholls didn't go to prison, she would probably never see him again after this trip.

And then, before she could think too hard about anything else, Jess eased herself silently out of the chair, letting the blanket fall to the floor. It took only four steps to reach the bed, and she hesitated, her bare toes curled in the acrylic carpet, even then not quite sure what she was doing. *You only live once.* And then in the near-total dark there was a faint movement and she saw Mr Nicholls turn to face her as she lifted the duvet and climbed in.

Jess was chest to chest against him, her cool legs against his warm ones. There was nowhere else to go in this tiny bed, with the sag of the mattress pushing them closer together and its edge like a cliff-drop just inches behind her. They were so close that she could breathe in the remnants of his aftershave, his toothpaste. She could feel the rise and fall of his chest, as her heart thumped erratically against his. She tilted her head a little, trying to read him. He put his right arm across the duvet, a surprisingly heavy weight, gathering her in closer to him. With his other, he took her hand and enclosed it slowly in his. It was dry and soft, and inches from her mouth. She wanted to lower her face to his knuckles and trace her lips along them. She wanted to reach her mouth up to his, and run her teeth gently along the soft curve of his upper lip.

You only live once.

She lay there in the dark, paralysed by her own longing, by the fact that just this once she did not know the answer, or even the question.

'Do you want to have sex with me?' she said, into the darkness.

There was a long silence.

'Did you hear what –'

'Yes,' he said. 'And . . . no.' He spoke again before she could turn completely to stone. 'I just think it would make things too complicated.'

'It's not complicated. We're both young, lonely, a bit pissed. And after tonight we're never going to see each other again.'

'How so?'

'You'll go back to London and lead your big city life, and I'll be down on the coast leading mine. It doesn't have to be a big deal.'

He was silent for a minute. 'Jess . . . I don't think so.'

'You don't fancy me.' She prickled with embarrassment, remembering suddenly what he'd said about his ex. Lara was a model, for Chrissakes. But even as she shifted away from him, his hand tightened around hers. His voice was a murmur in her ear. 'You're beautiful.'

She waited. His thumb brushed over her palm. 'So . . . why won't you sleep with me?'

He didn't say anything.

'Look. Here's the thing. I haven't had sex in three years. I sort of need to get back on the horse, and I think it – you – would be great.'

'You want me to be a horse.'

'Not like that. I need a metaphorical horse.'

'And now we're back to confusing metaphors.'

'Look, a woman you say you find beautiful is offering you no-strings sex. I don't understand the problem.'

'There's no such thing as no-strings sex.'

'What?'

'Someone always wants something.'

'I don't want anything from you.'

She felt him shrug. 'Not now, maybe.'

'Wow.' She turned onto her side. 'She really got to you, didn't she?'

'I just . . .'

Jess slid her foot along his leg. 'You think I'm trying to lure you in? You think this is me trying to entrap you with my womanly wiles? My womanly wiles, a nylon bedspread, pie and chips?' She interlinked her fingers with his. She let her voice drop to a whisper. She felt unleashed, reckless. She thought she might actually faint with how much she wanted him then. 'I don't want a relationship, Ed. With you or anyone. There's no room in my life for the whole one plus one thing.' She tilted her face so that her mouth was inches from his. She could almost taste the toothpaste sweetness of his breath. 'I'd've thought that would be obvious.'

He moved his hips an awkward fraction away from hers. 'You are . . . incredibly persuasive.'

'And you are . . .' She hooked her leg around him, pulling him closer. The hardness of him made her briefly giddy.

He swallowed.

Her lips were millimetres from his. All the nerves of her body had somehow concentrated themselves in her skin. Or maybe his skin: she could no longer tell.

'It's the last night. You know . . . you can drop us off tomorrow and we'll never see each other again. At worst we can exchange a glance over the vacuum cleaner and I'll just remember this as a nice night with a nice guy who actually was a nice guy.' She let her lips graze his chin. It carried the faint echo of stubble. She wanted to bite it. 'You, of course, will remember it as the greatest sex you ever had.'

'And that's it.' His voice was thick, distracted.

Jess moved closer. 'That's it,' she murmured.

'You'd have made a great negotiator.'

'Do you ever stop talking?' She moved forward, a fraction, until her lips met his. She almost jolted. She felt the electric pressure of his mouth on hers as he ceded to her, the sweetness of him, and she no longer cared about anything. She wanted him. She burnt with it. 'Happy birthday,' she whispered.

He pulled back a fraction. She felt, rather than saw, Ed Nicholls gazing at her. His eyes were black in the darkness, unfathomable. He moved his hand and as it brushed against her stomach she gave a faint, involuntary shiver.

'Fuck,' he said quietly. 'Fucking fuck.' And then, with a groan, he said, 'You will actually thank me for this tomorrow.'

And he gently disentangled himself from her, climbed out of bed, walked over to the chair, sat down and, with a great sigh, hauled the blanket over himself and turned away.

20.

ED

Ed Nicholls had thought that spending eight hours in a damp car park was the worst possible way to spend a night. Then he'd concluded that the worst way to spend a night was hoicking your guts up in a static caravan somewhere near Derby. He was wrong on both counts. The worst way to spend a night, it turned out, was in a tiny room a few feet from a slightly drunk, good-looking woman who wanted to have sex with you and whom you had, like an idiot, rebuffed.

Jess fell asleep, or pretended to: it was impossible to tell. Ed sat in the world's most uncomfortable chair, staring out of the narrow gap in the curtains at the black moonlit sky, his right leg going to sleep, and his left foot freezing cold where it wouldn't fit under the blanket and tried not to think about the fact that if he hadn't leapt out of that bed he could be there, curled around her right now, her arms around his neck, his lips pressed against her skin, those lithe legs looped around . . .

No.

He had done the right thing, he told himself. He must have done. His life was complicated enough without adding an impulsive cleaner with an eccentric family to the mix (he hated himself for letting the word 'cleaner' appear in that little mental riff). Even as Jess, uncharacteristically still in those last few moments, had lain against him and his brain had started to melt, he had tried to apply logic to the situation, and had concluded, with the few cells still functioning, that it couldn't end well. Either (a) the sex would have been terrible, they would have been mortified afterwards, and the five hours spent travelling to the Olympiad would have been excruciating. Or (b) the sex would have been fine, they would have woken up embarrassed and the journey would still have been excruciating. Worse, they could have ended up with (c): the sex would have been off the scale (he slightly suspected this one was correct – he kept getting a hard-on just thinking about her mouth), they would develop feelings for each other based purely on sexual chemistry and either (d) would have to adjust to the fact that they had nothing in common and were just completely unsuited in every other way or (e) they would find they were not entirely unsuited, but then he would be sent to prison. And none of this considered (f), which was that Jess had actual kids. Kids who needed stability in their lives and not someone such as him: he liked children as a concept, but in the same way that he liked the Indian subcontinent – i.e. it was nice to know it existed but he had no knowledge about it and had never felt any real desire to spend time there.

And all this was without the added factor of (g): that he was obviously crap at relationships, had only just come out of the two most disastrous examples anyone could imagine, and the odds of him getting it right with someone else on the basis of a lengthy car journey that had begun because he couldn't think how to get out of it were lower than a very low thing indeed.

Plus the whole horse conversation had been, frankly, weird.

And these points could be supplemented by the wilder possibilities that he had completely failed to consider. What if Jess was a psycho, and all that stuff about not wanting a relationship was just a way to reel him in? She didn't seem that sort of girl, sure.

But neither had Deanna.

Ed sat pondering this and other tangled things and wishing he could talk a single one of them through with Ronan, until the sky turned orange then neon blue and his leg became completely dead and his hangover, which had formerly manifested itself as a vague tightness at his temples, turned into an emphatic, skull-crushing head-ache. Ed tried not to look at the girl sleeping in the bed a few feet away as the outline of her face and body under the duvet became clear in the encroaching light.

And he tried not to feel wistful for a time when having sex with a woman you liked had just been about having sex with a woman you liked and hadn't involved a series of equations so complex and unlikely that probably only Tanzie could have got anywhere near understanding them.

'Come on. We're running late.' Jess shepherded Nicky – a pale, T-shirt-clad zombie – towards the car.

'I didn't get any breakfast.'

'That's because you wouldn't get up when I told you.

We'll get you something on the way. Tanze. Tanzie? Has the dog been to the loo?'

The morning sky was the colour of lead and seemed to have descended to a point around their ears. A faint drizzle promised heavier rain. Ed sat in the driving seat as Jess ran around, organizing, scolding, promising, in a fury of activity. She had been like this since he'd woken, groggily, from what seemed like twenty minutes' sleep, folding and packing, dragging bags downstairs, supervising breakfast. He didn't think she had met his eye once. Tanzie climbed silently into the back seat.

'You okay?' He yawned and looked at the little girl in the rear-view mirror.

She nodded silently.

'Nerves?'

She didn't say anything.

'Been sick?'

She nodded.

'It's all the rage on this trip. You'll be great. Really.'

She gave him the exact look he would have given any adult if they had said the same, then turned to stare out of the window, her face round and pale, her eyes mauve with exhaustion. Ed wondered how late she had stayed up revising.

'Right.' Jess shoved Norman into the back seat. He brought with him an almost overwhelming scent of wet dog. She checked that Tanzie had done up her belt, climbed into the passenger seat and finally turned to Ed. Her expression was unreadable. 'Let's go.'

*

284

Ed's car no longer looked like his car. In just three days its immaculate cream interior had acquired new scents and stains, a fine sprinkling of dog hair, jumpers and shoes that now lived on seats or wedged underneath them. The floor crunched underfoot with dropped sweet wrappers and crisps. The radio stations were no longer on settings he understood.

But something had happened while he had been driving along at forty m.p.h. The faint sense that he should actually have been somewhere else had begun to fade, almost without him being aware of it. He had stopped trying to anticipate what was going to happen next, stopped dreading the next phone call, stopped wondering whether there was any chance that Deanna Lewis would decide not to drag him down with her . . . and he had just started existing. Ed Nicholls drove mile after easy mile through the early-morning mist, slow enough to notice the landmarks, the subtle changes in landscape, the lives around him in little market towns, huge cities. He found himself glancing at the people they passed, buying food, driving their cars, walking their children to and from school in worlds completely different from his own, knowing nothing of his own little drama several hundred miles south. It made it all seem reduced in size, a model village of problems rather than something that loomed over him.

He drove on, and despite the pointed silence from the woman beside him, Nicky's sleeping face in the rear-view mirror ('Teenagers don't really do Before Eleven o'Clock,' Tanzie explained) and the occasional foul eruptions of the dog, it slowly dawned on him, as they crept closer to their destination, that he was feeling a complete lack of the relief he had expected to feel at the prospect of having his car, his life, back to himself. What he felt was more complex. Ed fiddled with the speakers, so that the music was loudest in the rear seats and temporarily silent in the front.

'You okay?'

Jess didn't look round. 'I'm fine.'

Ed glanced behind him, making sure nobody was listening. 'About last night,' he began.

'Forget it.'

He wanted to tell her that he regretted it. He wanted to tell her that his body had actually hurt with the effort of not climbing back into that sagging single bed. But what would have been the point? Like she'd said the previous evening, they were two people who had no reason to see each other ever again. 'I can't forget it. I wanted to explain –'

'Nothing to explain. You were right. It was a stupid idea.' She tucked her legs under her and stared away from him out of the window.

'It's just my life is too –'

'Really. It's not an issue. I just . . .' she let out a deep breath '. . . I just want to make sure we get to the Olympiad on time.'

'But I don't want us to end it all like this.'

'There's nothing to end.' She put her feet on the dashboard. It felt like a statement. 'Let's go.'

'How many miles is it to Aberdeen?' Tanzie's face appeared between the front seats.

'What, left?'

'No. From Southampton.'

Ed pulled his phone from his jacket and handed it to her. 'Look it up on the Maps app.'

She tapped the screen, her brow furrowed. 'About five hundred and eighty?'

'Sounds about right.'

'So if we're doing forty miles an hour we'd have had to do at least six hours' driving a day. And if I didn't get sick, we could have done it . . .'

'In a day. At a push.'

'One day.' Tanzie digested this, her eyes trained on the Scottish hillsides in the distance ahead. 'But we wouldn't have had such a nice time then, would we?'

Ed glanced sideways at Jess. 'No, we wouldn't.'

It took a moment before Jess's gaze slid back towards him. 'No, sweetheart,' she said, after a beat. And her smile was oddly rueful. 'No, we wouldn't.'

The car ate the miles sleekly and efficiently. They crossed the Scottish border, and Ed tried – failed – to raise a cheer. They stopped once for Tanzie to go to the loo, once twenty minutes later for Nicky to go ('I can't help it. I didn't want to go when Tanze did') and three times for Norman (two were false alarms). Jess sat silently beside him, checking her watch and chewing at her nails. She was still wearing flip-flops and he wondered fleetingly if her feet were cold. Nicky gazed groggily out of the window at the empty landscape, at the few flinty houses set into rolling hills. Ed wondered what would happen to him after this was over. He wanted to suggest fifty other things to help him, but he tried to imagine someone suggesting things to him at the same age, and guessed he would have taken no notice at all. He wondered how Jess would keep him safe when they returned home.

The phone rang and he glanced over, his heart sinking. 'Lara.'

'Eduardo. Baby. I need to talk to you about this roof.'

He was aware of Jess's sudden rigidity, the flicker of her gaze. He wished, suddenly, that he hadn't chosen to answer the call.

'Lara, I'm not going to discuss this now.'

'It's not a lot of money. Not for you. I spoke to my solicitor and he says it would be nothing for you to pay for it.'

'I told you before, Lara, we made a final settlement.'

He was suddenly conscious of the acute stillness of three people in the car.

'Eduardo. Baby. I need to sort this with you.'

'Lara –'

Before he could say anything more, Jess reached over and picked up the phone. 'Hello, Lara,' she said. 'Jess here. I'm awfully sorry but he can't pay for your roof, so there's really no point in ringing him any more.'

A short silence. Then an explosive: 'Who is this?'

'I'm his new wife. Oh – and he'd like his Chairman Mao picture back. Perhaps just leave it with his lawyer. Okay? In your own time. Thanks so much.'

The resulting silence had the same quality as the few

seconds before an atomic explosion. But before any of them could hear what happened next, Jess flipped the off button, and handed it back to him. He took it gingerly, and turned it off.

'Thank you,' he said. 'I think.'

'You're welcome.' She didn't look at him when she spoke.

Ed glanced into his rear-view mirror. He couldn't be sure, but he thought Nicky was trying very hard not to laugh.

Somewhere between Edinburgh and Dundee, on a narrow, wooded lane, they slowed and stopped for a herd of cows in the road. The animals moved around the car, gazing in at its inhabitants with vague curiosity, a moving black sea, eyes rolling in woolly black heads. Norman stared back, his body rigid with silent, confused outrage. Tanzie took off her glasses and rubbed her eyes, gazing back at them, half blind.

'Aberdeen Angus,' said Nicky.

Suddenly, without warning, Norman hurled his whole body, snarling and growling at the window. The car physically jolted to one side and his deafening bark bounced off the interior, amplified in the confined space. The back seat became a chaotic mass of arms and noise and writhing dog. Nicky and Jess fought to reach him.

'Mum!'

'Norman! Stop!' The dog was on top of Tanzie, his face hard against the window. Ed could just make out her pink jacket, flailing underneath him.

Jess lunged over the seat at the dog, grabbing for his collar. They dragged Norman back down from the window. He whined, shrill and hysterical, straining at their grasp, great gobs of drool spraying across the interior.

'Norman, you big idiot! What the hell –'

'He's never seen a cow before.' Tanzie, struggling upright, always defending him.

'Jesus, Norman.'

'You okay, Tanze?'

'I'm fine.'

The cows continued to part around the car, unmoved by the dog's outburst. Through the now steamed-up windows they could just make out the farmer at the rear, walking slowly and impassively, with the same lumbering gait as his bovine charges. He gave the barest of nods as he passed, as if he had all the time in the world. Norman whined and pulled against his collar.

'I've never seen him like that before.' Jess straightened her hair and blew out through her cheeks. 'Perhaps he could smell beef.'

'I didn't know he had it in him,' Ed said.

'My glasses.' Tanzie held up the twisted piece of metal. 'Mum. Norman broke my glasses.'

It was a quarter past ten.

'I can't see anything without my glasses.'

Jess looked at Ed. Shit.

'Okay,' he said. 'Grab a plastic bag. I'm going to have to put my foot down.'

*

They drove at speed, half frozen, the wind from the open windows a buffeting roar that thwarted conversation. The Scottish roads were wide and empty, and Ed drove so fast that the satnav had repeatedly to reassess its timing to their destination. Every minute they gained was an imaginary air punch in his head. Tanzie was sick twice. He refused to stop to allow her to vomit into the road.

'She's really ill.'

'I'm fine,' Tanzie kept saying, her face wedged into a plastic bag. 'Really.'

'You don't want to stop, sweetheart? Just for a minute?'

'No. Keep going. Bleurgh –'

There wasn't time to stop. Not that this made the car journey any easier to bear. Nicky had turned away from his sister, his hand over his nose. Even Norman's head was thrust as far out into the fresh air as he could get it.

Ed drove like someone in a luxury car advert, speeding through empty bends, along the winding base of ancient windswept hillsides. The car gripped the greasy roads as if it had been meant for this. He forgot he was cold, that his car interior was pretty much destroyed, his life a mess. There were moments, in that astonishing landscape, his whole being focused on driving as fast and as safely as he could, when it felt like an almost spiritual experience. A spiritual experience broken only by the occasional sound of a child gagging into a fresh plastic bag.

He would get them there. He knew this as surely as he

knew anything. He felt filled with purpose in a way that he hadn't done in months. And as Aberdeen finally loomed before them, its buildings vast and silver grey, the oddly modern high-rises thrusting into the distant sky, his mind raced ahead of them. He headed for the centre, watched as the roads narrowed and became cobbled streets. They came through the docks, the enormous tankers on their right, and that was where the traffic slowed, and slowly, unstoppably, his confidence began to unravel. They slowed and then sat in an increasingly anxious silence, Ed punching in alternative routes across Aberdeen that offered no time gain and often no sense. The satnav started to work against him, adding back the time it had subtracted. It was fifteen, nineteen, twenty-two minutes until they reached the university building. Twenty-five minutes. Too many.

'What's the delay?' said Jess, to nobody in particular. She fiddled with the radio buttons, trying to find the traffic reports. 'What's the hold-up?'

'It's just sheer weight of traffic.'

'That's such a lame expression,' said Nicky. 'Of course a traffic jam is sheer weight of traffic. What else would it be down to?'

'There could have been an accident,' said Tanzie.

'But the jam itself would still comprise the traffic. So the problem is still the sheer weight of traffic.'

'No, the volume of traffic slowing itself down is something completely different.'

'But it's the same result.'

'But then it's an inaccurate description.'

Jess peered at the satnav. 'Are we in the right place? I wouldn't have thought the docks would be near the university.'

'We have to get through the docks to get to the university.'

'You're sure?'

'I'm sure, Jess.' Ed tried to suppress the tension in his voice. 'Look at the satnav.'

There was a brief silence. In front of them the traffic-lights changed through two cycles without anybody moving. Jess, on the other hand, moved incessantly, fidgeting in her seat, peering around her to see if there was some clear route they might have missed. He couldn't blame her. He felt the same.

'I don't think we've got time to get new glasses,' he murmured to Jess, when they'd sat through the fourth cycle.

'But she can't see without them.'

'If we look for a chemist we're not going to make it there for midday.'

She bit her lip, then turned round in her seat. 'Tanze? Is there any way you can see through the unbroken lens? Any way at all?'

A pale green face emerged from the plastic bag. 'I'll try,' it said.

Traffic stopped and stalled. They grew silent, the tension within the car ratcheting up. When Norman whined, they growled, 'Shut up, Norman!' as one. Ed felt his blood pressure rising, even as the weight of responsibility for getting them there seemed to grow heavier. Why hadn't they left half an hour earlier? Why hadn't he worked this out better? What would happen if they missed it? He glanced sideways to where Jess was tapping her knee nervously and guessed that she was probably thinking the same thing. And then finally, inexplicably, as if the gods had been toying with them, the traffic cleared.

He flung the car through the cobbled streets, Jess yelling, 'GO! GO!' leaning forwards on the dashboard as if she were a coachman driving a horse. He skidded the car around the bends, almost too fast for the satnav, which actually started to burble, and entered the university campus on two wheels, following the small printed signs that had been placed haphazardly on random poles, until they found the Downes Building, an unlovely 1970s office block in the same grey granite as everything else.

The car screeched into a parking space in front of it, and everything stopped. Ed let out a long breath and glanced at the clock. It was six minutes to twelve.

'This is it?'

'This is it.'

Jess appeared suddenly paralysed, as if she couldn't believe they were actually there. She undid her seatbelt and stared at the car park, at the boys strolling in as if they had all the time in the world, some reading off electronic devices, others accompanied by tense-looking parents. They were all wearing the uniforms of minor public schools. 'I thought it would be . . . bigger,' she said.

Nicky gazed out through the dank grey drizzle. 'Yeah. Because advanced maths is such a crowd-puller.'

'I can't see anything,' said Tanzie.

'Look, you guys go in and register. I'll get her some glasses.'

Jess turned to him. 'But they won't be the right pre-scription.'

'I'll sort it. Just go. GO.'

He could see her staring after him as he skidded out of the car park and headed back towards the city centre.

It took seven minutes and three attempts to find a chem-ist large enough to sell reading glasses. Ed screeched to a halt so dramatic that Norman shot forward and his great head collided with his shoulder. He resettled him-self on the back seat, grumbling.

'Stay here,' Ed told him, and bolted inside.

The shop was empty, aside from an old woman with a basket and two assistants talking in lowered voices. He skidded around the shelves, past tampons and tooth-brushes, corn plasters and reduced Christmas-gift sets, until he finally found the stand by the till. Dammit. Why the hell hadn't he checked whether she was long- or short-sighted? He reached for his phone to ask, then remembered he didn't have Jess's number.

'Fuck. Fuck. Fuck.' Ed stood there, trying to guess. Tanzie's glasses looked as if they might be pretty strong. He had never seen her without them. Would that mean she was more likely to be short-sighted? Didn't all children tend to be short-sighted? It was adults who held things away from them to see, surely. He hesitated for about ten seconds and then, after a moment's indecision, he pulled them all from their rack, long- and short-sighted, mild and super-strength, and dumped them on the counter in a clear plastic-wrapped pile.

The girl broke off her conversation with the old woman. She looked down at them then up at him. Ed saw her clock the drool on his collar and tried to wipe it surreptitiously with his sleeve. This succeeded in smearing it across his lapel.

'All of them. I'll take all of them,' he said. 'But only if you can ring them up in less than thirty seconds.'

She looked over at her supervisor, who gave Ed a penetrating stare, then an imperceptible nod. Without a word, the girl began to ring them up, carefully positioning each pair in a bag. 'No. No time. Just chuck them in,' he said, reaching past her to thrust them into the plastic carrier.

'Do you have a loyalty card?'

'No. No loyalty card.'

'We're doing a special three for two offer on diet bars today. Would you like –'

Ed scrambled to pick up the glasses that had fallen from the counter. 'No diet bars,' he said. 'No offers. Thank you.'

'That'll be a hundred and seventy-four pounds,' she said finally. 'Sir.'

She peered over her shoulder then, as if half expecting the arrival of a prank television crew. But Ed stabbed out his PIN, grabbed the carrier bag and ran for the car. He heard, 'No manners,' in a strong Scottish accent, as he left.

There was nobody in the car park when he returned. He pulled up right outside the door, leaving Norman clambering wearily back onto the back seat, and ran inside, down the echoing corridor. 'Maths competition? Maths competition?' he yelled at anyone he passed. A man pointed wordlessly to a laminated sign. He bolted up a flight of steps two at a time, along another corridor, and into an anteroom. Two men sat behind a desk. On the other side of the room stood Jess and Nicky. She took a step towards him. 'Got them.' He held up the carrier bag, triumphantly. He was so out of breath he could barely speak.

'She's gone in,' she said. 'They've started.'

He looked up at the clock, breathing hard. It was seven minutes past twelve.

'Excuse me?' he said to the man at the desk. 'I need to give a girl in there her glasses.'

The man looked up slowly. He eyed the plastic bag Ed held in front of him.

Ed leant right over the desk, thrusting the bag towards him. 'She broke her glasses on the way here. She can't see without them.'

'I'm sorry, sir. I can't let anyone in now.'

Ed nodded. 'Yes. Yes, you can. Look, I'm not trying to cheat or sneak anything in. I just didn't know her glasses type so I had to buy every pair. You can check them. All of them. Look. No secret codes. Just glasses.' He held the bag open in front of him. 'You have to take them in to her so she can find a pair that fits.'

The man gave a slow shake of his head.

'Sir. We can't allow anything to disrupt the other —'

'Yes. Yes, you can. It's an emergency.'

'It's the rules.'

Ed stared at him hard for a full ten seconds. Then he straightened up, put a hand to his head and started to walk away from him. He could feel a new pressure building inside him, like a kettle juddering on a hotplate. 'You know something?' he said, turning around, slowly. 'It has taken us three solid days and nights to get here. Three days in which I have had my very nice car filled with vomit, and unmentionable things done to my upholstery by a dog. I don't even like dogs. I have slept in a car with a virtual stranger. Not in a good way. I have stayed places no reasonable human being should have to stay. I have eaten an apple that had been down the too-tight trousers of a teenage boy and a kebab that for all I know contained human flesh. I have left a huge, huge, personal crisis in London and driven five hundred and eighty miles with people I don't know – very nice people – because even I could see that this competition was really, really important to them. Vitally important. Because all that little girl in there cares about is maths. And if she doesn't get a pair of glasses that she can actually see through, she can't compete fairly in your competition. And if she can't compete fairly, she blows her only chance to go to the school that she really, really needs to go to. And if that happens, you know what I'll do?'

The man stared.

'I will go into that room of yours and I will walk around every single maths paper and I will rip it into teeny-tiny pieces. And I will do it very, very quickly, before you have a chance to call your security guards. And you know why I will do this?'

The man swallowed. 'No.'

'Because all this has to have been worth something.' Ed went back to him and leant close to him. 'It has to. And because right now, at this exact minute, I really, really don't feel like I have anything left to lose.'

Something had happened to Ed's face. He could feel it, in the way it seemed to have twisted itself into shapes he had never felt before. He could see it in the way the man was staring at him. And he could feel it in the way Jess stepped forward and gently put her hand on his arm and handed the man the bag of glasses.

'We'd be really, really grateful if you took her the glasses,' she said quietly.

The man stood up and walked around the desk towards the door. He kept his eyes on Ed at all times. 'I'll see what I can do,' he said. And the door closed gently behind him.

They walked out to the car in silence, oblivious to the rain. Jess unloaded the bags. Nicky stood off to the side, his hands thrust as far into his jeans pockets as he could manage. Which, given the tightness of his jeans, wasn't very far.

'Well, we made it.' She allowed herself a small smile.

'I said we would.' Ed nodded towards the car. 'Shall I wait here until she's finished?'

She wrinkled her nose. 'No. You're fine. We've held you up long enough.'

Ed felt his smile sag a little. 'Where will you sleep tonight?'

'If she wins, I might treat us to a fancy hotel. If she loses . . .' She shrugged. 'Bus shelter.' The way she said this suggested she didn't believe it.

She walked around to the rear door of the car. Norman, who had glanced at the rain and decided not to get out, looked up at her.

Jess stuck her head through the door. 'Norman, time to go.'

A small pile of bags sat on the wet ground behind the Audi. She hauled a jacket out of a bag and handed it to Nicky. 'Come on, it's cold.'

'So . . . is this . . . it?' The air held the salt tang of the sea. It made him think suddenly of Beachfront.

'This is it. Thank you for the lift. I . . . we . . . all appreciate it. The glasses. Everything.'

They looked at each other properly for the first time, and there were about a billion things he wanted to say.

Nicky lifted an awkward hand. 'Yeah. Mr Nicholls. Thanks.'

'Oh. Here.' Ed reached into his pocket for the phone he had pulled from the glove compartment, and tossed it to him. 'It's a back-up. I – um – don't need it any more.'

'Really?' Nicky caught it one-handed, and gazed at it, disbelieving.

Jess frowned. 'We can't take that. You've done enough for us.'

'It's not a big deal. Really. If Nicky doesn't take it I'll only have to send it off to one of those recycling places. You're just saving me a job.'

Jess glanced down at her feet as if she were going to say something else. And then she looked up, and hauled her hair briskly into an unnecessary ponytail.

'Well. Thanks again.' She thrust a hand towards him. Ed hesitated then shook it, trying to ignore the sudden flash of memory of the previous evening.

'Good luck with your dad. And the lunch. And the whole work thing. I'm sure it will come good. Remember, good things happen.' When she pulled her hand away he felt weirdly as if he'd lost something. She turned, and looked over her shoulder, already distracted. 'Right. Let's find somewhere dry to stick our stuff.'

'Hold on.' Ed hauled a business card from his jacket, scribbled a number and walked over to her. 'Call me.'

One of the numbers was smudged. He saw her staring at it.

'That's a three.' He altered it, then shoved his hands into his pockets, feeling like an awkward teenager. 'I'd like to know how Tanzie gets on. Please.'

She nodded, her face unreadable. And then she was gone, propelling the boy in front of her like a particularly vigilant shepherd. He sat and watched them, lugging their oversized holdalls and the huffing, recalcitrant dog, until they rounded the corner of the grey concrete building and were gone.

*

The car was silent. Even in the hours when nobody spoke, Ed had become used to the faintly steamed windows, the vague sense of constant movement that came from being in close confinement with other people. The muffled ping of Nicky's games console. Jess's constant fidgeting. Now he gazed around the car's interior at the long black hairs and ghostly trails of dried slobber across the middle of the rear seat where Norman had been, and felt as if he was standing in a deserted house. He saw the crumbs and the apple core that had been stuffed into the rear ashtray, the melted chocolate, the newspaper folded into the pocket of the seat. His damp clothes hung from wire hangers across the rear windows. He saw the maths book, half wedged down the side of the seat that Tanzie had evidently missed in her hurry to get out, and wondered whether to take it to her. But what was the point? It was too late.

It was too late.

He sat in the grey, bleak car park, watching the last of the parents walking to their cars, killing time as they waited for their charges. He leant forward and rested his head on the steering-wheel for some time. And then, when his was the only car left there, he put his key into the ignition and finally began to drive.

Ed had gone about twenty miles before he became aware of quite how tired he was. The combination of three nights of broken sleep, a hangover and hundreds of miles of driving hit him like a demolition ball, and he felt his eyes drooping. He turned up the radio, opened his windows, and when that failed, he pulled into a road-side café to get some coffee.

It was half empty despite it being lunchtime. In one corner a short-order chef fried something unseen on a griddle dark with grease, his hat pushed back on his head. A couple of suited men sat at opposite ends of the room, lost in mobile phones and paperwork, the wall behind them offering sixteen different permutations of sausage, egg, bacon, chips and beans. Ed grabbed a newspaper from the stand, and made his way to a table. He ordered coffee from the waitress.

'I'm sorry, sir, but at this time of day we reserve tables for those eating.' Her accent was strong enough that he had to think quite hard to work out what she had said.

'Oh. Right. Well, I –'

MAJOR UK TECHNOLOGY COMPANY IN INSIDER TRADING RIDDLE

He stared at the newspaper headline.
'Sir?'
'Mm?' His skin began to prickle.
'You have to order some food. If you want to sit down.'
'Oh.'

The Financial Services Authority confirmed last night that it is investigating a traded UK technology company for insider trading worth millions of pounds. The investigation is under-stood to be taking place on both sides of the Atlantic, and involves the London and New York stock exchanges, and the SEC, the US equivalent to the FSA.

Nobody has yet been arrested, but a source within the City of London police said that this was 'simply a matter of time'.

'Sir?'

She'd said it twice before he heard her. He looked up. A young woman, her nose freckled, her natural hair teased and fluffed into a kind of matted arrangement. She was waiting in front of him. 'What would you like to eat?'

'Whatever.' His mouth was the consistency of powder. A pause.

'Um. Do you want me to tell you today's specials? Or some of our more popular dishes?'

Simply a matter of time.

'We do an all-day Burns breakfast –'

'Fine.'

'And we . . . You want the Burns breakfast?'

'Yes.'

'Do you want white or brown bread with that?'

'Whatever.'

He felt her staring at him. And then she scribbled a note, tucked her pad carefully into her waistband and walked away. And he sat and stared at the newspaper on the Formica table. Over the past seventy-two hours he might have felt like the whole world had gone topsy-turvy, but that had been a mere taster for what had been about to come.

*

'I'm with a client.'

'This won't take a minute.' He took a breath. 'I'm not going to be at Dad's lunch.'

A short, ominous silence

'Please tell me I'm hallucinating through my ears.'

'I can't. Something's come up.'

'Something.'

'I'll explain later.'

'No. You wait. Hold on.'

He heard the muffled sound of a hand over a phone. Possibly a clenched fist. 'Sandra. I need to take this outside. Back in a . . .' Footsteps. And then, as if someone had turned the volume up to full blast: 'Really? Are you fucking kidding me? Really?'

Ed stared at the booth across the restaurant. An old couple sat side by side, saying nothing, eating their fish and chips with methodical accuracy. He had thought this would be a good time to do it. How could it have been any worse?

'I'm sorry.'

'I can't believe I'm hearing this. I can't believe it. It's tomorrow, Ed. Do you have any idea how hard Mum's worked to pull it together? Deirdre, Simon, the Grahams, that couple from down the road they're always going on about? They're all coming. They're coming because Mum and Dad want to show you off. Do you have any idea how much they're looking forward to seeing you? Dad sat down last week and worked out how long it had been since they last saw you. December, Ed. That's four months. Four months in which he's got more

305

and more sick and you have fucking well failed to do anything useful other than send him some stupid fucking magazines.'

'He said he liked the *New Yorker*. I thought it gave him something to do.'

'He can barely fucking see, Ed. As you'd know if you'd bothered to come up. He likes bloody magazines if there's someone to read them to him. And Mum gets so bored reading those long pieces that her brain actually starts to seep through her ears.'

On and on she went. It was like having a hairdryer turned on full strength in his ear.

'Mum is so freaking desperate to see you. She's actually cooked your favourite food rather than Dad's for their anniversary lunch. That's how much she wants to see you. And now, twenty-four hours before the actual thing, you just announce that you can't come? Just like that? No explanation? What the hell is this? I can't believe you. I defended you to Auntie Sheila when she said that that job was making you self-important, when she said you were getting too grand for your own family. Now I'm beginning to wonder whether she was right.'

His ears actually grew warm. He sat there, closed his eyes. When he opened them, it was twenty to two. The Olympiad would now be more than three-quarters through. He thought of Tanzie in that university hall, her head bent over her papers, the floor around her littered with redundant spectacles. He hoped for her sake that, faced with a page full of figures, she would relax and do the thing she was so plainly made to do. He

306

thought of Nicky, sloping around outside, perhaps trying to find somewhere for a sneaky smoke.

He thought of Jess, seated on a holdall, the dog at her side, her hands clasped together on her knees as if in prayer, convinced that if she wished hard enough, good things would finally happen.

'You are a bloody disgrace for a human being, Ed. Really.' His sister's voice was choked by tears.

'I know.'

'Oh, and don't think I'm going to tell them. I'm not doing your damned dirty work for you.'

'Gem. Please – there is a reason –'

'Don't even think about it. You want to break their hearts, then you do it. I'm done here, Ed. I can't believe you're my brother.'

Ed swallowed hard as she put down the phone. And then he let out a long slow, shuddering breath. What difference? It was only half of what they would all say if they knew the truth.

This way he could just be an uncaring, too-successful son. Too busy to see his family. Better than an utter failure. An embarrassment. A man who broke his father's heart.

It was there, in the half-empty restaurant, seated on a red leatherette banquette and facing a slowly congealing breakfast he didn't want that Ed finally understood how much he missed his father. He would have given anything just to see that reassuring nod, to watch that somehow oddly reluctant smile break over his face. He hadn't missed his home for the fifteen years since he had left it, yet suddenly he felt so homesick that it over-whelmed him. He sat in the restaurant staring out of the faintly greasy window at the cars whizzing past on the motorway and something he couldn't quite identify broke over him like the rolling of a vast wave. For the first time in his adult life – despite the divorce, the inves-tigation, the thing with Deanna Lewis – Ed Nicholls found he was fighting back tears.

He sat and pressed his hands into his eyes and tight-ened his jaw until he could think about nothing other than the feeling of his back teeth pressing against each other.

'Is everything okay?'

The young waitress's eyes were vaguely wary, as if she were trying to assess whether this man was going to be trouble.

'Fine,' he said. He had meant to sound reassuring, but his voice cracked on the word. And then, when she didn't seem convinced: 'Migraine.'

Her face relaxed immediately. 'Oh. Migraine. Sympa-thies. They're buggers. You got something for it?'

Ed shook his head, not trusting himself to speak.

'I knew there was something wrong.' She stood in front of him for a moment. 'Hold on.' She walked over to the counter, one hand reaching up to the back of her head, where her hair was pinned into an elaborate twist. She leant over, fumbling towards something he couldn't see, then walked back slowly. She glanced behind her, then dropped two pills in a foil casing on his table.

'I'm not meant to give customers pills, obviously, but

308

these are great. Only thing that works for mine. Don't drink any more coffee, though – it'll make it worse. I'll get you some water.'

He blinked at her, then down at the pills.

'It's okay. They're nothing dodgy. Just Migra-gone.'

'That's very kind of you.'

'They take about twenty minutes. But then – oh! Relief!' Her smile wrinkled her nose. Kind eyes, under all the mascara, he saw now. A sweet, open face. A face whose emotions had not yet been battered by experience.

She took away his coffee mug, as if to protect him from himself. Ed found himself thinking about Jess. Good things happen. Sometimes when you least expect them.

'Thank you,' he said quietly.

'You're welcome.'

And then his phone rang. The sound echoed in the roadside café and he gazed down at the screen as he stemmed the sound. Not a number he recognized.

'Mr Nicholls?'

'Yes?'

'It's Nicky. Nicky Thomas. Um. I'm really sorry to bother you. But we need your help.'

21.

NICKY

It had been obvious to Nicky that this was a bad idea from the moment they had pulled into the car park. Every other kid at that place – apart from maybe one or two at the most – was a boy. Every single one was at least two years older than Tanze. Most looked like they were not unfamiliar with the Asperger's scale. They wore wool blazers, bad haircuts, braces, the overly scruffy shirts of the properly middle class. Their parents drove Volvos.

The Thomas family were Aldi to their Waitrose, generic ketchup to their pesto. Tanzie, in her pink trousers and denim jacket with the sequins and felt flowers that Jess had sewn on, was as out of place as if she had been dropped there from outer space.

Nicky knew she was uncomfortable, even before Norman had broken her glasses. She had grown quieter and quieter in the car, locked in her own little world of nerves and car-sickness. He had tried to nudge her out of it – this was actually an act of epic selflessness as she smelt pretty bad – but by the time they had hit Aberdeen she had retreated so far inside herself that she was unreachable. Jess was so focused on getting there that she couldn't see it. She was all tied up with Mr Nicholls, the glasses and the sick bags. She hadn't considered for a minute that kids from private schools could be just as mean as kids from McArthur's.

Jess had been at the desk registering Tanzie and collecting her name tag and paperwork. Nicky had been checking out Mr Nicholls's phone, so he hadn't really paid any attention to the two boys who went and stood next to Tanzie, as she peered up at the desk plan at the entrance to the hall. He couldn't hear them because he had his ear-buds in, and he was listening to Depeche Mode without really noticing anything at all. Until he caught sight of Tanzie's crestfallen face. And he pulled an ear-bud from one ear.

The boy with the braces was staring at her, a slow up and down. 'You are at the right place? You know that the Justin Bieber fan convention is down the road?'

The skinnier boy laughed.

Tanzie looked at them with round eyes.

'Have you been to an Olympiad before?'

'No,' she said.

'Quel surprise. I can't say many Olympians bring furry pencil cases. Have you got your furry pencil case, James?'

'I think I forgot mine. Oh dear.'

'My mum made it for me,' Tanzie said stiffly.

'Your mum made it for you.' They looked at each other. 'Is it your lucky pencil case?'

'Do you know anything about string theory?'

'I think she's more likely to know about stink theory. Or . . . Hey, James, can you smell something unpleasant? Like vomit? Do you think someone's a bit nervous?'

Tanzie ducked her head and bolted past them into the loos.

'That's the Gents!' they cried, and fell about laughing.

As the boys made to walk into the main hall Nicky stepped forward and put his hand on the back of Braces' neck. 'Hey, kid. HEY.'

The boy spun round. His eyes widened. Nicky moved in, so that his voice was a low whisper. He was suddenly glad that he had a weird yellow tinge to his skin and a scar on the side of his face. 'Dude. A word. You ever speak to my sister like that again – anyone's sister – and I will personally come back here and tie your legs into a complex equation. You got that?'

He nodded, his mouth open.

Nicky gave him his best Fisher Psycho Stare. Long enough for the boy to do one of those massive Adam's-apple-bobbing gulps. 'Not nice being nervous, is it?'

The boy shook his head.

Nicky patted him on the shoulder. 'Good. Glad we're straight. Go do your sums.' He turned and began to walk towards the loos.

One of the teachers stepped in front of him then, one hand raised, his face questioning. 'Excuse me? Did I just see you . . .'

'. . . wishing him luck? Yes. Great kid. Great kid.' Nicky shook his head, as if in admiration, then headed for the Gents to fetch Tanzie.

*

When Jess and Tanzie emerged from the Ladies, Tanzie's top was damp where Jess had scrubbed at it with soap and water, her face blotchy and pale.

'You don't want to pay any attention to a little squit like that, Tanze,' Nicky said, climbing to his feet. 'He was just trying to put you off.'

'Which one was it?' Jess's expression was flinty. 'Tell me, Nicky.'

Yeah. Because Jess going in all guns blazing was going to be exactly the start to the competition that Tanzie needed. 'I . . . um . . . don't think I could recognize him. Anyway, I sorted it.'

He kind of liked the words. I sorted it.

'But I can't see, Mum. What am I going to do if I can't see?'

'Mr Nicholls is getting you some glasses. Don't worry.'

'But what if he doesn't? What if he doesn't even come back?'

I wouldn't have done, Nicky thought, if I were him. They had totalled his nice car. And he looked about ten years older than when they had set off.

'He'll come back,' Jess said.

'Mrs Thomas. We need to start. Your daughter has thirty seconds to take her seat.'

'Look, is there any way we can delay the start by a few minutes? We really, really need to get her some glasses. She can't see without them.'

'No, madam. If she's not in her place in thirty seconds I'm afraid we'll have to start without her.'

'Then can I go in? I could read her the questions?'

'But I can't write without my glasses.'

'Then I'll write for you.'

'Mum . . .'

Jess knew she was beaten. She looked over at Nicky and gave a vague shake of her head that said, I don't know what to do.

Nicky crouched beside her. 'You can do this, Tanze. You can. You can do this stuff standing on your head. Just hold the paper really, really close to your eyes and take your time.'

She was staring blindly into the hall. Beyond the door the students were shuffling into place, dragging chairs under desks, arranging pencils in front of them.

'And as soon as Mr Nicholls gets here we'll bring the glasses in to you.'

'Really. Just go in and do your best and we'll be waiting here. Norman will just be on the other side of the wall. We all will. And then we'll go and get some lunch. Nothing to stress about.'

The woman with the clipboard walked over. 'Are you going to take part in the competition, Costanza?'

'Her name's Tanzie,' Nicky said. The woman didn't seem to hear. Tanzie nodded mutely and allowed herself to be led to a desk. She looked so damned little.

'You can do it, Tanzie!' His voice burst out of him suddenly, bouncing off the walls of the hall, so that the man at the back tutted. 'Back of the net, Titch!'

'Oh, for goodness' sake,' someone muttered.

'Back of the net!' Nicky yelled again, so that Jess looked at him in shock.

And then a bell rang, the door closed in front of them with a solid thunk, and it was just Nicky and Jess on the other side, with a couple of hours to kill.

'Right,' said Jess, when she finally tore her gaze away from the door. She put her hands into her pockets, took them out again, straightened her hair and sighed. 'Right.'

'He will come,' said Nicky, who was suddenly not entirely sure he would.

'I know that.'

The silence that followed was long enough that they were forced to smile awkwardly at each other. The corridor emptied slowly, apart from one organizer who murmured to himself as he ran his pencil down a list of names.

'Probably stuck in traffic.'

'It was pretty bad.'

Nicky could picture Tanzie on the other side of the door, squinting at her papers, looking around for help that wouldn't come. Jess stared up at the ceiling, swore softly, then tied and retied her ponytail. He guessed she was doing the same.

And then there was the sound of a distant commotion and Mr Nicholls appeared, running down the corridor like a crazy man and holding aloft a plastic bag that looked as if it might be entirely full of pairs of glasses. And as he launched himself at the desk and started arguing with the organizers – the kind of argument that comes from someone who knows there is no way in the world he is going to lose – the relief Nicky felt was so overwhelming that he had to go outside, slump against the wall and drop his head to his knees until his breathing no longer threatened to turn into a huge, gulping sob.

It was weird saying goodbye to Mr Nicholls. They stood by his car in the drizzle and Jess was acting all oh-I-don't-care, even though she obviously did. And Nicky really wanted to thank him for the whole hacking thing, driving them all that way and just being, you know, weirdly decent, but then Mr Nicholls went and gave him his spare phone and he was so choked that all that came out was this weird strangulated 'Thanks.' And then that was it. And he and Jess were walking across the campus car park with Norman, and both of them were pretending they couldn't hear Mr Nicholls's car driving away.

They stopped by the corridor, and Jess stashed their bags in the cloakroom. Then she turned to Nicky and brushed non-existent fluff from his shoulder, and her voice was so brusque that for a moment he didn't notice her jaw was really really tight. 'Well,' she said, 'let's go and walk this dog, shall we?'

It was true that Nicky didn't talk much. It wasn't that he didn't have stuff to say. It was just that there was nobody he really wanted to say it to. Ever since he had gone to live with Dad and Jess, when he was eight, people had been trying to get him to talk about his 'feelings', like they were a big rucksack he could just drag around with him and open up for everyone to examine the contents. But half the time he didn't even know what he thought. He didn't have opinions about politics or the economy or what happened to him. He didn't even have an opinion about his birth mum. She was an addict. She liked drugs more than she liked him. What else was there to say?

Nicky went to the counselling for a bit, like they said. The woman seemed to want him to get mad about what had happened to him. Nicky had told her he wasn't angry because he understood that his mum couldn't look after him. It wasn't as if it was personal. If he had been any kid she would have dumped them just the same. She was just . . . sad. He had seen so little of her when he was small that he didn't even really feel like she was anything to do with him.

But the counsellor kept saying: 'You must let it out, Nicholas. It's not good for you to internalize what happened to you.' She gave him two little stuffed figures and wanted him to act out 'how your mother's abandonment made you feel'.

Nicky didn't like to tell her that it was the thought of having to sit in her office playing with dolls and being called Nicholas that made him feel destructive. He just wasn't a particularly angry person. Not with his real mum, not even with Jason Fisher, although he didn't expect anyone to understand. Fisher was just an idiot who didn't have the brainpower to do anything but hit out. Fisher knew on some deep level that he had nothing. That he was never going to be anything. He knew that he was a phoney, and that nobody liked him, not really. So he turned it all outwards, transferred his bad feelings to the nearest available person (See? The therapy had done something useful).

So when Jess said they should go for a walk, a little bit of Nicky was wary. He didn't want to get into some big conversation about his feelings. He didn't want to discuss any of it. He was all braced to deflect, and then she scratched her head a bit, and said, 'Is it just me, or does it feel a bit weird without Mr Nicholls?'

This was what they talked about:

The unexpected beauty of some of Aberdeen's buildings.

The dog.

Whether either of them had brought plastic bags for the dog.

Which of them was going to kick that thing under the parked car so that nobody trod in it.

The best way to clean the toes of your shoes on grass.

Whether it was actually possible to clean the toes of your shoes on grass.

Nicky's face, as in did it hurt. (Answer: no, not any more.)

Other bits of him, as in did they (no, no, and a bit, but it was improving.)

His jeans, as in why didn't he pull them up so that his pants weren't always showing?

Why his pants were actually his own business.

Whether they should tell Dad about the Rolls. Nicky told her she should pretend it had been nicked. What would he know? And it would serve him right. But Jess said she couldn't lie to him because that wouldn't be fair. And then she went quiet for a while.

Was he okay? Did he feel better for being away from

home? Was he worried about going home? This was where Nicky stopped talking and started shrugging. What was there to say?

This was what they didn't talk about:

Tanzie. She hung in the air between them the whole way around that university campus. Nicky could picture her, tongue wedged in the side of her mouth, head down, scribbling away in her own little world of numbers. He knew Jess was doing the same.

What it would be like if they actually went home with five thousand pounds.

If Tanzie went to that school and he left school before sixth form, whether Jess would want him to pick her up from St Anne's every day.

The takeaway that they would definitely get tonight in celebration. Possibly not a kebab.

That Jess was plainly freezing, even if she insisted she was fine. All the little hairs on her arms were standing bolt upright.

Mr Nicholls. Most notably, where Jess had actually slept the previous night. And why they had kept stealing looks at each other like a pair of teenagers all morning, even while they were grumping at each other. Nicky honestly thought she thought they were all stupid sometimes.

But it was kind of okay, the talking thing. He thought he might even do it more often.

They were waiting outside the doors when they finally opened at two o'clock. Tanzie walked out in the first batch, her furry pencil case clutched in front of her, and Jess held out her arms wide, all braced for celebration.

'So? How was it?'

She looked at them steadily.

'Did you muller them, Titch?' said Nicky, grinning.

And then, abruptly, Tanzie's face crumpled like it had done when she was little and fell over, and there was a three-second gap between whatever Bad Thing had just happened and a gigantic Bad Thing Wail coming out.

Jess grabbed her and pulled her close, maybe to re-assure her, maybe to hide the shock on her face, and Nicky put his arm around her on the other side, and Norman sat there on her feet, and as the other kids filed past, some of them chatting, a few silent as they looked at Tanzie, she told them what had happened, through muffled sobs.

'I lost the whole first half-hour. And I didn't under-stand some of their accents. And I couldn't see properly. And I got really nervous and I kept staring at my paper and then by the time I got the glasses it took me ages to find a pair that fitted me and then I couldn't even under-stand the first question.'

Jess scanned the corridor for the organizers. 'I'll talk to them. I'll explain what happened. I mean, you couldn't see. That's got to count for something. Maybe we could get them to adjust the score to take it into account.'

'No. I don't want you talking to them. I didn't under-stand the first question, even when I got the right glasses. I couldn't make it work the way they said it should work.'

'But maybe –'

'I messed it up,' Tanzie wailed. 'I don't want to go over it. I just want to go.'

'You didn't mess anything up, sweetheart. Really. You did your best. That's all that matters.' Jess kept stroking her back, as if that could make it all better.

'But it's not, is it? Because I can't go to St Anne's without the money.'

'Well, there must be . . . Don't worry, Tanze. I'll work something out.'

It was her least convincing smile ever. And Tanzie wasn't stupid. She cried like someone heartbroken.

Nicky had honestly never seen her like that. It actually made him want to cry a bit too. 'Let's go home,' he said, when it became unbearable.

But that made Tanzie cry harder.

Jess looked up at him, her face bleached and completely lost, and it was like she was asking him, Nicky, what shall I do? And the fact that just for once even Jess didn't know made him feel like something had gone really wrong with the world. And then he thought: I really, really wish Jess hadn't confiscated my stash. He didn't think he had ever needed a smoke more in his life.

They waited there in the hallway as the other competitors fell into groups or shared sandwiches or retreated into cars with their parents and just for once Nicky realized he did feel angry. He was angry with the stupid boys who had put his little sister off her stroke. He was angry with the stupid maths competition and its rules that wouldn't bend a tiny bit for a little girl who couldn't see. He was angry that they had come all this way across an entire country just to fail again. Like there was nothing this family could do that turned out right. Nothing at all.

When the hallway had emptied finally Jess reached into her back pocket and wrenched out a small rectangular card. She thrust it at him. 'Call Mr Nicholls.'

'But he's halfway home by now. And what can he do?'

Jess bit her lip. She half turned away from him, then back again. 'He can take us to Marty.'

Nicky stared at her.

'Please. I know it's awkward, but I can't think what else to do. Tanzie needs something to help her up again, Nicky. She needs to see her dad.'

He was back within half an hour. He had just been down the road, he said, having a bite to eat. Nicky thought afterwards that if he had been thinking more clearly he might have wondered why Ed hadn't gone very far, and why it had taken him so long to get a snack down him. But he was too busy arguing with Jess.

'I know you don't want to see your dad but –'

'I'm not going.'

'Tanzie needs this.' Her face had that determined set, where you knew she was making out that she was taking your feelings into account but actually she was just going to make you do what she wanted you to do.

'This is really not going to make anything better.'

'For you, maybe. Look, Nicky, I know you have very mixed feelings about your dad right now, and I don't blame you. I know it's been a very confusing time –'

'I'm not confused.'

'Tanzie is at rock bottom. She needs something to give her a lift. And Marty is not that far away.' She put out a hand and touched his arm. 'Look, if you really don't want to see him when we get there you can just stay in the car, okay? ... I'm sorry,' she said, when he didn't say anything. 'To be honest, I'm not exactly desperate to see him either. But we do have to do this.'

What could he tell her? What could he tell her that she would believe? And he supposed there was five per cent of him that still wondered if he was the one who was wrong.

Jess turned to Mr Nicholls, who had been leaning against his car watching silently. 'Please. Will you give us a lift to Marty's? His mum's, I mean. I'm sorry. I know you've probably had enough of us and we've been a complete pain, but ... but I haven't got anyone else to ask. Tanzie ... she needs her dad. Whatever I – we – think of him, she needs to see her dad. It's only a couple of hours from here.'

He looked at her.

'Okay, maybe more if we have to go slowly. But please – I need to turn this round. I really need to turn this round.'

Mr Nicholls stepped to one side and opened the passenger door. He stooped a little so that he could smile at Tanzie. 'Let's go.'

They all looked relieved. But it was a bad idea. A really bad idea. If only they'd asked him about the wallpaper Nicky could have told them why.

22.

JESS

The last time Jess had seen Maria Costanza was the day she had delivered Marty to her in Liam's brother's van. Marty had spent the last hundred miles to Glasgow asleep under a duvet, and as Jess stood in her immaculate front room and tried to explain her son's breakdown she had looked at her as if Jess had personally tried to kill him.

Maria Costanza had never liked her. She'd thought her son deserved better than a sixteen-year-old schoolgirl with a home-dye and glittery nails, and nothing Jess had ever done since had changed her fundamental low opinion of her. She thought what Jess did with the house was peculiar. She thought the fact that Jess made most of the children's clothes herself was wilfully eccentric. It never occurred to her to ask why she made their clothes, or why they couldn't afford to pay someone else to decorate. Or why when the overflow blocked it was Jess who ended up under the sink wrestling with the U-bend.

She had tried. She really had. She was polite, and didn't swear, or pick at bits of herself in public. She was faithful to Marty. She produced the world's most amazing baby, and kept her clean, fed and cheerful. It took

Jess about five years to grasp that it wasn't her. Maria Costanza was just one of life's lemon-suckers. Jess wasn't sure she had ever seen a smile break spontaneously over her face, unless it was to report some piece of news about one of her friends or neighbours: a slashed tyre or a terminal illness, maybe.

She had tried to ring her twice, on Mr Nicholls's phone, but got no answer.

'Granny's probably still at work,' she told Tanzie, ringing off. 'Or perhaps they've gone to see the new baby.'

'You still want me to head over there?' Mr Nicholls glanced at her.

'Please. I'm sure they'll be home by the time we get there. She never goes out in the evening.'

Nicky's eyes met hers in the mirror and slid away. Jess didn't blame him for being negative. If Maria Costanza's reaction to Tanzie had been lukewarm, her discovery that she had a grandson she hadn't even known about was met with the same enthusiasm as if they had announced a family case of scabies. Jess couldn't tell if she was offended that he had existed for so long without her knowledge, or whether her inability to explain him without referring to (a) illegitimacy and (b) that her son had been involved with an addict meant that she just found it easier to ignore him altogether. It was one of the reasons why, when Marty had announced, six months after he'd left, that he was feeling a bit better so they should all come up and stay, it had been quite easy to say no on the grounds of cost.

'You looking forward to seeing Daddy, Tanze?' Jess

turned in her seat. Tanzie was leaning against Norman, her face solemn and exhausted. Her eyes slid to Jess's and she gave the smallest of nods.

'It will be great to see him. And Granny,' Jess said brightly. 'I'm not sure why we didn't think of it sooner.'

It was as she went to ring Marty that she realized he'd been on voicemail for as long as she could remember. They only ever spoke via Skype or on his mobile, which was rarely switched on. That, she thought, was going to change. A lot of things were going to change.

They drove in silence. Tanzie dozed, resting against the dog. Nicky sat and watched the darkening sky in silence. She didn't feel like putting music on. She didn't dare let the children see how she felt about what had happened in Aberdeen. She couldn't let herself think about it. One thing at a time, she told herself. Just get Tanzie back on track. And then I'll work out what to do next.

'You okay?'

'Fine.' She could see he didn't believe her. 'She'll feel better once she sees her dad. I know it.'

'She could always do another Olympiad, next year. She'll know what to expect then.'

Jess tried to smile. 'Mr Nicholls. That sounds suspiciously like optimism.'

He turned to her and his eyes were full of sympathy.

She was relieved to be back in his car. She had begun to feel oddly safe there, like nothing really bad could happen while they were all inside it. She tried to imagine the reception they would get from Marty's mother, especially once the older woman discovered they were all going to have to stay with her overnight. Jess pictured being in the front room of Costanza's little house, trying to explain the events that had led them there. She pictured Marty's face when she told him about the Rolls-Royce. She saw them all waiting at a bus stop tomorrow, the first stage in an interminable journey home. She wondered briefly whether she could ask Mr Nicholls to mind Norman till they got back. Thinking about this made her remember how much this whole escapade had cost, and she pushed the thought away. One thing at a time.

And then she must have nodded off, because someone had hold of her arm.

'Jess?'

'Nngh?'

'Jess? I think we're here. That satnav says this is her address. Does this look right to you?'

She pushed herself upright, un-cricking her neck. The windows of the neat, white terraced house gazed unblinking back at her. Her stomach lurched reflexively.

'What's the time?'

'Just before seven.' He waited while she rubbed her eyes. 'Well, the lights are on,' he said. 'I'm guessing they're home.'

He turned in his seat as she pushed herself upright. 'Hey, kids, we're here. Time to see your dad.'

Tanzie's hand gripped Jess's tightly as they walked up the path. Nicky had refused to get out of the car, saying he'd wait with Mr Nicholls. Jess decided she'd let Tanzie go in before she went back and tried to reason with him.

'Are you excited?'

Tanzie nodded, her little face suddenly hopeful and, just briefly, Jess sensed that she had done the right thing. They would salvage something out of this trip, if it killed her. Whatever issues she and Marty had could be sorted out later. They paused to gaze at the peach-coloured rosebush that sat halfway along the path, placed, Jess always thought, to snag the unwary. Two new small barrels sat by the front steps, filled with a purple flower she didn't recognize. She straightened her jacket, smoothed the hair from Tanzie's face, leant forward and wiped a bit of something from the corner of her mouth, and then she rang the doorbell.

Maria Costanza saw Tanzie first. She gazed at her, and then up at Jess, and several expressions, none quite identifiable, flickered rapidly across her face.

Jess answered them with her cheeriest smile. 'Hey, Maria. We, um, were in the area, and I just thought we couldn't pass without seeing Marty. And you.'

Maria Costanza stared at her.

'We did try to call,' Jess continued, her voice a singsong, and odd to her ears. 'Quite a few times. I would have left a message but . . .'

'Hi, Granny.' Tanzie ran forwards and threw herself at her grandmother's waist. Maria Costanza's hand went down and she let it rest limply against Tanzie's back. She had dyed her hair a shade too dark, Jess noted absently. Maria Costanza stayed like that for a moment, then glanced at the car, where Nicky stared out impassively from the rear window.

God, would it kill you to express some enthusiasm, just once? Jess thought. 'Nicky will be over in a minute,' she said, keeping the smile firmly on her face. 'He's just woken up. I'm . . . giving him a moment.'

They stood and faced each other, waiting.

'So . . .' Jess said, when she didn't speak, and peered past the older woman down the hall.

'He – he's not here,' Maria Costanza said.

'Is he at work?' She had sounded more eager than she had intended. 'I mean, it's lovely if he's feeling . . . well enough to work.'

'He's not here, Jessica.'

'Is he ill?' Oh, Christ, she thought. Something's happened. And then she saw it. An emotion she was not sure she'd ever seen on Maria Costanza's features. Embarrassment.

Jess watched her attempt to cover it. She glanced behind her, folded her arms.

'So where is he?'

'You . . . I think you should talk to him.' Maria Costanza brought a hand to her mouth, as if to prevent herself saying more, then extricated herself gently from her grandchild. 'Hold on. I'll get you his address.'

'His address?'

She left Tanzie and Jess standing on the doorstep, and disappeared down the little hallway, half closing the door behind her. Tanzie looked up quizzically. Jess smiled reassuringly. It wasn't quite as easy as it had been.

The door opened again. She handed over a piece of paper. 'It will take you maybe one hour, maybe an hour and a half, depending on the traffic.' Jess registered her stiff features, then looked past her to the little hallway, where nothing had changed in the fifteen years she had known her. Nothing at all. And somewhere in the back of Jess's head a little bell began to chime.

'Right,' she said, and she wasn't smiling any more.

Maria Costanza couldn't hold her gaze. She stooped then, and put her palm against Tanzie's cheek. 'You come back and stay with your nonna soon, yes?' She looked up at Jess. 'You bring her back? It's been a long time.'

That look of mute appeal, of acknowledgement in her duplicity, was more unnerving than almost anything she had ever done in the years of their relationship.

Jess swept Tanzie towards the car.

Mr Nicholls looked up. He didn't say anything.

'Here.' Jess handed him the paper. 'We need to go here.' Wordlessly he began to program the postcode into the satnav. Her heart was thumping.

She looked in the rear-view mirror. 'You knew,' she said, when Tanzie finally put her earphones in.

Nicky pulled at his fringe, gazing out at his grand-mother's house. 'It was the last few times we've spoken to him on Skype. Granny would never have had that wallpaper.'

She didn't ask him where Marty was. She thought she probably had an idea, even then.

They drove the hour in silence. Jess wanted to be re-assuring, but she couldn't speak. A million possibilities ran through her head. Occasionally she looked into the mirror, watching Nicky. His face was closed, turned resolutely towards the roadside. She began slowly to reconsider his reluctance to come here, even to speak to his father these last few months, casting it in a new light.

They drove through the dusky countryside to the outskirts of a new town and an estate where the houses were box fresh, laid out in careful, sweeping curves, and new cars gleamed outside like statements of intent. Mr Nicholls pulled up in Castle Court, where four cherry trees stood like sentinels along the narrow pavement upon which she suspected nobody ever walked. The house was newly built; its Regency-style windows gleamed, its slate roof shone in the drizzle.

She stared at it out of the window.

'You okay?' They were the only two words Mr Nicholls had spoken the entire journey.

'You wait here a minute, kids,' Jess said, and climbed out.

She walked up to the front door, double-checked the address on the piece of paper, then rapped on the brass knocker. Inside she could hear the sound of a television, saw the vague shadow of someone moving under bright light.

She knocked again. She barely felt the rain.

Footsteps in the hallway. The door opened and a blonde woman stood in front of her. She wore a dark red wool dress and court shoes, and her hair was cut in one of those styles that women wear when they work in retail or banking but don't want to look like they've entirely given up on the idea of being a rock chick.

'Is Marty there?' Jess said. The woman made as if to speak, then looked Jess up and down, at her flip-flops, at her crumpled white trousers, and in the several seconds that followed, the faint hardening of her expression, Jess could see she knew. She knew about her.

'Wait there,' she said.

The door half closed, and Jess heard her shout down the narrow corridor. 'Mart? Mart?'

Mart.

She heard his voice, muffled, laughing, saying something about television, and then her voice dropped. She saw their shadows behind the frosted-glass panels. And then the door opened and he stood there.

Marty had grown his hair. He had a long, floppy fringe, swept carefully to one side like a teenager. He wore jeans she didn't recognize, in deep indigo, and he had lost weight. He looked like someone she didn't know. And he had gone quite, quite pale. 'Jess.'

She couldn't speak.

They stared at each other. He swallowed. 'I was going to tell you.'

Right up to that point a part of her had refused to believe it could be true. Right up to that point she had thought there must be some huge mistake, that Marty was staying with a friend or he was ill again and Maria Costanza, with her misplaced pride, just couldn't face admitting it. But there was no mistaking what was right in front of her.

It took her several seconds to find her voice. 'This? This is . . . where you've been living?'

She stumbled backwards, now taking in the immaculate front garden, the new three-piece suite, just visible through the window. Her hip bumped against a car on the drive and she put out her hand, to support herself, pulling it away as if burnt when she realized what it was. 'All this time? We've been scratching around for the last two years just to stay warm and fed and you're here with an executive home and a – a brand-new Toyota?'

Marty glanced awkwardly behind him. 'We need to talk, Jess.'

And then she saw the wallpaper in his dining room. The thick stripe. And it all fell into place. His insistence that they only speak at set times. The lack of a landline phone number. Maria Costanza's assurance that he was sleeping whenever she rang outside the usual time. Her determination to get Jess off the telephone as quickly as possible.

'We need to talk?' Jess was half laughing now. 'Yes, let's talk, Marty. How about I talk? For two years I've not made a single demand on you – not for money or time or childcare or help of any kind. Because I thought you were ill. I thought you were depressed. I thought you were living with your MOTHER.'

'I was living with Mum.'

'Till when?'

He compressed his lips.

'Till when, Marty?' Her voice was shrill.

'Fifteen months.'

'You were with your mum fifteen months?'

He looked at his feet.

'You've been here fifteen months? You've been here more than a year?'

'I wanted to tell you. But I knew that you'd –'

'What – kick off? Because you're here living a life of luxury while your wife and kids are back at home scrabbling around in the crap you left behind?'

'Jess . . .'

She was briefly silenced as the door opened abruptly. A little girl appeared behind him, her hair a virgin sheet of blonde, wearing a Hollister sweatshirt and Converse trainers. She tugged at his sleeve. 'It's your programme, Marty,' she began, and then she saw Jess and stopped.

'Go to your mum, babe,' he said quietly, his gaze flicking sideways. He put his hand gently on her shoulder. 'I'll be through in a minute.'

She looked at Jess warily, perhaps picking up on some strange vibration in the air. She was the same age as Tanzie. 'Go on.' He pulled the door behind him.

And that was when Jess's heart actually broke.

'She . . . she has kids?'

He swallowed. 'Two.'

Her hands went to her face, and then her hair. She turned and walked blindly back down the path. She didn't actually know where she was going. 'Oh, God. Oh, God.'

'Jess – I never set out to –'

She spun round and flew at him. She wanted to batter him. She wanted to smash his stupid face and his expensive haircut. She wanted him to know the pain he had put his children through. She wanted him to pay. He ducked behind the car and, almost without knowing what she was doing, she found she was kicking at it, at its oversized wheels, its gleaming panels, the stupid bright white shiny stupid immaculate stupid car.

'You lied! You lied to all of us! And I was trying to protect you! I can't believe . . . I can't –' She kicked and felt the faint satisfaction as the metal gave, even as the pain shot up her foot. She kicked again and again, not caring, her fists raining blows on the window.

'Jess! The car! Are you fucking mad?'

She rained blows down on that car because she could not rain the blows on him. She hit with her hands and her feet, not caring, sobbing with fury, her rasping breath loud in her ears. And when he wrenched her off it, wedging himself between her and the panels, his grip tight on her arms, she felt a momentary flicker of fear that they were into some new realm of craziness now, that her life had spun utterly out of control, and then she looked into his eyes, his coward's eyes, and there was a loud buzzing in her head. She wanted to smash –

'Jess.'

Mr Nicholls's arm was around her waist, easing her backwards.

'Get off me!'

'The kids are watching. Come on now.' A hand on her arm.

She couldn't breathe. A moan rose up through her whole body. She allowed herself to be pulled a few steps back. Marty was shouting something she couldn't hear through the din in her head.

'Come . . . come away.'

The kids. She looked at the car, and saw Tanzie's face, wide-eyed with shock, Nicky a motionless black silhouette behind her. She looked to the other side, at the executive house where two small, pale faces watched from the living room, their mother behind them. When she saw Jess looking she lowered the blind.

'You're mad,' yelled Marty, staring at the dented panels of the car. 'Completely effing mad.'

She had begun to shake. Mr Nicholls put his arms around her, and steered her into the car. 'Get in. Sit down,' he said, closing the door once she was inside. Marty was walking slowly down the pathway towards them, his old swagger suddenly visible now that she was the one in the wrong. She thought he was about to pick a fight, but when he was about fifteen feet away he peered into the car, stooping slightly as if to check, and then she heard the rear door open behind her and Tanzie was out and running towards him.

'Daddy!' she cried, and he swept her up in his arms and then Jess no longer knew what she felt about anything.

She wasn't sure how long she sat there, staring at the footwell. She couldn't think. She couldn't feel. She heard murmuring voices on the pathway, and at one point, Nicky reached forward and touched her shoulder lightly. 'I'm sorry,' he said, his voice cracking.

She reached behind and gripped his hand fiercely. 'Not. Your. Fault,' she whispered.

The door opened finally and Mr Nicholls put his head in. His face was wet, and rain dripped from his collar. 'Okay. Tanzie's going to stay here for a couple of hours.'

She stared at him, suddenly alert. 'Oh, no,' she began. 'He doesn't get to have her. Not after what he's —'

'This isn't about you and him, Jess.'

Jess turned towards the house. The front door was slightly ajar. Tanzie was already inside. 'But she can't stay there. Not with them . . .'

He climbed into the driver's seat, then he reached across and took her hand. His was ice cold and damp. 'Tanzie needs to see her dad.'

He spoke to her like someone explaining something to a difficult child. 'She's had a bad day and she asked if she could spend some time with him. And, Jess, if this really is his life now, then surely she has to be part of it.'

'But it's not —'

'Fair. I know.'

They sat there, the three of them, staring at the brightly lit little house. Her daughter was in there. With Marty's new family. It was as if someone had reached in, gripped her heart and ripped it out through her ribs.

She couldn't take her eyes from the window. 'What if she changes her mind? She'll be all alone. And we don't know them. I don't know this woman. She could be . . .'

'She's with her dad. She'll be okay.'

She stared at Mr Nicholls. His face was sympathetic. But his voice was oddly firm. 'Why are you on his side?' she whispered.

'I'm not on his side.' His fingers closed around hers.

'Look, we'll all go find somewhere to eat. We'll be back in a couple of hours. We stay close by and we can come back for her any time if she needs us.'

'No. I'll stay,' said a voice from behind. 'I'll stay with her. So that she's not by herself.'

Jess turned. Nicky was gazing out of the window. 'Are you sure?'

'I'll be fine.' His face was a blank. 'Anyway. I sort of want to hear what he says.'

Mr Nicholls saw Nicky to the front door. She watched her stepson, his long, lanky legs in his skinny black jeans, his diffident, awkward way of standing as the door opened to let him in. The blonde woman tried to smile at him. She peered surreptitiously past him at the car. It was possible, Jess observed distantly, that she was actually frightened of her. The door closed behind them. Jess shut her eyes, not wanting to see them there, in that house. Not wanting to imagine what was going on behind that door.

And then Mr Nicholls was in the car, bringing with him a blast of cold air. 'Come on,' he said. 'It's okay. We'll be back before you know it.'

They sat in a roadside café. She couldn't eat. She drank coffee, no longer caring if it would leave her awake. Mr Nicholls bought a sandwich and just sat there, opposite her. She wasn't sure he knew what to say. Two hours, she kept telling herself. Two hours and then I can have them back. She just wanted to be home then. She wanted to be back in the car with her children, away from here. Away from Marty and his lies and his new girlfriend and pretend family. She didn't care about anything else. She watched the clock hands edge round and let her coffee cool. Every minute felt like infinity.

And then, ten minutes before they were due to leave, the phone rang. Jess snatched it up. A number she didn't recognize. Marty's voice. 'Can you leave them with me tonight?'

It knocked the breath clean out of her.

'Oh, no,' she said, when she could find her voice. 'You don't get to keep them, just like that.'

'I'm just . . . trying to explain it all to them.'

'Well, good luck with that. Because I'm damned if I understand it.' Her voice lifted in the little café. She saw the people at the nearby tables turn their heads.

'I couldn't tell you, Jess, okay? Because I knew you'd react like you did.'

'Oh, so it's my fault. Of course it is!'

'We were over. You knew it as well as I did.'

She was standing. She wasn't aware of having got to her feet. Mr Nicholls, for some reason, stood too. 'I couldn't give a flying fuck about you and me, okay? But we've been living on the breadline since you left, and now I find out you're living with someone else, with your brand-new sofa and your shiny car, supporting her kids. Even as you said you couldn't lift a finger for ours. Yes, it's just possible I'm going to react badly to that one, Marty.'

'It's not my money I'm living on. It's Linzie's money. I can't use her money to pay for your kids.'

'My kids? *My* kids?' She was out from behind the table now, walking blindly towards the door. She was dimly aware of Mr Nicholls, summoning the waitress.

'Look,' said Marty, 'Tanzie really wants to stay over. She's obviously upset about this maths thing. She asked me to ask you. Please.'

Jess couldn't speak. She just stood in the cold car park, her eyes closed, her knuckles white around the phone.

'Plus I really want to sort things out with Nicky.'

'You are . . . unbelievable.'

'Just – just let me sort things out with the kids, please? You and I, we can talk afterwards. But just tonight, while they're here. I've missed them, Jess. I know, I know it's all my fault. I know I've been rubbish. But I'm actually glad it's all out there. I'm glad you know what's going on. And I just . . . I want to move forward now.'

She stared ahead of her at the car park. In the distance a police car's blue lights flashed. Her foot had begun to throb. She stood in the car park and put her hand against her face and finally she said, 'Put Tanzie on.'

There was a short silence, the sound of a door. Jess took a deep breath.

'Mum?'

'Tanze? Sweetheart? Are you okay?'

'I'm fine, Mum. They've got terrapins. One has a gammy leg. It's called Mike. Can we get a terrapin?'

'We'll talk about it.' She could hear a saucepan clash in the background, the sound of a tap running. 'Um, you really want to spend the night? You don't have to, you know. You just ... you do whatever makes you feel happy.'

'I would quite like to stay. Suzie's nice. She's going to lend me her *High School Musical* pyjamas.'

'Suzie?'

'Linzie's daughter. It's going to be like a sleepover. And she has those beads where you make a picture and stick it together with an iron.'

'Right.'

There was a brief silence. Jess could hear muffled talking in the background.

'So what time are you picking me up tomorrow?'

She swallowed, and tried to keep her voice level. 'After breakfast. Nine o'clock. And if you change your mind, you just call me, okay? Any time. And I'll pick you up straight away. Even if it's the very middle of the night. It doesn't matter.'

'I know.'

'I'll come any time. I love you, sweetie. Any time you want to call.'

'Okay.'

'Will you ... will you put Nicky on?'

'Love you. 'Bye.'

Nicky's voice was unreadable. 'I've told him I'll stay,' he said. 'But only to keep an eye on Tanze.'

'Okay. I'll make sure we're somewhere close by. Is she ... the woman ... is she okay? I mean, will you all be okay?'

'Linzie. She's fine.'

'And you – you're all right with this? He's not ...'

'I'm fine.'

There was a long silence.

'Jess?'

'Yes?'

'Are you okay?'

Her face crumpled then. She took a silent breath, put her hand up and wiped at the tears that were running silently down her cheeks. She hadn't known there were that many tears in her. She didn't answer Nicky until she could be sure they hadn't soaked her voice too. 'I'm fine, lovey. You have a good time and don't worry about me. I'll see you both in the morning.'

Mr Nicholls was behind her. He took his phone from her in silence, his eyes not leaving her face. 'I've found us somewhere to sleep where they'll let us take the dog.'

'Is there a bar?' Jess asked, wiping at her eyes with the back of her hand.

'What?'

'I need to get drunk, Ed. Really, really drunk.' He held out an arm and she took it. 'Plus I think I may have broken my toe.'

23.

ED

So, once upon a time Ed met a girl who was the most optimistic person he had ever known. A girl who wore flip-flops in the hope of spring. She seemed to bounce through life like Tigger; the things that would have felled most people didn't seem to touch her. Or if she did fall, she bounced right back. She fell again, plastered on a smile, dusted herself down and kept going. He never could work out whether it was the single most heroic or the most idiotic thing he'd ever seen.

And then he stood on the kerb outside a four-bedroomed executive home somewhere near Carlisle and watched as that same girl saw everything she'd believed in stripped away, until nothing was left but a ghost who sat in his passenger seat gazing unseeing through the windscreen; the sound of her optimism draining away was audible. And something cracked open in his heart.

He had booked a holiday cabin on the side of a lake, twenty minutes from Marty's – or rather his girlfriend's – house. He couldn't find a hotel within a hundred miles that would take the dog, and the last receptionist he had spoken to, a jovial woman who called him 'duck' eight times, suggested he just go self-catering, and told him of a new place she knew, run by her friend's daughter-in-law. He'd had to pay for three days – their minimum stay – but he didn't care. Jess didn't ask. He wasn't sure she even noticed where they were.

They picked up the keys from Reception, he followed the path through the trees, they pulled up in front of the cabin and he unloaded Jess and the dog and saw them inside. She was limping badly by then. He remembered suddenly the ferocity with which she had kicked the car. In flip-flops.

'Have a long bath,' he said, flicking on all the lights and closing the curtains. It was too dark outside by now to see anything. 'Go on. Try and relax. I'll go and get us some food. And maybe an ice pack.'

She turned and nodded. The smile she raised in thanks was barely a smile at all.

The closest supermarket was a supermarket in name only: there were two baskets of tired vegetables, and shelves of long-life food with brand names he hadn't heard of, sitting, as they might well have done for months, under flickering strip lights. He bought a couple of ready meals, some bread, coffee, milk, frozen peas and painkillers for her foot. As an afterthought he bought a couple of bottles of wine.

He was standing at the checkout when his phone beeped. He wrestled it out of his pocket, wondering if it was Jess. And then he remembered that her phone had run out of credit two days previously.

Hello darling. So sorry you can't make tomorrow. We do hope to see you before too long. Love Mum. PS Dad sends his love. Bit poorly today.

'Twenty-two pounds eighty.'

The girl had said it twice before he registered.

'Oh. Sorry.' He fished around for his card, and held it out to her.

'Card machine's not working. There's a sign.'

Ed followed her gaze. 'Cash or cheque only,' it said, in laboriously outlined ballpoint letters. 'You're kidding me, right?'

'Why would I be kidding you?' She chewed, meditatively, at whatever was in her mouth.

'I'm not sure I've got enough cash on me,' Ed said.

She gazed at him impassively.

'You don't take cards?'

"S what the sign says.'

'Well . . . do you not have a manual card machine?'

'Most people round here pay cash,' she said. Her expression said it was obvious that he was not from around here.

'Okay. Where's the nearest cash machine?'

'Carlisle.'

He thought she was joking. She wasn't.

'If you haven't got the money you'll have to put the food back.'

'I've got the money. Just give me a minute.'

He dug around in his pockets, ignoring the barely suppressed sighs and rolled eyes from those behind him and by some miracle from his inside jacket pocket and the bottom of his wallet he was able to scrape up cash for everything bar the onion bhajis. He counted it all out and she raised her eyebrows ostentatiously as she rang it up, and shoved the bhajis to one side, where they would doubtless be shoved back into a chiller cabinet some time later. Ed, in turn, shoved it all into a carrier bag that would give way even before he reached the car, and tried not to think about his mother.

He was cooking when Jess limped downstairs. At least, he had two plastic trays rotating noisily in the microwave, which was about as far as he had ever immersed himself in the culinary arts. She was wearing a towelling bathrobe and had her hair wrapped in a white bath-towel turban. He had never understood how women did that. His ex had done it too. He used to wonder if it was something women got taught, like periods and hand-washing. Her bare face was oddly beautiful.

'Here.' Ed held out a glass of wine.

She took it from him as if she barely noticed. He had started a fire, and she sat down in front of the flames, apparently still lost in her thoughts. He handed her the frozen peas for her foot, then busied himself with the rest of the microwave meals, following the instructions on the packaging.

'I texted Nicky,' he told her, as he stabbed the plastic film with a fork. 'Just to tell him where we were staying.'

She took another sip of her wine. 'Was he okay?'

'He was fine. They were just about to eat.' She flinched slightly as he said this, and Ed immediately regretted planting that little domestic tableau in her imagination. 'How's your foot?'

'Hurts.'

She took a huge swig of her wine and he saw she'd downed a glass already. She got up, wincing, so that the peas fell onto the floor and poured herself another. Then, as if she'd just remembered something, she reached into the pocket of the robe, before holding up a little clear plastic bag.

'Nicky's stash,' she said. 'I decided this qualified as an appropriate moment for appropriating his drugs.'

She said it almost defiantly, waiting for him to contradict her. When he didn't, she pulled out Nicky's papers and dragged a tourist guide from the glass coffee-table onto her lap, where she proceeded to roll a haphazard joint. She lit it, and inhaled deeply. She tried to smother a cough, then inhaled again. Her towel turban had started to slide and, irritated, she tugged it off, so that it was just her wet hair around her shoulders. She inhaled again, closed her eyes, and held it out towards him.

'Is that what I could smell when I came in?'

She opened one eye. 'You think I'm a disgrace.'

'No. I think one of us should be in a state to drive, just in case Tanzie wants picking up.'

Her eyes widened.

'It's fine,' he said. 'Really. You go ahead. I think . . . you need . . .'

'A new life? To pull myself together? A good seeing-to?' She laughed mirthlessly. 'Oh, no. I forgot. I can't even do that right.'

'Jess . . .'

She raised a hand. 'Sorry. Okay. Let's eat.'

They ate at the little laminated table beside the kitchen area. The curries were serviceable, but Jess barely touched hers, preferring to drink. She pushed the chicken biryani to and fro on her plate, until it was clear that she wasn't going to eat more than a few mouthfuls, and he offered to clear it away.

As he put the plates on the side and prepared to wash up, she faced him. 'I've been a total idiot, haven't I?'

Ed leant back against the kitchen units, a plate in his hand. 'I don't see how –'

'I worked it all out in the bath. I've been blathering to the kids all these years about how if you look out for people and do the right thing it will all be okay. Don't steal. Don't lie. Do the right thing. Somehow the universe will see you right. Well, it's all bullshit, isn't it? Nobody else thinks that way.'

Her voice was slightly slurred, its edges frayed with pain.

'It's not –'

'No? Two years I've been flat broke. Two years I've been protecting him, not adding to his stress, not bothering him about his own children. And all the while he's been living like that, in his executive home, with his highlights and his designer jeans and his new girlfriend.' She shook her head in wonder. 'I didn't suspect a thing. Not for one minute. And I worked it out, while I was in the bath . . . that whole "do as you would be done by" thing? Well, it only works if everyone else does it. And nobody does, any more. The world is basically full of people who couldn't give a shit. They'll tread all over you if it means they get what they want. Even if it's their own kids they're treading on.'

'Jess . . .'

He walked around the kitchen units until he was inches from her. He couldn't think what to say. He wanted to put his arms around her, but something about her held him back. She poured herself another glass of wine, and lifted it towards him.

'I don't care about that woman, you know. That's not it. Me and Marty were over a long time ago. But all that crap about not being able to help his own kids? Refusing to even think about helping Tanze with school fees?' She took a long gulp of her drink and blinked slowly. 'Did you see that girl's top? That designer top? You know how much they cost? Sixty-seven pounds. Sixty-seven pounds for a child's sweatshirt. I saw the price tag when Druggie Aileen brought one round.' She wiped angrily at her eyes. 'You know what he sent Nicky for his birthday in February? A ten-pound voucher. A ten-pound voucher for the computer-games shop. You can't even buy a computer game for ten pounds. Only second-hand. And they don't always wipe the second-hand ones so someone else will have got all the points. And the stupid thing is we were all really pleased. We thought it meant that Marty was getting better. I told the kids that ten pounds, when you're not working, is actually quite a lot of money.'

She started to laugh. An awful, desolate sound. 'And all the time . . . all the time he was in that executive home with his immaculate new sofa and his matchy-matchy curtains and his bloody boy-band haircut. And he didn't even have the balls to tell me.'

'He's a coward,' he said.

'Yup. But I'm the idiot. I've dragged the kids halfway around the country on some wild goose chase because I thought I could somehow better their chances. I've put us thousands of pounds into debt. I've lost my job at the pub. I've pretty much destroyed Tanzie's self-confidence by putting her through something I should never have made her do. And for what? Because I refused to see the truth.'

'The truth?'

'That people like us never get on. We never move upwards. We just rattle around at the bottom, scrabbling over the other people at the bottom like rats in a cellar, everyone trying to keep out of the wet.'

'That's not how it is.'

'What do you know?' There was no anger in her voice, just confusion. 'How could you possibly understand? You're being done for one of the most serious crimes in the City. Strictly speaking, you did do it. You told your girlfriend what shares to buy so that she would make herself a heap of money. But you'll get off.'

His glass stopped somewhere near his mouth.

'You will. You'll get a couple of weeks inside, maybe a suspended sentence even, and a big fine. You've got expensive lawyers who will keep you out of any real trouble. You've got people who will argue for you, fight for you. You have houses, cars, resources. You don't really need to worry. How could you possibly understand what it's like for us?'

'That's not fair,' he said gently.

'Don't talk to me about fair,' she snapped.

She turned away, and inhaled. She inhaled like someone who wanted to actually black out. She pulled on the joint again and again, closing her eyes and exhaling upwards, the sweet smoke drifting towards the ceiling.

Ed sat down beside her and took it from between her fingers. 'I think maybe that isn't such a good idea.'

She snatched it back. 'Don't tell me what's a good idea.'

'I don't think this is going to help.'

'I don't care what you –'

'I'm not the enemy here, Jess.'

She shot him a look, then turned and stared at the fire. He couldn't tell if she was waiting for him to get up and leave. Or maybe shout back at her. Just for once, he thought, I'm not going anywhere. I'm going to sit this out.

'I'm sorry,' she said eventually, and her voice was stiff, like card.

'It's fine.'

'It's not fine.' She sighed. 'I shouldn't . . . I shouldn't take it out on you.'

'It's okay. It's been a crappy day. Look, I'm going to have a bath, and then I think we should just get some sleep.'

'I'll be up when I've finished this.' She inhaled again.

Ed waited for a moment, then left her staring at the fire. It was a mark of how tired he was that he didn't think any further than the bath.

He must have nodded off in the water. He had run it deep, pouring in whatever unguents and potions he could find on the side without looking to see what they were, and sinking in gratefully, letting the hot water ease out some of the tensions of the day. He tried not to think. Not about Jess, downstairs, staring bleakly into the flames, not about his mother, a couple of hours away, awaiting a son who wouldn't come. He just needed a few minutes of not having to think about anything. He lowered his head as far as he could into the water while still breathing.

He dozed. But some strange tension seemed to have crept into Ed's bones: he couldn't quite relax, even as he closed his eyes. And then he became aware of the sound: a distant revving noise, uneven and dissonant, a whining chainsaw, or a driver learning how to accelerate. He opened an eye, wishing it would just go away. He had thought that this place, of all places, might offer the tiniest bit of peace. Just one night with no noise or drama. Was it really so much to ask?

'Jess?' he called, when it became too irritating. He wondered if there was a music system downstairs. Something she could turn on to drown it out.

And then he realized the cause of his vague discomfort. It was his own car he could hear.

He sat there, bolt upright, for a split second, then leapt from the bath, wrapping a towel around his waist. He ran down the stairs two at a time, past the empty sofa, past Norman, who lifted his head quizzically from his spot in front of the fire, and wrestled with the front door until he had it open. A blast of cold air hit him. He was just in time to see his car bunny-hopping its way forward from its place in front of the cabin, and along the curved gravel drive. He leapt off the steps and as he ran he could just make out Jess at the wheel, craning forward to see through the windscreen. She didn't have any headlights on.

'Jesus Christ. JESS!' He sprinted across the grass, still dripping, one hand clutching at the towel around his waist, trying to cross the lawn to block her before she could get round the drive to the road. Her face swivelled briefly towards him, her eyes widening as she saw him. There was an audible crunch as she wrestled with the gears.

'JESS!'

He was at the car. He threw himself at the bonnet, thumping it, then at the side, wrenching at the driver's door. It opened before she could fumble for the lock, sending him swinging sideways.

'*What the hell are you doing?*'

But she didn't stop. He was running now, unnaturally long steps, braced against the swinging door, one hand on the wheel, the gravel sharp under his feet. The towel had long since disappeared.

'Get off!'

'*Stop the car! JESS, STOP THE CAR!*'

'Get off, Ed! You'll get hurt!' She batted at his hand, and the car swerved dangerously to the left.

'What the –' With a leap he managed to wrestle the keys from the ignition. The car juddered and stalled abruptly. His right shoulder collided hard with the door. Jess's nose hit the steering-wheel with a crack. The air-bag, as if in afterthought, inflated with a *whoosh*.

'*FUCK.*' Ed landed heavily on his side, his head hitting something hard. 'FUCK IT.' He lay on the ground winded, his head spinning. It took a second for his thoughts to clear, and then he scrambled unsteadily to his feet, hauling himself up by the still-open door. He could see, through blurred vision, that they were feet from the lake, its shoreline an inky black near his wheels. Jess's arms rested against the airbag, her face buried in the gap between them, a faint wisp of smoke curling upwards from its seams. He reached across her and pulled on the handbrake, before she could somehow set the thing in motion again.

'*What the hell were you doing? What were you DOING?*' Adrenalin and pain coursed through him. The woman was a nightmare. She was chaos. What the hell had she been thinking? What the hell had *he* been thinking, agreeing to any part of this? 'Jesus, my head. Oh, no. Where's my towel? Where's the damn towel?'

Lights were flicking on in the other cabins. He glanced up, and there were silhouettes in windows that he hadn't known were there, figures looking out at him. He cupped himself as best he could with one hand and half walked, half ran for the towel, which was lying, muddied, half-way along the path, a glowing, crumpled pennant. As he walked, he lifted his other hand towards them as if to say, Nothing to see here (given the cold night air, this had swiftly become true), and a couple of them shut their curtains hurriedly.

She was sitting where he had left her. 'Do you know how much you've drunk tonight?' he yelled, through the open door. 'How much dope you've smoked? You could have killed yourself. You could have killed us both.'

He wanted to shake her, to show her the madness of what she had just done. 'Are you really so determined to dig yourself deeper and deeper into more crap? What the hell is *wrong* with you?'

And then he heard it. She had her head in her hands and she was crying into them, a soft, desolate sound. 'I'm sorry.'

Ed deflated a little, hitched the towel around his waist. 'What the hell were you doing, Jess? You must know this is crazy behaviour.'

'I wanted to get them. I couldn't leave them there. With him.'

He took a breath, made a fist and released it. 'But we've discussed this. They're absolutely fine. Nicky said he'd call if there were any problems. And we're going to get them first thing tomorrow. You know that. So what the hell –'

'I'm scared, Ed.'

'Scared? Of what?'

Her nose was bleeding, a dark scarlet trickle winding its way down to her lip, her eyes smudged black with mascara. 'I'm scared that . . . I'm scared that they'll like it at Marty's.' Her face crumpled. 'I'm scared they won't want to come back.'

And Jess Thomas came to rest, gently, against him, her face buried in his bare chest. And finally Ed put his arms around her and held her close and let her cry.

He had heard religious people talk about having revelatory experiences. Like there was one moment where everything became clear to them and all the crap and ephemera just floated away. It had always seemed pretty unlikely to him. But then Ed Nicholls had one such moment in a log cabin beside a stretch of water that might have been a lake, or might well have been a canal for all he could tell, somewhere near Carlisle. You see, he had once known a woman who had told herself she could do anything – and then decided she could do nothing; a woman who, finding herself at her lowest, did her best to push everyone away. And he realized in that moment that he had to make things right. He felt her injustices more fiercely than he had ever felt anything for himself. He realized, as he held her to him and kissed the top of her head and felt her cling to him, that he would do anything he could to make her happy, and her kids, and to keep them safe and give them a fair chance.

He didn't ask himself how he could know this after

four days. It just seemed clearer to him than anything he had worked out in entire decades before.

And so he told her. He told her, in the quiet tones of someone offloading a confession, that it would be okay. That he would make it okay. Because she was the most amazing woman he had ever met, and it was as simple for him as knowing that he couldn't not make it okay. And when she lifted her swollen eyes to his, frowning as she tried to make sense of what she was hearing, Ed Nicholls mopped her bleeding nose, and he dropped his lips gently onto hers, and he did what he had wanted to do for the past forty-eight hours, even if he had been initially too dumb to know it. He kissed her. And when she kissed him back – tentatively at first, and then with a fierce, gratifying passion, her hand stealing up to his neck, her eyes closing – he picked her up (he was starting with the broken toe), carried her back to the house, and in the only way he could offer that he was sure wouldn't be misunderstood, he tried to show her.

Because, in that one moment, Ed Nicholls saw that he had been more like Marty than he was like Jess. He had been that coward, who spent his life running from things rather than facing up to them. And that something had to change.

'Jess?' he said, softly, into her skin, some time later, as he lay awake, marvelling at the 180-degree swings of life in general. 'Will you do something for me?'

'Again?' she said sleepily. Her hand rested lightly on his chest. 'Good God.'

'No. Tomorrow.' He leant his head into hers.

She shifted, so that her leg slid across his. He felt her lips on his skin. 'Sure. What do you want?'

He gazed up at the ceiling. 'Will you come with me to my dad's?'

24.

NICKY

So Jess's favourite saying, next to 'It's all going to be fine' and 'We'll work something out' and 'Oh, Christ, NORMAN' is that families come in all different shapes and sizes. 'It's not all 2.4 now,' she says, like if she says it enough times we'll all have to actually believe it.

Well, if our family was a weird shape before, it's pretty much insane now.

I don't really have a full-time mum, not like you probably have a mum, but it looks like I've acquired another part-time version. Linzie. Linzie Fogarty. I'm not sure what she makes of me: I can see her watching me out of the corner of her eye, trying to work out if I'm going to do something dark and Gothic, or chew up a terrapin or something. Dad said she does something high up in the local council. He said it like he was really proud, like he's gone up in the world. I'm not sure he ever looked at Jess the way he looks at her.

For about the first hour after we got here I just felt really awkward, like I basically just acquired one more place to feel like I didn't fit. The house is really tidy and they don't have any books, unlike ours, where Jess has stuffed them into pretty much every room except the bathroom and there's usually one by the loo anyway. And I kept staring at Dad because I couldn't believe he'd been living here like a totally normal person while lying to us all the time. It made me hate her, like I hate him.

But then Tanzie said something at supper, and Linzie burst out laughing, and it was this really goofy, honking laugh – FOGHORN FOGARTY, I thought – and she clamped her hand over her mouth and she and Dad exchanged a look like it was a sound she should have tried really, really hard not to make, and something about the way her eyes wrinkled up made me think maybe she was okay.

I mean, her family has just taken on a weird shape too. She had two kids, Suze and Josh, and Dad. And suddenly there's me – Gothboy, as Dad calls me, like that's funny – and Tanze, who has taken to wearing two pairs of glasses on top of each other because she says the one pair isn't quite right, and Jess going nutso on her drive, and kicking holes in her car, and Mr Nicholls, who definitely has a thing about Mum, hanging around and calmly trying to sort everyone out like the only grown-up in the place. And no doubt Dad has had to tell her about my biological mum, who might also end up on her drive shouting one day, like that first Christmas after I moved in with Jess where she threw bottles at our windows and screamed herself hoarse until the neighbours called the police. So, all things considered, Foghorn Fogarty might legitimately be feeling like her family isn't quite the shape she expected either.

I don't really know why I'm telling you this. It's just it's three thirty a.m. and everyone else in this house is asleep and I'm in Josh's room with Tanzie and he has his own computer (both of them have their own computers, Apple Macs, no less) and I can't remember his codes to do any gaming, but I've been thinking about what Mr Nicholls said about blogging and how somehow if you write it and put it out there your people might come.

You probably aren't my people. You're probably people who made a typo while doing a search on discount tyres or porn or something. But I'm putting it out here anyway. Just in case you happen to be anything like me.

Because this last twenty-four hours has made me see something. I might not fit in the way that you fit with your family, neatly, a little row of round pegs in perfectly round holes. In our family we've had to whittle at our pegs and our holes because they all belonged somewhere else first, and they're all sort of jammed in and a bit lopsided. But here's the thing. I realized something when Dad sat down and told me it was good to see me and his eyes got all moist: my dad might be an arse, but he's my arse, and he's the only arse I've got. And feeling the weight of Jess's hand as she sat by my hospital bed, or hearing her try not to cry down the phone at the thought of leaving me here – and watching my little sister, who is trying to be really, really brave about the whole school thing, even though I can tell her world has basically ended – it all made me see that I do sort of belong somewhere.

I think I sort of belong to them.

25.

JESS

Ed lay propped against the pillows, watching her do her makeup, painting out the bruises on her face with a little tube of concealer. She had just about covered the blue bruise on her temple where her head had bounced off the airbag. But her nose was purple, the skin stretched tight over a bump that hadn't been there before, and her upper lip bore the swollen, oversized look of a woman who had ill-advisedly indulged in backstreet fillers. 'You look like someone punched you in the nose.'

Jess rubbed her finger gently over her mouth. 'So do you.'

'It did. My own car, thanks to you.'

She tilted her head, gazing at his reflection behind her. He had this slow lopsided grin, and his chin was a giant bristly shadow. She couldn't not smile back.

'Jess, I'm not sure there's really any point trying to cover it. You're going to look bashed up whatever you do.'

'I thought I'd tell your parents, sorrowfully, that I walked into a door. Maybe with a bit of a furtive sideways look at you.'

362

He let out a sigh and stretched, closing his eyes. 'If that's the worst they think of me by the end of today, I suspect I'll be doing quite well.'

She gave up on her face, and shut her makeup bag. He was right: short of spending the day pressed against an ice-pack, there was little she could do to make it look less battered. She ran a speculative tongue over her sore upper lip. 'I can't believe I didn't feel this when we were . . . well, last night.'

Last night.

She turned and crawled up the bed until she was lying full length along him. She knew this man. She knew every inch of him. She couldn't believe that they had not even properly met each other a week previously. He opened his eyes, sleepily, reached out and toyed lazily with a lock of her hair.

'That'll be the sheer power of my animal magnetism.'

'Or the two joints and a bottle and a half of Merlot.'

He hooked his arm around her neck and pulled her into him. She closed her eyes briefly, breathing in the scent of his skin. He smelt pleasingly of sex. 'Be nice,' he growled softly. 'I'm a bit broken today.'

'I'll run you a bath.' She traced the mark on his head where it had hit the car door. They kissed, long and slow and sweet, and it raised a possibility.

'Are you okay?'

'Never felt better.' He opened one eye.

'No. About lunch.'

He looked briefly serious, and let his head fall back on

the pillow. She regretted mentioning it. 'No. But I guess I'll feel better when it's done.'

She sat in the loo, agonizing in private, then rang Marty at a quarter to nine and told him she had something to sort out and that she would now pick the children up between three and four. She didn't ask. From now on, she had decided, she was just going to tell him how it was going to be. He put Tanzie on the phone and she said nothing about the evening but demanded to know how Norman had coped without her. The dog was stretched out in front of the fire, like a three-dimensional rug. She wasn't entirely sure he'd moved in twelve hours, apart from to eat breakfast.

'He survived. Just.'

'Dad said he's going to make bacon sandwiches. And then we might go to the park. Just him and me and Nicky. Linzie's taking Suze to ballet. She has ballet lessons twice a week.'

'That sounds great,' Jess said. She wondered whether being able to sound cheerful about things that made her want to kick something was her superpower.

'I'll be back some time after three,' she said to Marty, when he came back on the phone. 'Please make sure Tanzie wears her coat.'

'Jess,' he said, as she was about to ring off.

'What?'

'They're great. The pair of them. I just –'

Jess swallowed. 'After three. I'll ring if I'm going to be any later.'

She walked the dog, left him stretched out in the front room, and when she returned Ed was up and breakfasted. They drove the hour to his parents' house in silence. He had shaved, and changed his T-shirt twice, even though they were both exactly the same. She sat beside him and said nothing, and felt, with the morning and the miles, the intimacy of the previous evening slowly seep away. Several times she opened her mouth to speak and then found she didn't know what to say. She felt as if someone had peeled a layer of skin off her, leaving all her nerve endings exposed. Her laugh was too loud, her movements unnatural and self-conscious. She felt as if she had been asleep for a million years and someone had just blasted her awake.

What she really wanted to do was touch him, to wind her hand into his, to rest a hand on his thigh and yet she wasn't sure whether, now they were out of the bedroom and in the unforgiving light of day, that was appropriate any more.

She wasn't sure what he thought had just happened. And she was afraid to ask.

Jess lifted her bruised foot and placed the bag of frozen peas back onto it. Taking it off and putting it back on again.

'You okay?'

'Fine.' She had mostly done it for something to do. She smiled fleetingly at him and he smiled back.

She thought about leaning across and kissing him. She thought about running her finger lightly along the back of his neck so that he would look over at her like he had

365

the previous night, about undoing her seatbelt and edging across the front seat and forcing him to pull over, just so she could take his mind off things for another twenty minutes. And then she remembered Nathalie, who, three years previously, in an effort to be impulsive, had given Dean a surprise blow-job while he was driving the truck. He had yelled, 'What the hell do you think you're doing?' and ploughed straight into the back of a Mini Metro, and before he'd had a chance to do himself up, Nathalie's aunt Doreen had come running out of the supermarket to see what had happened. She had never looked at Nathalie in quite the same way again.

So maybe not. As they drove she kept stealing looks at him. She found she couldn't see his hands without picturing them on her skin, that soft mop of hair travelling slowly down her bare stomach. She thought about the smell of him, the tough muscle and the smooth skin of him. Oh, God. She crossed her legs and stared out of the window.

But Ed's mind was elsewhere. He had grown quieter, the muscle in his jaw tightening, his hands a fraction too fixed on the wheel.

She turned to the front, adjusted the frozen peas, and thought about trains. And lampposts. And Maths Olympiads.

I am the woman who doesn't need a relationship, she told herself. I have simply confused myself by stirring up hormones, like a sort of needy soup.

I am the woman who does not get involved. And, frankly, there's enough that's complicated around here right now without this adding to it. It's just a few days out of my life. Jess gazed out of the window and repeated the words silently until they ceased to have any meaning.

Ed's parents lived in a grey stone Victorian house at the end of a terrace, the kind of street where neighbours try to outdo each other with the neatness of their window boxes, and the recycling bins are hidden when not in use. Ed pulled up, let the engine tick down, and gazed out of the window at his childhood home, the freshly painted gate, and the lawn that looked as if somebody had been over it with nail scissors. He didn't move.

Almost without thinking, she reached out and touched his hand and he turned to her as if he'd forgotten she was there. 'You sure you don't mind coming in with me?'

'Of course not,' she stuttered.

'I'm really grateful. I know you wanted to get the kids.'

She rested her hand on his briefly. 'It's fine. Let's get it over with.'

They walked up the path, and Ed paused, as if checking what he was wearing, then knocked sharply on the front door. They glanced at each other, smiled awkwardly, and waited. And waited some more.

After about thirty seconds, he knocked again, louder this time. And then he crouched to peer through the letterbox.

He straightened up and reached for his phone. 'Odd. I'm sure Gem said the lunch was today. Let me check.' He flicked through some messages, nodded, confirming it, then knocked again.

'I'm pretty sure if anyone was there they would have

heard,' Jess said. The thought occurred, in passing, that it would be quite nice just for once to walk up to a house and have a clue what was happening on the other side of the door.

They started at the stuttering sound of a sash window being raised above their heads. Ed took a step back and peered up at next door.

'Is that you, Ed?'

'Hi, Mrs Harris. I'm after my parents. Any idea where they are?'

The woman grimaced. 'Oh, Ed dear, they've gone to the hospital. I'm afraid your father took ill again early this morning.'

Ed put his hand up to his eyes. 'Which hospital?'

She hesitated, as if she couldn't believe he didn't know. 'The Royal, dear. It's about four miles away if you head for the dual carriageway. You want to go left at the end of the road . . .'

He was already stepping away. 'It's okay, Mrs Harris. I know where it is. Thank you.'

'Give him our best,' she called, and Jess heard the window being pulled down. Ed was already opening the car door.

They reached the hospital in a matter of minutes. Jess didn't speak. She had no idea what to say. At one point she ventured, 'Well, at least they'll be glad to see you,' but it was a stupid thing to say and he was so deep in thought that he didn't seem to hear. He gave his father's name at the information desk and they traced him to

Victoria Ward. 'You know where Oncology is, yes?' the receptionist added helpfully, looking up from her screen. Ed flinched visibly at the word.

They entered a steel lift and travelled up two floors. The doors opened, and the sign for the ward was in front of them. Ed gave his name on the intercom, cleaned his hands with the antibacterial lotion by the door and, when the doors finally clicked open, she followed him through.

A woman walked down the hospital corridor towards them. She was wearing a felt skirt and coloured tights. Her hair was cut in the short feathery style that women use when they insist they're too busy to worry about their hair.

'Hey, Gem,' he said, slowing as she drew near.

She looked at him, disbelieving. Her jaw dropped and for a moment Jess thought she was going to say something.

'It's good to s–' he began. From nowhere, the woman's hand shot out and she smacked him hard. The sound actually echoed down the corridor.

Ed staggered backwards, clutching his cheek. 'What the –'

'You fucking wanker,' she said. 'You fucking, fucking wanker.'

The two of them stared at each other, Ed lowering his hand as if to check for blood. Her jaw was clenched, as if she were waiting for him to say something, do something, but he did nothing.

She shook her hand then, staring at it as if she had

surprised herself, and then after a moment, she held it gingerly towards Jess. 'Hello, I'm Gemma,' she said.

Jess hesitated, then shook it carefully. 'Um . . . Jess.'

She frowned. 'The one with a child in need of urgent help.'

When Jess nodded, she looked her up and down slowly. Her smile was weary, rather than unfriendly. 'Yes, I rather thought you might be. Right. Mum's down the end, Ed. You'd better come and say hello.'

'Is he here? Is it Ed?' The woman's hair was gunmetal grey, pinned up in a neat twist. 'Oh, Ed! It is you. Oh, darling. How lovely. But what have you done to yourself?'

He hugged her, then pulled back, ducking his face when she tried to touch his nose, and giving Jess the swiftest sideways look. 'I . . . I walked into a door.'

She pulled him close again, patting his back. 'Oh, it is so good to see you.'

He let her hold him for a few minutes, then gently disentangled himself. 'Mum, this is Jess.'

'I'm . . . Ed's friend.'

'Well, how lovely to meet you. I'm Anne.' Her gaze travelled briefly over Jess's face, taking in her bruised nose, the faint swelling on her lip. She hesitated just a moment, then perhaps decided not to ask. 'I'm afraid I can't say Ed's told me an awful lot about you but he never does tell me an awful lot about anything, so I'm very much looking forward to hearing it from you.' She put her hand on Ed's arm and her smile wavered a little. 'We did have a rather nice lunch planned but . . .'

Gemma took a step closer to her mother and began rummaging around in her handbag. 'But Dad was taken ill again.'

'He was so looking forward to this lunch. We had to put Simon and Deirdre off. They were just setting out from the Peak District.'

'I'm sorry,' Jess said.

'Yes. Well. Nothing to be done.' She seemed to pull herself together. 'You know, it really is the most revolting disease. I have to work quite hard not to take it all personally.' She leant into Jess with a rueful smile. 'Sometimes I go into our bedroom and I call it the most dreadful names. Bob would be horrified.'

Jess smiled at her. 'I'll give it a few from me, if you like.'

'Oh, please do! That would be wonderful. The filthier the better. And loud. It has to be loud.'

'Jess can do loud,' Ed said, dabbing at his lip.

There was a short silence.

'I bought a whole salmon,' Anne said, to nobody in particular.

Jess could feel Gemma studying her. Unconsciously she pulled at her T-shirt, not wanting her tattoo to show above her jeans. The very words 'social worker' always made her feel scrutinized, as if the woman had already worked out where Jess came from and was assessing her.

And then Anne had moved past and was holding out her arms. The hungry way she pulled Ed to her again made Jess wince a little. 'Oh, darling. Darling boy. I know I'm being a terrible clingy mum but do indulge me. It really is so lovely to see you.' He hugged her back, his eyes raising to Jess's briefly, guiltily.

'My mother last hugged me in 1997,' murmured Gemma. Jess wasn't sure she was aware that she had said it out loud.

'I'm not sure mine ever did,' Jess said.

Gemma looked at her as if she'd forgotten she was there. 'Um . . . about the whole whacking-my-brother thing. He's probably told you what I do for a living. I just feel obliged to stress that I don't usually hit people.'

'I don't think brothers count.'

There was a sudden flicker of warmth behind Gemma's eyes. 'That's a very sensible rule.'

'No problem,' Jess said. 'Anyway, I've wanted to do it quite often myself over the past few days.'

Bob Nicholls lay in a hospital bed, a blanket up to his chin and his hands resting gently on its surface. It was clear from the pallor of his skin and the way the bones of his skull were almost visible that he was not a well man. His breathing was laboured and his head swivelled slowly towards the door as they entered. An oxygen mask sat on a bedside table, and two faint indents on his cheek told of its recent use. He was painful to look at.

'Hey, Dad.'

Jess watched Ed struggle to hide his shock. He stooped towards him and hesitated, before touching his father lightly on the shoulder.

'Edward.' His voice was a croak, but there was still something weighty within it.

'Doesn't he look well, Bob?' said his mother.

His father studied him from under shadowed lids. When he spoke, it was slowly, and with deliberation, as if he had an allotted number of words to use.

'No. He looks like someone beat the living daylights out of him.'

Jess could see the new colour on Ed's cheekbone where his sister had hit him. She found herself reaching unconsciously towards her injured lip.

'Where's he been, anyway?'

'Dad, this is Jess.'

His father's eyes slid towards her. His eyebrow lifted a quarter of an inch. 'And what the hell happened to your face?' he whispered to her.

'I had an argument with a car. My fault.'

'Is that what happened to him?'

She didn't blink. 'Yes.'

He regarded her for a moment longer. 'You look like trouble,' he said. 'Are you trouble?'

Gemma leant forwards. 'Dad! Jess is Ed's friend.'

He dismissed her. 'If there's one small advantage to having very little time left then surely it's that I can say whatever I like. She doesn't look offended. Are you offended? I'm sorry, I've forgotten your name. I don't seem to have any brain cells any more.'

'Jess. No. I'm not offended.'

He kept staring.

'And, yes, I probably am trouble,' she said, holding his gaze.

His smile was slow to arrive, but when it came she

could see, fleetingly, how he must have looked before he got ill. 'Glad to hear it. I always liked girls who were trouble. And this one has been head-down in front of a computer for far too long.'

'How are you, Dad?'

His father blinked. 'I'm dying.'

'We're all dying, Dad,' Gemma said.

'Don't give me your social-worker sophistry. I am dying uncomfortably rapidly. I have few faculties left, and very little dignity. I will probably not make the end of the cricket season. Does that answer your question?'

'I'm sorry,' Ed said quietly. 'I'm sorry I haven't been.'

'You've been busy.'

'About that . . .' Ed began. His hands were thrust deep in his pockets. 'Dad. I need to tell you something. I need to tell you all something.'

Jess stood up hurriedly. 'Why don't I go and get us some sandwiches? Leave you to talk.'

Jess could feel Gemma assessing what she knew. 'I'll get drinks too. Tea? Coffee?'

Bob Nicholls's head turned towards her. 'You've only just got here. Stay.'

Her eyes met Ed's. He gave a tiny shrug, like it was really not going to make any difference.

'What is it, dear?' His mother put a hand out to him. 'Are you all right?'

'I'm fine. Well. I'm sort of fine. I mean I'm healthy. But . . .' He swallowed. 'No I'm not fine. There's something I have to tell you.'

'What?' Gemma said.

'Okay.' He took a deep breath. 'Well, here it is.'

'What?' said Gemma. 'Jesus, Ed. What?'

'I'm being investigated for insider trading. I've been suspended from my company. Next week I have to go to a police station where I will in all likelihood be charged and I may go to prison.'

To say the room fell silent was an understatement. It was as if someone had come in and sucked out all the available air. Jess thought she might pass out briefly from lack of oxygen.

'Is this a joke?' said his mother.

'No.'

'I really could go and get some tea,' Jess said.

Nobody paid her any attention. Ed's mother sat down slowly on a plastic chair.

'Insider trading?' Gemma was the first to speak. 'This – that's serious, Ed.'

'Yeah. I do get that, Gem.'

'Actual insider trading, like you see on the news?'

'That's the one.'

'He's got good lawyers,' Jess said.

Nobody seemed to hear.

'Expensive ones.'

His mother's hand had risen halfway to her mouth. She lowered it slowly. 'I don't understand. When did this happen?'

'A month or so ago. The insider-trading bit, anyway.'

'A month ago? But why didn't you tell us? We could have helped you.'

'You couldn't, Mum. Nobody can help.'

'But prison? Like a criminal?' Anne Nicholls had gone quite pale.

'I think if you're sent to prison you pretty much are a criminal, Mum.'

'Well, they'll have to sort it out. They'll see that there's been some kind of mistake, but they'll sort it out.'

'No, Mum. I'm not sure it's going to work out like that.'

There was another long silence.

'Are you going to be all right?'

'I'll be fine, Mum. As Jess said, I have good lawyers. I have resources. They have already established that there was no financial gain for me.'

'You didn't even make money out of it?'

'It was a mistake.'

'A mistake?' said Gemma. 'I don't get it. How do you do insider trading by mistake?'

Ed straightened his shoulders and gazed steadily at her. He took a breath, and his gaze flickered towards Jess. And then he looked up at the ceiling. 'Well, I had sex with a woman. I thought I liked her. And then I realized she wasn't who I thought she was and I sort of wanted her to go away without it all getting messy. And what she wanted to do was travel. So I made a snap decision and told her a way I thought she could make a little extra money to pay off her debts and go travelling.'

'You gave her inside information.'

'Yup. On SFAX. Our big product launch.'

'Jesus Christ.' Gemma shook her head. 'I can't believe I'm hearing this.'

'And my name hasn't come out in the press yet. But it will.' He put his hands into his pockets and looked steadily at his family. Jess wondered if only she could detect that his hand was shaking. 'So . . . um . . . that's why I haven't been home. I was hoping I could keep it from you, maybe even sort it out so that you didn't have to know anything about it. But it turns out that's going to be impossible. And I wanted to say I'm sorry. I should have told you and I should have spent more time here. But I – I didn't want you to know the truth. I . . . didn't want you to see what a mess I'd made of everything.'

Nobody spoke. Jess's right leg had begun to jiggle involuntarily. She found a really interesting bit of skin beside her thumbnail and tried to make the jiggling stop. When she finally looked up, Ed was staring at his father. 'Well?'

'Well what?'

'You're not going to say anything?'

Bob Nicholls lifted his head slowly from his pillow. 'What do you want me to say?'

Ed and his dad gazed at each other.

'You want me to say you've been an idiot? I'll say you've been an idiot. You want me to say you've ballsed up a brilliant career? I'll say that too.'

'Bob . . .'

'Well, what do you –' Abruptly, he started to cough, a hollow, rasping sound. Anne and Gemma lurched forward to help him, handing over tissues, glasses of water, fussing and clucking like a pair of hens. It was as if everyone was grateful for being given something to do.

Ed was standing at the foot of his father's bed.

'Prison?' his mother said again. 'Actual prison prison?'

'That's what he said, Mum.'

'But this is awful.'

'Sit down, Mum. Deep breaths.' Gemma steered her mother into a chair.

Nobody moved towards Ed. Why didn't somebody hug him? Why could they not see how alone he felt right at that minute?

'I'm sorry,' he said quietly.

Nobody seemed to hear.

'Can I say something?' Jess could bear it no longer. She heard her voice, clear and slightly too loud. 'I just want to tell you that Ed helped my two children when I couldn't. He drove us the length of the country, because we were desperate. As far as I'm concerned your son is . . . wonderful.'

They all looked up. Jess turned to his father. 'He's kind, smart and clever, even if I don't agree with all the things he does. He's nice to people he barely knows. Insider trading or no, if my son turns out half the man your son is then I'll be very happy. More than happy. I'll be ecstatic.'

They were all staring at her.

She added: 'And I thought that even before I had sex with him.'

Nobody spoke. Ed stared fixedly at his feet.

'Well,' Anne gave a faint nod, 'that's, er, that's . . .'

'Enlightening,' said Gemma.

Anne's voice tailed away. 'Oh, Edward.'

Bob sighed and closed his eyes. 'Let's not get all Hollywood about this.' He opened them again and signalled for the head of the bed to be raised a little. 'Come here, Ed. Where I can see you. Wretched eyesight.' He motioned for the glass again and his wife held it to his lips.

He swallowed painfully, then tapped the side of his bed, so that Ed sat down on it. He reached out a hand and rested it lightly on his son's. He was unbearably frail. 'You're my son, Ed. You might be idiotic and irresponsible, but it doesn't make the slightest difference to what I feel about you.' He frowned. 'I'm pissed off that you could have thought it would.'

'I'm sorry, Dad.'

His father gave a slow shake of his head. 'I'm afraid I can't be much help. Stupid breathless . . .' he pulled a face, then swallowed painfully. His hand tightened around Ed's. 'We all make mistakes. Go and take your punishment, then come back and start again.'

Ed looked up at him. And Jess saw the boy he must have been: hurt, desperate for his father's approval. And determined never to let that show.

'Do even better next time. I know you can.'

It was at that point that Anne started to cry, abrupt, helpless tears that she buried in her sleeve. Bob turned his head slowly towards her. 'Oh, darling,' he said softly. And that was where Jess acknowledged that she had finally become an intruder. She opened the door silently and slid out.

She put some credit on her phone in the hospital shop, texted Ed to say where she was, and waited in A&E to get her foot looked at. Badly bruised, said a young Polish doctor, who didn't bat an eyelid when she told him how she had done it. He strapped it up, wrote a prescription for strong painkillers, handed her back her flip-flop, and advised her to rest. 'Try not to kick any more cars,' he said, without looking up from his clipboard.

Jess hobbled back upstairs to Victoria Ward, sat on one of the plastic chairs in the corridor, and waited. It was warm and the people around her spoke in whispers. She may have nodded off briefly. She woke abruptly when Ed emerged from the room. She held out his jacket and he took it without a word. A moment later Gemma appeared in the corridor. They stood facing each other silently. His sister put her hand gently to the side of his face. 'You bloody idiot.'

His head dipped, hands shoved deep in his pockets, like Nicky.

'You stupid bloody stupid idiot. Call me.'

He pulled back. His eyes were red-rimmed.

'I mean it. I'll come with you to court. I might know some people in probation who could help get you into an open prison. I mean, you're not going to be category A, as long as you haven't done anything else.' Her eyes flickered towards Jess and back to him. 'You haven't done anything else, right?'

He leant forward and hugged her, and maybe it was only Jess who noticed the way his eyes closed really tightly when he pulled away.

*

They emerged from the hospital into the luminous white of a spring day. Real life, inexplicably, seemed to have continued regardless. Cars reversed into too-small spaces, buggies were disgorged from buses, a workman's radio blared as he painted a nearby railing. Jess found herself taking deep breaths, grateful to be away from the stale, medical air of the ward, the almost tangible spectre of death that hung over Ed's father. Ed walked and looked straight ahead. He reminded her, briefly, of Nicky before they had come here, when all his energies seemed to be focused on showing nothing, feeling nothing. They crossed the car park until they reached his car and he paused. The doors unlocked with an audible clunk. Then he stopped. It was as if he couldn't move. He just stood there, one arm slightly outstretched, staring blankly at his car.

Jess waited for a minute, and then she walked slowly around it. She took the key fob from his hand. And, finally, when his gaze slid towards her she went to him and slid her arms tight around his waist. She held him until his head came slowly down to rest, a soft, dead weight, upon her shoulder.

26.

TANZIE

Nicky actually started a conversation at breakfast. They had been sitting eating around the table like a television family – Tanzie had multigrain hoops, and Suzie and Josh had chocolate croissants, which Suzie said they had every day because it was was their favourite – and it was a bit weird sitting there with Dad and his other family but not actually as bad as she'd thought. Dad was eating a bowl of bran flakes because he said he had to stay in trim now and patted his stomach a lot although she wasn't sure why because it wasn't like he had an actual job. 'Things in the pipeline, Tanze,' he said, whenever she asked what he was actually doing, and she wondered if Linzie had a garage full of air-conditioning units that didn't work too. Linzie didn't seem to eat anything. Nicky was toying with some toast – he never usually ate breakfast: until this trip he had never usually been up for breakfast – when he just looked at Dad and said, 'Jess works all the time. All the time. And I don't think it's fair.'

Dad's spoon stopped halfway to his mouth and Tanzie wondered whether he was going to get really angry, like he used to if Nicky said anything he felt was disrespectful. Nobody said anything for a minute. Then Linzie put her hand on Dad's and smiled. 'He's right, love.'

And Dad went a bit pink and said, yes, well, things were going to change a bit from now on and we all made mistakes, and because she felt a bit braver then, Tanzie said, no, strictly speaking, not all of us did make mistakes. She had made a mistake with her algorithms and Norman had made a mistake because of the cows and breaking her glasses, and Mum had made a mistake with the Rolls-Royce and getting arrested, but Nicky was the one person in their family who hadn't made any mistakes. But halfway through her saying it Nicky kicked her hard under the table and gave her that look.

What? her eyes said to him.

Shut it, his said to her.

GRRR, don't tell me to shut it, hers said to him.

And then he wouldn't look at her.

'Would you like a chocolate croissant, love?' Linzie said, and put one on her plate before Tanzie had even answered.

Linzie had washed and dried Tanzie's clothes overnight and they smelt of orchid and vanilla fabric conditioner. Everything in that house smelt of something. It was as if nothing was allowed to just smell of itself. She had little plug-in things that released 'a luxurious scent of rare blossoms and rainforests' dotted around her skirting, and bowls of pot-pourri that she sprayed from little bottles of scent, and she had about a billion candles in the bathroom ('I do love my scented candles'). Tanzie's nose itched the whole time they were indoors.

After they'd got dressed Linzie took Suze to ballet. Dad and Tanzie went to the park even though she hadn't been to the park in about two years because she had sort of grown out of it. But she didn't want to hurt Dad's feelings so she sat on the swing and let him push her a few times and Nicky stood and watched, with his hands stuffed into his pockets. He had left his Nintendo in Mr Nicholls's car and she knew he really, really wanted a cigarette but she didn't think he felt brave enough to smoke one in front of Dad.

There were chip-shop chips for lunch ('Don't tell Linze,' Dad said, patting his stomach), and Dad asked questions about Mr Nicholls, trying to sound all casual: 'Who is he then, that bloke? Your mum's boyfriend?'

'No,' said Nicky, in a way that made it hard for Dad to ask another question. Tanzie thought Dad was a bit shocked at how Nicky spoke to him. Not that he was rude, exactly, it's just that he didn't seem to care what Dad thought. Plus Nicky was now taller than him but when Tanzie pointed it out Dad didn't seem to think that was amazing at all.

And then Tanzie got cold because she hadn't brought her coat so they went back and Suze was already home from ballet so Nicky went upstairs to go on the computer, and they played some games and then they played with her terrapin and then they just went to her room and she said they could watch a DVD because she had a DVD player and that she watched a whole one by herself every night before she went to sleep.

'Doesn't your mum read to you?' Tanzie said.

'She doesn't have time. That's why she got me the DVD player,' Suze said. She had a whole shelf of films, all her favourites, that she could watch up there when they were watching something she didn't like downstairs.

'Marty likes gangster films so they watch those,' she said, her nose wrinkling, and it took Tanzie a few minutes to realize she was actually talking about her dad. And she didn't know what to say.

'I like your jacket,' Suze said, peering into Tanzie's bag.

'My mum made it for me for Christmas.'

'Your mum actually made it?' She held it up, so that the sequins Mum had sewn into the sleeves glinted in the light. 'Oh, my God, is she like a fashion designer or something?'

'No,' Tanzie said. 'She's a cleaner.'

Suze laughed as if she was joking.

'What are all those?' she said, when she saw the maths papers in her bag.

This time Tanzie kept her mouth closed.

'Is that maths? Oh, my God, it's like . . . squiggles. It's like . . . Greek.' She giggled, flicking through them, then holding them from two fingers, like they were something horrible. 'Are they your brother's? Is he, like, a maths freak?'

'I don't know.' Tanzie blushed because she was not very good at lying.

'Ugh. What a brainiac. Freaky. Geeky.' She tossed them to one side, while she pulled out Tanzie's other clothes.

Tanzie didn't say anything. She left them there on the floor because she didn't want to have to explain. And she didn't want to think about the Olympiad. And she just thought maybe it would be easier if she tried to be like Suze from now on because she seemed really happy and Dad seemed really happy here and then she said maybe they should watch television downstairs because she really didn't want to think about anything any more.

They were three-quarters of the way through *Fantasia* when Tanzie heard Dad calling, 'Tanze, your mum's here.' Mum stood on the doorstep with her chin up like she was ready for an argument, and when Tanzie stopped and stared at her face, she put a hand to her lip as if she had only just remembered it was split, and said, 'I fell over,' and then Tanzie looked behind her to Mr Nicholls who was sitting in the car, and Mum said, quick as anything, 'He fell over too.' Even though she hadn't actually been able to see his face and she had just wanted to see whether they were getting in the car or if they were going to have to get a bus after all.

And Dad said, 'Does everything you come into contact with, these days, suffer some kind of injury?' Mum gave him a look and he muttered something about repairs, then said he'd go and get her bag, and Tanzie let out a big breath and ran into Mum's arms because although she'd had a nice time at Linzie's house, she'd missed Norman and she wanted to be with Mum and she was suddenly really, really tired.

The cabin that Mr Nicholls had rented was like something out of an advertisement for what old people want to do when they retire, or maybe pills for urine problems. It was on a lake and there were a few other houses but they were mostly set back behind trees or at angles so that no single window looked directly at any other house. There were fifty-six ducks and twenty geese on the water and all but three were still there by the time they'd had tea. Tanzie thought Norman might chase them but he just flopped down on the grass and watched.

'Awesome,' said Nicky, even though he didn't really like the outdoors at all. He inhaled deeply. She realized he hadn't smoked a cigarette for four days.

'Isn't it?' said Mum. She gazed out at the lake and didn't say anything for a while. She started to say something about paying their share, and Mr Nicholls held up his hands and made this 'no-no-no-no' noise like he didn't even want to hear it, and Mum went a bit pink and stopped.

They had dinner on a barbecue outside, even though it was not really barbecue weather, because Mum said it would be a fun end to the trip, and when did she ever get time to do a barbecue, anyway? She seemed determined to make everyone happy and just chatted away about twice as much as anyone else, and she said she'd blown the budget because sometimes you had to count your blessings and live a little. It seemed like it was her way of saying thank you. So they had sausages and chicken thighs in spicy sauce and fresh rolls and salad, and Mum had bought two tubs of the good ice cream, not the cheap stuff that came in the white plastic cartons. She didn't ask anything about Dad's new house, but she did hug Tanzie a lot and said that she'd missed her and wasn't that silly because it was only one night after all.

They each told jokes, and even though Tanzie could only remember the one about a stick being brown and sticky, everyone laughed, and they played the game where you put a broom to your forehead and run around it in circles until you fall over, which always made every-one laugh. Mum did it once, even though she could barely walk with her foot all strapped up, and kept say-ing, 'Ow ow ow,' as she went round in a circle. And that made Tanzie laugh because it was just nice to see Mum being silly for a change. And Mr Nicholls kept saying, no, no, not for him thanks, he would just watch. And then Mum limped over to him and said something really quiet in his ear and he raised his eyebrows and said, 'Really?' And she nodded. And he said, 'Well, all right, then.' And when he crashed over he actually made the ground vibrate a little. And even Nicky, who never did anything, did it, his legs sticking out like a daddy-long-legs's, and when he laughed his laugh was really strange like this huh huh huh sound and then Tanzie decided she hadn't heard him laugh like that for ages. Maybe ever.

And she did it about six times until the world bucked and rolled beneath her and she collapsed on her back on the grass and watched the sky spin slowly around her and thought that was a bit like life for their family. Never quite the way up it was meant to be.

They ate the food, and Mum and Mr Nicholls had some wine, and Tanzie took all the scraps off the bones and gave them to Norman because dogs die if you give them chicken bones. And then they put their coats on and just sat out on the nice wicker chairs that went with the cabin, all lined up in a row in front of the lake, and watched the birds on the water until it got dark. 'I love this place,' said Mum, into the silence. Tanzie wasn't sure anyone was meant to see it, but Mr Nicholls reached over and gave Mum's hand a squeeze.

Mr Nicholls seemed a bit sad most of the evening. Tanzie wasn't sure why. She wondered if it was because they'd reached the end of the little trip. But she heard the geese and ducks quacking and splashing on the far side of the lake, and then just the water lapping against the shore and it was really calm and peaceful and then she must have fallen asleep because she sort of remembered Mr Nicholls carrying her upstairs and Mum tucking her in and telling her she loved her, but what she mostly remembered about that whole evening was that nobody talked about the Olympiad and she was just really, really glad.

Because here's the thing. While Mum was getting the barbecue set up Tanzie asked to borrow Mr Nicholls's computer and looked up the statistics for children of low-income families at private schools. And she saw within a few minutes that the probability of her actually going to St Anne's had always been in single-figure per-centages. And she understood that it didn't matter how well she had done in that entrance test, she should have checked this figure before they had even left home because you only ever went wrong in life when you didn't pay attention to the numbers. Nicky came upstairs, and when he saw what she was doing he stood there without saying anything for a minute, then patted her arm and said he would speak to a couple of people he knew in the year below him at McArthur's to make sure they looked out for her.

When they were at Linzie's, Dad had told her that pri-vate school was no guarantee of success. He'd said it three times. 'Success is all about what's inside you,' he'd said. 'Determination.' And then he said Tanzie should get Suze to show her how she did her hair because maybe hers would look nice like that too.

Mum said she would sleep on the sofa that night so that Tanzie and Nicky could have the second bedroom but Tanzie didn't think she did because she woke up really thirsty in the middle of the night because of Mum's cooking and she went downstairs and Mum wasn't there. And in the morning Mum was wearing Mr Nicholls's grey T-shirt that he wore every single day and Tanzie waited twenty minutes watching his door because she was curious to know what he was going to come down in.

A faint mist hung across the lake in the morning. It rose off the water like a magician's trick as everyone packed up the car. Norman sniffed around the grass, his tail wagging slowly. 'Rabbits,' said Mr Nicholls (he was wearing another grey T-shirt). The morning was chill and grey and the wood pigeons cooed softly in the trees and Tanzie had that sad feeling like you've been somewhere really nice and it's all come to an end.

'I don't want to go home,' she said quietly, as Mum shut the boot.

She flinched. 'What, love?'

'I don't want to go back home,' Tanzie said.

Mum glanced at Mr Nicholls and then she tried to smile, walked over slowly and said, 'Do you mean you want to be with your dad, Tanze? Because if that's what you really want I'll –'

'No. I just like this house and it's nice here.' She wanted to say, 'And there's nothing to look forward to when we get back because everything is spoiled and, besides, here there are no Fishers,' but she could see from Mum's face that that was what she was thinking too, because she immediately looked at Nicky and he shrugged.

'You know, there's no shame in having tried to do something, right?' Mum gazed at them both. 'We all did our best to make something happen, and it didn't happen, but some good things have come out of it. We got to see some parts of the country we would never have seen. We learnt a few things. We sorted it out with your dad. We made some friends.' It's possible she meant Linzie and her children but her eyes were on Mr Nicholls when she said it. 'So all in all I think it was a good thing that we tried, even if it didn't go quite the way we'd planned. And, you know, maybe things won't be so bad once we get home.'

Nicky's face didn't show anything. Tanzie knew he was thinking about all the money.

And then Mr Nicholls, who had said barely anything all morning, walked around the car, opened the door for her and said, 'Yes. Well. I've been thinking about that. And we're going to make a little detour.'

27.

JESS

They were a muted little group in the car on the way home. Nobody asked to play music, and there was little conversation. Even the dog no longer whined, as if he had accepted that this car was now his home. The whole time Jess had planned the trip, through the strange, frenetic few days of travelling, she had imagined no further than getting Tanzie to the Olympiad. She would get her there, she would sit the test, and everything would be okay. She hadn't given a thought to the possibility that the entire trip might take three days longer than she had planned or that she would blow the budget in the process. She'd never once considered that they might need to stay somewhere on the way home. Or that she would be left with precisely £13.81 in cash to her name and a bank card that she was too frightened to feed into a cashpoint in case it didn't come back.

Jess mentioned none of this to Ed. He was silent, his gaze trained on the road ahead, perhaps lost in thoughts of his father. Nicky, behind him, tapped away on Ed's laptop, ear-buds wedged into his ears, his brow furrowed with concentration. Jess suspected there was some weird gadget of Ed's that allowed him access to the Internet.

She was so grateful that he was talking and eating and sleeping that she didn't query it. Tanzie was silent, her hand resting on Norman's great head, her eyes fixed on the speeding landscape through the window. Whenever Jess asked her if she was okay, she would simply nod.

None of it seemed to matter as much as it should. Because something fundamental had shifted in her.

Ed. Jess repeated his name silently in her head until it ceased to have any real meaning. She sat inches from this man, who, she now understood, was quite simply the greatest man she had ever known. She was only surprised that nobody else seemed to have realized it. When he smiled, Jess couldn't help smiling. When his face stilled in sadness, something inside her broke a little. She watched him with her children, the easy way in which he showed Nicky some feature on his computer, the serious manner in which he considered some passing comment of Tanzie's – the kind of comment that would have caused Marty to roll his eyes to Heaven – and she wished he had been in their lives long ago. When they were alone and he held her close to him, his palm resting with a hint of possession on Jess's thigh, his breath soft in her ear, she felt with a quiet certainty that it would all be okay. It wasn't that Ed would make it okay – he had his own problems to deal with – but that somehow the sum of them added up to something better. They would make it okay. He was the first person Jess had ever met with whom she understood the saying: They were just really good together.

She was afraid to ask him what any of this meant. She

was afraid that she had rattled on for so long about how she didn't need anyone, how she was quite self-sufficient, thank you, and how, what with her work and the two kids and the dog, there was no room for anyone else in her life, that he might have taken her seriously.

Because she wanted Ed Nicholls. She wanted to wake up with him, to drink with him, to feed him toast from sticky fingers. She wanted to wrap her legs around him in the dark and feel him inside her, to buck against him as he held her. She wanted the sweat and the pull and the solidity of him, his mouth on hers, his eyes on hers. They drove and she recalled the previous two nights in hot, dreamy fragments, his hands, his mouth, the way he had to stifle her as she came so that they wouldn't wake the children, and it was all she could do not to reach across and bury her face in his neck, to slide her hands up the back of his T-shirt for the sheer pleasure of feeling his skin against hers.

She had spent so long thinking only about the children, about work and bills and money. Now her head was full of him. When he turned to her she blushed. When he said her name she heard it as a murmur, spoken in the dark. When he handed her a coffee the brief touch of his fingers sent an electric pulse fizzing through her. She liked it when she felt his eyes settle on her, something distant in his gaze, and she wondered what he was thinking.

Jess had no idea how to communicate any of this to him. She had been so young when she met Marty, and apart from one night in the Feathers with Liam Stubbs's hands up her shirt, she had never had even the beginnings of a relationship with anyone else since.

Jess Thomas had not been on an actual date since school. It made her sound ridiculous, even to herself. She just wanted to show him.

She ached with it.

'We'll keep going to Nottingham, if you guys are all okay,' he said, turning to look at her. He still had the faintest bruise on the side of his nose. 'We'll pitch up somewhere late. That way we'll make it home in one run on Thursday.'

And then what? Jess wanted to ask. But she put her feet up on the dashboard, and said, 'Sounds good.'

They stopped for lunch at a service station. The children had given up asking if there was any chance they could eat anything but sandwiches, and now eyed the fast-food joints and upmarket coffee shops with something close to indifference. They unfolded themselves, and paused to stretch.

'How about sausage rolls?' said Ed, pointing towards a concession. 'Coffee and hot sausage rolls. Or Cornish pasties. My treat. Come on.'

Jess looked at him.

'I need some trash food. Some calorific greasy junk. Who wants some greasy carbohydrate, kids?' He motioned to Jess. 'Come on, you food Nazi. We'll eat some fruit afterwards.'

'You're not afraid? After that kebab?'

His hand was above his brow, shielding his eyes from

the sun so that he could see her better. 'I've decided I like living dangerously.'

He had come to her the previous night, after Nicky, who had been tapping silently away at Ed's laptop in the corner of the room, had finally gone to bed. She had felt like a teenager sitting there on the other sofa to him, pretending to watch the television, waiting for everyone else to go to bed just so she could touch him. But when Nicky finally sloped off, Ed had opened up the laptop rather than move straight to her.

'What's he doing?' she had said, as Ed peered at the screen.

'Creative writing,' he said.

'Not gaming? No guns? No explosions?'

'Nothing.'

'He sleeps,' she had whispered. 'He has slept every night we've been away. Without a spliff.'

'Good for him. I feel like I haven't slept for several years.'

He seemed to have aged a decade in the short time they had been away. Jess wondered if she should apologize, if spending too much time with her chaotic little family would do that to any man. She remembered what Chelsea had said about her chances of having any kind of love life. And then, as she sat, suddenly unsure what to do next, he had reached out a hand to her and pulled her into him. 'So,' he had said softly, 'Jessica Rae Thomas. Are you going to let me get some sleep tonight?'

She studied his lower lip, absorbing the feel of his hand on her hip. Feeling suddenly joyous. 'No,' she said.

'Excellent answer.'

She thought they might have had three hours. It was hard to tell.

Now they changed direction, walking away from the mini-mart, weaving their way through clumps of disgruntled travellers looking for cashpoint machines or overcrowded toilets. Jess tried not to look as delighted as she felt at the thought of not making another round of sandwiches. She could smell the buttery pastry of the hot pies from yards away.

The children, clutching a handful of notes and Ed's instructions, disappeared into the long queue inside the shop. He walked towards her, so that they were shielded from them by the crowds of people.

'What are you doing?'

'Just looking.' Every time he stood close to her Jess felt like she was a few degrees warmer than she should have been.

'Looking?'

'I find it impossible being close to you.' His lips were inches from her ear, his voice a low rumble through her skin.

Jess felt her skin prickle. 'What?'

'I just imagine myself doing filthy things to you. Pretty much the whole time. Completely inappropriate things. Disgraceful things.'

He took hold of the front of her jeans and pulled her to him. A bolt of such heat went through her that she was amazed nobody could see it. Jess drew back a little, craning her neck to make sure they were out of sight.

'That's what you were thinking about? While you were driving? All that time while you weren't speaking?'

'Yup.' He glanced behind her towards the shop. 'Well, that and food.'

'My two favourite things, right there.'

His fingers traced the bare skin under her top. Her stomach tensed pleasurably. Her legs had become oddly weak. She had never wanted Marty like she wanted Ed.

'Apart from sandwiches.'

'Let's not talk about sandwiches. Ever again.'

And then he placed the flat of his hand on the small of her back, so that they were as close as they could decently be. 'I know I shouldn't be,' he murmured, 'but I woke up really happy.' His face scanned hers. 'I mean, like, really, stupidly happy. Like even though my whole life is a complete disaster, I just . . . I feel okay. I look at you, and I feel okay. I feel like we're going to get through this.'

A great fat lump had risen in her throat. 'Me too,' she whispered.

He squinted against the sun, trying to gauge her expression. 'So I'm not . . . just a horse?'

'You are so not a horse. Well. In the nicest way I could say that you were –'

He dropped his head and kissed her. He kissed her and it was a kiss of utter certainty, the kind of kiss during which monarchs die and whole continents fall without you even noticing. When Jess extricated herself it was only because she didn't want the children to see her lose the ability to stand. Her finger traced his lips, just for the pleasure of touching them, and he grinned.

'They're coming,' he said.

Jess found herself staring at him goofily.

'Trouble.' He glanced back at her as they approached, bearing their paper bags aloft. 'That's what my dad said.'

'Like you hadn't worked that one out by yourself.' Her lips tingled. Her thoughts swam sweet and sticky, like honey. Jess felt like he was imprinted all over her. She held back, watching Ed chat to Nicky, the opening of paper bags as Nicky revealed what they'd chosen, waiting for the colour on her cheeks to fade. She felt the sun on her skin, heard birdsong over people talking, revving cars, smelt petrol fumes and cheap food, and the words echoed through her head, unbidden: this is what happiness feels like.

They set off slowly back to the car, faces already buried in paper bags. Jess watched her daughter walking a few paces ahead, her skinny legs trailing behind the others and it was then that she noticed something was missing.

'Tanze? Where are your maths books?'

She didn't turn around. 'I left them at Dad's.'

'Oh. Do you want me to call him?' She fumbled in her bag for her mobile phone. 'I'm sure I can get him to pop them straight in the post. They'll probably arrive back before we do.'

'No,' she said. She inclined her head slightly towards her, but not quite meeting Jess's eye. 'Thank you.'

Nicky stopped, as he reached the car. His gaze slid to Jess and back to his sister. And something heavy settled in her stomach.

*

By the time they reached their final overnight stop it was almost nine o'clock and they were drooping. The children, who had been snacking on biscuits and sweets for most of the last leg of the journey, were exhausted and cranky, and headed straight upstairs to examine the sleeping arrangements. Ed carried the bags and Tanzie tugged the dog behind her.

The hotel was vast and white and expensive-looking, the kind of place Mrs Ritter might have shown Jess on her camera-phone and she and Nathalie would have sighed about afterwards. Ed had booked it over the phone and when Jess had started to protest about the cost there was a slight edge to his voice: 'We're all tired, Jess. And my next bed may be at Her Majesty's Pleasure. Let's just stay somewhere nice tonight, okay?'

Three interlocking rooms, in a corridor that seemed to double as an annex to the main hotel. 'My own room.' Nicky sighed with relief as he unlocked number twenty-three. He lowered his voice as Jess pushed open the door. 'I love her and everything, but you have no idea how much the Titch snores.'

'Norman will like this,' said Tanzie, as Jess opened the door to room twenty-four. The dog, as if in agreement, immediately flopped down at the side of the bed. 'I don't mind sharing with Nicky, Mum, but he really does snore badly.'

Neither of them seemed to question where Jess would be sleeping. She couldn't work out if they knew and didn't mind, or whether they just assumed either she or Ed was still sleeping in the car.

Nicky borrowed Ed's laptop. Tanzie worked out how to operate the remote control for her television, and said she would watch one programme then go to sleep. She wouldn't talk about the missing maths books. She actually said, 'I don't want to talk about it.' Jess didn't think Tanzie had ever said those words to her.

'Just because something doesn't work out once, sweetheart, doesn't mean you can't try again,' she said, laying out Tanzie's pyjamas on her bed.

Tanzie's expression seemed to contain a knowledge that hadn't been there before. And her words broke Jess's heart. 'I think it's best if I just work with what we've got, Mum.'

'What do I do?'

'Nothing. She's just had enough for now. You can't blame her.' Ed dropped the bags in the corner of the room. Jess sat on the side of the huge bed, trying to ignore her throbbing foot.

'But this isn't like her. She loves maths. Always has. And now she's acting like she doesn't want anything to do with it.'

'It's been two days, Jess. She's had a massive upheaval. Just . . . let her be. She'll work it out.'

'You're so sure.'

'They're smart kids.' He walked over to the switch and turned the lights down, gazing up at them until he'd got it dark enough. 'Like their mother. But just because you bounce back like a rubber ball, it doesn't mean they always will.'

She looked at him.

'That's not a criticism. I'm just saying that it's been a pretty intense week. I think if you give her some time to decompress, she'll be okay. She is who she is. I can't see that changing.'

He pulled his T-shirt over his head in a fluid motion and dropped it onto a chair. Her thoughts muddled immediately. Jess couldn't see his bare torso without wanting to touch it. A little too thick around the middle to be perfect, perhaps. But that made it somehow more beautiful.

'How did you get so wise?' she said, gazing at him.

'Dunno. I guess it rubbed off.' He took two steps towards her, and then he knelt down and pulled off her flip-flops, removing the one on her injured foot with extra care. 'How's it feeling?'

'Sore. But fine.'

He reached for her top. He unzipped it slowly and without asking, his eyes fixed on the skin it exposed. He seemed almost distant then, as if his thoughts were on her, yet miles away. The zip caught near the end, and she took it from him gently, her hands over his, unhitching the two sides so that he could peel it from her shoulders. He stood there for a moment, just gazing at her.

He kissed her then, and said softly, 'I don't think we should think about it any more.' He kissed her shoulder. 'I think we shouldn't think full stop.' He kissed her neck. 'It's our last night on the road and there's nothing much we can do about anything. For tonight at least.'

He reached for her belt, undid it, then her jeans, his

fingers measured and precise. She watched them and her heart began to pulse in her ears.

'It's time, Jessica Rae Thomas, that someone looked after you.'

Edward Nicholls washed her hair, his legs around her waist, as she lay back against him in the oversized bath. He rinsed it gently, smoothing it and wiping her eyes with a facecloth to stop shampoo getting into them. She went to do it herself, but he shushed her. Nobody had ever washed her hair, outside a hairdresser's. It made her feel vulnerable and oddly emotional. When he was done, he lay in the steaming, scented water with his arms wrapped around her and kissed the tips of her ears. And then, as if some part of them agreed jointly that this had been quite enough romantic stuff, thank you, she felt him rise under her and swivelled, lowered herself onto him, and they fucked until the water sluiced out of the bath, and she couldn't work out whether the pain of her foot was greater than her need to feel him inside her.

Some time later, they lay half submerged, legs entwined. And they started to laugh. Because it was a cliché to fuck in a shower but it was sort of ridiculous to do it in a bath, and it was even more ridiculous to be in this much trouble and yet this happy. Jess twisted so that she lay along the length of him, and draped her arms around his neck and pressed her wet chest to his, and she felt with utter certainty that she would never be as close to another human being again. God, I love you, she told him silently. And then so that she didn't let those words burst, unbidden, from her mouth, she smothered him with kisses. She held his face in her hands and she kissed his jaw and his poor bruised temple, and his lips, and she felt his arms holding her to him and told herself that whatever happened she would always remember how this felt.

He brought his hand down over his face, wiping the moisture from it. He looked suddenly serious. 'Do you think this is a bubble?'

'Um, there's lots of bubbles. It's a –'

'No. This. A bubble. We're on this weird journey, where the normal rules don't apply. Real life doesn't apply. This whole trip has been . . . like time out of real life.'

She noticed that the water was pooling on the bathroom floor.

'Don't look at that. Talk to me.'

She dropped her lips to his collarbone, thinking. 'Well,' she said, lifting her head again, 'in a little over five days, we've dealt with illness, distraught children, sick relatives, unexpected acts of violence, nearly broken feet, police and car accidents. I'd say that was quite enough real life for anyone.'

'I like your thinking.'

'I like your everything.'

'We seem to spend a lot of time talking rubbish to each other.'

'Well, I like that too.'

The water had started to cool. She wriggled out of his arms, and stood, reaching for the heated towel rail. She handed him a warm towel, wrapping one around herself.

Oh, the utter sensual pleasure of fluffy hotel towels. He stood, rubbing at his hair vigorously with one hand.

She wondered, briefly, whether Ed was so used to fluffy hotel towels that he didn't even notice. She watched him and felt suddenly bone-weary. She brushed her teeth, switched off the bathroom light, and when she turned back he was already in the enormous hotel bed, holding back the covers to allow her in. He flicked off the bedside lamp and she lay there beside him in the dark, feeling his damp skin against her own, wondering what it would be like to have this every night. To have a man all to herself for ever.

'I don't know what's going to happen to me, Jess,' he said, into the dark, as if he could hear her thoughts. His voice was a warning.

'You'll be okay.'

'Seriously. You can't do your optimism tricks on this one. Whatever happens, I'm probably going to lose everything.'

'So? That's my default position.'

'But I might have to go away.'

'You won't.'

'I might, Jess.' His voice was uncomfortably firm.

And she spoke before she knew what she was saying. 'Then I'll wait,' she said.

She felt his head tilt towards her, a question. 'I'll wait for you. If you want me to.'

He took three calls on the final leg home, all on hands-free. His lawyer, a man with an accent so grand he should have been announcing the arrival of the Royal Family at dinner, told him he was due at the police station the following Thursday. No, nothing had changed. Yes, said Ed, he understood what was happening. And, yes, he had spoken to his family. The way he said it made her stomach tense. She couldn't help herself afterwards. She reached over and took his hand. When he squeezed it back he didn't look at her.

His sister rang to say his dad had had a better night. They had a long conversation about some insurance bonds that his father had been concerned about, some keys that were missing from a filing cabinet, and what Gemma had had for lunch. Nobody talked about dying. She said to say hello and Jess shouted hello back and felt a bit self-conscious and a bit pleased at the same time.

After lunch he took a call from a man called Lewis, and they discussed market values and percentages and the state of the mortgage market. It took Jess a while to realize he was talking about Beachfront.

'Time to sell,' he said, when he rang off. 'Still. Like you said, at least I have assets to dispose of.'

'What's it all going to cost you? The prosecution?'

'Oh. Nobody's saying. But reading between the lines, I think the answer is "most of it".'

She couldn't work out if he was more upset than he was letting on.

He tried to call someone else, but the answer phone kicked in. 'It's Ronan here. Leave a message.' He hung up without saying anything.

With every mile, real life moved steadily towards them

like an encroaching tide, cold, unstoppable. Jess thought about the fact that there was a whole swathe of his life she knew nothing about, and tried not to think about bubbles.

They finally arrived back shortly after four. As the Audi pulled into the street the rain had eased to a fine drizzle, the road looked oily with damp, the sprawling Danehall estate struggling to show spring promise. There was the little house, somehow smaller and scruffier than Jess remembered it and, oddly, like something that had nothing to do with her. Ed pulled up outside, and she peered out of the window at the peeling paintwork on the upstairs windows that Marty had never got round to painting because he said, really, you had to do a proper job, sanding it first and taking off the old paint and using filler to plug the gaps, and he had always been either too busy or too tired to do any of it. Just for a moment, she felt a wave of depression wash over her at the thought of all the problems that had been sitting there waiting for them on their return. And all the greater ones that she had created in her absence. And then she looked at Ed, who was helping Tanzie with her bag, and laughing at something Nicky said, leaning over to hear him better, and it passed.

He had stopped at a DIY superstore about an hour out of town – his detour – emerging with a great box of stuff that he had to wrestle into the back alongside their bags. It was possible he needed to tidy his house before he sold it. Jess couldn't think what you would do to that house to make it any nicer.

He dropped the last of the bags by the front door and stood there, holding the cardboard box. The children had disappeared immediately to their rooms, like creatures in some sort of homing experiment. Jess felt embarrassed then by the cluttered little house, the wood-chip wallpaper, the long row of battered paperbacks that snaked along the hall.

'I'm going back to my dad's tomorrow.'

A reflexive twinge at the thought of his absence. 'Good. That's good.'

'Just for a few days. Until the police thing. But I thought I'd put these up first.'

Jess looked down at the boxes.

'Security camera and motion-activated light. It shouldn't take more than a couple of hours.'

'You bought that for us?'

'Nicky got beaten up. Tanzie plainly doesn't feel safe. I thought it would make you all feel better. You know . . . if I'm not here.'

She stared at the box, at what it meant. She felt suddenly overwhelmed by the fact that this man had considered these things and wanted to protect them. She spoke before she knew what she wanted to say. 'You – you don't have to do that,' she stammered. 'I'm good at DIY. I'll do it.'

'On a ladder. With a busted foot.' He raised an eyebrow. 'You know, Jessica Rae Thomas, at some point you're going to have to let someone help you.'

'At some point you're going to have to stop calling me Jessica Rae Thomas.'

'I can't help it. I like it.'

She liked it too. 'Well, what shall I do, then?'

'Sit down. Stay still. Put your injured foot up. And then afterwards I'll walk into town with Nicky and we'll buy a disgustingly unhealthy waste-of-money takeaway because it might be the last one I get for a while. And then we'll sit here and eat it and afterwards you and I will lie around gazing in awe at the size of each other's stomachs.'

'Oh, my God, I love it when you talk dirty.'

So she sat. Doing nothing. On her own sofa. And Tanzie came and sat with her for a while and Ed went up a ladder outside and waved the drill at her through the window and pretended that he was going to fall off until it made her anxious. 'I've been in two different hospitals in eight days,' she yelled at him through the window, crossly. 'I do not want to make it a third.' And then, because she was not very good at sitting still, she sorted some dirty washing and put a load in, but after that she sat down again and just let everyone else move because she had to admit that resting her foot was a lot less painful than trying to do things on it.

And there was something so good about having everyone just potter around her, listening to the sound of Ed's drill and catching his eye through the window as he attached the camera and called at her to come, come and look. She couldn't remember the last time someone had done something to the house and it hadn't been her. 'Is that okay?'

She limped outside to see him. He stood back on the garden path, gazing up at the front of the house. 'I figured if I put it there it'll catch anyone who comes not just in your front garden but who hangs around outside. It's got a convex lens, see?' She tried to look interested. She was wondering whether once the children had gone to bed she could persuade him to stay over.

'And often, with these sorts of things, you find that just having a camera there is a deterrent.'

Would it really be that bad? He could always sneak out before they woke up. But, then, who were they really kidding? Nicky and Tanzie must have guessed something was going on, surely.

'Jess?'

He was standing in front of her.

'Mm?'

'All I have to do is drill a hole there, and feed the wires in through that wall. Hopefully I can put a little junction just inside and it should be fairly simple to connect it all up.'

He wore the satisfied look that men assume when in possession of power tools. He patted his pocket, checking for screws, then looked at her carefully. 'Were you listening to a single thing I've said?'

Jess grinned at him guiltily.

'Oh, you're incorrigible,' he said, after a minute. 'Honestly.'

Glancing around to make sure nobody was looking, he hooked his arm gently around her neck, pulled her close and kissed her. His chin was thick with stubble. 'Now let me get on. Undistracted. Go and dig out that takeaway menu.'

Jess limped, grinning, into the kitchen, and began rootling through the drawers. She couldn't remember the last time she had ordered a takeaway. She was pretty sure none of the menus were up to date. Ed went upstairs to connect up the wiring. He shouted down that he was going to need to move some furniture to get at the skirting.

'Fine by me,' she yelled back. She heard the rumbling, thunderous sound of large things being dragged around the floor above her head, as he tried to access the electricity, and marvelled again that somebody other than her was going to do it.

And then she lay back on the sofa, put a fresh bag of ice on her foot, and started going through the fistful of old menus that she had uncovered in the tea-towel drawer, unpicking the pages of those splashed with sauce, or yellowed with age, weeding out the restaurants that were miles away, or long closed. She was pretty sure the Chinese didn't exist any more. Some business with environmental health. The pizza place was unreliable. The curry-house menu looked pretty standard, but she couldn't shake the thought of that curly little hair in Nathalie's Jalfrezi. Still, chicken balti. Pilau rice. Poppadums. She thought of what he'd said about the two of them, side by side, gazing in awe at each other's stomachs. And then she forgot the curry and just thought about his naked stomach.

She was so distracted that she didn't hear his footsteps as he came slowly down the stairs. 'Jess?'

'I think this one will do it.' She held up the menu. 'I've

decided a hair of unknown provenance is a small price to pay for a decent jal –'

It was then that she saw his expression. And what he held, disbelieving, in his hand.

'Jess?' he said, and his voice sounded as if it belonged to someone else. 'Why would my security pass be in your sock drawer?'

28.

NICKY

Jess stayed in bed for almost two days.

Nicky came downstairs and she was just sitting on the sofa staring straight ahead of her, like she was in a trance. The Black & Decker drill sat on the windowsill and the ladder was still propped against the front of the house.

'Has Mr Nicholls gone to get the takeaway?' Nicky was a little annoyed that he didn't get to ask for onion bhajis.

She didn't seem to hear him.

'Jess?'

Her face was sort of frozen. She gave a little shake of her head and said, quietly, 'No.'

'He is coming back, though, right?' he said, after a minute. He opened the fridge door. He didn't know what he expected to find. There was a pack of shrivelled lemons and a half-empty jar of Branston pickle.

There was a long pause. 'I don't know,' she said. And then, like she'd forgotten she'd said it, 'I don't know.'

'So . . . we're not getting a takeaway?'

'No.'

Nicky let out a groan of disappointment. 'Well, I guess he'll have to come back at some point. I've got his laptop upstairs.'

They'd obviously had some kind of row, but she wasn't behaving like she did when she and Dad had had a row. Then she would slam a door and you'd hear her muttering, 'Dick,' under her breath, or wearing that really tight expression that said, *Why do I have to live with this idiot?* yet not saying anything when he shouted at her because of the children. Now she looked like someone who'd just been given six months to live.

'Are you okay?'

She blinked and put a hand to her forehead, like she was taking her temperature. 'Um. Nicky. I need . . . I need to lie down. Can you . . . can you sort yourself out? There's stuff. Food. In the freezer.'

In all the years Nicky had lived with her, Jess had never asked him to sort himself out. Even that time she'd had flu for two weeks. Before he could say anything, she turned and limped upstairs, really slowly, leaving him with it all.

At first when she didn't come down he had thought it was just because she and Mr Nicholls had had an argument, and she was being all melodramatic about it. He and Tanzie hovered outside her bedroom, discussing it in whispers. Then they took her in some tea and toast but she was just staring at the wall, even though the window was still open and it was getting cold outside. She hadn't seemed to notice. Nicky closed the window and put the ladder and the drill back in the garage, which seemed really enormous without the Rolls in it. And when he came back a couple of hours later to collect her plate the tea and toast were still there, just congealing on the bedside table beside her.

'She's probably exhausted from all the travelling,' said Tanzie, like an old lady.

But the next day Jess stayed in bed. When Nicky went in, the covers were barely rumpled and she was still wearing the exact same clothes she'd gone to bed in.

'Are you ill?' he said, opening the curtains. 'Do you want me to call the doctor?'

'I just need a day in bed, Nicky,' she said quietly.

'Nathalie came round. I said you'd call her. Something about cleaning.'

'Tell her I'm ill.'

'But you're not ill. And the police pound rang up to ask when you're picking up the car. And Mr Tsvangarai rang up but I didn't know what to say to him so I just let him leave a message on the answerphone.'

'Nicky. Please?' Her face was so sad that he felt bad for even saying anything. She waited a moment, then pulled the duvet up to her chin and turned away.

Nicky got breakfast for Tanzie. He felt oddly useful in the mornings now. He wasn't even missing his stash. He let Norman into the garden and cleaned up after him. Mr Nicholls had left the security light out by the window. It was still in its box, which had become damp because of the rain, but nobody had nicked it. Nicky picked it up, brought it inside and sat there, looking at it.

He thought about ringing Mr Nicholls, but he didn't know what he would say if he did. And he felt a bit weird asking Mr Nicholls to come back a second time. If someone wanted to be with you, after all, they just made it happen. Nicky knew that better than anyone. Whatever had gone on between him and Mum seemed serious enough that he wasn't sure he should interfere. It was serious enough that he hadn't come back for his laptop.

He sorted out his room. He went online for a while, but he was bored of gaming. He stared out of the window at the roofs of the high street and the distant orange brick of the leisure centre and he knew he didn't want to be an armour-clad droid shooting aliens out of the sky any more. He didn't want to be stuck in this room. Nicky thought back to the open road, and the feeling of Mr Nicholls's car taking them vast distances, that endless time when they didn't even know where they were headed next, and he realized that, more than anything, he wanted to be out of this little town.

He wanted to find his tribe.

Nicky had given it some considerable thought and concluded that by the afternoon of Day Two he was entitled to feel a little freaked out. School was due to start again after the weekend, and he wasn't sure how he was meant to look after Jess as well as Titch and the dog and everything else. He vacuumed the house and rewashed the load of damp laundry that he found sitting in the washing-machine, which had started to smell musty, and Tanzie helped him peg it out. He walked with her to the shop and they bought some bread and milk and dog food, and although he didn't show it to Tanze he was quite relieved that there was nobody hanging around

417

outside to call him 'fagboy' or 'freak' or whatever. And Nicky thought maybe, just maybe, Jess had been right and that things did change. And that maybe a new stage of his life was finally beginning.

A short time later, as he was going through the post, Tanzie arrived in the kitchen. 'Can we go back to the shop?'

He didn't look up. He was wondering whether to open the official letter addressed to Mrs J. Thomas. 'We've just been to the shop.'

'Then can I go by myself?'

He looked up then, and started a little. She had done something weird to her hair, putting it up on one side with a load of glittery slides. She didn't look like Tanzie.

'I want to get Mum a card,' she said. 'To cheer her up a bit.'

Nicky was pretty sure a card wasn't going to do it. 'Why don't you make her one, Titch? Save your money.'

'I always make her one. Sometimes it's nice to get a shop card.'

He studied her face. 'Have you got makeup on?'

'Only a bit of lipstick.'

'Jess wouldn't let you wear lipstick. Take it off.'

'Suze wears it.'

'I don't think that's going to make Jess any happier about it, Titch. Look, take it off and I'll give you a proper makeup lesson when you get back.'

She pulled her jacket from the hook and left. Mum had let Tanzie walk to the shop and back since she was nine.

'I'll rub it off on the way,' she called, over her shoulder.

'Take Norman with you,' he yelled. Then he made a cup of coffee and carried it upstairs. It was time to sort Jess out. Saying those words to himself made Nicky feel weirdly grown-up. It was time to sort Jess out.

The room was dark. It was a quarter to three in the afternoon but she hadn't even bothered opening the curtains. 'Leave it on the side,' she murmured. The room held the fug of unwashed bodies and undisturbed air.

'It's stopped raining.'

'Good.'

'Jess, you need to get up.'

She didn't say anything.

'Really. You need to get up. It's starting to honk in here.'

'I'm tired, Nicky. I just need . . . a rest.'

'You don't need rest. You're . . . you're the household Duracell Bunny.'

'Please, love.'

'I don't get it, Jess. What's going on?'

She turned over, really slowly, then propped herself up on one elbow. Downstairs the dog had begun to bark at something, insistent, erratic. Jess rubbed at her eyes. 'Where's Tanzie?'

'Shop.'

'Has she eaten?'

'Yes. But mostly cereal. I can't really cook anything more than fish fingers and she's sick of those.'

She looked at Nicky, then out towards the window, as if weighing something up. And then she said, 'He's not coming back.' And her face sort of crumpled.

The dog was really barking outside now, the idiot. Nicky tried to stay focused on what Jess was saying. 'Really? Never?'

A great fat tear rolled down her cheek. She wiped it away with the flat of her hand and shook her head. 'You know the really stupid bit, Nicky? I actually forgot. I forgot I did it. I was so happy while we were away, it was like all the time before had happened to someone else. Oh, that bloody dog.'

She wasn't really making sense. He wondered if she actually was ill.

'You could call him.'

'I tried. He's not picking up.'

'Do you want me to go over there?'

Even as he asked he slightly regretted it. Because even though he really liked Mr Nicholls he knew better than anyone that you couldn't make someone stay with you. There was no point trying to hang on to someone who didn't want you.

It's possible she'd told him because she didn't have anyone else to tell. 'I loved him, Nicky. I know it sounds stupid after such a short time, but I loved him.' It was a shock to hear her say it. All that emotion, just blurted out there. But just for once it didn't make him want to run. Nicky sat on the bed, leant over and, although he still felt a bit weird about actual physical contact, he hugged her. And she felt really small, even though he'd always thought of her as sort of bigger than he was. And she rested her head against him and he just felt really, really sad because for once he did want to say something but he didn't know what.

It was at that point that Norman's barking got hysterical. Like when he saw the cows in Scotland. Nicky pulled back, distracted. 'He sounds like he's going insane.'

'Bloody dog. It'll be that chihuahua from fifty-six.' Jess sniffed and wiped at her eyes. 'I swear it torments him on purpose.'

Nicky climbed off the bed and walked over to the window. Norman was in the garden, barking hysterically, his head thrust through the gap in the fence where the wood was rotten and two of the panels had half broken away. It took him a few seconds to register that he didn't look like Norman. The dog was weirdly upright, his hair bristling. Nicky pulled the curtain back further, and it was then that he saw Tanzie across the road. There were two Fishers and a boy he didn't recognize and they had backed her up against the wall. As Nicky watched, one of them grabbed at her jacket and she tried to bat his hand away. 'Hey! Hey!' he yelled, but they didn't hear him. His heart thumping, Nicky wrestled with the sash window but it refused to budge. He banged on the glass, trying to make them stop. 'HEY! Shit. HEY!'

'What?' said Jess, swivelling in the bed.

'Fishers.'

They heard Tanzie's high-pitched scream. As Jess dived out of bed, Norman stilled for a split second, then hurled himself against the weakest section of the fence. He went through it like a canine battering ram, sending pieces of wood splintering into the air around him. Straight towards the sound of Tanzie's voice. Nicky saw the Fishers spin round to see this enormous black missile coming for them and their mouths opened. And then he heard the screech of brakes, a surprisingly loud whumph, Jess's Oh, God, oh, God and then a silence that seemed to go on and on for ever.

29.

TANZIE

Tanzie had sat in her room for almost an hour trying to draw Mum a card. She couldn't work out what to put on it. Mum seemed like she was sick, but Nicky said she wasn't really sick, not like Mr Nicholls had been sick, so it didn't seem right to write a Get Well Soon card. She thought about writing 'Be Happy!' but it sounded like an instruction. Or even an accusation. And then she thought about just writing 'I Love You' but she'd wanted to do it in red and all her red felt-tips had run out. So then she thought she'd buy a card because Mum always said that Dad had never bought her a single one, apart from a really cheesy padded Valentine's Day card once when they were courting. And she burst out laughing at the word 'courting'.

Mostly Tanzie just wanted her to cheer up. A mum should be in charge, taking care of things and bustling around downstairs, not lying up there in the dark, like she was really a million miles away. It made Tanzie fearful. Ever since Mr Nicholls had gone, the house had felt weirdly quiet and a massive lump had lodged itself in her stomach, like something bad was about to happen. She had crept into Mum's room that morning when she woke up and crawled into bed with her for a cuddle and Mum had put her arms around her and kissed the top of her head. Her hair was a bit greasy and she had no makeup on but Tanzie nestled into her anyway. 'Are you ill, Mum?' she'd said.

'I'm just tired, Tanze,' Mum's voice did sound like the saddest, tiredest thing in the world. 'I'll get up soon. I promise.'

'Is it . . . because of me?'

'What?'

'Not wanting to do maths any more. Is that what's making you sad?'

And then Mum's eyes filled with tears and Tanzie felt like she'd somehow made things even worse. 'No, Tanze,' she said, and pulled her close. 'No, darling. It is absolutely nothing to do with you and maths. That is the last thing you should think.'

But she didn't get up.

So Tanzie was walking along the road with two pounds fifteen in her pocket that Nicky had given her, even though she could tell he thought a card was a stupid idea, and wondering if it was better to get a cheaper card and some chocolate or if a cheap card spoiled the whole point of a card full stop when a car pulled up alongside. She thought it was someone going to ask for directions to Beachfront (people were always asking for directions to Beachfront) but it was Jason Fisher.

'Oi. Freak,' he said, and she kept walking. His hair was gelled up in spikes and his eyes were narrowed, like he spent his whole life squinting at things he didn't like.

'I said, Freak.'

Tanzie tried not to look at him. Her heart had begun to thump. She began to walk a little bit faster.

He pulled forward a bit, so that she thought maybe he was going to go away. But he stopped the car and got out and swaggered over so that he was in front of her and she couldn't actually go any further without pushing past him. He leant to one side, like he was explaining something to someone stupid.

'It's rude not to answer someone when they're talking to you. Did your mum never tell you that?'

Tanzie was so frightened that she couldn't talk. She just shook her head.

'Where's your brother?'

'I don't know.' Her voice came out as a whisper.

'Yes, you do, you little four-eyed freak. Your brother thinks he's been a bit clever messing around with my Facebook.'

'He didn't,' she said. But she was a really bad liar and she knew as soon as she'd said it that he knew she was lying.

He took two steps towards her. 'You tell him that I'm going to have him, the cocky little shit. He thinks he's so clever. Tell him I'm going to mess with his profile for real.'

The other Fisher, the cousin whose name she never remembered, muttered something to him that Tanzie couldn't hear. They were all out of the car now, walking slowly towards her.

'Yeah,' Jason Fisher said. 'Your brother needs to understand something. He messes with something of mine, we mess around with something of his.' He lifted

425

his chin and spat noisily on the pavement. It sat there in front of her, a great green slug. Tanzie hesitated, not wanting to tread in it.

She wondered if they could see how hard she was breathing.

'Get in the car.'

'What?'

'Get in the fucking car.'

'No.' She began to back away from them. She glanced around her, trying to work out if anyone was coming down the road. Her heart hammered against her ribs like a bird in a cage.

'Get in the fucking car, Costanza.' He said it like her name was something disgusting. She wanted to run then but she was really bad at running – her legs always swung out to the sides at the wrong angle – and she knew they would catch her. She wanted to cross the road and turn back towards home but she knew that as soon as she started to run they would get her. And then a hand landed on her shoulder.

'Look at her hair.'

'You know about boys, Four Eyes?'

'Course she doesn't know about boys. Look at the state of her.'

'She's got lipstick on, the little tart. Still fugly, though.'

'Yeah, but you don't have to look at its face, do you?' They started laughing. Her voice came out sounding like someone else's: 'Just leave me alone. Nicky didn't do anything. We just want to be left alone.'

'We just want to be left alone.' Their voices were

mocking. Fisher took a step closer. His voice lowered. 'Just get into the fucking car, Costanza.'

'Leave me alone!'

He started grabbing at her then, his hands snatching at her clothes. Panic washed over her in an icy wave, tightening her throat, pushing her heart against her ribs. She tried to push him away. She might have been shouting but nobody came. The two of them grabbed her arms and were pulling her towards the car. She could hear their grunts of effort, smell their deodorant, as her feet scrabbled for purchase on the pavement. And she knew like she knew anything that she should not get inside. Because as that door opened in front of her, like the jaws of some great animal, she suddenly remembered an American statistic for girls who got into strange men's cars. Your odds of survival dropped by 72 per cent as soon as you put your foot in that footwell. That statistic became a solid thing in front of her. Tanzie took hold of it and she hit and she kicked and she bit and she heard someone swear as her foot made contact with soft flesh and then something hit the side of her head and she reeled and spun and there was a crack as she hit the ground. Everything went sideways. There was scuffling, a distant shout. And she lifted her head and her sight was all blurry but she thought she saw Norman coming towards her across the road at a speed she'd never seen, his teeth bared and his eyes black, looking not like Norman at all but some kind of demon, and then there was a flash of red and the squeal of brakes and all Tanzie saw was something black flying into the air like a ball of washing and all she heard was the scream, the screaming that went on and on, the sound of the end of the world, the worst sound you ever heard, and she realized it was her it was her it was the sound of her own voice.

30.

JESS

He was on the ground. Jess ran, breathless, barefoot, into the street and the man was standing there, both hands on his head, rocking on his feet, saying, 'I never even saw it. I never saw it. It just ran straight out into the road.'

Nicky was on the ground beside him, cradling his head, white as a sheet and murmuring, 'Come on, fella. Come on.' Tanzie was wide-eyed with shock, her arms rigid at her sides.

Jess knelt. Norman's eyes were glass marbles. Blood seeped from his mouth and ear. 'Oh, no, you daft old thing. Oh, Norman. Oh, no.' She put her ear to his chest. Nothing. A great sob rose into her throat.

She felt Tanzie's hand on her shoulder, her fist grabbing a handful of her T-shirt and pulling at it again and again. 'Mum, make it all right. Mum, make him all right.' Tanzie dropped to her knees and buried her face in his coat. 'Norman. Norman.' And then she began to howl.

Beneath her shrieking, Nicky's words emerged garbled and confused. 'They were trying to get Tanzie into the car. I was trying to get you but I couldn't open the window. I just couldn't open it and I was shouting and he just went through the garden fence. Before I could get there. He knew. He went straight through. He was trying to help her.'

Nathalie came running down the road, her shirt fastened with the wrong buttons, hair half done in rollers. She wrapped her arms around Tanzie and held her close, rocking her, trying to stop the noise.

Norman's eyes had stilled. Perhaps focused on some distant piece of food. Jess lowered her head to his and felt her heart break.

'I've called the emergency vet,' someone said.

She stroked his big soft ear. 'Thank you,' she whispered.

'We've got to do something, Jess.' He said it again, more urgently. 'Now.'

She put a trembling hand on Nicky's shoulder. 'I think he's gone, sweetheart.'

'No. You don't say that. You're the one who said we don't say that. We don't give in. You're the one who says it's all going to be okay. You don't say that.'

And as Tanzie began to wail again, Nicky's face crumpled. And he began to sob, one elbow bent across his face, huge, gasping sobs, as if a dam had finally broken.

Jess sat in the middle of the road, as the cars crawled around her, and the curious neighbours hovered on the front steps of their houses, and she held her old dog's enormous bloodied head on her lap and she lifted her face to the heavens and said silently, What now? WHAT THE HELL NOW?

*

She didn't see Jason Fisher climb into the car and drive away.

But the CCTV did.

31.

TANZIE

Her mother brought her indoors. Tanzie didn't want to leave him. She didn't want him to die out there on the Tarmac, alone, strangers staring at him with open mouths and murmured whispers, but Mum wouldn't listen. Nigel from next door came running out and said he would take over and the next thing Mum was pulling her indoors, her arms tight around Tanzie, and as she kicked and screamed for him, her voice was close in Tanzie's ear, arms clasped around her middle, 'Sweetheart, it's all all right, sweetheart, come on inside, don't look, it's all going to be okay.' But even as she closed the front door, head against hers, pulling Tanzie to her, and her eyes were blind with tears, Tanzie could hear Nicky sobbing behind them in the hallway, weird jagged sobs like it wasn't even something he knew how to do, and Mum was finally lying to her because it wasn't going to be okay, it never could be, because it was actually the end of everything.

32.

ED

'Sometimes,' Gemma said, glancing behind her at the puce, screaming child, arching its back at the next table, 'I think the worst sort of parenting is not actually witnessed by social workers but by baristas.' She stirred her coffee briskly, as if biting back a natural urge to say something.

The mother, her blonde corkscrew curls cascading stylishly over her back, continued to ask the child in soothing tones to stop and drink its 'babycino'. It ignored her, possibly unable to hear her over the self-created noise levels.

'I don't see why we couldn't go to the pub.'

'At eleven fifteen in the morning? Jesus, why doesn't she just tell him to stop? Or take him out? Does nobody know how to distract a child any more?'

The child screamed louder. Ed's head had begun to hurt.

'We could go.'

'Go where?'

'The pub. It would be quieter.'

She stared at him, and then she ran a speculative finger across his chin. 'Ed, how much did you drink last night?'

He had emerged from the police station spent. They had met his barrister afterwards – Ed had already forgotten his name – with Paul Wilkes and two other solicitors, one of whom specialized in insider-trading cases. They sat around the mahogany table and spoke as if choreographed, laying out the prosecution case baldly, so that Ed was in no doubt about what lay ahead. Against him: the email trail, Deanna Lewis's testimony, her brother's phone calls, the FSA's new determination to stamp down on perpetrators of insider trading. His own cheque, complete with signature.

Deanna had sworn that she had not known what she was doing was wrong. She stated Ed had pressed the money on her. She said that had she known what he was suggesting was illegal she would never have done it. Nor would she have told her brother.

The evidence for him: that he had plainly not gained a cent from the transaction. His legal team said – in his opinion, a little too cheerfully – that they would stress his ignorance, his ineptitude, that he was new to money, the ramifications and responsibilities of directorship. They would claim that Deanna Lewis knew very well what she was doing; that his and Deanna's short relationship was actually evidence of her and her brother's entrapment. The investigating team had been all over Ed's accounts and found them gratifyingly unrewarding. He paid the full whack of tax every year. He had no investments. He had always liked things simple.

And the cheque was not addressed to her. It was in

her possession, but her name was in her own writing. They would assert that she had taken a blank cheque from his home at some point during the relationship, they said.

'But she didn't,' he said.

Nobody seemed to hear.

It could go either way with the prison sentence, they told him, but whatever happened Ed was undoubtedly looking at a hefty fine. And obviously the end of his time with Mayfly. He would be banned from holding a directorship, possibly for some considerable time. Ed needed to be prepared for all these things. They began to confer among themselves.

And then he had said it: 'I want to plead guilty.'

'What?'

The room fell silent.

'I did tell her to do it. I didn't think about it being illegal. I just wanted her to go away so I told her how she could make some money.'

They stared at each other.

'Ed –' his sister began.

'I want to tell the truth.'

One of the solicitors leant forward. 'We actually have quite a strong defence, Mr Nicholls. I think that given the lack of your handwriting on the cheque – their only substantive piece of evidence – we can successfully claim that Ms Lewis used your account for her own ends.'

'But I did give her the cheque.'

Paul Wilkes leant forward. 'Ed, you need to be clear

about this. If you plead guilty, you substantially increase your chance of a custodial sentence.'

'I don't care.'

'You will care, when you're doing twenty-three hours in solitary in Winchester for your own safety.'

He barely heard her. 'I just want to tell the truth. That's how it was.'

'Ed,' his sister grabbed at his arm, 'the truth has no place in a courtroom. You're going to make things worse.'

But he shook his head and sat back in his chair. And then he didn't say anything more.

He knew they thought he was odd, but he didn't care. He couldn't bring himself to look exercised by any of it. He sat there, numb. His sister asked most of the questions. He heard Financial Services and Markets Act 2000 *blah blah blah*. He heard open prison and punitive fines and Criminal Justice Act 1993 *blah blah blah* and he sat there and he honestly couldn't make himself care less about any of it. So he was going to prison for a bit? So what? He had lost everything anyway, twice over.

'Ed? Did you hear what I said?'

'Sorry.'

Sorry. It's all he seemed to say these days. Sorry, I didn't hear you. Sorry, I wasn't listening. Sorry I fucked it all up. Sorry I was stupid enough to fall in love with someone who actually believed I was an idiot.

And there: the now familiar clench at the thought of her. How could she have lied to him? How could they

436

have sat side by side in that car for the best part of a week, and she hadn't even begun to let on what she had done?

How could she have talked to him of her financial fears? How could she have talked to him of trust, have collapsed into his arms, all the while knowing that she had stolen money right out of his pocket?

She hadn't even needed to say anything in the end. It was her silence that told him. The fractional delay between her registering the sight of the security card that he held, disbelieving, in his hand, and her stuttering attempt to explain it.

I was going to tell you.

It's not what you're thinking. The hand to the mouth.

I wasn't thinking.

Oh, God. It's not –

She was worse than Lara. At least Lara had been honest, in her way, about his attractions. She liked the money. She liked how he looked, once she had shaped him according to what she wanted. He thought they had both understood, deep down, that their marriage was a kind of deal. He had told himself that everybody's marriages were, one way or another.

But Jess? Jess had behaved as if he were the only man she had ever truly wanted. Jess had let him think it was the real him she liked, even when he was puking, or with his face bashed up, or afraid to meet his own parents. She had smiled sweetly and let him think it was him.

'Ed?'

'Sorry?' He lifted his head from his hands.

'I know it's tough. But you will survive this.' His sister reached across and squeezed his hand. Somewhere behind her the child screamed. His head pulsed.

'Sure,' he said.

The moment she left he went to the pub.

They had fast-tracked the hearing, following his revised plea, and Ed spent the last few days before it took place with his father. It was partly down to choice, partly because he no longer had a flat in London that contained any furniture, everything having been packed for storage, ready for the completion of the sale.

It had sold for the asking price without a single viewing. The estate agent didn't seem to find this surprising. 'We have a waiting list for this block,' he said, as Ed handed him the spare keys. 'Investors, wanting a safe place for their money. To be honest, it will probably just sit there empty for a few years until they feel like selling it.'

It dawned on him then that nearly all the flats around him had slowly emptied; the evenings he had arrived home and been surprised by how few lights were on in the block now made sense. For a brief moment Ed wanted to snatch back the keys. How can that be right? What about all the people who need somewhere to live? But he swallowed his protest. As soon as both properties were sold, he had to find some smaller, cheaper option, once he knew what was left. Once he knew where, and whether, he was likely to be able to get another job. It felt weird not to know where that was likely to be.

For three nights Ed stayed at his parents' house, sleeping in his childhood room, waking in the small hours and running his fingers across the surface of the woodchip wallpaper behind his headboard, recalling the sound of his teenage sister's feet thundering up the stairs, the slam of her bedroom door as she digested whatever insult their father had apparently directed her way this time. In the mornings he sat and had breakfast with his mother in the too-silent kitchen and slowly grasped that his father was never coming home. That they would never see him there again, flicking his paper irritably into straight corners, reaching without looking for his mug of strong black coffee (no sugar). Occasionally she would burst into tears, apologizing and waving him away as she pressed a napkin to her eyes. I'm fine, I'm fine. Really, love. Just ignore me.

In the overheated confines of Room Three, Victoria Ward, Bob Nicholls spoke less, ate less, did less. Ed didn't need to speak to a doctor to see what was happening. The flesh seemed to be disappearing from him, melting away, leaving his skin pulled translucent over his skull, his eyes great, bruised sockets: Death was claiming him.

They played chess. Talking tired him but, oddly, he could play chess. He often fell asleep mid-game, drifting off during a move, and Ed would sit patiently at his bedside and wait for him to wake again. And when his eyes opened, and he took a moment or two to register where he was, his mouth closing, and his eyebrows lowering as he took in the state of play on the board, Ed would move a piece and act as if it had been a minute, not an hour, that he had been missing from the game.

They talked. Not about the important stuff. Ed wasn't sure either of them were built that way. They talked about cricket, and the weather, and the ridiculous cost of the pay-as-you-go entertainment system at the foot of the bed. Ed's father talked about the nurse with the dimples who always thought up something funny to tell him. He asked Ed to look after his mother. He worried she was doing too much. He worried that the man who cleared the guttering would overcharge her if he wasn't there. He was annoyed that he had spent lots of money in the autumn having the moss removed from the lawn and he wouldn't get to see the results. Ed didn't try to argue. It would have seemed patronizing.

'So, where's the firecracker?' he said, one evening. He was two moves from checkmate. Ed was trying to work out how to block him.

'The what?'

'Your girl.'

'Lara? Dad, you know we got —'

'Not her. The other one.'

Ed took a breath. 'Jess? She's . . . uh . . . she's at home, I think.'

'I liked her. She had a way of looking at you.' He pushed his castle forward slowly onto a black square.

'I'm glad you have her.' He gave a slight nod. 'Trouble,' he murmured, almost to himself, and smiled.

Ed's strategy went to pieces. His father beat him in three moves.

33.

JESS

The bearded man emerged from the swing doors wiping his hands on his white coat. He paused in the doorway, like someone who had walked into a room and couldn't remember why they'd gone in.

'Norman Thomas?'

Jess had never considered their dog might have a surname.

'Norman Thomas? Large, indeterminate breed?' he said, lowering his chin and looking straight at her.

She scrambled to standing in front of the plastic chairs. 'He has suffered massive internal injuries,' he said, with no preamble. 'He has a broken hip and several broken ribs and a fractured front leg and we won't know what's going on inside until the swelling's gone down. And I'm afraid he's definitely lost the left eye.' She noticed there were bright smears of blood on his blue plastic shoes.

She felt Tanzie's hand tighten in hers. 'But he's still alive?'

'I don't want to give you false hope.' His voice held the careful modulation of someone who had witnessed drowning men cling to the smallest pieces of driftwood. 'The next forty-eight hours will be critical.'

Beside her Tanzie gave a low moan of something that might have been joy or anguish, it was hard to tell.

'Walk with me.' He took Jess's elbow, turning his back on the children, and lowered his voice. 'I have to say that I'm not sure, given the extent of his injuries, if the kindest thing wouldn't be to let him go.'

'But if he does survive forty-eight hours?'

'Then he may stand some chance of recovery. But as I said, Mrs Thomas, I don't want to give you false hope. He really isn't a well lad.'

Around them the waiting clients were watching silently, their cats in pet carriers cradled on their laps, their small dogs panting gently under chairs. Nicky was staring at the vet, his jaw set in a tense line. His mascara was smudged around his eyes.

'And if we do proceed, it's not going to be cheap. He may need more than one operation. Possibly even several. Is he insured?'

Jess shook her head.

Now the vet became awkward. 'I need to warn you that going forwards his treatment is likely to cost a significant sum. And there are no guarantees of recovery. It's very important that you understand that before we go any further.'

It was her neighbour Nigel who had saved him. He had run from his house carrying two blankets, one to wrap around the shivering Tanzie, the other to cover the body of the dog. Go indoors, he had instructed Jess. Take the kids indoors. But as he drew the tartan rug gently over Norman's head, he had paused, and said to Nathalie, 'Did you see that?'

She hadn't heard him at first, over the sound of the crowd, and Tanzie's muffled wailing and the children crying nearby because even though they didn't know him they understood the utter sadness of a dog lying motionless in the road.

'Nathalie? His tongue. Look. I think, he's panting. Here, pick him up. Get him in the car. Quick!' It had taken three of Jess's neighbours to lift him. They had laid him carefully on the rear seat, and had driven in a blur to the big veterinary practice on the outskirts of town. It wasn't as quick as Mr Miller by the crossroads, but they had an operating theatre and hotlines to all sorts of specialists. Nathalie had cradled Norman on the back seat, crouching in the footwell so that she could support his head. Jess loved Nigel for not once mentioning the blood all over his upholstery. They had rung her from the vet's and told her to get down there as fast as she could. Under her jacket, she was still in her pyjamas.

'So what do you want to do?'

Lisa Ritter had once told Jess about a huge deal her husband had done that had gone wrong. 'Borrow five thousand and you can't pay it back, and it's your problem,' she said, quoting him. 'Borrow five million and it's the bank's problem.'

Jess looked at her daughter's pleading face. She looked at Nicky's raw expression: the grief and love and fear

444

that he finally felt able to express. She was the only person who could make this right. She was the only person who would ever be able to make it right.

'Do whatever it takes,' she said. 'I'll find the money. Just do it.'

The short pause told her he thought she was a fool. But of a kind he was well used to dealing with. 'Come this way, then,' he said. 'I need you to sign some paperwork.'

Nigel drove them home. She tried to give him some money but he waved her away gruffly and said, 'What are neighbours for?' Belinda cried as she came out to greet them.

'We're fine,' she muttered dully, her arm around Tanzie, who still shook intermittently. 'We're fine. Thank you.'

They would call, the vet said, if there was any news.

Jess didn't tell the kids to go to bed. She wasn't sure she wanted them to be alone in their rooms. She locked the door, bolted it twice, and put an old film on. She went around the house and secured every window, drawing the curtains and propping a chair underneath the back-door handle just for good measure. Then she made three mugs of cocoa, brought her duvet down and sat under it, one child on each side of her, watching television that they didn't see, each alone with their thoughts. Praying, praying that the telephone wouldn't ring.

34.

NICKY

This is the story of a family who didn't fit in. A little girl who was a bit weird and geeky and liked maths more than makeup. And a boy who liked makeup and didn't fit into any tribes. And this is what happens to families who don't fit in – they end up broken and skint and sad. No happy ending here, folks.

Mum doesn't stay in bed any more, but I catch her wiping her eyes as she washes up or gazing down at Norman's basket. She's busy all the time: working, cleaning, sorting out the house. She does it with her head down and her jaw set. She packed up three whole boxes of her paperback books and took them back to the charity shop because she said she'd never have time to read them and, besides, it's pointless believing in fiction.

I miss Norman. It's weird how you can miss something you only ever complained about. Our house is weirdly quiet without him. But since the first forty-eight hours went past, and Mr Adamson said he was in with a chance, and we all cheered down the phone, I've started to worry about other stuff. We sat on the sofa last night after

Tanzie went to bed and the phone still didn't ring and then I said to Mum, 'So what are we going to do?'

She looked up from the television.

'I mean, if he lives.'

She let out a long breath, like this was something that had already occurred to her. And then she said, 'You know what, Nicky? We didn't have a choice. He's Tanzie's dog, and he saved her. If you don't have a choice then it's actually quite simple.'

I could see that even though she really did believe this, and it might actually be quite simple, the extra debt is like a new weight settling on her. That with each new problem she just looks a bit older, and flatter and wearier.

She doesn't talk about Mr Nicholls.

I couldn't believe after how they'd been together that it could just end like that. Like one minute you can seem really happy and then nothing. I thought you got all that stuff sorted when you get older, but clearly you don't. So that's something else to look forward to.

I walked up to her then, and I gave her a hug. And that might not be a big deal in your family, but I can tell you in mine it is. It's about the only stupid difference I can make.

So this is the thing I don't understand. I don't understand how our family can basically do the right thing and yet always end up in the crap. I don't understand how my little sister can be brilliant and kind and some sort of damn

447

genius, and yet pretty much everything she loves has disappeared, just because she's a bit different. I don't understand how it is that she now wakes up crying and having nightmares and I have to lie awake listening to Mum pottering across the landing at four a.m. trying to calm her down, and how she stays inside in the day, even though it's finally warm and sunny, because she's too afraid to go outside any more in case the Fishers come back to get her. And how in six months' time she'll be at a school whose main message is that she should be like everyone else or she'll get her head kicked in, like her freak of a brother did. I think about Tanzie without maths, and it just feels like the whole universe has gone mad. It's like . . . Morecambe without Wise, or Jaffa Cakes without the orange. I just can't imagine who Tanze will even be if she doesn't do maths any more.

I don't understand why I had just got used to sleeping and now I lie awake listening for non-existent sounds downstairs, and how now when I want to go to the shop to buy a paper or some sweets I feel sick again and have to fight the urge to look over my shoulder.

I don't understand how a big, useless, soppy dog, who has basically never done anything worse than dribble on everyone, had to lose an eye and get his insides rearranged just because he tried to protect the person he loves.

Mostly, I don't understand how the bullies and the thieves and the people who just destroy everything – the arseholes – get away with it. The boys who punch you in your kidneys for your dinner money, and the police who think it's funny to treat you like you're an idiot, and the kids who take the piss out of anyone who isn't just like them, whether they're posh and at a maths competition, or a stupid, ignorant idiot who doesn't know the difference between a username and a password. Or the dads who walk right out and just start afresh somewhere new that smells of Febreze with a woman who drives her own Toyota and owns a three-piece with no marks on it and laughs at all their stupid jokes like they're God's gift and not actually a slimeball who lied to all the people who loved him for two whole years. Two whole years.

Mum always told us that good things happen to good people. Guess what? She doesn't say that any more.

I'm sorry if this blog has just got really depressing but that's how our life is right now. My family, the eternal losers. It's not a story, really, is it? It's a flipping cautionary tale.

35.

JESS

The police came on the fourth day after Norman's accident. Jess watched the officer coming up the garden path through the living-room window and for one stupid minute she thought she had come to tell her Norman had died. A young woman; red hair pulled back in a neat pony tail. One Jess hadn't seen before.

She was coming in response to reports about an RTA, she said, as she opened the door.

'Don't tell me,' Jess said, walking back down the hall to the kitchen. 'The driver's going to sue us for damaging his car.' It was Nigel who had warned her this might happen. She had actually started to laugh when he said it.

The officer looked at her notebook. 'Well, not at the moment, at least. The damage to his car seems to be minimal. And there have been conflicting statements as to whether he was exceeding the speed limit. But we've had various reports about what happened in the lead-up to the accident and I was wondering if you could clarify a few things?'

'What's the point?' Jess said, turning back to the washing-up. 'You lot never take any notice.'

She knew how she sounded: like half the residents of this estate – antagonistic, braced for confrontation, hard-done-by. She no longer cared. But the officer was too new, too keen, to play that game.

'Well, do you think you could tell me what happened anyway? I'll only take five minutes of your time.'

So Jess told her, in the flat tones of someone who no longer expected to be believed. She told her about the Fishers, and their history with them, and the fact that she now had a daughter who was afraid to play in her own garden, even though Jess had repaired the hole in the fence. She told her about her daft cow-sized dog who was racking up bills at the vet's roughly equivalent to if she had bought him a suite in a luxury hotel. She told her how her son's sole aim now was to get as far from this town as possible, and how, thanks to the Fishers having made a misery of his exam year at school, this was unlikely to happen.

The officer didn't look bored. She stood, leaning against the kitchen cabinets, and taking notes. Then she asked Jess to show her the fence. Jess didn't bother going outside. 'There,' she said, pointing through the window. 'You can see where I've mended it, by the lighter wood. And the accident, if that's what we're calling it, happened about fifty yards up on the right.' She watched her walk outside, and turned back to the sink. Aileen Trent, pulling her shopping trolley, gave her a cheery wave over the hedge. Then, when she registered who was in the garden, she ducked her head and walked swiftly the other way.

PC Kenworthy was out there for almost ten minutes. Jess almost forgot about her. She was unloading the washing-machine when the officer let herself back in.

'Can I ask you a question, Mrs Thomas?' she said, closing the back door behind her.

'That's your job,' Jess said.

'You've probably been through this a dozen times already. But your CCTV camera. Does it have any film in it?'

Jess watched the footage three times after PC Kenworthy called her into the station, sitting beside her on a plastic chair in Interview Suite Three. It chilled her every time: the tiny figure, her sequined sleeves glinting in the sun, walking slowly along the edge of the screen, pausing to push her spectacles up her nose. The car that slows, the door that opens. One, two, three of them. Tanzie's body language. The slight step backwards, the nervous glance behind, back down the road. The raised hands. And then they're on her and Jess cannot watch.

'I'd say that was pretty conclusive evidence, Mrs Thomas. And on good-quality footage. The CPS will be delighted,' she said cheerfully, and it took Jess several seconds to grasp that she was serious about this. That somebody was actually taking them seriously.

At first Fisher had denied it, of course. He said they were 'having a joke' with Tanzie. 'But we have her testimony. And two witnesses who have come forward. And we have screenshots of Jason Fisher's Facebook account discussing how he was going to do it.'

'Do what?'

Her smile faded for a minute. 'Something not very nice to your daughter.'

Jess didn't ask anything else.

They had received an anonymous tip that he used his name as his password. The div, PC Kenworthy said. She actually said 'div'. 'Between us,' she said, as she let Jess out, 'that hacked evidence may not be strictly admissible in court. But let's just say it gave us a leg up.'

The case was reported in vague terms at first. Several local youths, the local papers said. Arrested for assault of a minor and attempted kidnap. But they were in the newspapers again the following week, and named. Apparently the Fisher family had been instructed to move out of their council house. The Thomases were not the only people they had been harassing. The housing association was quoted as saying the family had long been on a last warning.

Nicky held up the local newspaper over tea and he read the story aloud. They were all silent for a moment, unable to believe what they had heard.

'It actually says the Fishers have to move somewhere else?'

'That's what it says,' Nicky said.

'But what will happen to them?' Jess said, her fork still halfway to her mouth.

'Well, it says here, they're going to move to Surrey, to near his brother-in-law.'

'Surrey? But –'

'They're not the housing association's responsibility

any more. None of them. Jason Fisher. And his cousin and his family. They're moving in with some uncle. And, even better, there's an exclusion order preventing them from returning to the estate. Look, there's two pictures of his mum crying and saying they've always been misunderstood and Jason wouldn't hurt a fly.' He pushed the newspaper across the table towards her.

Jess read the story twice, just to check he'd understood it correctly. That she'd understood it correctly. 'They actually get arrested if they come back here?'

'See, Mum?' he said, chewing on a piece of bread. 'You were right. Things can change.'

Jess sat very still. She looked at the newspaper, then back at him, until he realized what he had called her, and she could see him colouring, hoping she wouldn't make a big deal out of it. So she swallowed and then she wiped both her eyes with the heels of her palms and stared at her plate for a minute before she began eating again. 'Right,' she said, her voice strangled. 'Well. That's good news. Very good news.'

'Do you really think things can change?' Tanzie's eyes were big and dark and wary.

Jess put down her knife and fork. 'I think I do, love. I mean, we all have our down moments. But, yes, I do.'

And Tanzie looked at Nicky and back at Jess, and then she carried on eating.

Life went on. Jess walked to the Feathers on a Saturday lunchtime, hiding her limp for the last twenty yards, and pleaded for her job back. Des told her he'd taken on a girl from the City of Paris. 'Not the actual city of Paris. That would be uneconomical.'

'Can she take apart the pumps when they go wrong?' Jess said. 'Will she fix the cistern in the men's loos?'

Des leant on the bar. 'Probably not, Jess.' He ran a chubby hand through his mullet. 'But I need someone reliable. You're not reliable.'

'Give me a break, Des. One missed week in two years. Please. I need this. I really need this.'

He said he'd think about it.

The children went back to school. Tanzie wanted Jess there to pick her up every afternoon. Nicky got up without her having to go in six times to wake him. He was actually eating breakfast when she got out of the shower. He didn't ask to renew his prescription of anti-anxiety medication. The flick on his eyeliner was point perfect.

'I was thinking. I might want to do sixth form at McArthur's after all. And then, you know, I'll be around when Tanzie starts big school.'

Jess blinked. 'That's a great idea.'

She cleaned alongside Nathalie, listening to her gossip about the final days of the Fishers – how they had pulled every plug socket off the walls, and kicked holes in the plaster in the kitchen before they'd left the house on Pleasant View. Someone – she pulled a face – had set fire to a mattress outside the housing-association office on Sunday night.

'You must feel relieved, though, eh?' she said.

'Sure,' Jess said.

Nathalie straightened and rubbed her back. 'I meant

to ask you. What was it like going all the way to Scotland with Mr Nicholls? It must have been weird.'

Jess leant over the sink, and paused, gazing out of the window at the infinite crescent of the sea. 'It was fine.'

'Didn't you run out of things to say to him, stuck in that car? I know I would.'

Jess's eyes prickled with tears so that she had to pretend to be scrubbing at an invisible mark on the stainless steel. 'No,' she said. 'Funnily enough. I didn't.'

Here was the thing: Jess felt the absence of Ed like a thick blanket, smothering everything. She missed his smile, his lips, his skin, the bit where a trace of soft dark hair snaked up towards his belly button. She missed feeling like she had when he was there, that she was somehow more attractive, more sexy, more everything. She missed feeling as if anything was possible. She couldn't believe losing someone you had known such a short time could feel like losing part of yourself, that it could make food taste wrong and colours seem dull. Some nights after Nicky went to bed she didn't go into her too-big bed, but just dozed on the sofa in front of the television, her knees pressed into her chest to try to stop the empty feeling inside.

Jess saw now that when Marty had left, everything she had felt had been related to practical matters. She had felt unsafe. She had worried about how the children would feel with him gone. She had worried about money, about who would mind them if she had to do an evening shift at the pub, about who would take the bins out on a Thursday. But what she mostly felt was a vague relief that she was no longer governed by his moods. That she didn't have to act as referee between him and the children. That she no longer had to try to convince herself that this was a relationship worth saving.

More than anything she hated the fact that a man who had seen only the best of her now thought the worst. To Ed she was now no better than any of the other people who had let him down or messed him up. In fact, she was probably worse. And it was all her own fault. That was the thing she could never escape from. It was entirely her own fault.

She thought about it for three nights, then she wrote him a letter.

So, in one ill-thought-out minute, I became the person I have always taught my children not to be. We are all tested eventually, and I failed.

I'm sorry.

I miss you.

PS I know you'll never believe me. But I was always going to pay it back.

She put her phone number on it and twenty pounds in an envelope, marked First Instalment. And she gave it to Nathalie and asked her to put it with his post at Beach-front Reception. The next day, Nathalie said a for-sale sign had gone up outside number two. And she watched her reaction just slightly too closely and then she stopped asking questions about Mr Nicholls.

When five days had gone by and Jess realized he wasn't going to respond, she spent an entire night awake, and then she told herself firmly that she could lie around feeling miserable no longer. It was time to move on. Heartbreak was a luxury too costly for the single parent.

On Monday she made herself a cup of tea, sat down at the kitchen table and called the credit-card company; she was told that she needed to up her minimum monthly payment. She opened a letter from the police who said that she would be fined a thousand pounds for driving without tax and insurance and that if she wanted to appeal against the penalty she should apply for a court hearing in the following ways. She opened the letter from the pound, which said she owed a hundred and twenty pounds up to the previous Thursday for the safe-keeping of the Rolls. She opened the first bill from the vet and shoved it back in the envelope. There was only so much news you could digest in one day. She got a text from Marty, who wanted to know if he could come and see the kids at half-term.

'What do you think?' she said to them, over breakfast. They shrugged.

After her cleaning shift on Tuesday she walked into town to the low-cost solicitors and paid them twenty-five pounds to draft a letter to Marty asking for a divorce, and for back payments in child support.

'How long?' the woman asked.

'Two years.'

She didn't even look up. Jess wondered what kinds of

stories she heard every day. She tapped in some figures, then turned the screen to Jess's side of the desk. 'That's what it comes to. Quite a sum. He'll ask to pay in instalments. They usually do.'

'Fine.' Jess reached for her bag. 'He has someone to help him.'

She worked her way methodically through the list of things she needed to sort out, and she tried to see a bigger picture beyond that small town. Beyond a little family with financial problems, and a brief love story that had snapped in two before it had really begun. Sometimes, she told herself, life was a series of obstacles that just had to be negotiated, possibly through a sheer act of will. She walked the length of her seaside town and she vowed that she would hide the full extent of her financial worries from the two of them. It was important that they were allowed to hope, to dream, even if she no longer would. If she could give them nothing else she could give them that. She stared out at the muddy blue of the endless sea, gulped in the air, lifted her chin and decided that she could survive this. She could survive most things. It was nobody's right to be happy, after all.

Jess walked along the pebbly beach, her feet sinking, stepping over the groynes, and counted her blessings on three fingers, as if she was playing a piano in her pocket: Tanzie was safe. Nicky was safe. Norman was getting better. That was what it all boiled down to, in the end, wasn't it? The rest was just detail.

If she said it often enough she might start believing it.

*

Two evenings later, they sat in the garden on the old plastic furniture. Tanzie had washed her hair and was on Jess's lap while Jess tugged the comb through the wet tangles. She told them why Mr Nicholls wouldn't be coming back.

Nicky stared at her. 'From his pocket?'

'No. It had fallen out of his pocket. It was in a taxi. But I knew whose it was.'

There was a shocked silence. Jess couldn't see Tanzie's face. She wasn't sure she wanted to look at Nicky's. She kept combing gently, smoothing her daughter's hair, her voice calm and reasonable, as if that might bring reason to what she had done.

'What did you do with the money?' Tanzie's head had become unusually still.

Jess swallowed. 'I can't remember now.'

'Did you use it for my registration?'

She kept combing. Smooth and comb. Tug, tug, release. 'I honestly can't remember, Tanzie. Anyway, what I did with it is irrelevant.'

Jess could feel Nicky's eyes on her the whole time she spoke.

'So why are you telling us now?'

Tug, smooth, release.

'Because . . . because I want you to know that I made a terrible mistake and I'm sorry. Even if I planned to pay it back I should never have taken that money. There was no excuse for it. And Ed – Mr Nicholls was well within his rights to leave when he found out because, well, the most important thing you have with another human

460

being is trust.' She tried to keep her voice measured and unemotional. It was becoming harder. 'So, I want you to know that I'm sorry I let you both down. I'm conscious that I've always told you how to behave, and then I did the complete opposite. I'm telling you because not telling you would make me a hypocrite. But I'm also telling you because I want you to see that doing the wrong thing has a consequence. In my case I lost someone I cared about. Very much.'

They were both silent.

After a minute, Tanzie reached a hand round. Her fingers sought Jess's, and closed briefly around them. 'It's okay, Mum,' she said. 'We all make mistakes.'

Jess closed her eyes.

When she opened them again, Nicky lifted his head. He looked genuinely bemused. 'He would have given it to you,' he said, and there was a faint, but unmistakable trace of anger in his voice.

Jess stared at him.

'He would have given it to you. If you'd asked.'

'Yes,' she said, and her hands stilled on Tanzie's hair. 'Yes, that's the worst bit. I think he probably would have done.'

36.

NICKY

A week went by. They caught the bus to see Norman every day. The vet had sewn up his eye socket where the eye had had to be taken out; there wasn't an actual hole but it still looked pretty grim. The first time Tanzie saw his face she burst into tears. They said he might bump into things for a while once he was up and about. They said he would spend a lot of time sleeping. Nicky didn't like to tell them he wasn't sure anyone would be able to tell the difference. Jess stroked his head and told him he was a wonderful brave boy, and when his tail thumped gently on the tiled floor of his veterinary pen she blinked a lot and turned away.

On the Friday Jess asked Nicky to wait in Reception with Tanzie and she walked over to the front desk to speak to the woman about the bill. He guessed it was about the bill. They printed out a sheet of paper, then a second sheet, then, incredibly, a third, and she ran her finger the whole way down each page and swallowed visibly when it reached the bottom. They had walked home that day, even though Jess was still limping.

The town started to get busier, as the sea turned from mucky grey to glinting blue. It felt weird at first, the

Fishers being gone. It was as if no one could actually believe it. Someone said that they'd gone to Sussex, not Surrey. Someone else said that Fisher's dad had been arrested for aggravated assault in Northampton. Nobody's tyres got slashed. Mrs Worboys started to walk to bingo in the evenings again. Nicky got used to being able to walk to the shop and back and realized that the butterflies he still felt in his stomach didn't have to be there. He told them this repeatedly, but they refused to get the message. Tanzie didn't come outside at all unless Jess was with her.

Nicky didn't look at his blog for almost ten days. He had written that post when Norman was hurt and he was so full of anger that he had had to get it out somewhere. He had never felt rage, real rage, where he had wanted to break stuff and hit people before, but for days after the Fishers had done what they did, Nicky felt it. It boiled in his blood like poison. It made him want to scream. For those awful few days at least, writing it down and putting it out there had actually helped. It had felt like he was telling someone, even if that someone didn't really know who he was and probably didn't care. He just needed to know that someone would hear what had happened, would see the injustice of it.

And then, after his blood had cooled, and they heard that the Fishers were going to have to pay, Nicky felt, weirdly, like an idiot. It felt like that thing when you tell someone a bit too much and you feel exposed and spend the following weeks praying they'll forget what you told them, afraid they might use it against you. And what was the point of putting it out there, anyway? The only people who'd want to look at a blog like that were the kind of people who slowed down to look at car crashes.

He opened it up at first because he was going to delete it. And then he thought, No, people will have seen it. I'll look even more stupid if I take it down. So he decided to write a short thing about the Fishers being evicted and that would be the end of it. He wasn't going to name them, but he wanted to post something good so that if anyone ever did come across what he had written they wouldn't think his whole family were completely tragic. He read through what he'd written the previous week – the emotion and the rawness of it – and his toes actually curled with shame. He wondered who out there in cyber-space had read it. He wondered how many people in the world now thought he was an idiot as well as a freak.

And then he reached the bottom. And he saw the comments.

Hang on in there, Gothboy. People like that make me sick.

Your blog got sent to me by a friend and it made me cry. I hope your dog is okay. Please post and let us know when you get a chance.

Hey Nicky. I'm Viktor from Portugal. I don't know you but my friend linked to your blog on Facebook and I just wanted to say that I felt like you did a year back and things did get better. Don't worry. Peace!

He scrolled down some more. There was message after message. Kind, helpful, friendly. He put his blog into a search engine: it had been copied and linked hundreds, then thousands of times. Nicky looked at the statistics, then sat back in his chair and stared in disbelief: 2,876 people had read it. In a single week. Almost three thousand people had read his words. More than four hundred of them had taken the trouble to send him a message about it. And only two had called him a wanker.

But that wasn't all. People had sent money. Actual money. Someone had opened an online donation account to help with the vet's fees because they wanted Norman to be okay and left a message telling him how he could access it using a PayPal account.

I can't donate enough to put your sister through school, but I can put something towards a new puppy for your sister if your dog doesn't make it. I'm glad she has you.

Hey Gothboy (is that your real name??) have you thought of a rescue dog? That way something good might come out of it. I enclose a contribution! Rescue centres always need donations ;-)

A little something to help with the vet's bills. Give your sister a hug from me. I'm so mad at what happened to you all.

My dog got hit by a car and was saved by the PDSA. I'm guessing you don't have one near you. I thought it would be nice, as someone helped me, to help you a little. Please accept my £10 towards his recuperation.

From a fellow girl maths geek. Please tell your little sister
to keep on. Don't let them win.

It had gone viral. There were 459 shares. Nicky
counted a hundred and thirty names on the donations
page, two pounds being the smallest donation, and two
hundred and fifty the highest. A total stranger had sent
two hundred and fifty pounds. The final tally sat at
£932.50, the last having come in an hour previously. He
kept refreshing the page and staring at the figure, wondering if they had put a full stop in the wrong place.

His heart was doing something really strange. He
placed his palm against his chest, wondering if this was
what it felt like to have a heart attack. He wondered if he
was going to die. What he wanted to do, though, he discovered, was laugh. He wanted to laugh at the
magnificence of total strangers. At their kindness and
their goodness and the fact that there were actual people
out there being good and nice and giving money to
people they had never met and never would. And
because, most crazy of all, all that kindness, all that magnificence, was sitting there just because of his words.

Jess was standing by the cupboard holding a parcel of
pink tissue when he scooted into the living room. 'Here,'
he said. 'Look.' He pulled at her arm, dragging her over
to the sofa.

'What?'

'Put that down.'

Nicky opened the laptop and placed it on her lap. She

almost flinched, as if it was actually painful for her to be so close to something that belonged to Mr Nicholls.

'Look.' He pointed at the donations page. 'Look at this. People have sent money. For Norman.'

'What do you mean?'

'Just look, Jess.'

She squinted at the screen, moving the page up and down as she read, then reread it. 'But . . . we can't take that.'

'It's not for us. It's for Tanzie. And Norman.'

'I don't understand. Why would people we don't know send us money?'

'Because they're upset about what happened. Because they can see it wasn't fair. Because they want to help. I don't know.'

'But how did they know?'

'I wrote a blog about it.'

'You did what?'

'Something Mr Nicholls told me. About finding your people. I just . . . put it out there. What was happening to us.'

'Show me.'

Nicky switched pages then and showed her the blog. She read it slowly, her brow furrowed in concentration, and he felt a bit strange, like he was showing her part of himself that he didn't show anyone. Somehow it was harder to show all that emotional stuff to someone you knew.

'So, how much is the vet?' he said, when he could see that she'd finished.

She spoke like someone in a daze. 'Eight hundred and seventy-eight pounds. And forty-two pence. So far.'

Nicky lifted his hands in the air. 'So we're okay, yes? Look at the total. We're okay!'

She looked at him and he could see on her face the exact expression he must have worn half an hour previously.

'The kindness of strangers,' he said.

She lifted her hand to her mouth. 'I just can't believe that people would send money to someone they don't even know.'

'It's like you said. Good things do happen.' Nicky wanted her to smile. He wanted her to feel like he did, like a door had opened onto a world he hadn't even known about, full of kind people and the possibility of happiness.

'It's good news, Jess! Be pleased!' And for a minute her eyes brimmed with tears. And then she looked so confused that he leant forward and hugged her. This was his third voluntary hug in three years.

'Mascara,' she said, when she pulled back.

'Oh.' He wiped under his eyes. She wiped hers.

'Good?'

'Fine. Me?'

She leant forward and ran a thumb under the outer edge of his eye.

Then she let out a breath and suddenly she was a bit like the old Jess again. She stood up and brushed down her jeans. 'We'll have to pay them all back, of course.'

'Most of them are, like, three pounds. Good luck with working that out.'

'Tanzie will sort it.' Jess picked up the pink tissue parcel, and then, almost as an afterthought, she shoved it into a cupboard. She pushed her hair from her face. 'And you have to show her the messages about maths. It's really important she sees those.'

Nicky looked upstairs towards Tanzie's bedroom. 'I will,' he said, and just for a minute his mood dipped. 'But I'm not sure it's going to make any difference.'

37.

JESS

Norman came home. Mr Adamson gave them a discount because, he said, the case had been 'fascinating'. Jess had thought he was referring to Norman's injuries, but it turned out one of the veterinary nurses had read Nicky's blog after Tanzie had mentioned it, and the vet had meant he was fascinated that Norman had, against all expectations and his normal characteristics, roused himself to try to protect Tanzie.

'And we have to help a hero, don't we, old chap?' he said, patting Norman's side. The way the vet spoke to him, and the way that Norman immediately flopped to the ground for a tummy scratch, made Jess think this was not the first time he'd done it. As the vet dropped right down onto the floor she caught a glimpse of the man beyond the careful professional manner. His broad smile, the way his eyes crinkled when he looked at the dog. And she heard Nicky's phrase running through her head, as it had done for days: the kindness of strangers.

'I'm glad you made the decision you did, Mrs Thomas,' he said, pushing himself back onto his feet while they diplomatically ignored the pistol crack of his knees. Norman stayed on his back, his tongue lolling, ever hopeful. Or perhaps just too fat to get up. 'He deserved his chance. If I'd known how his injuries had come about I would have been a bit less reticent about proceeding.'

Jess paid with her pre-loaded credit card. She put twenty pounds in the animal charity box. Yes, it could probably have been usefully spent elsewhere, but it felt like the right thing to do.

Tanzie stayed pressed close to Norman's enormous black body as they lumbered home, clutching his lead like a lifeline. The walk from the vet's was the first time she had been outside in three weeks and hadn't insisted on holding Jess's hand.

Jess had hoped that having him back would lift her daughter's spirits. But Tanzie was still a little shadow, tailing her silently around the house, peering around corners, waiting anxiously beside her form teacher at the end of the day for Jess's arrival at the school gates. At home she read in her room, or lay silently on the sofa watching cartoons, one hand resting on the dog beside her. Mr Tsvangarai had been off since term restarted – some family emergency – and Jess felt a reflexive sadness when she pictured him discovering Tanzie's determination to push mathematics from her life, the disappearance of the singular, quirky little girl she'd been. Sometimes she felt as if she had simply traded one unhappy, silent child for another.

St Anne's rang to discuss Tanzie's orientation day at the school, and Jess had to tell them that she wasn't coming. The words were a squat dry frog in her throat.

'Well, we do recommend it, Mrs Thomas. We find the children settle a lot better if they've familiarized themselves a little. It's good for her to meet a few fellow pupils as well. Is it a problem with getting time off from her current school?'

'No. I mean she – she's not coming.'

'At all?'

'No.'

A short silence.

'Oh,' said the registrar. Jess heard her flicking through papers. 'But this is the little girl with the ninety per cent scholarship, yes? Costanza?'

She felt herself colour. 'Yes.'

'Is she going to Petersfield Academy instead? Did they offer her a scholarship too?'

'No. That's not it,' Jess replied. She closed her eyes as she spoke. 'Look, I don't suppose ... Is there any way you could ... increase the scholarship any further?'

'Further?' She sounded taken aback. 'Mrs Thomas, it was already the most generous scholarship we've ever offered. I'm sorry, but there's no question.'

Jess pressed on, glad that nobody could see her shame. 'If I could get the money together by next year would you consider deferring her place?'

'I'm not sure whether that would be possible. Or even if it would be fair to the other candidates.' She hesitated, perhaps suddenly conscious of Jess's silence. 'But of course we'd certainly look at her favourably if ever she did want to reapply.'

Jess stared at the spot on the carpet where Marty had

brought a motorbike into the front room and it had leaked oil. A huge lump had risen into her throat. 'Well, thank you for letting me know.'

'Look, Mrs Thomas,' the woman said, her voice suddenly conciliatory, 'there's still another week to go before we have to close the place. We'll hold it for you until the last possible minute.'

'Thank you. That's very kind of you. But, really, there's no point.'

Jess knew it and the woman knew it. It wasn't going to happen for them. Some leaps were just too big to make.

She asked Jess to pass on her best wishes to Tanzie for her new school. As she put the phone down Jess could hear her already scanning her lists for the next suitable candidate.

She didn't tell Tanzie. She suspected she already knew. Two nights previously she discovered Tanzie had removed all her maths books from her cupboard and stacked them with Jess's remaining books on the upstairs landing, inserting them carefully between thrillers and a historical romance so that she wouldn't notice. Jess removed them carefully and put them in a neat pile in her wardrobe, where they couldn't be seen. She wasn't sure if this was saving Tanzie's feelings or her own.

Marty received the solicitor's letter and rang, protesting and blustering about why he couldn't pay. She told him it was out of her hands. She said she hoped they could be civil about it. She told him his children needed shoes. He didn't mention coming down at half-term.

She got her job back at the pub. The girl from the City of Paris had apparently disappeared to the Texas Rib Shack three shifts after she'd started. Tips were better and there was no Stewart Pringle making random grabs at your backside.

'No loss. She didn't know not to talk during the guitar solo of "Layla",' Des mused. 'What kind of barmaid doesn't know to keep quiet during the guitar solo of "Layla"?'

She cleaned four days a week with Nathalie, and avoided number two Beachfront. She preferred jobs like scrubbing ovens, where she was unlikely to accidentally look through the window and catch sight of it, with its jaunty blue and white for-sale placard. If Nathalie thought she was behaving a little oddly, she didn't say anything.

She put an advert in the local newsagent's offering her services as a handy-woman. No Job Too Small. Her first job came in less than twenty-four hours later: putting up a bathroom cabinet for a pensioner in Aden Crescent. The old woman was so happy with the result that she gave Jess a five-pound tip. She said she didn't like having men in her house and that in the forty-two years she had been married to her husband he had only ever seen her with her good wool vest on. She recommended Jess to a friend in the sheltered housing who had a washer needed replacing and a carpet gripper. Two other jobs followed, also pensioners. Jess sent a second instalment of cash to number two Beachfront. Nathalie dropped it in. The for-sale sign was still up.

Nicky was the only one in the family who seemed genuinely cheerful. It was as if the blog had given him a new sense of purpose. He wrote it most evenings, posting about Norman's progress, chatting with new friends. He met up with one of them IRL, he said, translating that for Jess: 'In Real Life'. He was all right, he said. And, no, not like that. He wanted to go to open days at two different colleges. He was speaking to his form tutor about how to apply for a hardship grant. He'd looked it up. He smiled, often several times a day and without being bribed, dropped to his knees with pleasure when he saw Norman wagging his tail in the kitchen, waved unselfconsciously at Lola, the girl from number forty-seven, who, Jess noticed, had dyed her hair the exact same shade as his, and played an air-guitar solo in the front room. He walked into town frequently, his skinny legs seeming to gain a longer stride, his shoulders not exactly back, but not slumped, defeated, as they had been weeks earlier. Once he wore a yellow T-shirt.

'Where's the laptop gone?' Jess said, when she went into his room one afternoon and found him working away on their old computer.

'I took it back.' He shrugged. 'Nathalie let me in.'

'Did you see him?' she said, before she could stop herself.

Nicky's eyes slid away. 'Sorry. His stuff's there but it's all boxed up. I'm not sure he stays there any more.'

It shouldn't have been a surprise but as Jess made her way downstairs she found herself holding her stomach with both hands, as if she had been winded.

38.

ED

His sister accompanied him to court several weeks later, on a day that woke still and hot, and the traffic crawled as if the heat had slowed the very movement in London's veins. Ed had told his mother not to come too. By that time they were never sure, day by day, whether it was a good idea to leave Dad for any length of time. As they crawled across London, his sister leant forwards in her taxi seat, her fingers tapping impatiently on her knee, her jaw set in a tight line. She was clearly even tenser than he was. Ed felt strangely, perversely relaxed. The weight of other, future, losses hung over him, making today's troubles seem trivial.

The courtroom was almost empty. Thanks to the unholy combination of a particularly grisly murder at the Old Bailey, a political love scandal, and the public meltdown of a young British actress, the two-day trial had not registered as a big news story, just enough for an agency court reporter and a trainee from the *Financial Times*. And Ed had already pleaded guilty, against the advice of his legal team.

Deanna Lewis's claims of innocence had been somewhat undermined by the evidence of a friend, a banker, who had apparently informed her in no uncertain terms that what she was about to do was indeed insider trading. The friend was able to produce an email she had sent informing Deanna as much, and one in return from Deanna accusing the friend of being 'picky', 'annoying', and 'frankly a little too involved in my business. Don't you want me to have a chance to move forward?'

Ed stood and watched the court reporter scribbling away, and the solicitors leaning in to each other, pointing to bits of paper, and it all felt oddly anti-climactic.

'I am minded that you confessed your guilt and that, as far as Miss Lewis and yourself are concerned, this appears to be isolated criminal behaviour, motivated by factors other than money. This cannot be said of Michael Lewis.'

The FSA, it turned out, had tracked other 'suspicious' trades Deanna's brother had made, spread bets and options.

'It is necessary, however, that we send a signal that this kind of behaviour is completely unacceptable, however it may have come about. It destroys investors' confidence in the honest movement in markets, and it weakens the whole structure of our financial system. For that reason I am bound to ensure that the level of punishment is still a clear deterrent to anyone who may believe this to be a "victimless" crime.'

Ed stood in the dock trying to work out what to do with his face and was fined £750,000 and costs, and given a six-month sentence, suspended for twelve months.

And it was over.

Gemma let out a long, shuddering breath, and

dropped her head into her hands. Ed felt curiously numb. 'That's it?' he said quietly, and she looked up at him in disbelief. A clerk opened the door of the dock and ushered him out. Paul Wilkes clapped him on the back as they emerged into the corridor.

'Thank you,' Ed said. It seemed like the right thing to say.

He caught sight of Deanna Lewis in the corridor, in animated conversation with a red-headed man. He looked like he was trying to explain something to her and she kept shaking her head, cutting him off. He stood staring for a moment, and then, almost without thinking, he walked through the throng of people and straight up to her. 'I wanted to say I'm sorry,' he said. 'If I had thought for one minute –'

She spun round, her eyes widening. 'Oh, fuck off,' she said, her face puce with fury, and pushed past him. 'You fucking loser.'

The faces that had swivelled at the sound of her voice registered Ed, then turned away in embarrassment. Somebody sniggered. As Ed stood there, his hand still half lifted as if to make a point, he heard a voice in his ear.

'She's not stupid, you know. She would always have known she shouldn't have told her brother.'

Ed turned, and there, behind him, stood Ronan. He took in his checked shirt and his thick black glasses, the computer bag slung over his shoulder, and something in him deflated with relief. 'You . . . you were here all morning?'

'Bit bored at the office TBH. I thought I'd come and see what a real-life court case was like.'

Ed couldn't stop looking at him. 'Overrated.'

'Yeah. That's what I thought.'

His sister had been shaking hands with Paul Wilkes. She appeared at his side, straightening her jacket. 'Right. Shall we go and ring Mum, give her the good news? She said she'd leave her mobile on. If we're lucky she'll have remembered to charge it. Hi, Ronan.'

He leant forward and kissed her cheek. 'Nice to see you, Gemma. Been a long time.'

'Too long! Let's go to mine,' she said, turning to Ed. 'It's ages since you saw the kids. I've got a spag bol in the freezer we can have tonight. Hey, Ronan. You can come too if you like. I'm sure we could bung some extra pasta in the pot.'

Ronan's gaze slid away, as it had done when he and Ed were eighteen. He kicked at something on the floor. Ed turned to his sister. 'Um . . . Gem . . . would you mind if I left it? Just for today?' He tried not to register the way her smile fell. 'I'll definitely come another time. I just — There's a few things I'd really like to talk to Ronan about. It's been . . .'

Her gaze flickered between them. 'Sure,' she said brightly, pushing her fringe from her eyes. 'Well. Call me.' She hoisted her bag onto her shoulder, and began to make her way towards the stairs.

And he yelled across the busy corridor, so that several people looked up from their papers. 'Hey! Gem!'

She turned, her bag under her arm.

'Thanks. For everything.'

She stood there, half facing him.

'Really. I appreciate it.'

She nodded, a ghost of a smile. And then she was gone, lost in the crowds on the stairwell.

'So. Um. Fancy a drink?' Ed tried not to sound pleading. He wasn't sure he was entirely successful. 'I'm buying.'

Ronan let it hang there. Just for a second. The bastard. 'Well, in that case . . .'

It was Ed's mother who had once told him that real friends were the kind where you pick up where you'd left off, whether it be a week since you'd seen each other or two years. He'd never had enough friends to test it. He and Ronan nursed pints of beer across a wobbling wooden table in the busy pub, a little awkwardly at first, and then increasingly freely, the familiar jokes popping up between them like Whac-A-Moles, targets to be hit, with discreet pleasure. Ed had an almost physical sense of relief at having him nearby, as if he had been untethered for months and someone had finally tugged him in to land. He found himself gazing at his friend surreptitiously, noticing the things he remembered – his laugh, his enormous feet, the way he slumped over, even at a pub table, as if peering into a screen – and those things he hadn't seen about him before: how he laughed more easily, his new, designer-framed glasses, a kind of quiet confidence. When he opened his wallet to pull out some cash, Ed caught a glimpse of a photograph of a girl, beaming into his credit cards.

'So . . . how's Soup Girl?'

'Karen? She's good.' He smiled, the kind of smile that denotes private happiness, the kind where you have nothing to prove. 'She's good. Actually, we're moving in together.'

'Wow. Already?'

He looked up almost defiantly. 'It's been six months. And with rental prices as they are in London, those not-for-profit soup charities don't exactly make a fortune.'

'That's great,' Ed stuttered. 'Fantastic news.'

'Yeah. Well. It's good. She's great. I'm really happy.'

They sat there, silent for a moment. He'd had his hair cut, Ed noticed. And that was a new jacket. 'I'm really pleased for you, Ronan. I always thought you two would be great together.'

'Thanks.'

He smiled at him, and Ronan grinned back, pulling a face, like all this happiness stuff was a bit embarrassing.

Ed stared at his pint, trying not to feel left behind. Trying not to think about the fact that his own life was basically a mess while his oldest friend was sailing on to a happier, brighter future. Around them the pub was filling up with end-of-the-day office workers, secretaries in too-high shoes and young men trying to prove they were, actually, men. He suddenly had a sense of limited time, of the importance of laying things out, straight, in front of him.

'I'm sorry,' he said.

'What?'

'About everything. About Deanna Lewis. I don't know

why I did it.' His voice emerged as a croak. 'I hate how I've messed things up. I mean, I'm sad about the job, yes, but mostly I'm just gutted that I messed us up.' He couldn't look at him yet it was a relief to say it.

Ronan took a swig of his drink. 'Don't worry. I've thought about it a lot these past months and, while I kind of don't want to admit it, there's a good chance that if Deanna Lewis had come on to me I would have done the same.' A rueful smile. 'It was Deanna Lewis.'

'She's . . . really not what we thought she was.'

'Believe it or not, I get that.' Ronan grinned.

'Seriously, though, I'm sorry about all of it. Messing it all up. Our company. Our friendship. If you knew what I've been like this last –'

Ronan shrugged, as if Ed should say no more.

They sat in silence. Ronan leant back in his chair. He bent a beer mat into two, and then into four. 'You know . . . it's been kind of interesting with you not being there any more,' he said finally. 'It made me understand something. I don't much like working at Mayfly. I liked it better when it was just you and me. All the suits, the profit-and-loss stuff, shareholders, it's not me. It's not what I liked about it. It's not why we started it.'

'Me too. I miss you, but I don't miss them.'

'I mean the endless meetings . . . having to run ideas past marketing people even to proceed with basic code. Having to justify every hour's activity. You know they want to bring in time-sheets for everyone? Actual time-sheets?'

Ed waited.

'You're not missing much, I tell you.' Ronan shook his head, as if he had something more to say but felt he shouldn't.

It felt momentous. It felt a little like that moment in a date, where you're about to confess your feelings to the other person, not quite sure how they're going to respond.

'Ronan?

'Yeah?'

'I had this idea. This last week or two. About a new piece of software. I've been fiddling around, working on a piece of predictive software – really simple stuff – that will help people plan their finances. A sort of spreadsheet for people who don't like spreadsheets. For people who don't know how to handle money. It would have alerts that pop up whenever the user was about to incur a charge from their bank. It would have an option calculation to show how much different interest charges would add up to over a set period of time. Nothing too complicated. I was thinking it's the kind of thing they could give away at Citizens' Advice Bureaux.'

'Interesting.'

'It would need to be able to fit cheap computers. Software that might be a few years old. And cheaper mobile phones. I'm not sure it would make much money but it's just something that I've been thinking about. I've outlined it. But . . .'

Ronan was thinking. Ed could see his mind working away, already chewing over the parameters.

'The thing is, it would need someone who is really good at coding. To build it.'

Ronan watched his pint, his face neutral. 'You know you can't come back to Mayfly, right?' he said.

Ed nodded. His best friend since college. 'Yeah. I know.'

Ronan met his eyes and suddenly they were grinning.

39.

ED

All these years, and he didn't know his own sister's number off by heart. All those years of her living in the same house, and he still had to look up her address. Those two things alone made Ed feel bad. He seemed to have an ever-growing list of things to feel bad about.

He had stood outside the King's Head as Ronan headed off to the Tube station and a nice girl who made soup, whose presence in his life had given him a whole extra dimension, and he knew he could not go home to an empty flat, surrounded by boxes, the chill breath of its next owner in his lungs.

It took six rings for her to pick up the phone. And then he heard someone screaming in the background before she actually answered.

'Gem?'

'Yes?' she said, breathlessly. 'LEO, DON'T YOU THROW THAT DOWN THE STAIRS.'

'Does that offer of spaghetti bolognese still stand?'

They were embarrassingly pleased to see him. The door of the little house in Finsbury Park opened and he walked in through the bikes and the piles of shoes and the overloaded coat rack that seemed to extend the entire way along the hall. Upstairs, the relentless beat of pop thumped through the connecting walls. It competed with the cinematic sounds of a war game on some kind of games console.

'Hey, you!' His sister pulled him to her and hugged tight. She was out of her suit, wearing jeans and a jumper. 'I can't even remember the last time you came here. When was the last time he was here, Phil?'

'With Lara,' came the voice from down the corridor.

'Two years ago?'

'Where's the corkscrew, love?'

All was noise and chaos. The kitchen was filled with steam and the smell of garlic. At its far end two clothes-horses sagged under several loads of washing. Every surface, mostly stripped pine, was covered with books, piles of paper or children's drawings. Phil stood and shook his hand, then excused himself. 'Got a few emails to answer before supper. You don't mind?'

'You must be appalled,' his sister said, plonking a glass in front of him. 'You'll have to excuse the mess. I've been on late shifts, Phil has been flat out and we haven't had a cleaner since Rosario left. All the others are a bit pricey.'

He had missed this chaos. He missed the feeling of being embedded in a noisy, thumping heart. 'I love it,' he said, and her eyes scanned his swiftly for sarcasm. 'No. Seriously. I love it. It feels . . .'

'Messy.'

'That too. It's good.' He sat back in his chair at the kitchen table and let out a long breath.

'Hey, Uncle Ed.'

Ed blinked. 'Who are you?'

A teenage girl with burnished gold hair and several thick layers of mascara on each eye grinned at him. 'Funny.'

He looked at his sister for help. She raised her hands. 'It's been a while, Ed. They grow. Leo! Come and say hello to Uncle Ed.'

'I thought Uncle Ed was going to prison,' came the cry from the other room.

'Excuse me for a minute.'

His sister left the pan of sauce and disappeared into the hall. Ed tried not to hear the distant yelp.

'Mum says you lost all your money,' said Justine, sitting down opposite and peeling the crust from a piece of French bread.

Ed's brain was desperately trying to marry the awkward, reed-thin child he had last seen with this tawny miracle who stared at him with faint amusement, as if he were a museum curio. 'Pretty much.'

'Did you lose your swanky flat?'

'Any minute now.'

'Damn. I was going to ask you if I could have my sixteenth-birthday party there.'

'Well, you saved me the trouble of a refusal.'

'That's exactly what Dad said. So are you happy that you didn't get banged up?'

'Oh, I think I'm still going to be the family cautionary tale for a while.'

She smiled. *'Don't be like naughty Uncle Edward.'*

'Is that how it's being pitched?'

'Oh, you know Mum. No moral lesson left unlearnt in this house. "You see how easy it is to end up on the wrong path? He had absolutely everything and now . . ."'

'. . . I'm begging for meals and driving a seven-year-old car.'

'Nice try. But ours still beats yours by three years.' She glanced towards the hall, where her mother was speaking to her brother in low tones. 'Actually, you mustn't be mean about Mum. You know she spent all of yesterday on the phone working on how to get you into an open prison?'

'Really?'

'She was properly stressed about it. I heard her telling someone you wouldn't last five minutes in Pentonville.'

He felt a pang of something he couldn't quite identify at his utter ignorance of his sister's efforts on his behalf. So deep in self-pity had he been that he hadn't considered how others would be affected if he was sent to prison. 'She's probably right.'

Justine pulled a lock of hair into her mouth. She seemed to be enjoying herself. 'So what are you going to do now you're a family disgrace with no job and possibly no home?'

'No idea. Should I take up a drugs habit? Just to round it off?'

'Ugh. No. Stoners are so boring.' She peeled her long legs off the chair. 'And Mum's busy enough as it is. Although, actually, I should say yes. Because you've totally taken the heat off me and Leo. We now have so little to live up to.'

'Glad to be of help.'

'Seriously. Nice to see you, though.' She leant forward and whispered, 'You've actually made Mum's day. She won't say so, but she was really, really pleased you came. Like, embarrassingly so. She even cleaned the downstairs loo in case you turned up.'

'Yeah. Well. I'm going to make sure I do it more often.'

She narrowed her eyes, as if she were trying to work out whether he was being serious, then turned and disappeared back up the stairs.

'So what's going on?' Gemma helped herself to green salad. 'What happened to the girl at the hospital? Joss? Jess? I thought she'd be there today.'

It was the first home-cooked meal he had eaten in ages, and it was delicious. The others had finished and left, but Ed was on his third helping, having suddenly reacquired the appetite that had disappeared for the last few weeks. His last mouthful had subsequently been a little over-ambitious and he sat there chewing for some time before he could answer. 'I don't want to talk about it.'

'You never want to talk about anything. C'mon. Price of a home-cooked meal.'

'We split up.'

'What? Why?' Three glasses of wine had made her garrulous, opinionated. 'You seemed really happy. Happier than you were with Lara, anyway.'

'I was.'

'So? God, you're an idiot sometimes, Ed. There is a woman who actually seems normal, who seemed to have a handle on you, and you run a mile.'

'I really don't want to talk about it, Gem.'

'What was it? Too frightened to commit? Too soon since the divorce? You're not still hankering after Lara, are you?'

He took a bit of bread and wiped it around some sauce on the plate. He chewed for a minute longer than he needed to. 'She stole from me.'

'She what?'

It felt like a trump card, laying it down like that. Upstairs the children were arguing. Ed found himself thinking of Nicky and Tanzie, placing bets in the back seat. If he didn't tell somebody the truth he might actually explode. So he told her.

Ed's sister pushed her plate across the table. She leant forwards, her chin resting in her hand, a faint frown bisecting her brow as she listened. He told the tale of the CCTV, how he had pulled out the drawers of the chest to move it across the room, and how there it had been, sitting on some neatly folded blue socks – his own laminated face.

I was going to tell you.

It's not how it looks. The hand to the mouth.

I mean it is how it looks but, oh, God, oh, God –

'I thought she was different. I thought she was the greatest thing, this brave, principled, amazing ... But, fuck it, she was just like Lara. Just like Deanna. Only interested in what she could get out of me. How could she do that, Gem? Why can't I spot these women a mile off?' He finished, leant back in his chair, and waited.

She didn't speak.

'What? You're not going to say anything? About my poor judge of character? About the fact that yet again I've let a woman screw me out of what's mine? About how I'm an idiot on yet another count?'

'I certainly wasn't going to say that.'

'What were you going to say?'

'I don't know.' She sat staring at her plate. She registered no surprise whatsoever. He wondered if ten years of social work did that, whether it was now ingrained in her to appear visibly neutral whatever shocking thing she heard. 'That I see worse?'

He stared at her. 'Than stealing from me?'

'Oh, Ed. You have no idea what it is to be truly desperate.'

'It doesn't make it okay to steal someone else's stuff.'

'No, it doesn't. But . . . um . . . one of us has just spent the day in court pleading guilty to insider trading. I'm not entirely sure that you're the greatest moral arbiter around here. Stuff happens. People make mistakes.' She pushed herself upright and began to clear the plates. 'Coffee?'

He was still staring at her.

'I'll take that as a yes. And while I'm clearing the plates you can tell me a little more about her.' She moved with a graceful economy around the little kitchen while he talked, never meeting his eye. She had her thinking face on. When he couldn't think of anything to do other than sit there with a slack jaw, Ed got up and helped her put the plates into the sink.

She pushed a drying-up cloth towards him. 'So here's how I see it. She's desperate, right? Her kids are being bullied. Her son gets his head kicked in. She's afraid it'll happen to the little girl next. She finds a wad of notes at the pub or wherever. She takes them.'

'But she knew they were mine, Gem.'

'But she didn't know you.'

'And that makes a difference?'

His sister shrugged. 'A nation of insurance fraudsters would say so.'

Before he could protest again, she said, 'Honestly? I can't tell you what she thought. But I can tell you that people in tight spots do things that are stupid and impulsive and ill thought-out. I see it every day. They do idiotic things for what they think are the right reasons, and some people get away with it and others don't.'

When he didn't reply, she said, 'Okay, so you never took a ballpoint home from work?'

'It was five hundred pounds.'

'You never "forgot" to pay a parking meter and cheered when you got away with it?'

'That isn't the same.'

'You've never exceeded the speed limit? Never done a job for cash? Never bounced off someone else's Wi-Fi?' She leant forward. 'Never exaggerated your expenses for the taxman?'

'That isn't the same thing at all, Gem.'

'I'm just pointing out that quite often how you see a crime depends on where you're standing. And you, my little brother, were a fine example of that today. I'm not saying she wasn't wrong to do it. I'm just saying maybe that one moment shouldn't be the whole thing that defines her. Or your relationship with her.'

She finished the washing-up, peeled off the rubber gloves and laid them neatly across the draining board. Then she poured them both a mug of coffee and stood there, leaning against the sink unit. 'I don't know. Maybe I just believe in second chances. Maybe if you had the litany of human misery trudging through your working day that I do, you would too.' She straightened up and looked at him. 'Maybe if it were me I'd at least want to hear what she had to say.'

He couldn't think of a reply.

'Do you miss her?'

Did he miss her? Ed missed her like he would miss a limb. He spent every day trying to evade thoughts of her, running from the direction of his own mind. Trying to dodge the fact that everything he came across – food, cars, bed – reminded him of her. He had a dozen arguments with her before breakfast, and a thousand passionate reconciliations before he went to sleep.

Upstairs in a bedroom a thumping beat broke the silence. 'I don't know if I can trust her,' he said.

Gemma gave him the same look she had always given him when he told her he couldn't do something. 'I think you do, Ed. Somewhere. I think you probably do.'

*

494

He finished the rest of the wine alone, then drank the bottle he had brought with him, crashing out on his sister's sofa. He woke sweaty and dishevelled at a quarter past five in the morning, left his sister a thank-you note, let himself out silently and drove down to Beachfront to settle up with the managing agents. The Audi had gone to a dealer the previous week, along with the BMW he had kept in London, and he was now driving a seven-year-old Mini with a dented rear bumper. He had thought he'd mind more than he did.

It was a balmy morning, the roads were clear, and even at ten thirty, when he arrived, the holiday park was alive with visitors, the main stretch of bars and restaurants filled with people making the most of rare sunlight. Others were walking, laden with bags of towels and umbrellas, to the beach. Well-dressed children skipped past the open-air restaurant with the outdoor pizza oven or dragged reluctant parents towards the covered pool. Tubs of seasonal flowers punctuated the pavement with perfectly laid-out, gaudy displays. He drove through them slowly, feeling irrationally furious at the sight of them – at this sterile semblance of a community, one in which everyone was in the same income bracket and nothing as messy as real life ever intruded as far as the perfectly aligned flower displays. He drove slowly past them all into the residential sector and pulled into the immaculate drive at number two, pausing to listen to the sound of the waves as he stepped out of the car.

He let himself in and realized he didn't care that this would be the last time he came here. There was just a week left until he completed on the sale of his London flat. The vague plan was that he would spend the remaining time with his father. He had nothing planned beyond that.

The hallway was lined with boxes bearing the name of the storage company that had packed them in his absence. He closed the door behind him, hearing the sound of his footsteps echo through the empty space. He walked upstairs slowly, making his way past the empty rooms. Here and there he saw evidence of the storage men's efforts: a stray roll of packing tape or an offcut of bubble wrap. But essentially the whole house was packed and otherwise empty. Next Tuesday the van would come, load the boxes and take them away, until Ed could work out what to do with his stuff. That was the problem with owning more than one property: what did you do with spare sofas, spare beds, when you were struggling to see how you would fit one lot into a one-bedroom flat?

Right up until then, he supposed, he had ploughed resolutely through what had been the worst few weeks of his life. If you had looked at him from the outside you might have seen someone grimly determined, sucking up their punishment. He had put his head down and kept moving on. Perhaps drinking a little too much but, hey, considering he'd lost a job, a home, a wife, and was about to lose a parent, all in a little over twelve months, he thought he could have argued that he was doing okay.

And then he spotted the four buff envelopes propped up on the kitchen work-surface, his name scribbled on them in ballpoint pen. At first he assumed they were administrative letters, left by the managing agents, but then he opened one and was confronted by the filigree purple print of a twenty-pound note. He extracted it, then pulled out the accompanying note, which said simply, 'THIRD INSTALMENT'.

He opened the others, tearing the envelope carefully when he reached the first. As he read her note, an image of her sprang, unbidden, to mind and he was shocked by her sudden proximity, by the way she had been waiting there all along. Her expression, tense and awkward while writing, perhaps crossing out the words and reworking them. Here she would pull her ponytail from its band and retie it.

I'm sorry.

Her voice in his head. *I'm sorry.* And it was then that something started to crack. Ed held the money in his hand and didn't know what to do with it. He didn't want her apology. He didn't want any of it.

He walked out of the kitchen and back down the hall, the crumpled notes clutched in his hand. He wanted to throw it all away. He wanted never to let it go. He felt as if something in him was about to combust. He walked from one end of the house to the other, backwards and forwards, trying to work out what he needed to do. He gazed around him at the walls he'd never had a chance to scuff, and the sea view that no guests had ever enjoyed. He had never felt at home there. He wasn't sure he'd ever felt at home.

The thought of it: that he would never feel at ease

anywhere, belong anywhere, was suddenly overwhelming. He paced the length of the hallway again, exhausted and restless, still overcome by the feeling that he should be doing something. He opened a window, hoping to be calmed by the sound of the sea, but the shouts of the happy families outside felt like a rebuke.

A free newspaper sat folded on one of the boxes, obscuring something beneath. Exhausted by the relentless circling of his thoughts, he stopped and absentmindedly lifted it. Underneath sat a laptop and a mobile phone. It was such an unlikely sight that he had to think for a minute to work out why they might be there. Ed hesitated, then picked up the phone, turning it over. It was the handset he had given Nicky back in Aberdeen, carefully hidden from the casual view of passers-by.

For weeks he had been fuelled by the anger of betrayal. When that initial heat dissipated, a whole part of him had simply iced over, become glacial. He had been secure in his outrage, safe in his sense of injustice. Now Ed held a mobile phone that a teenage boy who possessed next to nothing had felt obliged to return to him. He heard his sister's words and something began to open up, almost audibly, inside him. What the hell did he know about anything? Who was he to judge anyone?

Fuck it, he told himself. I can't go and see her. I just can't.

Why should I?

What would I even say?

He walked from one end of his empty house to the

other, his footsteps echoing on the wooden floors, his fist tight around the notes.

What kind of a fool would forgive?

He stared out of the window at the sea and wished, suddenly, that he had gone to jail. He wished that his mind had been filled with the immediate physical problems of safety, logistics, survival.

He didn't want to think about her.

He didn't want to see her face every time he closed his eyes.

He would go. He would leave here, and get a new place, and a new job, and he would start again. And he would leave all this behind. And things would be easier.

A shrill noise – a ringtone he didn't recognize – shattered the silence. His phone, recalibrated with Nicky's preferences. He stared at it, at the rhythmically glowing screen. Caller unknown. After five rings, when the sound became unbearable, he finally snatched it up.

'Is Mrs Thomas there?'

Ed held the phone briefly away from himself, as if it were radioactive. 'Is this a joke?' he said, putting it back to his ear.

A nasal voice, sneezing: 'Sorry. Awful hay fever. Have I got the right number? Parents of Costanza Thomas?'

'What – who is this?'

'My name's Andrew Prentiss. I'm calling from the Olympiad.'

It took him a moment to collect his thoughts. He sat down on the stairs.

'The Olympiad? I'm sorry – how did you get this number?'

'It was on our contacts list. You left it during the exam. I have got the right number?'

Ed remembered Jess's phone being out of credit. She must have given the number of the phone he'd given to Nicky instead. His head dropped into his free hand. Someone up there had quite a sense of humour.

'Yes.'

'Oh, thank goodness. We've been trying you for days. Did you not pick up any of my messages? I'm calling about the exam . . . The thing is, we discovered an anomaly when we were marking the papers. The first one contained a misprint, which made the algorithm question impossible to solve.'

'What?'

He spoke as if reciting a well-worn series of statements. 'We noticed it after the final results were collated. The fact that every single student failed the first question was a giveaway. It wasn't picked up on initially as we had several different people marking. Anyway, we're very sorry – and we'd like to offer your daughter the chance to resit. We're doing the whole thing again.'

'Resit the Olympiad? When?'

'Well, that's the thing. It's this afternoon. It had to be a weekend as we couldn't expect students to miss school to do it. We've actually been trying to reach you all week on this number but we got no response. I only tried you the one last time on the off-chance.'

'You're expecting her to get to Scotland in . . . four hours?'

Mr Prentiss paused to sneeze again. 'No, not Scotland

this time. We had to take the space available to us. But looking at your details I see this might work out better for you, seeing as you live on the south coast. The event is scheduled to take place in Basingstoke. Are you happy to pass the message on to Costanza?'

'Uh . . .'

'Thanks so much. I suppose these things are only to be expected in our first year. Still, one more down! I only have one more entrant to reach! The rest of the info is on the website if you need it.'

An almighty sneeze. And the phone went dead.

And Ed was left in his empty house, staring at the handset.

40.

JESS

Jess had been trying to persuade Tanzie to open the door. The school counsellor had told her it would be a good way to start rebuilding her confidence in the outside world, as long as she was in the house. She would answer the door, safe in the knowledge that Jess was behind her. That confidence would slowly stretch to other people, to being in the garden. It would be a stepping stone. These things were incremental.

It was a nice theory. If Tanzie would only agree to do it. 'Door. Mum.'

Her voice carried over the sound of the cartoons. Jess was wondering when to get tough with her on the television-watching. She had calculated last week that Tanzie now spent upwards of five hours a day lying on the sofa. 'She has had a shock,' Mrs Liversedge had said. 'But I think she'd feel better sooner if she was doing something a little more constructive.'

'I can't answer it, Tanze,' she called down. 'I'm standing here with my hands in a bowlful of bleach.'

Her voice, a whine, a new development these last days: 'Can't you get Nicky to open it?'

'Nicky's gone to the shop.'

Silence.

The sound of canned laughter echoed up the stairs. Jess could feel, if not see, the presence of whoever was waiting at the door, the shadow behind the glass. She wondered if it was Aileen Trent. She had arrived uninvited four times over the last two weeks with 'unmissable bargains' for the children. She wondered if she'd heard about Nicky's blog money. Everyone on the estate seemed to know about it.

Jess yelled down, 'Look, I'll stand at the top of the stairs. All you have to do is open it.'

The doorbell rang again, twice.

'Come on, Tanze. It's not going to be anything bad. Look, put Norman on the lead and bring him with you.'

Silence.

Out of sight, she let her head drop down and wiped her eyes in the crook of her arm. She couldn't ignore it: Tanzie was getting worse, not better. In the last fortnight she had taken to sleeping in Jess's bed. She no longer woke, crying, but crept across the hallway in the small hours and simply climbed in, so that Jess woke beside her with no idea of how long she had been there. She hadn't had the heart to tell her not to, but the counsellor said pointedly that she was a little old to do that indefinitely.

'Tanze?'

Nothing. The doorbell rang a third time, impatient now.

Jess waited, her ears trained on the silence. She was going to have to go down and do it herself.

'Hold on,' she called wearily. She began to peel off her

rubber gloves, and then she stopped as she heard the footfall in the hallway. The lumbering, wheezing sound of Norman being tugged along. Tanzie's sweet voice entreating him to come with her, a tone she only used with him these days.

And then the front door opening. Her satisfaction at the sound was tempered by the sudden realization that she should have told Tanzie to tell Aileen to go away. Given half a chance she would be in with her black bag on wheels and straight past her, settling herself on the sofa and her 'bargains' spread out on the living-room floor.

But it wasn't Aileen's voice she heard.

'Hey, Norman.'

Jess froze.

'Whoa. What happened to his face?'

'He only has one eye now.' Tanzie's voice.

Jess tiptoed to the top of the stairs. She could see his feet. His Converse trainers. Her heart began to thump.

'Did he have some kind of accident?'

'He saved me. From the Fishers.'

'He what?'

And then Tanzie's voice – her mouth opening and the words coming out in a rush. 'The Fishers tried to get me in a car and Norman bust through the fence to save me but he got hit by a car and we had no money but all these people sent money to us because of what Nicky wrote and then the vet let us off half the bill because he said he'd never met such a brave dog.'

Her daughter. Talking as if she wouldn't stop.

Jess took one step down, and then another.

'He nearly died,' Tanzie said. 'He nearly died and the vet didn't even want to give him an operation because he was so sick with infernal injuries and he thought we should just let him go. But Mum said she didn't want to and that we should give him a chance. And then Nicky wrote this blog about how everything had gone wrong and some people just sent him money. Well, lots of people sent little bits of money. For no reason. And we had enough to save him. So Norman saved me and people we don't even know saved him, which is sort of cool. But he only has one eye now and he gets really tired because he's still in recovery and he doesn't do very much.'

She could see him now. He had crouched down, and was stroking Norman's head. And she stared at him as if she couldn't tear her eyes away: the dark hair, the way his shoulders fitted his T-shirt. That grey T-shirt. Something rose up in her and a muffled half-sob came out so that she had to press her arm against her mouth. And then he looked up at her daughter from his low position and his face was deadly serious. 'Are you okay, Tanzie?'

She lifted a hand and twisted a lock of her hair, as if deciding how much to tell him. 'Sort of.'

'Oh, sweetheart.'

Tanzie hesitated, her toe rotating on the floor behind her, and then she simply stepped forward and walked into his open arms. He closed them around her, as if he had been waiting for just that thing, letting her rest her head against his shoulder and they just stayed there, her wrapped in his arms, in the hallway. Jess watched him close his eyes, and she had to take one step back up to where she couldn't be seen because she was afraid if he saw her she wouldn't be able to stop crying.

'Well, you know, I knew,' he said finally, when he pulled back, and his voice was oddly determined. 'I knew there was something special about this dog. I could see it.'

'Really?'

'Oh, yes. You and him. A team. Anyone with any sense could see it. And you know what? He looks pretty cool with one eye. He looks kind of tough. Nobody's going to mess with Norman.'

Jess didn't know what to do. She didn't want to go downstairs because she couldn't bear him to look at her the way he did before. She couldn't move. She couldn't go down and she couldn't move.

'Mum told us why you don't come round any more.'

'She did?'

'It was because she took your money.'

A painfully long silence.

'She said she made a big mistake and she didn't want us to do the same thing.' Another silence. 'Have you come to get it back?'

'No. That's not why I've come at all.' He looked behind him. 'Is she here?'

There was no avoiding it. Jess took one step down. And then another, her hand on the banister. She stood on the stairs with her rubber gloves on and waited as his eyes lifted to hers. And what he said next was the last thing she had expected him to say. 'We need to get Tanzie to Basingstoke.'

'What?'

'The Olympiad. There was a mistake with the paper last time. And they're resitting it. Today.'

Tanzie turned and looked up the stairs at her, frowning, as confused as Jess was. And then she looked as if a light-bulb had just gone on in her head. 'Was it question one?' she said.

He nodded.

'I knew it!' And she smiled, an abrupt, brilliant smile. 'I knew there was something wrong with it!'

'They want her to resit the whole paper?'

'This afternoon.'

'But that's impossible.'

'Not in Scotland. Basingstoke. It's doable.'

She didn't know what to say. She thought of all the ways in which she had destroyed her daughter's confidence by pushing her to the Olympiad the previous time. She thought of her mad schemes, of how much hurt and damage their single trip had caused. 'I don't know . . .'

He was still balanced on his haunches. He reached out a hand and touched Tanzie's arm. 'You want to give it a go?'

Jess could see her uncertainty. Tanzie's grip on Norman's collar tightened. She shifted her weight from one foot to the other. 'You don't have to, Tanze,' she said. 'It doesn't matter one bit if you'd rather not.'

'But you need to know that nobody got it right.' Ed's voice was calm and certain. 'The man told me it was impossible. Not a single person in that examination room got question one correct.'

Nicky had appeared behind him, holding a plastic bag full of stationery from his shopping trip. It was hard to tell how long he'd been there.

'So, yes, your mum is quite right, and you absolutely don't have to go,' Ed said. 'But I have to admit that, personally, I would quite like to see you whup those boys at maths. And I know you can do it.'

'Go on, Titch,' Nicky said. 'Go and show them what you're really made of.'

She looked round at Jess. And then she turned back and pushed her glasses up her nose.

It's possible that all four people held their breath.

'Okay,' she said. 'But only if we can bring Norman.'

Jess's hand went to her mouth. 'You really want to do this?'

'Yes. I could do all the other questions, Mum. I just panicked when I couldn't get the first one to work. And then it all went a bit wrong from there.'

Jess took two more steps down the stairs, her heart racing. Her hands had started to sweat in her rubber gloves. 'But how will we get there in time?'

Ed Nicholls straightened up, and looked her in the eye. His expression was both determined and oddly unreadable. 'I'll take you.'

It's not easy driving four people and a large dog in a Mini, especially not on a hot day and in a car with no air-conditioning. Especially if the dog's intestinal system is even more challenged than it once was, and if time constraints mean you have to go at speeds of more than forty miles an hour with all the inevitable consequences that brings. They drove with all of the windows open, in near silence, Tanzie murmuring to herself as she tried to remember all of the things she'd become convinced she'd forgotten, and occasionally pausing to bury her face in a strategically placed plastic bag.

Jess map-read, as Ed's new car had no built-in satnav, and tried to steer a route away from motorway traffic jams and clogged shopping centres. Within an hour and three-quarters, all conducted in a peculiar near-silence, they were there: a 1970s glass and concrete block with a piece of paper marked OLYMPIAD flapping in the wind, taped to a sign that said 'Keep Off the Grass'.

This time they were prepared. Jess signed Tanzie in, handed her a spare pair of spectacles ('She never goes anywhere without a spare pair, now,' Nicky told Ed), a pen, a pencil and a rubber. Then they all hugged her and reassured her that this didn't matter, not one bit, and stood in silence as Tanzie walked in to do battle with a bunch of abstract numbers, and possibly the demons in her own head. The door closed behind her.

Jess hovered at the desk and finished signing the paperwork, acutely conscious of Nicky and Ed chatting on the grass verge through the open door. She watched them with surreptitious sideways looks. Nicky was showing Mr Nicholls something on Mr Nicholls's old phone. Occasionally Mr Nicholls would shake his head. She wondered if it was his blog.

'She'll be cool, Mum,' said Nicky, cheerfully, as Jess emerged. 'Don't stress.' He was holding Norman's lead.

He had promised Tanzie they would not go more than five hundred feet from the building, so that she could feel their special bond even through the walls of the examination hall.

'Yeah. She'll be great,' said Ed, his hands thrust deep in his pockets.

Nicky's gaze flicked between the two of them, then down at the dog. 'Well. We're going to take a comfort break. The dog's. Not mine,' he said. 'I'll be back in a while.' Jess watched him wander slowly along the quadrant and fought the urge to say that she would go with him.

And then it was just the two of them.

'So,' she said. She picked at a bit of paint on her jeans. She wished she had had the chance to change into something smarter.

'So.'

'Yet again you save us.'

'You seem to have done a pretty good job of saving yourselves.'

They stood in silence. Across the car park a car skidded in, a mother and a young boy hurling themselves from the back seat and running towards the door.

'How's the foot?'

'Getting there.'

'No flip-flops.'

She gazed down at her white tennis shoes. 'No.'

He ran his hand over his head and stared at the sky. 'I got your envelopes.'

She couldn't speak.

'I got them this morning. I wasn't ignoring you. If I'd known . . . everything . . . I wouldn't have left you to deal with all that alone.'

'It's fine,' she said briskly. 'You'd done enough.' A large piece of flint was embedded in the ground in front of her. She kicked at some dirt with her good foot, trying to dislodge it. 'And it was very kind of you to bring us to the Olympiad. Whatever happens I'll always be –'

'Will you stop?'

'What?'

'Stop kicking stuff. And stop talking like . . .' He turned to her. 'Come on. Let's go and sit in the car.'

'What?'

'And talk.'

'No . . . thank you.'

'What?'

'I just . . . Can't we talk out here?'

'Why can't we sit in the car?'

'I'd rather not.'

'I don't understand. Why can't we sit in the car?'

'Don't pretend you don't know.' Tears sprang to her eyes. She wiped at them furiously with the palm of her hand.

'I don't know, Jess.'

'Then I can't tell you.'

'Oh, this is ridiculous. Just come and sit in the car.'

'No.'

'Why? I'm not going to stand out here unless you give me a good reason.'

'Because . . .' her voice broke '. . . because that's where

we were happy. That's where I was happy. Happier than I've been for years. And I can't do it. I can't sit in there, just you and me, now that . . .'

Her voice failed. She turned away from him, not wanting him to see what she felt. Not wanting him to see her tears. She heard him come and stand close behind her. The closer he got the more she couldn't breathe. She wanted to tell him to go but she couldn't bear it if he did.

His voice was low in her ear. 'I'm trying to tell you something.'

She stared at the ground.

'I want to be with you. I know we've made an unholy mess of it but I still feel more right with you doing wrong than I feel when everything's supposedly right and you're not there. Fuck. I'm no good at this stuff. I don't know what I'm saying.'

Jess turned slowly. He was gazing at his feet, his hands in his pockets. He looked up suddenly.

'They told me what Tanzie's wrong question was.'

'What?'

'It was about the theory of emergence. Strong emergence says that the sum of a number can be more than its constituent parts. You know what I'm saying?'

'No. I'm crap at maths.'

'I don't want to go back over it all. What you did. It's not like I'm perfect. But I just . . . I want to try. It might prove to be a huge fuck-up. But I'll take that chance.'

He reached out then and gently took hold of the belt loop of her jeans. He pulled her slowly towards him. She couldn't tear her eyes from his hands. And then, when she finally did lift her face to his, he was gazing straight at her and Jess found she was crying and smiling, perhaps the first time she had smiled properly in about a million years.

'I want to see what we can add up to, Jessica Rae Thomas. All of us. What do you say?'

41.

TANZIE

So the uniform for St Anne's is royal blue with a yellow
stripe. You can't hide in a St Anne's blazer. Some girls in
my class take them off when they're going home, but it
doesn't bother me. When you work hard to get somewhere,
it's quite nice to show people where you belong. The
funny thing is that when you see another St Anne's
student outside school it's the custom to wave to each
other, like people who drive Fiat 500s. Sometimes it's a big
wave, like Sriti, my best friend, who always looks like she's
on a desert island trying to attract a passing plane, and
sometimes it's just a tiny lifting of your fingers down by
your school bag, like Dylan Carter, who gets embarrassed
about talking to anyone, even his own brother. But
everyone does it. You might not know the person waving,
but you wave at the person in the uniform. It's what the
school's always done. It shows that we're all a family,
apparently.

I always wave, especially if I'm on the bus.

Ed picks me up in the car on Tuesdays and Thursdays
because that's when I have maths club and Mum works
late at her handywoman thing. She has three people

working for her now. She says they work 'with' her, but she's always showing them how to do stuff and telling them which jobs to go to and Ed says she's still a bit uncomfortable with the idea of being a boss. He says she's getting used to it. He pulls a face when he says it, like Mum's the boss of him, but you can tell he likes it.

She takes Friday afternoons off and meets me at school and we make biscuits together, just me and her. It's been nice, but I'm going to have to tell her I'd rather stay late at school, especially now I'm going to do my A level in the spring. Dad hasn't had a chance to come down yet, but we Skype every week and he says he's definitely going to. He's got two job interviews next week, and lots of irons in the fire.

Nicky is at sixth-form college in Southampton. He wants to go to art school. He has a girlfriend called Lila, which Mum said was a surprise on all sorts of counts. He still wears lots of eyeliner but he's letting his hair grow out to its natural colour, which is sort of a dark brown. He's now a whole head taller than Mum and sometimes when they're in the kitchen he thinks it's funny to rest his elbow on her shoulder, like she's a bar or something. He still writes in his blog sometimes, but mostly he says he's too busy so it would be okay if I take it over for a bit. Next week it will be less personal stuff and more about maths. I'm really hoping lots of you like maths.

We paid back 77 per cent of the people who sent us money for Norman. Fourteen per cent said they would rather we just gave the money to charity, and we were never able to trace the other nine per cent. Mum says it's fine, because the important thing was that we tried, and that sometimes it's okay just to accept people's generosity as long as you say thank you. She said to say thank you and she'll never forget the kindness of strangers.

Ed is here literally ALL the time. He sold his house at Beachfront and he now owns a really small flat in London and Nicky and I have to sleep on a put-you-up bed when we're there but most of the time he stays with us. He works in the kitchen on his laptop and talks to his friend in London on this really cool set of headphones and he goes up and down for meetings in the Mini. He keeps meaning to get a new car, as it's really hard to fit all of us in when we want to go somewhere, but in a weird way none of us really wants him to. It's kind of nice in the little car, all squashed together, and in that car I don't feel so guilty about the drool.

Norman is happy. He does all the things the vet said he'd be able to do, and Mum says that's enough for us. The law of probability combined with the law of large numbers states that to beat the odds, sometimes you have to repeat an event an increasing number of times in order to get you to the outcome you desire. The more you do, the closer you get. Or, as I explain it to Mum, basically, sometimes you just have to keep going.

I've taken Norman into the garden and thrown the ball for him eighty-six times this week. He still never brings it back.

But I think we'll get there.

Acknowledgements

Thank you as ever to my amazing Penguin teams on both sides of the Atlantic. At Penguin UK I am in particular indebted to Louise Moore, Clare Bowron, Francesca Russell, Elizabeth Smith, as well as Mari Evans and Viviane Basset. In the US thank you to Pamela Dorman, Kiki Koroshetz, Louise Braverman, Rebecca Lang, Annie Harris and Carolyn Coleburn. Thank you, too, to all the lovely media escorts – Cindy Hamel Sellers, Carolyn Kretzer, Debb Flynn Hanrahan, Esther Levine, Larry Lewis and Mary Gielow, who have spent so much time with me over there this year. In Germany, thank you to Katharina Dornhofer, Marcus Gaertner and Grusche Junker, and all the team at Rowohlt for your wonderful work.

At Curtis Brown, thank you yet again to my indefatigable agent Sheila Crowley, and to Rebecca Ritchie, Katie McGowan, Sophie Harris, Rachel Clements, Alice Lutyens as well as Jessica Cooper, Kat Buckle, Sven van Damme and of course Jonny Geller.

Thank you to Robin Oliver and Jane Foran for advice on insider trading law. I have had to skew the legal procedure slightly to fit the plot, so any errors or anomalies are entirely my own.

More generally thank you to Pia Printz, Damian

Barr, Alex Heminsley, Polly Samson, David Gilmour, Cathy Runciman, Jess Ruston and Emma Freud as well as the gang at Writersblock for excellent narrative interruptions. Also for excessive levels of help, advice and general loveliness, Ol Parker and Jonathan Harvey – thank you.

Thanks nearer home to Jackie Tearne, Chris Luckley, Claire Roweth, Vanessa Hollis and Sue Donovan, without whom I couldn't fit in the actual writing.

Thank you to Kieron and Sharon Smith and their daughter Tanzie, after whom the main character in this book was named, thanks to their generous bid in a charity auction in aid of the Stepping Stones Down Syndrome support group.

And thanks to my parents – Jim Moyes, Lizzie and Brian Sanders – and most importantly Charles, Saskia, Harry and Lockie, for being the point of it all.

The One Plus One
Reading Group Questions

- Do you think that Jess's family, with its complex relationships, is becoming the norm in contemporary society? Is it a good thing that the lines of what constitutes family are becoming more blurred?

- How did you feel when Marty was brought into the story? Were you sympathetic towards him despite his previous behaviour?

- What Ed does for Jess and her family is a kind deed, given they are virtually strangers. Do you think what Ed does for Jess is a rarity these days?

- How do you feel about the message that the only way for Tanzie to escape the same bullying that Nicky was subjected to is for her to go to the private school, St Anne's? If you were in Jess' shoes, would you feel the same?

- Do you think that it was morally wrong of Jess to take the money? Was Ed's reaction when he finds out what she did justified? Do you think he was right to forgive her?

- Nicky grows in confidence as the novel progresses. Why do you think this is? Is Ed a good influence on him? Do you think Nicky feels a responsibility to protect Jess and Tanzie (from both his own problems as well as from theirs)? And if so, why?

- Ed makes a huge mistake when he gets involved with his old university crush and consequently nearly loses everything. Did you feel any sympathy for him? Or did you think he got what he deserved?

- Both Ed and Jess make big mistakes that are out of character. How far do you think the mistakes they made led to them being a good match for one another? Do you think they would've got together had they both not been in such difficult situations when they met?

Jojo Moyes

We spend our lives trying not to be stuck in cars. Everyone has a horror story to tell about a long car journey. Most involve epic jams, or bladder accidents, especially when they involve transporting small children.

But over the last few years I've come to realize that I've made some big emotional discoveries on these long journeys – and not just that I've taken the wrong turning off the M27. Sometimes the miles of road ahead of you can give you breathing space that other types of journey don't allow.

I still remember clearly at the age of nineteen driving to the North West to meet a man who I had loved passionately, and who had dumped me, breaking my heart. A year on, he decided he had made a huge mistake and wanted me back, calling and writing endless emotional letters. Guardedly, I had finally agreed to drive up and see him.

Something happened on that journey. I set out full of nervous anticipation, my case packed with matching underwear, wondering if I was brave enough to open my heart to him again. Around two hours into the six hour drive I had begun to wonder what I was doing. By hour four I had recalled all the things I had never liked about him, things that had been obscured by being heartbroken. By the time I got there I had realized: I no longer loved him, and I never would again.

I spent an excruciating evening trying to let him down far more gently than he had done me. And then next morning I left him behind, along with the whole traumatic love affair, and drove back with the roof down, singing at the top of my voice.

A two-day drive to Italy to holiday to stay with a friend in need was one of the worst journeys with small children I can remember. My memories are of a heatwave, and endless traffic jams, and overheated, screaming toddlers, and the discovery when my husband and I finally got there that the friend in need had also invited a companion we didn't like, without telling us.

That was the drive that taught me that it is okay to say no to people, sometimes. And also never to embark on a summer driving holiday through Europe in a car that doesn't have air-con.

My husband reminded me that it was on one such summer holiday trip that I wrote my first book, while my infant daughter slept in the back, and he navigated the French motorway system. While he swerved around the Peripherique I was tapping away on a laptop in the passenger seat, conscious that as a working parent it was going to be one of the few uninterrupted times for writing that I would get.

But sometimes the road trips that look like the worst ideas can turn out to be the most useful. When our third child was born profoundly deaf, we were initially shell-shocked. We adapted quickly, but I realize now that the way it came at us – unexpected and devastating – had a long-reaching effect on my confidence. The prospect of putting our baby son into major surgery – to give him a cochlear implant – was even more terrifying.

We were still coming to terms with this, when I was due to travel on a book tour of Australia and New Zealand. I had agreed to go on condition that I could bring all the children, including the six-month-old baby, and as a result, having completed the Australian section mostly by air, we set off on a long road trip from the South Island to the North, in a people carrier with a travel cot and an unflappable publicist called Rae, who didn't mind frequent stops for breastfeeding, nappy changing or three-year-old's wee breaks.

Looking back, it was insane. Takng three children, including a six-month-old baby, and two parents half-demented with stress halfway across the world, while tying in an intense publicity schedule and numerous flights (I was pathologically afraid of flying).

And yet – it was the best family trip we have ever had. During those long stretches of road, our family rediscovered its sense of adventure. We chatted and played games, and, freed from the stresses of everyday life, just opened our eyes again to the world beyond us.

We used our spare time to run around on beaches, to whale watch, and reminded ourselves in doing so that life could be wonderful, instead of just a series of unpleasant shocks and fearful outcomes. We discovered that one of the joys of having a deaf baby was that he would sleep in the noisiest of motels. And watching him charm everyone he met made me see that he would still be someone fantastic, just a different person to the one we had originally expected.

More importantly, when we returned and I told people what we had just done ('You took how many young children? To where?') I realized we could do anything. We could overcome anything, if we were together.

More recently, my car journeys have been less exotic. A close relative has spent years dying a slow death from a cruel and debilitating illness. The long journey up to see her in her care home, in recent months, was always filled with a vague dread of what I might find this time, and the journey home simply profoundly sad.

I don't generally eat fast food, but for some reason I developed a routine of stopping at a drive-thru on the way home – the comforting stodge of salt and carbohydrate – eaten soggy with tears. But that journey, sad and saturated-fat-filled as it always was, also gradually became a time to reflect, both on her life, on happier times that we had spent together, and simply on the importance of living – really living – while you can.

It is hard to feel angry about sitting in traffic when you have just left behind someone who would have given anything to be able to even move beyond the four walls of her room. It is hard not to see simple joy in the mere act of travelling, when you have sat with someone for whom it is impossible.

For all these reasons I used a car journey on which to hang the personal trajectories of the characters in my new book. Forced into close proximity over long distances, they have to consider themselves a new, and how far the journey is as important as the destination, if not more so.

Because how you approach a long car journey is a lot like how you approach life. If even before you have set out, you view it as a trial, likely to be full of unexpected obstacles, either frightening and full of dangerous possibilities, or slower and more wearying than you might have wanted, then that is probably how you will experience it.

Or you could learn to see each long journey as an opportunity – to spot something new and unexpected, to think – each full of possibilities and diversions that could lead you somewhere totally unexpected. You could find simple joy in the act of moving forward.

Don't miss the greatly anticipated third
Lou Clark novel, following the number one
international bestsellers *Me Before You*
and *After You*

Coming 25th January 2018

Read on for an extract . . .

Chapter One

It was the moustache that reminded me I was no longer in England; a solid, grey millipede firmly obscuring the man's upper lip; a Village People moustache, a cowboy moustache, the miniature head of a broom that meant business. You just didn't get that kind of moustache at home. I couldn't tear my eyes from it.

'Ma'am?'

The only person I had ever seen with a moustache like that at home was Mr Naylor, our maths teacher, and he collected Digestive crumbs in his; we used to count them during algebra.

'Ma'am?'

'Oh. Sorry.'

The man in the uniform motioned me forward with a flick of his stubby finger. He did not look up from his screen. I waited at the booth, long-haul sweat drying gently into my shirt. He held up his hand, waggling four fat fingers. This, I grasped after several seconds, was a demand for my passport.

'Name.'

'It's there,' I said.

'Your name, ma'am.'

'Louisa Elizabeth Clark.' I peered over the counter. 'Though I never use the Elizabeth bit. Because my mum realized after they named me that it would make me Lou Lizzy. And if you say that really fast it sounds like lunacy. Though my dad says that's kind of fitting. Not that I'm a lunatic. I mean, you wouldn't want lunatics in your country. Hah!' My voice bounced nervously off the Perspex screen.

The man looked at me for the first time. He had solid shoulders and a gaze that could pin you like a Tazer.

He did not smile. He waited until my own faded.

'Sorry,' I said. 'People in uniform make me nervous.'

I glanced behind me at the immigration hall, at the snaking queue that had doubled back on itself so many times it had become an impenetrable, restless sea of people. 'I think I'm feeling a bit odd from standing in that queue. That is honestly the longest queue I've ever stood in in my life. I'd begun to wonder whether to start my Christmas list.'

'Put your hand on the scanner.'

'Is it always that size?'

'The scanner?' He frowned.

'The queue.'

But he was no longer listening. He was studying something on his screen. I put my fingers on the little pad. And then my phone dinged.

Mum: *HAVE YOU LANDED?*

I went to tap an answer with my free hand but the man turned sharply toward me.

'Ma'am, you are not permitted to use cell phones in this area.'

'It's just my mum. She wants to know if I'm here.' I surreptitiously tried to press the thumbs-up emoji as I slid the phone out of view.

'Reason for travel?'

WHAT IS THAT? came Mum's immediate reply. She had taken to texting like a duck to water and could now text faster than she could speak. Which was basically warp speed.

YOU KNOW MY PHONE DOESN'T DO THE LITTLE PICTURES. IS THAT AN SOS? LOUISA TELL ME YOU'RE OKAY.

'Reason for travel, ma'am.' The moustache twitched with irritation. He added slowly: 'What are you doing here in the United States?'

'I have a new job.'

'Which is?

'I'm going to work for a family in New York. Central Park.'

Just briefly, the man's eyebrows might have raised a millimetre. He checked the address on my form, confirming it.

'What kind of job?'

'It's a bit complicated. But I'm sort of a paid companion.'

'A *paid companion.*'

'It's like this – I used to work for this man. I was his companion but also I would give him his meds and take him out and feed him – that's not as weird as it sounds, by the way – he had no use of his hands. It wasn't like something pervy. But the thing is it's hard not to get close to people you look after and Will – the man – was amazing and we . . . well, we fell in love . . .' Too late, I felt the familiar welling of tears. I wiped at my eyes briskly. 'So I think it'll be a bit like that. Except for the love bit. And the feeding.'

I looked up. The immigration officer was staring at me. I tried to smile. 'Actually I don't normally cry talking about jobs. I'm not like a genuine lunatic, despite my name. Hah! But I loved him. And he loved me. And then he . . . well, he chose to end his life. And so this is sort of my attempt to start over.'

The tears were now leaking relentlessly, embarrassingly, from the corners of my eyes. I couldn't seem to stop them. I couldn't seem to stop anything. 'Sorry. Must be the jet lag. It's something like two o'clock in the morning in normal time, right? Plus I don't really talk about him anymore. I mean, I have a new boyfriend. And he's great! He's a paramedic! And hot! That's like winning the boyfriend lottery, right? A hot paramedic?'

I scrabbled around in my handbag for a tissue. When I looked up, the man was holding out a box.

I took one.

'Thank you. So anyway, my friend Nathan – he's from New Zealand – works here and he helped get me this job and I don't really know what it involves yet apart from looking after this rich man's wife who gets depressed. But I've decided this time I'm going to live up to what Will wanted for me, because I didn't get it right before. I just ended up working in an airport.'

I froze. 'Not – uh – that there's anything wrong with working in an airport! I'm sure Immigration is a very important job. *Really* important. But I have a plan. I'm going to do something new every week that I'm here and I'm going to say yes.'

'Say yes?'

'To new things. Will always said I shut myself off from new experiences. So this is my plan.'

The officer studied my paperwork.

'You didn't fill the address section out properly. I need a zip code.'

He pushed the form towards me. I checked the number on the sheet that I had printed out and filled it in with trembling fingers. I looked to my left, where the queue at my section was growing restive. At the front of the next queue a Chinese family was being questioned by two officials. As the woman protested, they were led into a side room. I felt suddenly very alone.

The immigration officer glanced down the line at the people waiting. And then, abruptly, he stamped my passport. 'Good luck, Louisa Clark,' he said.

I stared at him. 'That's it?'

'That's it.'

I smiled. 'Oh, thank you! That's really kind. I mean, it's quite weird being on the other side of the world by yourself for the first time and now I feel a bit like I just met my first nice new person and –'

'You need to move along now, ma'am.'

'Of course. Sorry.'

I gathered up my belongings and pushed a sweaty frond of hair from my face.

'And, ma'am . . .'

'Yes?' I wondered what I had got wrong now.

He didn't look up from his screen. 'Be careful what you say yes to.'

Nathan was waiting in Arrivals, as he had promised. I scanned the crowd, feeling self-conscious, secretly convinced that nobody would come, but there he was, his huge hand waving above the shifting bodies around him. He raised his other arm, a smile breaking across his face, and pushed his way through to meet me, picking me up off my feet in a gigantic hug.

'Lou!'

At the sight of him, something in me constricted un-expectedly – something linked to Will and loss and the raw emotion that comes from sitting on a slightly too bumpy flight for seven hours – and I was glad that he held me tight, so that I had a moment to compose my-self. 'Welcome to New York, shorty! Not lost your dress sense, I see.'

He held me at arm's length, grinning. I straightened my 1970s tiger-print shirt. I had thought it might make me look like Jackie Kennedy, the Onassis years. If Jackie Kennedy had spilled half her airline coffee on her lap. 'It's so good to see you.'

He swept up my leaden suitcases like they were filled with feathers. 'C'mon. Let's get you back to the house.

The Prius is in for servicing so Mr G lent me his driver's car. Traffic's terrible, but you'll get there in style.'

Mr Gopnik's driver's car was sleek and black and the size of a bus and the doors closed with that emphatic, discreet *thunk* that signalled a six-figure price tag. Nathan shut my cases in the boot and I settled into the passenger seat with a sigh. I checked my phone, answered Mum's fourteen texts with one that told her simply that I was in the car and would call her tomorrow. And then answered Sam's, which told me he missed me, with *Landed xxx.*

'How's the fella?' said Nathan, glancing over at me.

'He's good, thanks.' I added a few more xxxxs just to make sure.

'Wasn't too sticky about you heading over here?'

I shrugged. 'He thought I needed to come.'

'We all did. Just took you a while to find your way, is all.'

I put my phone away, sat back in my seat, and gazed out at the unfamiliar names that dotted the highway, Milo's Tire Shop, Richie's Gym, the ambulances and U-Haul trucks, the rundown houses with their peeling paint and wonky stoops, the basketball courts and drivers sipping from oversized plastic cups. Nathan turned on the radio and I listened to someone called Lorenzo talking about a baseball game, and felt, briefly, as if I were in some kind of suspended reality.

'So you've got tomorrow to get straight. Anything you want to do? I thought I might let you sleep in and then drag you out to brunch. You should have the full NY diner experience on your first weekend here.'

'Sounds great.'

'They won't be back from the country club till tomorrow evening. There's been a bit of strife this last week. I'll fill you in when you've had some sleep.'

I stared at him. 'No secrets, right? This isn't going to be –'

'They're not like the Traynors. It's just your average dysfunctional multimillionaire family.'

'Is she nice?'

'She's great. She's . . . a handful. But she's great. He is too.'

That was as good a character reference as you were likely to get from Nathan. He lapsed into silence – Nathan never was big on gossip – and I sat in the smooth, air-conditioned Mercedes GLS and fought the waves of sleep that kept threatening to wash over me. I thought about Sam, now fast asleep several thousand miles away in his railway carriage. I thought of Treena and Thom, tucked up in my little flat in London. And then Nathan's voice cut in.

'There you go.'

I looked up through gritty eyes and there it was across the Brooklyn Bridge – Manhattan – shining like a million jagged shards of light; awe-inspiring, glossy, impossibly condensed and beautiful, a sight that was so familiar from television and films that I couldn't quite accept I was seeing it for real. I shifted upright in my seat, dumbstruck as we sped towards it, the most famous metropolis on the planet.

'Never gets old, that view, eh? Bit grander than Stortfold.'

I don't think it had actually hit me until that point. *My new home.*

'Hey, Ashok. How's it going?' Nathan wheeled my cases through the marble lobby as I stared at the black-and-white tiles and the brass rails and tried not to trip, my footsteps echoing in the cavernous space. It was like the entrance to a grand, slightly faded hotel: the elevator in burnished brass, the floor carpeted in a red and gold livery, the reception a little darker than was comfortable. It smelt of beeswax and polished shoes and money.

'I'm good, man. Who's this?'

'This is Louisa. She'll be working for Mrs G.'

The uniformed porter stepped out from behind his desk and held out a hand for me to shake. He had a wide smile and eyes that looked like they had seen everything.

'Nice to meet you, Ashok.'

'A Brit! I have a cousin in London. Croy-down. You know Croy-down? You anywhere near there? He's a big fella, you know what I'm saying?'

'I don't really know Croydon,' I said. And then when his face fell: 'But I'll look out for him the next time I'm passing through.'

'Louisa. Welcome to the Lavery. You need anything, or you want to know anything, you just let me know. I'm here twenty-four seven.'

'He's not kidding,' said Nathan. 'Sometimes I think he sleeps under that desk.'

'Three kids under five, man,' said Ashok. 'Believe me, being here keeps me sane. Can't say it does the same for my wife.' He grinned. 'Seriously, Miss Louisa. Anything you need, I'm your man.'

'As in drugs, prostitutes, houses of ill repute?' I whispered as the elevator doors closed around us.

'No. As in theatre tickets, restaurant tables, best places to get your dry-cleaning done,' Nathan said. 'This is Fifth Avenue. Jesus. What have you been doing back in London?'

The Gopnik residence comprised seven thousand square feet on the second and third floors of a red-brick Gothic building, a rare duplex in this part of New York, and testament to generations of Gopnik family riches. This, the Lavery, was a scaled-down imitation of the famous Dakota building, Nathan told me, and was one of the oldest co-ops on the Upper East Side. Nobody could buy or sell an apartment here without the approval of a board of residents who were staunchly resistant to change. While the glossy condominiums across the park housed the new money – Russian oligarchs, pop stars, Chinese steel magnates, and tech billionaires – with communal restaurants, gyms, child care and infinity pools, the residents of the Lavery liked things Old School.

These apartments were passed down through generations; their inhabitants learned to tolerate the 1930s plumbing system, fought lengthy and labyrinthine battles for permission to alter anything more extensive than a light switch, and looked away politely from the way that New York was changing around them in the same way one might ignore a beggar with a cardboard sign.

I barely glimpsed the grandeur of the duplex itself, with

its parquet floors, elevated ceilings, and floor-to-ceiling damask drapes, as we headed straight to the staff quarters, which were tucked away at the far end of the second floor, down a long narrow corridor that led off from the kitchen – an anomaly left over from a distant age. The newer or refurbished buildings had no staff quarters: housekeepers and nannies would travel in from Queens or New Jersey on the dawn train and return after dark. But the Gopnik family had owned these tiny rooms since the building was first constructed. They could not be developed or sold, but were tied through deeds to the main residence, and lusted after as storage rooms. It wasn't hard to see why they might naturally be considered storage.

'There.' Nathan opened a door and dropped my bags.

My room measured approximately twelve feet by twelve feet. It housed a double bed, a television, a chest of drawers and a closet; a small armchair, uphol-stered in beige fabric, sat in the corner, its sagging seat testament to previous exhausted occupants. A small window may have looked south. Or north. Or east. It was hard to tell, as it was approximately six feet from the blank brick rear of a building so tall that I could only see the sky if I pressed my face to the glass and craned my neck.

A communal kitchen set nearby on the corridor, to be shared by me, Nathan and a housekeeper, whose own room was across the corridor.

On my bed sat a neat pile of five dark-green polo shirts and what looked like black trousers, bearing a cheap Teflon sheen.

'They didn't tell you about the uniform?'

I picked up one of the polo shirts.

'It's just a shirt and trousers. The Gopniks think a uniform makes it simpler. Everyone knows where they stand.'

'If you want to look like a pro golfer.'

I peered into the tiny bathroom, tiled in limescale-encrusted brown marble, which opened off the bedroom. It housed a loo, a small basin that looked like it dated from the 1940s and a shower. A paper-wrapped soap and a can of cockroach killer sat on the side.

'It's actually pretty generous by Manhattan standards,' Nathan said. 'I know it looks a little tired but Mrs G says we can give it a splosh of paint. A couple of extra lamps and a quick trip to Crate and Barrel and it'll –'

'I love it,' I said. I turned to him, my voice suddenly shaky. 'I'm in New York, Nathan. I'm actually here.'

He patted me on the shoulder. 'Yup. You really are.'

I managed to stay awake just long enough to unpack, eat some takeaway with Nathan (he called it takeout, like an actual American), flick through some of the 859 channels on my little television, the bulk of which seemed to be on an ever-running loop of American football, adverts for digestive issues, or badly lit crime shows I hadn't heard of, and then I zonked out before waking with a start at four forty-five a.m. For a few discombobulating minutes I was confused by the distant sound of an unfamiliar siren, the low whine of a reversing truck – then flicked on the light switch, remembered where I was, and a jolt of excitement whipped through me.

I pulled my laptop from my bag and tapped out a chat message to Sam. **You there? xxx** I waited, but nothing came back. I couldn't remember what he had said his plans were, and was too befuddled to work out the time difference. I put my laptop down and tried briefly to get back to sleep (Treena said when I didn't sleep enough I looked like a sad horse). But the unfamiliar sounds of the city were a siren call, and at six I finally climbed out of bed and showered, trying to ignore the rust in the sputtering water that exploded out of the shower head. I dressed (denim pinafore sundress and a vintage turquoise short-sleeved blouse bearing a picture of the Statue of Liberty) and went in search of coffee.

I padded along the corridor, trying to remember the location of the staff kitchen that Nathan had shown me the previous evening. I opened a door and a woman turned and stared at me. She was middle-aged and stocky around the middle, with her hair set in neat dark waves, like a 1930s movie star. Her eyes were beautiful and dark but her mouth dragged down at the edges, as if in permanent disapproval.

'Um . . . good morning!'

She kept staring at me.

'I – I'm Louisa? The new girl? Mrs Gopnik's . . . assistant?'

'She is not Mrs Gopnik.' The woman left this statement hanging in the air.

'You must be . . .' I racked my jet-lagged brain but no name was forthcoming. Oh, come on, I willed myself. 'I'm so sorry. My brain is like porridge this morning. Jet lag.'

'My name is Ilaria.'

'Ilaria. Of course, that's it. Sorry.' I stuck out my hand. She didn't take it.

'I know who you are.'

'Um . . . can you show me where Nathan keeps his milk? I just wanted to get a coffee.'

'Nathan doesn't drink milk.'

'Really? He used to.'

'You think I lie to you?'

'No. That's not what I was s—'

She stepped to the left and gestured towards a wall cupboard that was half the size of the others and ever so slightly out of reach. 'That is your cupboard.'

Then she opened the fridge door to replace her juice and I noticed the full two-litre bottle of milk on her shelf. She closed it again and gazed at me implacably.

'Mr Gopnik will be home at six-thirty this evening. Dress in uniform to meet him.' And she headed off back down the corridor, her slippers slapping against the soles of her feet.

'Lovely to meet you! I'm sure we'll be seeing loads of each other!' I called after her.

I stared at the fridge for a moment, and then decided it probably wasn't too early to go out for milk. After all, this was the city that never slept.

*

New York might be awake, but the Lavery was cloaked in a silence so dense it suggested communal doses of zopiclone. I walked along the corridor, closing the front door softly behind me and checking eight times that I had remembered both my purse and keys. I had planned to use the service lift, but figured the early hour and the sleeping residents gave me licence to look a little closer at where I had ended up.

As I tiptoed along, the plush carpet muffling my steps, from inside one of the doors a dog started to bark – a yappy, outraged protest – and an elderly voice shouted something muffled that I couldn't make out. I hurried past, not wanting to be responsible for waking up the other residents, and instead of taking the main stairs, headed down in the service lift.

There was nobody in the lobby so I let myself out onto the street and stepped straight into a clamour of noise and light so overwhelming that I had to stand still for a moment just to stay upright. In front of me the green oasis of Central Park extended for what looked like miles. To my left, the side streets were already busy – enormous men in overalls unloaded crates from an open-sided van, watched by a cop with arms like sides of ham crossed over his chest. A road sweeper hummed industriously. A taxi driver chatted to a man through his open window. I counted off the sights of the Big Apple in my head. Horse-drawn carriages! Yellow taxis! Impossibly tall buildings! As I stared, two weary tourists with children in buggies pushed their way past me clutching Styrofoam coffee cups, still operating perhaps on some distant time zone.

Manhattan stretched in every direction, enormous, sun-tipped, teeming and glowing.

My jet lag evaporated with the last of the dawn. I took a breath and set off, aware that I was grinning but quite unable to stop myself.

I walked eight blocks without seeing a single convenience store. I walked over to Madison Avenue, past huge glass-fronted luxury stores with their doors locked, and, dotted between them, the occasional restaurant, windows darkened like closed eyes, or a gilded hotel whose liveried doorman didn't look at me as I passed.

I walked another five blocks, realizing gradually that this wasn't the kind of area where you could just nip to the grocer's. I had pictured New York diners on every corner, staffed by brassy waitresses and men with white pork-pie hats, but everything looked huge and glossy and not remotely like a cheese omelette or a mug of tea might be waiting behind its doors. Most of the people I passed were tourists, or fierce, jogging hard-bodies, sleek in Lycra and oblivious between earphones, stepping nimbly around homeless men who glared from furrowed, lead-stained faces. Finally I stumbled upon a large coffee bar, one of a chain, in which half of New York's early risers seemed to have congregated, bent over their phones in booths or feeding preternaturally cheerful toddlers, with generic easy listening music filtering through speakers on the wall.

I ordered a cappuccino and a muffin, which, before I could say anything, the barista sliced in two, heated, and slathered in butter, all the while never breaking his conversation about a baseball game with the barista next to him.

I paid, sat down with the muffin, wrapped in foil, and took a bite. It was, even without the clawing jet-lag hunger, the most delicious thing I had ever eaten.

I sat in a window seat gazing out at the early-morning Manhattan street for half an hour or so, my mouth alternately filled with claggy, buttery muffin or scalded by hot, strong coffee, giving free rein to my ever present internal monologue (*I am drinking New York coffee in a New York coffeehouse! Just been walking along a New York street! Like Meg Ryan! Or Diane Keaton! I am in Actual New York!*) and, briefly, I understood exactly what Will had been trying to explain to me two years previously; for those few minutes, my mouth full of unfamiliar food, my eyes filled with strange sights, I existed only in the moment. I was fully present, my senses alive, my whole being open to receive the new experiences around me. I was in the only place in the world I could possibly be.

And then, apropos of apparently nothing, two women at the next table launched into a fist fight, coffee and bits of pastry flying across the tables, baristas leaping to pull them apart. I dusted the crumbs off my dress, closed my bag, and decided it was probably time to return to the peace of the Lavery.

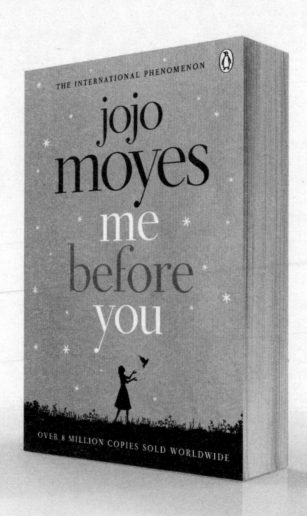

THE INTERNATIONAL PHENOMENON

jojo
moyes
me
before
you

OVER 8 MILLION COPIES SOLD WORLDWIDE

The stunning sequel to *Me Before You*

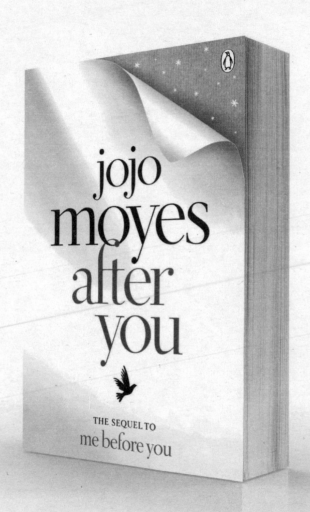

jojo
moyes
after
you

THE SEQUEL TO
me before you

An irresistible collection of eleven
romantic short stories

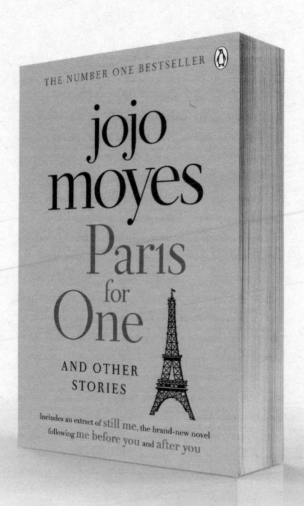

THE NUMBER ONE BESTSELLER

jojo
moyes

Paris
for
One

AND OTHER
STORIES

Includes an extract of still me, the brand-new novel
following me before you and after you

Also by

jojo
moyes

jojo
moyes
the
girl you left
behind

'Heart-stoppingly
brilliant'
Marie Claire

'A masterclass'
Elle

He just wanted a decent book to read ...

Not too much to ask, is it? It was in 1935 when Allen Lane, Managing Director of Bodley Head Publishers, stood on a platform at Exeter railway station looking for something good to read on his journey back to London. His choice was limited to popular magazines and poor-quality paperbacks – the same choice faced every day by the vast majority of readers, few of whom could afford hardbacks. Lane's disappointment and subsequent anger at the range of books generally available led him to found a company – and change the world.

'We believed in the existence in this country of a vast reading public for intelligent books at a low price, and staked everything on it'
Sir Allen Lane, 1902–1970, founder of Penguin Books

The quality paperback had arrived – and not just in bookshops. Lane was adamant that his Penguins should appear in chain stores and tobacconists, and should cost no more than a packet of cigarettes.

Reading habits (and cigarette prices) have changed since 1935, but Penguin still believes in publishing the best books for everybody to enjoy. We still believe that good design costs no more than bad design, and we still believe that quality books published passionately and responsibly make the world a better place.

So wherever you see the little bird – whether it's on a piece of prize-winning literary fiction or a celebrity autobiography, political tour de force or historical masterpiece, a serial-killer thriller, reference book, world classic or a piece of pure escapism – you can bet that it represents the very best that the genre has to offer.

Whatever you like to read – trust Penguin.